THE RECKONING OF ADRIENNE MONET

ALSO BY GENE RITCHINGS

Frankenrocker

Winter in a Summer Town

THE RECKONING
OF
ADRIENNE MONET

GENE RITCHINGS

Rebel in the Rubble Books
NEW YORK

THE RECKONING OF ADRIENNE MONET. Copyright © 2025 by Gene Ritchings. All rights reserved. Printed in the United States of America. No part of this book may be used or reproduced in any manner whatsoever without written permission except in the case of brief quotations embodied in critical articles or reviews. For permission to use for other purposes, email the author at generitchings@gmail.com.

Designed by Lauren Naslund

Cover images from Shutterstock

Quote from Elaine May from an interview with Haden Guest, Harvard Film Archive, November 12, 2010. Used by permission.

ISBN - 979-8-9985997-4-3

To the memory of Nate Ranger

"I probably should have kept making movies. So for all you women here, let that be a lesson. Just don't stop."

Elaine May

ONE *The night of January 9, 2018*

With a shaky hand, I light one of Jonathan's cigarettes, and after a couple puffs his living room doesn't smell so much like gun smoke and spilled blood. I slide back the glass door, step out on the terrace, and breathe in the cold, windy night.

I lean over the parapet high above the city and watch people hurrying along the sidewalk far below and the traffic passing up and down Central Park West. A bus engine's rattle, a car horn, a far-off siren, echo up to me. Across the street the park spreads out dark and vast, the pale moonlight gleaming on the freshly fallen snow under the trees. In the glow of a streetlamp on a path, a woman in a black overcoat with earmuffs over her blonde hair stops, thumbs out a text on her phone, and disappears into the shadows.

I feel such envy. Why can't I just disappear into the dark and forget about tonight? None of my usual problem-solving hacks are going to help me now. If I was on a film set, and I didn't have an answer with a crew member waiting for a decision or an actor needing direction, we'd collaborate, we'd work it out, or at least I'd try to be decisive, even though they might still walk away grumbling, "Well, that figures. Typical woman, she doesn't know what she's doin'." Tonight I've got nobody to collaborate with, and the police are on the way. The worst thing is, I keep wishing I was somewhere else, which makes it hard to get a grip on the situation. I wish I could wake up one last time beside A.J., so warm, so in love, so at peace with myself and the world. But that love and that life are over, and there's no darkness deep enough for me to hide.

I put the cigarette between my lips, kick one leg over and straddle the stone parapet. Go ahead, I tell myself. Don't think too much about it. Stand up, and just let yourself drop. What have you got left to live for? At least you won't be disgusted when the media treats your death like just another trashy show business tragedy.

Actor-director Adrienne Monet died last night, after she fell or jumped from the terrace of the Central Park West penthouse of actor Jonathan Lehane. After directing three successful films Monet attracted notoriety as the controversial creator of the hit reality TV show "Men R Dawgs".

At least you won't be around when they remind everybody your fourth film was a flop and you didn't direct another for over ten years. You won't have to grind your teeth when some creep writes in their Hollywood blog that your fifth film, starring Jonathan and scheduled to drop next year, is rumored to be your best work yet, just so they can say, whoa, so even that wasn't enough to keep her from jumping off a building? Like, WTF?

Cigarette between my lips, I lean forward, tuck my knees under me, roll back on my feet, and slowly stand up, surrounded by nothing but the huge indifferent universe. I stiffen my knees to stop them from trembling. I lift my arms and spread my fingers and my hands grasp only emptiness.

I slide one foot forward. It's okay. A second step. Still, all good. I take the next step and a sudden gust of wind whips my hair over my eyes, catches my jacket like a sail, and tries to blow me off the building. For an endless moment I rock on one foot, the sidewalk far below, arms spinning, my pulse punching in my stomach, my brain screaming *Careless! Reckless! Stupid!* Then the wind drops off, and I'm back on two feet. I dash to the end of the parapet, seize the neighbor's wrought-iron fence, and hold tight, gasping.

What goes through the mind of a jumper, falling faster and faster, body spinning, clothes flapping and shoes falling off as the pavement rushes up? *Goodbye?* It would be just like me, as I begin to drop, to realize *Oh my God! I changed my mind!*

I try to tell myself I can always hop down on the terrace, go back inside Jonathan's penthouse and try to go on living, but no... I can't... Not that...

My numb fingers let go of the fence. I turn and step back into empty space. Very focused and unafraid, I inch back down the parapet between my choice of disasters. On one side, a few screaming seconds of free fall, a crash, and a final answer to everything. On the other side, the world as I just left it.

At the middle of the parapet I carefully lower myself back down and hang a leg over each side. Well, that didn't clarify anything, but it made my indecision worse. It's maddening. I've struggled my whole life for insight into the mystery that is me, and now when it matters the most, it seems like I don't know a thing.

Down below a siren keeps rising and falling, coming closer. The traffic on Central Park West moves aside for a speeding police car with its lights flashing. The car stops in front of this building and two policemen get out and hurry inside. Time's up, Adrienne.

Then, an idea occurs to me, arriving at the worst moment, a distraction, yes, but irresistible. I have an interesting scene here. How can I shoot it? The most challenging, most thrilling way would be one unbroken take.

EXTERIOR — CENTRAL PARK WEST. A winter night. Bare tree limbs arc over the sidewalk. Parked cars lay buried under snowdrifts. A row of massive buildings dissolves into the darkness. We ZOOM slowly, ominously, then PAN toward

The elegant façade of a posh pre-war apartment building. Strings of tiny Christmas lights the color of champagne adorn the evergreens flanking the glass doors. People in winter coats pass under the building's awning, its lights brightening the sidewalk and welcoming the fortunate ones who live here.

Out steps MICKEY the doorman in a visor cap and a large greatcoat with shiny buttons. His eyes flicker back and forth in that sly New York doorman's all-seeing way. Sure that no one is watching, he clears his throat and spits into the shrubbery, the little man's statement of contempt for the residents of the building who look down their noses every day at working stiffs like Mickey.

A police cruiser enters the frame. Two uniformed officers get out. Pushing Mickey ahead of them, they hustle into the building.

MUSIC BEGINS, solo piano in a minor key.

The camera slowly rises up the front of the building.
In window after window we see brief vignettes of people
being tender, disgusting, noble, brutal, silly,
decadent, careless, sexy, despairing, farcical, the
whole human tragicomedy in one apartment building in
New York.

The camera stops on ADRIENNE straddling the parapet,
hugging herself and shivering, cigarette in her
trembling fingers. Tears gleam in her eyes.

She grows bigger in the frame and her face blurs as the
camera passes her, crosses the terrace, and the shot
DISSOLVES through the glass doors into the living room.

INTERIOR - LIVING ROOM. The room is nearly dark except
for a bright wedge of light across the carpet.

On the floor at the wide end of that light is A.J.
UPTON's bare foot in a brown penny loafer.

The wedge of light on the carpet narrows to the other
end of the room, where JONATHAN LEHANE is lying on his
back. In his outstretched hand the light gleams off a
chrome revolver.

First of all, Adrienne, it's probably been done before. And sitting here dreaming up a shot, that's easy. To capture it, you'd need truckloads of equipment, permits from the city, actors with impeccable timing, a team of efficient assistant directors and crew members, location deals with the building management and each apartment owner, a skilled rigging and lighting crew, a camera operator who's a wizard at shooting with the SkyCam or a drone, a lot of money, producers practiced in the art of pacifying the studio suits when they kvetch about the cost, and the stamina to do it over and over again. But if you even come close to what's in your head, maybe your one-shot will one day be spoken of with your favorite oners, like Scorsese's Steadicam shot as Henry squires Karen into the Copa in *"Goodfellas"*, or like Altman's opening shot of *"The Player"* in the studio parking lot that introduces almost every major character. Like, for that matter, the opening shot of *"Psycho"* that descends from the clouds into a hotel room where a man and woman have been having daytime sex.

Then I realize I have made the decision. What I will do is work, and keep making movies that pulse with more life than life itself. That's all I've ever cared about anyway. I can't let tonight detour me from the path I started on so long ago. With A.J. gone, work is all I have left. I'll live for that, like I always have, and I'll survive, however I have to.

I swing around and drop down to the terrace, take a deep breath, and pump my legs, stiff from the cold. Through the glass doors, details in the living room emerge from the shadows, a bent knee in blue jeans, a wave of gray hair, Jonathan's wide-open eyes seeing nothing. I step into the glow of the terrace light and the glass door throws my reflection back at me, an intense and determined looking woman with a cigarette in her lips dressed in black, tight jeans, tight tee, and leather jacket, ready to do a desperate dance with the police and, once the cameras arrive, with the whole wired world.

On a sticky sweltering Friday afternoon last August, I was curled up on the sofa in my office at Alpha Bitch Productions, my company in the Cinema Arts Building on Times Square at 49th and Broadway. I was exhausted and trying to sleep but nagging guilt over my behavior on the set the night before wouldn't let me rest.

My crew and I had been struggling for 12 hours to shoot the final episode of *"Men R Dawgs"*, my reality TV series about adultery for The Lily Channel. After working six-day weeks through a scorching summer, we were a gang of short-tempered, staggering zombies. Crew call had been 6 p.m. but by daybreak the following day we were still working in a scruffy studio in Jersey City, all because of one actor named Adam.

He was a short young studly driver for a car share service, with a thick moustache and greasy Jheri curls and bulging muscles. He had auditioned well, but my usually acute casting instincts failed me, because once shooting began, he choked, even when I tried to establish a rapport. He got a glazed look in his eyes and became tongue-tied and deaf to my direction. I should've recast the role, but we didn't have the time or the money, so I convinced myself I could work with him. When we were ready to shoot his bedroom scene, he froze up and forced the young woman playing another man's cheating wife to improvise like mad. In the penultimate scene between the husbands, they were supposed to share all the funky details without knowing they'd had sex with each other's wives, but Adam couldn't even talk about sex like a real guy. The second husband was Kurt, a slim handsome blonde-haired guy whose raunchy descriptions of sex with Adam's wife got better with each take.

Patiently, I kept trying to find some life in his performance., and for my trouble Adam got surly and pissy. I called for another take of that scene. I told the guys to get down and dirty and build up to anger when they realize what they'd unwittingly done with each other's wives. That's when I caught Adam sneaking a glance at his wristwatch, and I finally lost it. It wasn't fair to take out my fury on him, but this episode was the season climax, and we all knew it was failing, so to speak, to rise. Unprofessional for a director and not my style at all, I needed to get radical to activate Adam while the cameras were rolling and we were all still awake after 12 hours.

"For God's sake, Adam," I said, in a voice of calm precise malice that everyone could hear. "Kurt just called your wife 'a hot piece of ass.' Said he screwed her silly and she loved it, and all you can do is just stand there? I mean, if you can't find anything to say, do something, or jerk off, or at least act like you've been listening to him."

"You know what?" Adam whirled on me. "Fuck you."

"Would you even know how?" The crew laughed, and he turned red from his curly head to his toenails.

"Y'know," he hissed, "I'm sick of you –"

"You're sick? We've been laughing at you behind your back this whole fucking episode." Titters and chuckles from some crew members. Adam looked around at them, hurt. "Where'd you learn how to act, anyway? Oh, I forgot. You don't know how to act."

He lunged and threw a punch at me. I knew it was coming, dodged, and I fell back and was caught by Tawana Barber, my 1st A.D. I didn't have to tell my shooters to keep the cameras rolling. Long hard workdays had wired us together until we were telepathic, so they captured the next moment when Adam seized my director's chair and smashed it to a tangle of wood and canvas on the floor of the studio.

The two local bar bouncers we'd hired to work security jumped in. They wrestled him down and cuffed his hands behind his back, then one held Adam up and the other idiot pepper-sprayed him.

"My eyes!" Adam wailed. "My fucking eyes!"

"What's the matter with you?" I yelled at the bouncers. "Now I'm short one actor. All right, damn it, let's take him to the emergency room."

They dragged him outside and pushed him into the back seat of a 15-passenger van. Rather than stand around in the studio with nothing to shoot, I grabbed Gabriella, our director of photography, and Bobby our sound recordist, and we climbed into the van. The ride to the medical center was ten minutes of rolling chaos, with Adam screaming "My eyes! My eyes!" and fighting the security guards holding him down. Gabriella shot it hand-held with the Redcam, I shot iPhone footage, and Bobby clipped his iPhone onto the end of his mike boom over Adam's face. I was thrilled that Adam's kicks fell just inches short of the cameras. The audience would flinch in front of their screens.

We got to the ER entrance and the bouncers wrestled Adam out of the van. It took two male nurses to force Adam into a wheelchair. We scrambled beside them, still rolling cameras. I felt sorry that Adam got hurt, but it was his own fault for getting violent. At least I got a few minutes of hot cinema verité, a season finale gifted to me by the gods. Before the hospital security guards pushed and shoved me and my crew out the door, I got close up footage on my iPhone of his face, streaming tears and snot and screaming that I was an evil cunt.

Without a pause I turned my phone on myself. "He means me, folks." I shrugged. "But I was sure he had at least one good scene in him." Gabriella laughed so hard Bobby had to hug her or she would've dropped a $25,000 camera.

Back at the studio, the trucks were loaded and ready to go.

"Sign the bouncers to non-union one day deals," I told Tawana as we mounted up. "I'd like to fire them both, but now they're in the show."

"We'll get 'em," she said.

I belted myself into the passenger seat of the director van. We left the studio and started back toward Manhattan with the rising sun in the east in our bloodshot eyes. In morning rush hour traffic, we crawled toward the Holland Tunnel bumper to bumper, each foot by frustrating foot bringing me closer to home and bed. I changed glasses to my dark Wayfarers. I was desperate to be anywhere but here. My mood soured into exhaustion and sadness over the end of shooting and dread of the days to come without a shot list and a crew to work with, my basic requirements for a potentially happy day.

Men R Dawgs, salacious junk TV for a niche streaming channel, had put me back on the street directing a crew for the first time in 10 years. This summer I'd felt my life reborn by the stress and the hard work with my crew and the camaraderie I'd missed for so many years. Now I'd lose the daily rush of shooting and have to settle into regular office hours and the tedium of post-production. I could feel the collapse coming that I'd fought off to survive the weeks of 14 and 16-hour workdays. I promised myself as soon as I got home, I'd sit with myself and accept the stress burnout of my mind and body and start a healing routine. But my poor beat up soul couldn't contain the grief and relief any longer. I closed my eyes and took a deep breath, and on came the tears, embarrassing but impossible to hold back. My driver Tony noticed, reached over and took my hand in his rough, hairy paw.

I turned and crooned sadly to my exhausted comrades. "The party's over..."

Silence. Blank stares. Then Sharona, our droll makeup artist, yawned and said, "Yeah... we're all so-o-o sad." That sent a quiet, tired laugh rippling through the van.

"What'll I do without you guys to torture every day?" I pretended to whine. "I'm tough on my office kids, but they can't take a punch like you."

A few of them laughed wearily, like, okay, let the boss have her fun. Others were probably giving me the finger below the back of the seat. After a long hot summer of me demanding more than they could give, some of them would need time for the bruises to heal.

I tried to cheer myself up by counting my blessings, but I couldn't think of any. Certainly not money. My company had the post-production budget of *"Men R Dawgs"* to carry us for a while, but we were working from check to check. Certainly not my love life, either. With shooting over and time on my hands, I knew I'd have to resist the urge to try to get back with Nadia Gummo, a hustling young actress and night life blogger who dumped me and broke my heart in mid-summer when I wouldn't put her in the show. Better to write that one off, I knew, and keep going forward. Shooting was finished more or less on time and on budget, so at least the network would be happy. The pilot episode that we shot back in May was scheduled to drop at 9 p.m. tonight, so I soon might be doing more interviews with geeky show biz reporters to hype a show that embarrassed me but I couldn't disown.

Still, talking about the series was better than being asked about my long-gone career, when I lived and worked on both coasts and directed four films, and had money, fame, a passionate workaholic schedule, high times and beautiful lovers. In those days I never thought about if, or how quickly, it all could end, but I found out. With one flop that wasn't my fault my filmmaking career had stalled, grew colder with every unsuccessful pitch and every phone call never returned, and finally died.

Then last fall I came roaring out of my depression when Donald Trump was elected president, even after bragging about grabbing women by the pussy. I sat down and poured my anger into a proposal for my own reality TV show, an improv series of 30-minute episodes using fake married couples mocking the sexism and toxic masculinity and lowbrow trash TV that Trump epitomized. To make it as offensive as possible, I called it *"Men R Dawgs"*. I got it out of my system and sent it to my agent Marshall and forgot all about it. But to my complete amazement my old friendly rival Sylvia Strawn, now an executive producer at the Lily Channel, fell in love with the idea and fast-tracked it into production. Was this decision the network's poor taste, or was I in-sync with the culture?

Who cared? It was work, and I needed it. We set men up to be liars and brazen crisscross adulterers who get busted by their wives, while the wives get to have a sexual adventure *and* the last word. The series presented male promiscuity and infidelity so caustically it absolutely titillated the executives at Lily. Based on focus group tests, their promo people had high hopes the show would be a hit. The audience didn't care that we weren't using real couples, they liked the premise, most of all the shaming of the husbands. At least I'd make some money, thank God. But I'd also have to keep lying to interviewers and saying I was proud of this crude hairball my dark side coughed up as a *Fuck You* to a vulgar misogynist who mistook his gold-plated toilet for a throne.

My phone spit out a blues riff. Marshall, my agent, was calling. Experience told me to let it go to voicemail. Whenever Marshall called so early in the morning it was always buzzkill for breakfast. He liked to offload bad news early while I was asleep so there was no time wasted talking to me and he could get to work for clients who made him more money.

"Yo, it's me. Sorry about this, but I got a call back from your favorite people, Lenny and Juno Victor. So, like, they're gonna pass on producing 'After Lena'. I guess you expected that, right? Anyway, if you have anybody else you want me to pitch to, lemme know."

I'd put aside pride and my painful history with them and sent the Victors my screenplay for *"After Lena."* The film was based on a mother's memoir of coping with her teenage daughter's suicide after the girl was harassed and cyber-bullied by a sadistic self-pitying ex-boyfriend. To be rejected by the Victors ripped open wounds I thought had healed long ago. All my old grievances with them started echoing angrily in my head and I was enjoying the rage too much to hit STOP.

Inside the van it got dark as we entered the tunnel and picked up speed, hurrying me toward what already looked like a pretty shitty day.

I lived in a rent-stabilized one-bedroom apartment in a rehabbed old brownstone on a quiet, leafy block in Chelsea. The rent was low when I signed the lease in 2004 and I could still just barely afford it. I'd covered the floors with gray industrial carpet, painted the walls pale blue, and installed my crammed bookcases, wide screen TV, and posters of my films. My neighbors were a mix of gay and straight couples because there were no units large enough for even a small family. My place had plenty of light from large windows front and back, a kitchen with room for a table and four chairs, and a large rear fire escape landing that I used as a balcony and herb garden.

I turned on the air conditioners, pulled down the shades, and threw my sweaty clothes on the Eames chair in the corner. I rolled out my yoga mat on the living room floor and, ignoring how I smelled after a hard night's work, practiced the Sun Salute over and over until my body felt relaxed enough to sleep. I got into bed and wrapped myself in a cool sheet. But my over-stimulated brain kept flickering with memories of the all-night shoot and echoing with raspy walkie talkie voices. Finally, I gave up. I crawled out of bed, blasted myself wide awake under a hot and cold shower, and ate an apple and a slice of whole wheat toast for breakfast. I pulled on jeans and a white linen blouse, kicked my bare feet into Cons and combed my wet hair back off my forehead to dry in the heat, and headed to work.

I caught the C train at 8th and 23rd and got off at the West 50th Street station. On the subway walls I saw a poster for "Men R Dawgs" for the first time: a well-dressed young woman making a scornful face, holding a leash around the neck of a chubby balding boyfriend or husband, his tongue wagging over a sexy girl passing by. That was the Lily gang for you, risking no subtlety. I texted Sylvia to thank her and the girls for capturing the essence of the show in one image.

With "Men R Dawgs" done shooting my office staff was working with fresh enthusiasm. I quickly glanced at my email Inbox and saw nothing urgent, including a screenplay for a lesbian Western sent by an NYU film student who somehow got my address. Large cup of coffee in hand, I drove myself through a morning of concentrated work in the dim confines of the editing cave with my editor Layne McPeek.

Our office PA brought in deli sandwiches for lunch, and while we ate, McPeek and her assistant Betty Ann kept replaying the footage of Adam smashing up the furniture and screaming at me.

"Awesome," Betty Ann marveled.

"I might be able to cut it," McPeek said, scratching her gray buzz cut and peering critically at the screen, "so it seems like he's screaming and smashing shit because of the wife."

"Luckily Adam is only half the episode," Betty Ann said. "At least the blonde guy is hot."

McPeek sat back. "I can do something cool with this. Let me play with it."

"How about this?" I said. "In the van and at the hospital, we shot Adam, but we also shot each other shooting him. We could break the fourth wall."

"Really?"

"'The breakdown of a film shoot.' We go verité and show a director struggling with a character gone berserk. It's one way to end the season. Let's try that. Go crazy. Make it fun."

"I'd have to use his worst takes," McPeek grumbled.

"But in a perverse way," Betty Ann said, "that might be more entertaining."

All I could do was sigh.

"His performance was a disaster, so let's play it that way. You get what I want, right? A chaos episode to end the season."

"Keep the profanity in?"

"Yeah. We're only gonna get one season anyway."

By mid-afternoon I was drained, a mumbling, stumbling wreck. I used to be able to work around the clock before I felt tired, but I didn't have that kind of energy anymore. I could bum an Adderall from one of my office kids, but I was no longer a kid myself. I swore years ago after some intermittent tachycardia that I'd never risk my health on drugs again. My middle-aged addictions were pretty basic: the gym, strong coffee, sex with soulful women and rough men, and above all, work.

I let McPeek keep working, crept to my office, and told my assistant Megan to send my calls to voicemail. I shut the door, turned off the lights, and closed the venetian blinds to shade the office from the sun beating down on Times Square and grilling the masses of tourists shuffling around in the blue haze.

I felt bad about how I'd treated Adam. But the dude deserved a beating for not doing his job. I also failed as a director and I took it out on him. But so what? The only thing that really mattered was that we got the shot. I was excited because his performance would be a shocking break from the husbands we'd had all season, none of whom broke any furniture or tried to hit me and all of whom could act. Last night's captures looked great and McPeek would work her usual magic. I turned off my phone, put on a sleep mask, lay back on the sofa, unsnapped my jeans and slipped my hand down between my legs, and melted into the cushions.

Megan was gently shaking my shoulder.

"Marshall's on Hold."

I must've been out for a couple hours. I'd fallen deep asleep, but now I wasn't fully awake, and I was in no mood for more bad news.

"Tell him to call me later."

"He says it's urgent."

"Ugh, shit. Okay."

I slid into the chair behind my desk, took a deep breath, yawned so hard it shook me down to my toes, and grabbed the phone.

"A-Girl!" No Hello, just straight to business. Marshall likes his speakerphone because he can stalk around his office yelling at the phone. "We've got a situation! Lenny and Juno are bombarding me with calls!"

That woke me up.

"They changed their mind about Lena?"

"Nope nope nope. They got a huge problem with this thing they're producing. The script needs a rewrite and you're the writer they want."

"A rewrite?"

Was this a joke? The Victors were notorious for hiring writers then forcing them to sue to get paid. Even after all these years Lenny and Juno were an open wound in my psyche and Marshall knew it. So why was he doing this to me? I often wondered what mutant genes produced guys like him: aggressive, head-driven, trash-talking young agents wearing brown shoes with dark slacks, wheeling and dealing their way through a business jungle where envy, vanity, contempt, and Schadenfreude were the daily emotional weather.

"They're way into prep, and now, I mean, like, today, their director told them the script still needs a lot of work."

"What director?"

"Egon" – slowly, for effect – "*Swift.*"

"Oh wow," I whispered, mocking Marshall's awe. "Egon...Swift."

A pampered Hollywood brat whose father was a big studio executive, Egon, in New York film crew lingo, was a "silver spoon," as in born with one in his mouth. Most women I knew hated his films, ultra-violent psycho-thrillers with undisguised borrowings from Hitchcock, De Palma, and Tarantino. He was famous for his flashy camera work, simple-minded plots, disturbed male characters, and their sexy female victims, who were always emotionally abused and graphically killed. His first two films so glamorized cruelty and violence against women that he was called out by male and female critics alike for his sadistic misogyny. I wasn't one of those women who wanted to string him up by his balls, but if someone did, I'd approve. His movies grossed nine hundred million dollars worldwide catering to the lowest audience tastes and made him a Hollywood player at the age of thirty. Then, his imagination apparently exhausted, came his third film, a strained mashup of his over-used ideas, and it bombed, or, as the studios liked to say of their precious male directors, it underperformed.

"They begged me to call you," Marshall said, "can you believe that shit?"

They begged? I hoped they squirmed in shame. But that was impossible because Lenny and Juno Victor were the most shameless people I knew. For years I'd seen a psychiatrist to try to stop blaming them for the failure of my fourth film. I spent most of those sessions ranting and raving and trying to purge my rage by smashing the exam couch with a tennis racket and screaming "No!" at the top of my lungs. It didn't work, because they *were* to blame. When my health insurance stopped paying the shrink because I wasn't making progress, I quit going. I stopped trying to forgive them, owned my real feelings, and created my own guided-imagination exercise. I fantasized that I cornered the Victors, drenched them with a bucket of gasoline, and set them on fire. That usually mellowed me out. The only reason I asked Marshall to pitch *"After Lena"* to them was because I'd been rejected all the way down to the bottom of my list of possible producers, and there they were.

"Marshall," I sighed. "I don't want to work with Egon Swift. You know the kind of movies he makes."

"No, no, this is not his usual thing. It's based on a play about 9/11 called *'Lonely Sky'*. It's a big Off Broadway hit."

"Yeah, I know about it. I haven't seen it."

"It's heavy. All about loss and mourning and grief and shit. And yeah, okay, 9/11, not exactly a fresh idea. But they read *Lena* and they think you have a talent for painful material."

"So why didn't they ask me to direct?"

"Adrienne —"

"Call them back. Tell them I'm unavailable." Let's see how they handle painful material. "Anything else?"

"C'mon Adrienne."

"The director is unhappy with the script. The producers are desperate. The clock is running, money is burning up. You know what this is? It's a glue trap for any writer dumb enough to go for the cheese."

"Yeah, okay. It's also a job."

"If the movie works and makes money, they'll take all the credit. If it flops, they'll blame me and my script."

"How do you know that'll happen?"

"Instinct. And I can't risk another flop."

Ten years ago, Lenny and Juno abandoned me in my fight against the studio's insipid marketing campaign for my fourth film. It failed at the box office and that killed my career in feature films. I try never to think about that bleak summer, the snarky self-esteem-crushing reviews, the film playing for two weeks to empty theaters, and how I'd wake up in the wee lonesome hours, angry and sick at heart. I'm sure the experience took years off my life.

"This could be an opening to make features again," Marshall said. "And you know you need the money."

"I need a vacation, and I'm too tired and depressed to keep talking about this. Tomorrow I'm going out to Cherry Grove for two weeks rest. Goodbye, Marshall."

"No no no! They want you to see the play tonight, go talk with them and the director, and do a rewrite, like, tomorrow. They're looking for a savior. They think you're it."

"Did they actually say that?"

"Yeah, yeah," he chuckled, echoing my astonishment, "they did."

"Wait a second."

I put him on hold, got down on my knees in front of my couch, and began pounding it with my fists, crying and cursing, "Get out of my life! Get out of my life! Get the fuck out of my life!"

I heard Megan outside the door. "Adrienne? Are you okay?"

"Yes, I'm fine." I got up and wiped my eyes, feeling better. Marshall's call was still blinking at me.

"This is the best offer anyone's made since '*Men R Dawgs*," he said, calmer this time. "If you go in, do a rewrite that works, people will know you saved the show. It'll improve your brand."

"I have directed four films."

"You're only as hot as your last film. You know that."

"Then how come his last film bombed two years ago and he's already making a new one?" Of course, he wouldn't even try to answer that. "Just tell them 'no.'"

"Maybe the writing gig will start something we can leverage to get them to produce Lena."

"Why are men deaf to the word 'No' when it's spoken by a woman?"

"Look, okay, I get it, I do," he said. When Marshall meets resistance, he always sounds like he's strangling on his vocal chords. "You hate Lenny and Juno, fine, I know you've got your reasons. But go see the play at least? Please? Then if you say no, you'll at least have looked at the material. Saying no won't seem so much like a 'Fuck you.' The *Dawgs* wrap party's tonight, right? Can you fit it in before the party?" When I didn't answer, he said, "Do it as a favor to me? Please? They're calling me every fifteen minutes."

The fucking nerve of those two. They were really asking for it.

"All right. Tell them I'll see it. Get me a ticket for tonight. And have them email me the play."

"Okay! And you know, maybe the play doesn't suck."

I didn't care about that. This was an opportunity to serve up a cold dish of revenge. I was so pissed off at this intrusion that I decided to teach the Victors a painful lesson in good manners. I'd see the play, take a meeting, act nice to them, pay for my own drinks, and try not to talk through gritted teeth. I'd raise their hopes, make them wait while I pretended to consider their offer, waste as much of their precious time as I could, then reject their offer and flick them away like dead flies off a windowsill.

I went home and got ready for a night on the town. I pumped L'Occitane Verbena liquid soap on a loofah and scrubbed myself, imagining I was shedding old skin, until I glowed. I used baby shampoo and a conditioner that gave my black hair a dramatic shine. It's a cliché that French girls use cosmetics so cleverly you can't tell that they're wearing any, but it's also true. All I ever used was light sunblock and a swipe of clear lip gloss. I stepped back from the full-length mirror on the bedroom door. I still loved the woman I saw in the mirror, and I was proud that even in my worst times I never let myself sit in front of the TV at night stuffing my face. I got hooked on fitness in my twenties, and in my mid-forties I was still lean and muscled and luckily small-breasted, so I was still defying gravity. I finished fluffing out my hair and plucked out a few gray strands.

When I was a skinny punky middle school girl, before I grew into my face and body, my dimwitted classmates nicknamed me The Little Crow because I always dressed in black. Someone wrote in my yearbook, *Quietly weird*, and she was a friend. Except for exploring my sexuality and shooting my early camcorder movies with friends, high school was a torturous bore, and I endured it like a convict counting the days left in a prison sentence. I was unpopular and considered stuck up, but high school was where I trained myself to intuit what people were thinking and feeling so I'd know how real a threat or possible friend they might be. In my 1988 yearbook photo, amongst all the big hair and shoulder pads and mullets and friendly clueless looks, my eyes almost burn off the page. *Friend or foe?*

I've been lucky as an actor, because I've played roles that I wrote for myself. In a casting director's database I'd be described as "Pretty, nerdy, emo-gamine," and my picture would show a pale-faced brunette wearing glasses, with high cheekbones, a small pointy nose, a thick mane of raven hair, strong jawline, and a small mouth with pouty lips. An added note, "looks older in close-up," meant I didn't try to hide the wrinkles around those dark, troubled eyes.

I pulled on a white lace thong and bra, dabbed a Dior fragrance called Ambre Nuit between my breasts and just below my belly button, and slipped into a sleeveless white linen dress hemmed above the knee. Tonight, once I'd seen the play and mind-gamed the Victors, I planned to go to the *Dawgs* wrap party and seduce the hottest man or woman I could get. Male, female, both, whatever. I needed steam, hot naked skin on skin, a night of rough, smelly, sweaty, mind-blowing sex to mark the end of shooting. I stepped into my dancing shoes and tossed my hair back on my shoulders.

A call rang on my iPhone from PRIVATE. I let it go to voicemail, then I listened. A deep resonant male voice, throbbing with feeling, crooned, off-key, a song by Irving Berlin called *"What'll I do?"*

Aldo. Oh no. Oh God. No-no-no! I got to the Eames chair in my living room, my safe place, and sat down. I saved the voicemail and swiped through my contacts for my lawyer's cell number, which I hadn't called in months. A recorded message said the number had been disconnected, so I called her office.

"Levy and Associates," a voice said. It sounded like a new receptionist.

"Annie, please. It's Adrienne Monet."

"I'm sorry, she's gone for the weekend."

"Can I have her cellphone number, please?"

"I'm sorry, I'm not allowed to give that out."

That jerked me bolt upright in the chair. "I'm a client."

"I'm so sorry, but —"

"This is urgent. Like, life or death, okay? Can you find her and conference us?"

"One moment please." On hold, I jumped up and rushed around the apartment making sure all the windows were locked and the chain was on the front door.

Not this! Not him again! Not now, when my workdays were about to become regular, leaving me lots of time for paranoia. 'Aldo,' a one name legend in his own mind, was the alter ego of a pretty-boy slacker from Los Angeles, none-too-bright and living on a trust fund. He hung around New York where his sloth and lifestyle weren't so visible to his rich family. Aldo had an obsession with the dissolute jazz trumpeter Chet Baker. He had the same brooding beauty, thick chestnut hair and high cheekbones, full pouty lips and deep-set blue eyes. He wore dark suits and white shirts and skinny ties like a 1950s cool jazz musician and carried a trumpet in an alligator-hide case. He also used heroin and cocaine like his idol, and dope was slowly destroying his lean, tautly muscled body. Aldo called himself a trumpet player, but he was often too stoned to practice and his playing sucked. No-one dared to say that to Aldo's face, because despite the cool mask he could suddenly become a very angry dude. Emotionally, Aldo could pinball from charming to truculent to dangerous in a blink.

The night we met, he chatted me up outside a club downtown, saying he liked my performance in my second film, *"Girl in the City"*. His charm and rugged good looks, his obvious wealth, and his jittery energy swept me up immediately. After a couple drinks, I let him take me up to his room in a posh hotel near Gramercy Park. That night he played his trumpet for me and I pretended to be impressed. Luckily, the people in the next room complained and he had to stop. That night I discovered Aldo's real talent was for the kind of rough sex that got me scared and excited but didn't go too far. I floated out at eight o'clock the next morning, yawning, sore, and at peace with the world. Angry self-destructive guys are sometimes just the thing for exciting sex, better than the petting, licking, and dull fucking a girl gets from nice, sensitive men. I liked how he treated me like a bad girl who needed to be taught a lesson without crossing into threatening behavior. That came later.

I tried to keep the affair uncomplicated, like most of my hookups with men. The final break up was driven by our respective maladjustments. I knew I should quit him, but I found the sex irresistible, despite the risk he would pick up a disease from another junkie and infect me. The harder I tried to pull away, the more possessive he got.

Eventually he took the bullying too far and I finally found the nerve to end it. Afterward, I went hunting again among the lower primates, hoping for a new no-strings hookup with a handsome thug. Instead I met Nadia Gummo, bad luck that I made worse by falling in love.

"Miss Monet? Annie's on the line, go ahead."

"Adrienne?" my lawyer said. "What's wrong?"

"He's back."

"Who's back?"

"Aldo."

"Oh God. Him again?"

"He's never going to stop."

"All right, calm down. What happened?"

"A lovesick voicemail. Somehow he got my new cell number."

"But you haven't seen him? Hanging around?"

"Not yet."

"Good."

"Yeah, until he kills me."

"Call the police. You have to report this."

"What good did it do last time?"

"We got the order of protection."

"A piece of paper."

"Which he violated by calling you."

"Great. Next time he tries to cut my throat, I'll wave it in his face."

"I'm trying to be helpful –"

But nobody could help. That throb in Aldo's voice as he sang me a love song meant he was out of his mind again. I hung up and grabbed my keys. I had to get out of the apartment before I gave in to fear and stayed home. Skip the play, skip the wrap party, cower in my apartment? No way. Before I left for my night on the town, I rummaged around in the junk drawer under my kitchen counter, found my vial of jogger's pepper spray, and put it in my shoulder bag.

Would I really have to go back to looking over my shoulder, scanning faces, afraid to check my phone messages and email? Because Aldo had taken getting dumped badly. He begged me to reconsider. He wept. He gave up and crept away. Later, he came bopping back into my life, and when I ignored him, he flipped out and trapped me one morning in the foyer of my old office building in Tribeca, shoving me around and threatening me with a knife, sputtering that I was no longer his 'No. 1 Lady,' just a cruel, sneaky bitch who used him for sex then dumped him. Which was true, of course, but I didn't trick poor Aldo into anything. He was just too dumb to get the deal. He'd been a cool playmate until he let his delusion that we were in love run away with him. Such a beautiful young man, such an exciting beast in bed, but weak at the core, like most men who bully women. By sheer luck I was saved that morning by a husky building custodian who slammed Aldo into a wall, took away his knife, and sent him sniveling out the door. I moved my offices up to Times Square, glad that I'd never let him know where I lived. My lawyer also got that order of protection from the court, but by then Aldo had vanished. My bruises soon faded but the nightmares never quite went away.

That night in the theater as the cast of *"Lonely Sky"* took one curtain call after another, I stood there sobbing, clapping and yelling "Bravo!" in awe at how deeply the brave wounded characters had touched me and moved the entire audience. People were either on their feet clapping and roaring or still sitting in stunned silence. Finally, the cast waved and blew kisses and walked off.

I sat back down in my seat as the people shuffled out, thinking about what I'd just experienced. The playwright Joel Garner had woven together three separate stories about people in New York still struggling to recover one year after the horror of 9/11. The stories developed in radically different directions. In "The Day Before Doomsday," a comically paranoid East Village hipster keeps exhausting his young wife with schemes to fortify their railroad flat against the dangers he's sure are coming – another terrorist attack, a killer pandemic, an Atlantic tsunami, a dirty bomb in the middle of Manhattan – imprisoning himself and his wife in anxiety and suffocating their marriage. "I'm A Stranger Here" was the harrowing story of the dignified patriarchal Muslim owner of a Brooklyn travel agency. After false arrest, a year of imprisonment, rendition and torture, he is dumped back on his doorstep by the CIA and tries to resume his life, while his teenage son struggles to come to terms with his manhood in the country that brutalized his father by mistake.

The performance I couldn't get out of my head was a spooky story called "Constant Companion." A tall handsome actor named Jonathan Lehane played investment banker David Sawyer, who kissed his wife as she left for her law office at the World Trade Center on 9/11 and never heard from her again. A year later, still unable to accept her death, he hallucinates her as a living presence in their Upper East Side townhouse. Lehane's beauty made Sawyer's misery poignant; it seemed unfair that such a handsome man should suffer so profoundly.

In a daze, I floated out of the air-conditioned lobby and into that hot August night thick with humidity and bus exhaust, into a world that felt so much richer, so much more alive than the world before the play. I wandered down 42nd Street to 10th Avenue, caught in the rush of the Friday evening crowd, feeling a powerful, sweet sad empathy for my fellow human beings. Weren't all of us struggling against the odds to live the best life we can? Never had a night in the theater made me feel so alive, or so radically changed my hope for my future. I forgot all about my fantasy of wreaking vengeance on the Victors. They had a potential masterpiece of a movie on their hands.

Meanwhile, at that moment The Lily Channel was streaming the premiere episode of "*Men R Dawgs*." I had no difficulty admitting to myself that I was so deeply moved by *"Lonely Sky"* because the play's compassion for its characters was the opposite of the contempt for the cheating husbands and the hypocritical triumph of the wives offered by my brazen, smutty reality TV show. To achieve the distasteful Schadenfreude that *"Dawgs"* promised to arouse, I had to go 100 percent for that vulgar pleasure while I was directing it. But *"Lonely Sky"* and the nobility of its struggling characters filled me with compassion and a tragic sense of life as it really was.

It also gave me a powerful and totally unrealistic hope. I knew exactly how I could turn the play into a brilliant movie, one that would challenge my talents and force me to grow as an artist, exactly what I needed after ten years of fruitless effort and aching frustration. But the rights were owned by producers I hated and mistrusted, and my only way onto the show was to write for a director who glamourized brutality against women. Any self-respecting writer with taste and common sense would pass; but not if she'd seen this play, and not if she'd struggled for the past ten years with so little to show.

I found Lenny Victor smoking a cigar and pacing in front of the West Bank Café in a heated conversation with someone on the Bluetooth buds sticking out of his ears. Since I'd last seen him his reckless hedonism had turned him into a gross, dissipated cherub, fatter in the belly and jowls, his eyes sunken deeper and darker. His thinning gray hair was moussed-up into an absurdly youthful brush cut and stubble covered his cheeks and neck. His wardrobe was still hopelessly 1980s: cracked unpolished cowboy boots, wrinkled linen slacks, a tent-like Hawaiian shirt, and a double-breasted linen suit jacket hanging open, the sleeves shoved up to his elbows exposing his thick hairy forearms.

He waved and gave me the 60-year-old version of little boy Lenny's twinkly eyes and toothy grin. He stashed his half-smoked cigar in a screw-top case and pocketed it and swung toward me with his arms out and a wounded look that said *Rescue me!* but really meant *I'm coming to steal your soul!* The hug was unbearable, reeking of sweat and cigar breath. But he didn't grab my ass, so that told me he really needed something from me, which meant I was holding his big furry balls in the palm of my hand.

"So!" he growled. "You saw the play?"

"Just now."

"Incredible, right?"

"Well, we should talk."

"Yeah! Let's go!" As he led me to the rear of the cafe, Lenny said, "How's your TV show doing?" I was surprised he even knew what I was working on.

"Episode 1 drops tonight. The network thinks we have a hit."

"Good for you, Adrienne," he said, adding with a smarmy chuckle, "didn't I always say you have many talents?"

That motherfucker! He still can't help himself! We both knew what he was talking about and suddenly, as if no years had passed and I was still an 18-year-old newcomer to the business, my pulse started pounding, my mouth went dry, and I was afraid to be too close to him.

"Is Juno here?"

"Yeah, yeah," he sighed. "She's in the back. We're proud of you, Adrienne, especially me, since I gave you your start in the business."

Juno was perched on a back corner banquette, her phone at her ear. She was wearing a beige pants suit and open-collared blouse and a look of distress. Her long-jawed, bronzed face was framed with shoulder-length hair, now gray, that she kept flipping nervously back. She muttered into the phone and slid over for Lenny to sit beside her, but she held me off with a raised hand for privacy. Hello Juno, I thought, and fuck you, too.

This meeting would go easier with a dose of anesthesia. I didn't care that I'd only had two hours sleep in the last thirty-six. I wandered over to the bar and asked for a St. Germain Royale, ice cold champagne with a dash of a liqueur made from elderflowers. It arrived in a chilled tulip glass, and I took a long drink and congratulated myself for finishing a long hot summer's work.

Lenny and Juno waved me over to join them. I drained my Royale and brought a second drink to the table. There were smiles and hugs and kisses all around, murmurs of counterfeit affection, and we settled in around the banquette. I sat back and sipped my drink with a pleasant smile on my face and my loathing on a low burn, waiting for them to crawl to me.

"So," Lenny said, "when I read Lana —"

"*Lena.*"

"— I knew you were the answer to our Joel Garner problem. The way your writing brings out the humanity of your characters."

"Sorry we passed on your new script, honey," Juno droned through her nose. "We just didn't fall in love with it."

I shrugged. "I'm sure somebody will."

Lenny said, "Our problem is, we signed Joel to adapt his play, but he's on the fifth draft and the writing is getting worse, not better."

"Egon's frustrated," Juno said. "And now he won't even talk to Joel. It's, like, over between those two."

"There were five curtain calls tonight," I said. "Everybody walked out in tears. With impact like that, how could you have a bad script?"

"Because he didn't write a screenplay!" Juno said. "He stuck a lot of camera angles into his play that he thinks are Egon's style. None of it makes any sense. The script isn't shaped, it doesn't flow, it has no voice —"

"No locations!" Lenny gasped. "But Joel, him we have to deal with every day."

"Such a pain in the ass," Juno said in a languid drawl. "Always bitching and demanding something."

Probably to get paid, I thought.

"In the screenplay," I said, "the three stories have to harmonize as perfectly as they do onstage," preparing to make the obvious point: Egon Swift was the wrong director for such complex material.

But Juno cleared her throat. "It's about people struggling courageously to recover. They're all dealing with loss – the death of a beloved wife, the loss of a sense of freedom and safety, of the immigrant's hope for a better life in America and belief in a father's strength. They all have to decide, live free, or become walled-in by fear, illusion, terror, or hatred."

I almost laughed. Juno had quoted, like a parrot, from a poster enlargement of a review that stood in the lobby of the theater. She'd always been clever like that, in a vacuous sort of way.

"True," I said. "But that's not why people are so moved by it."

"No?" she said irritably. A highly educated know-it-all, she hated to be corrected, which was too bad, because she wasn't as smart as she thought.

"The play puts us right back in the emotional impact of 9/11," I said. "When we share the character's struggles to rebalance their lives, we feel closer to our fellow Americans, which I think is so important at this moment when the country is so divided and angry. 9/11 supposedly gave us national unity from shared tragedy. I always thought that was wishful thinking, but tonight I saw I was wrong. With this play, we get that connection with each other back for a couple hours. And we need that now, more than ever." Lenny and Juno glanced at each other, wary but impressed. "I walked out feeling compassion for everybody in this country. It was a huge relief. Great cast, by the way."

"Yes, except Egon decided to get new actors," Juno said. "The only one he kept in the film is Jonathan Lehane."

"He's brilliant."

"Yeah," Lenny said. "And he won the Best Actor Obie."

"I'm surprised I don't know his work."

"He's been under the radar for a long time," Lenny said.

"His performance is uncanny."

"We have a chance here to make a wonderful film," Lenny said, "but the time factor is insane. The start and wrap dates are set in stone, because Egon's availability is limited. He's gotta be back in L.A. by Christmas to start prep on a new thriller."

The surge of outrage made my head spin. The sexist brat was going to toss off his New York art film before he rushed back to Hollywood to squeeze out another big budget turd.

"This isn't Egon's kind of material," I said, as pleasantly as I could. "Why'd you ask him to direct this, anyway?"

"He came to us," Juno said. "Egon and his wife were on a shopping trip in the city. They saw the play and he just fell in love with it."

"He offered us a serious chunk o' change for the rights," Lenny grinned. "We wouldn't sell, but he was still hot to direct."

Juno explained, "We bought the rights before it even opened. We read it two years before it got to the stage."

"The chick who used to be our personal assistant lives with Joel."

"They needed money. We were able to cut a deal."

"Egon has made a shit ton of money for Emerge International and they want to keep him happy."

"They came up with a small budget for '*Lonely Sky*' as a passion project for him."

"So everybody's working for scale. Or else deferred," said Lenny. "That's how we can do it for so little money. But that doesn't apply to you. We need you on this."

I was half-listening to them. Losing Egon would mean no financing and no movie, so it was pointless to pitch myself to direct. There was still the re-write gig, but that was no consolation. I was about to finish my drink, say I'd think about it, and cry all the way over to the "*Dawgs*" wrap party when Lenny looked past me, waved toward the bar, and called out, "Oh, hi!" He lowered his voice. "Here comes Jonathan." Then he called out, "Hello, hello! Join us!" Lenny twisted in his seat, looking for the waiter.

I heard a deep bass voice behind me: "'Ey-y-y Lenny... and Juno baby," ogling and mocking Juno's homeliness, which caused my jaw to tighten.

Juno replied with a steely grin. "Have you met Adrienne Monet?"

Jonathan Lehane leaned into my line of sight and looked me over from head to foot.

"Well hello." His voice went right through me, like a phrase on a cello.

I nodded. "Pleased to meet you."

He offered his hand, and we shook. I moved over, inviting him to sit beside me. He hesitated for a moment, then sat down and gave us all a smile that was hearty but wary.

He looked older off stage and without makeup, maybe 65 going on 45, with no signs of cosmetic surgery. He was dressed in faded blue jeans and a matching sleeveless denim jacket and no undershirt. He was over six feet tall and slender, with thick gray Irish hair, long expressive eyebrows and bright blue eyes, a perfect nose and high cheekbones and strong jaw, and full lips that would have been sexy on a woman. Beside me, he smelled like salty sweat and cigarette smoke, and he stared at me like a cartoon cat who's cornered a mouse.

"Well, Adrienne," he said. "First time we meet, and here you are in very disreputable company." Lenny gave a little forced laugh, but Juno just settled into a droll stare.

"Just having a drink with old friends."

"We're trying to sign Adrienne to do a rewrite," Lenny said.

"Well, somebody better do one. What else have you done?"

"I've written and directed four films."

"So how would you write this one?"

"I just saw the play. The impact on the audience —"

"It's every night," Lenny said.

"Obviously the emotions from 9/11 are now wired into the collective consciousness. To take a movie audience into that pain the writing has to be wise and compassionate."

"Yeah." He nodded. "And don't forget our director isn't Mike Nichols." He resented Lenny and Juno for signing a hack like Egon Swift to direct his award-winning vehicle. Could've predicted that.

"I'll arrange Adrienne's meeting with Egon," Lenny said, grabbing his cell phone.

With his elbow on the table, Jonathan turned toward me, and I found myself in an intimate space with him. My most seductive instincts arose quite naturally.

"You directed something with 'sperm' in the title, right?" he said. "That was a while ago."

"That title was the studio's idea. And it didn't work."

"I remember the story. Interesting characters. And you didn't take sides."

"Well, how could I? They're all me."

I got the kind of condescending grin he might give an amateur. That told me he'd already decided I was not the writer to adapt *"Lonely Sky"*.

Across the table Lenny and Juno were passing the phone back and forth as they jabbered noisily with Egon Swift. I leaned my shoulder on the banquette and turned so I could only be heard by Jonathan.

"You made me cry tonight," I said softly. "You made your dead wife come alive, right out of thin air."

"Well, I had a lot of help from the playwright."

"Film would allow us to show her. It could deepen the audience's empathy with them both."

"Depends on the writing, and who plays the wife."

"I think the audience will want to see her." He thought about that a moment then shrugged. "To write her side of the scenes, there's plenty to work with, because Sawyer's lines are excellent. The playwright deserves a lot of credit."

"Yes, he does." Jonathan lowered his voice, glancing across the table. "But he's not getting much help from Egon, and those two think he's a pain in the ass." I just shrugged. Some people, what can you do? "So, you live in the city?" he said.

Under the table I suddenly felt a warm, dry hand grip my bare thigh under my skirt, high up on the inside.

"Chelsea," I heard myself say, looking him in the eye, all my attention on that hand and the smirk on his face. I was offended, yet also excited. Despite those killer looks, or maybe because of them, he was just a typical man, grabbing what he wanted without any wit or charm. His audacity intrigued me for a second or two, then I considered breaking his perfect blade of a nose. But that would definitely be counterproductive. So instead of smacking him or turning the table over, and because the butterflies fluttering in my belly seemed to be trying to pour out of my vagina, I sipped my drink and just stared. If he wanted to shock me, he'd have to be a lot bolder than a sneaky hand stroking my thigh.

"Oh, too bad," he said. "I'm going uptown, or else I'd offer you a ride."

I could have invited him to come with me to the "*Dawgs*" wrap party so I could get to know him. But that hand on my thigh changed the dynamic, and now I'd have to be careful with how I encouraged Jonathan Lehane.

"So, Adrienne," he said, "if you take the gig, you better be good."

"I'm better than you seem to think." I reached down, squeezed his hand holding my thigh, then removed it.

Grinning, he plucked a pen from his jacket pocket. "Here's my number. Call me." He wrote it on my napkin. "I can tell you things about the play from the inside out."

"I'm sure your insights would be helpful." And by the way, does your cock match your big opinion of yourself?

"See ya." He rose, flipped a dismissive wave to the Victors, and headed for the exit, leaving the Heineken they bought him sweating untouched on its coaster. He strolled with ease and confidence, like an athlete or a dancer. As he passed two young men at the bar they stopped talking, watched him leave, then turned to each other, drank up and tossed some money down, and headed out the door.

"Tough luck fellas," Lenny chuckled. "He's queer for girls."

Juno was on a FaceTime call, calmly and patiently pitching me to Egon Swift. "We've worked with her. Her name is Adrienne Monet."

His voice was light and calm and without any apparent attitude. Mellow, y'know?

"Never heard of her."

"She's a first-rate writer, one of the best."

"Then why don't I know about her?"

"She's New York-based."

"So are plenty of other writers."

"You've never worked in New York, otherwise you'd know about her."

"So, what's she done?"

"She's written and directed four films and we respect her work very highly. We think she's the writer you need. Here, talk to her."

Juno handed me the phone. On screen was a young man with a wide, square-jawed face, a small tightly pursed mouth and curly black hair. The look in his eyes was arrogant, cool and confident. He was wearing a dark jacket and white dress shirt. In the room behind him, a piano, bass, and drums played a slow shuffle behind a trumpet player, causing me a brief trill of Aldo terrors, as jazz always did.

"Hello Egon."

"Oh hi Adrienne," he said briskly. "So you're our new writer?"

"Once I hear your vision for the film, I'll know if I can write it."

I felt ridiculous using the word vision with him, but Egon Swift was a creature of Hollywood, a place where you don't have a career, you have a journey, and where even your flimsiest idea can prove you're a visionary if you get somebody to finance it.

"I just need the play translated to the screen with as much taste and elegance as you can bring."

Of course. A tasteful, elegant art film to dress up his sordid reputation.

"Are you available tomorrow?"

"I'll be at my place in East Hampton. Lenny and Juno have the address."

"I'll be there—"

Abruptly the screen went blank.

"So Adrienne," Juno said, taking the phone from me. "Can we call Marshall and talk about your deal?"

"I'll call you tomorrow. After I meet with Egon."

Lenny kept clearing his throat and pushing up his jacket cuffs like he was ready to get to work, while Juno just looked at her watch and sighed. Tick tock, tick tock...

On Saturday morning the East Hampton jitney was totally booked and so were the planes from Teterboro and LaGuardia, so I had to settle in for a long train ride to the east end of Long Island. The night before, I'd left the "*Dawgs*" wrap party with one of the Lily execs on one arm and her boyfriend on the other, both of them tripping on mushrooms that I politely declined, and we made a long erotic night of it at their place in Williamsburg. I was tired and hungover by the time I raced up to Penn Station and the LIRR. But I had the playscript for "*Lonely Sky*" to read, which was more stimulating than a 24-ounce cup of coffee.

My taxi stopped beside a tall hedge on Lily Pond Lane, at a gate manned by a security guard in uniform with a pistol on his belt. I rolled down the window and gave my name. He looked me up on a tablet, took my picture, tapped the screen, and the gate swung open. We drove toward the house up a long shady driveway bordering an emerald green lawn that glowed in the salty oceanside sunlight. Egon's house was a brand-new replica of a classic, brown-shingled Hamptons beach mansion with lots of gables and white porch railings.

Ordinarily I'd have no desire to meet Egon Swift. We were in the same business, his movies were hits, he was a Hollywood player and world famous and everybody wanted to befriend him, work with him, go to bed with him, get high with him. But he was all wrong as the director of "*Lonely Sky*". Nothing in his past work suggested he had the talent to direct it with any taste or intelligence. So why did he think he could? Was this a sudden burst of creative testosterone? A spiritual upshift to a more enlightened Hollywood consciousness? I couldn't wait to hear whatever insights he was undoubtedly eager to share.

A cool dry breeze swept across the car park, lifted the hair off my forehead, unstuck my linen blouse from my back and invaded the wide cuffs of my shorts. Even the wind out here was the best money could buy. In the shade beneath a row of towering hemlocks, a Mercedes SUV was parked beside a BMW convertible and a Range Rover, all of them black with smoked windows.

A man's voice murmured behind me, "Adrienne?"

"Hello Egon."

He stepped down the broad granite staircase with his hand extended and his small lips twisted in a pout. I guessed he was thirty. He was about six feet tall and broad shouldered, with a buffed-out chest under a white linen shirt. His handshake was as limp as his voice.

"It took you so long to get here. Didn't you fly?"

"I couldn't get a flight on short notice, so I had to take the train."

"Well, okay, but I'm a little pressed for time. Come on, let's get comfortable."

Walking through the house was like flipping the pages of a feature story in Architectural Digest. In the living room, two sofas faced each other across a marble and mahogany coffee table on natural fiber carpet, near a fireplace big enough to roast more than one peasant at a time. Passing through the dining room, we rounded a table set for twelve under two chandeliers of electric candles. The kitchen had a wide-plank oak floor, glass-front cabinetry, stainless steel appliances, and a wine cabinet behind glass doors holding at least fifty bottles.

We stepped out the back door onto a covered terra cotta deck overlooking the swimming pool, beyond which the backyard sloped down to the dunes and the gray-green Atlantic. Egon led me to two wicker sofas facing each other across a low glass table. He gestured to someone behind me, and when I glanced back, I caught the flicker of a white apron.

"Is coffee okay for you?" he said, pulling out his smart phone and peering at it. "Or would you like something stronger?"

"Coffee's perfect."

"Good, coming right up. One second." His thumbs attacked the phone.

The coffee came in a glass French press on a silver tray with a pitcher of cream, a bowl of sugar cubes and a pair of tongs, and was strong, hot, and delicious. A maid in uniform silently poured a Red Bull into a tall glass for my host.

Egon's lips moved as he read the text message, then he sent it.

"On the phone last night the light was so dim I couldn't see you," he said. "I was expecting a writer who was all business, you know, hunchback, chronic headache, chain-smoker. You're a very nice surprise."

"Who says I'm not all business?" I said with a friendly grin.

He chuckled, then glanced over my shoulder and his grin vanished. From behind me a lithe, dark haired woman appeared, tanned and fit in a two-piece bathing suit and herding two smaller versions of Egon, one boy and one girl. She held out her hand to me. Her grip was strong, assured.

"Hello, I'm Rita Swift," she said, smiling, but curious. Her husband watched us nervously.

"Adrienne Monet."

"Your name is familiar."

"I've made a few films. I'm here to talk about writing for your husband."

"Ah. Well, welcome." Rita's voice quickened as she turned to her husband. "We're going to the beach."

The little girl sidled up beside Egon and put her arm over his shoulders.

"Daddy, are you coming to the beach with us?"

"Not now, honey, Daddy's working." He kissed her cheek, and she slid away from him, disappointed.

"The beach?" Egon said. "You're going to the beach now?"

"Just for a while," Rita said with forced patience. "The kids need something to do." Her eyes dropped to me. "Nice meeting you, Adrienne."

"Nice meeting you too. Bye, kids."

"Don't forget later," Egon called out as his family walked away. "We have that thing."

"I know, I know," Rita said over her shoulder. "I'll be here for your thing."

He watched Rita walk away. He pondered for a moment, then said, "Sorry. Excuse me for a second."

He stood up, dialing the phone, and walked over beside the pool. He talked for a minute, lowered his voice and spoke emphatically at one point, then returned, shaking his head.

"The work never ends," Egon said, staring at his phone and flicking it with his fingertip. "So... Juno said you used to direct."

"I still do. My reality TV series dropped last night. Maybe you saw it. *'Men R Dawgs'*?"

"*'Men R Dawgs'*?" He chuckled. "That's yours?"

"My latest."

"Congratulations. As we know, it's a rough business for women."

"Yeah. I guess we've both had our ups and downs."

He gave me a vague smirk.

I raised my coffee cup. "Here's to more ups than downs."

With his free hand he raised his Red Bull and drank. He obviously didn't know about any of my films. That didn't surprise me, since I made my last film when he was barely out of school. But no way was I going to present my CV like some pathetic job seeker. I wanted to hear how he'd answer the most important question.

"So, Egon, what attracted you to *'Lonely Sky'*?"

"Well, I'm obviously very gratified that the public has embraced me and my films, but I've got to re-brand. Show a new maturity in my work." I waited for more, and, looking uncomfortable, he went on. "Rita took me to see the play. I knew immediately I had to do it. It's rare to find 9/11 material that isn't the usual, you know, clichés."

"But the script needs work."

"Yes it does." His phone rang. "One second, sorry. I have to take this."

He stepped away again, walking past the pool towards the beach. He started shaking his head and I heard him say, "No, no, that's not what I want." He listened for a time, nodding, then shook his head and said loudly, "No. Definitely not. I want you to get back to me. Today."

He returned and sat back down, frowning.

"Where were we? Oh yeah. I guess it was the weave of the three stories together, that strategy, that I thought was intriguing."

"An emotional and thematic unity holds those stories together. That's why the impact is greater than the sum of all three stories. That's what gives the play its power."

He was listening to me, but his eyes were on his phone. Lucky for him he was too far away for me to grab it and throw it in the pool. But I knew how to get his complete attention.

"Anyway, I doubt your psycho-thriller fans will come to see '*Lonely Sky*'."

He shot me a surprised, hostile glance. I'd finally penetrated his cool indifference.

"Of course, some will come because your name will be on it, but the genre and the subject will appeal to people who've never seen your work. This film should help you reach a new audience."

"Well, that's the idea."

It was time to get down to details.

"Let's talk about locations for scenes. Any thoughts about that?"

He seemed surprised by the question.

"You're from New York, right?"

"Yes."

"Well, you can do that better than me."

"Okay. Anything else on your mind?"

He stared at me and scrunched his forehead as if he could squeeze out an idea. What he came up with was, I guess, the best he could do.

"I can see what I want the film to be, but it's kind of hard to put into words, Adrienne. I'm eager to see what you come up with."

I waited for more. Hard to put into words! Lenny and Juno had a much bigger problem than they knew. Egon wanted a script rewrite, but he couldn't offer even a vague idea of how he wanted it done, and that was making me uneasy.

He tapped his finger on his chin.

"You know what I've been thinking? All my films have explored violence in a certain way. Operatically, let's say. But here, there's no violence to put on screen. This movie is about the aftermath. Same theme I've always worked with but requiring different treatment."

"You have no family drama to speak of in your films. And in 'Lonely Sky' we have two, plus a Gothic love story."

He nodded. He seemed to be fighting to concentrate despite the shot of caffeine from the Red Bull.

"Yeah, I guess so. But there's comedy here and there, too."

"And the characters and situations are so emotionally complicated."

"Oh yeah." He cocked his fist, and said vaguely, "That's one of the real strengths of the piece."

"So we've got to get it right, or people will say we're exploiting a national tragedy. Disrespecting the dead."

He tilted his head back. "Oh yeah. Very serious stuff." Then he looked back at the phone and shook his head. "Jesus Christ! I'm sorry. One second." He got up and went into the house. In a moment I heard him shouting at someone but what he was saying wasn't clear. I checked my wristwatch. It was already late afternoon.

I could almost *smell* what had gone wrong with Egon Swift. There must have been a moment when he got excited by the potential of *"Lonely Sky"* to lend prestige to his career, and with reckless confidence and little self-examination, he took it on. Then when he realized directing it was beyond his abilities, he choked. He couldn't give me any ideas for the script rewrite because the whole project was beyond his skills and imagination. Judging by his attitude toward me, he was counting on the talent and energy of his collaborators to make up for his shortcomings. I was thinking about that, and about how little time we had, when he returned and dropped back into his chair, looking exasperated.

"So, the script," he said.

"Anything else you want me to focus on?"

"No. I'm looking forward to reading your first draft."

So, was that the deal? Because he couldn't tell me what he wanted, I was free to write whatever I liked? Yeah, sure, until he didn't like it. Then I'd be entangled, writing for someone who didn't know and couldn't say what he wanted. He'd tell me "Try this," then "No, try that," and his whims and uncertainty would run me ragged. I loved the project, but I had to be careful not to trap myself in a writing gig that could potentially be torture, butting heads every day with a spoiled mediocrity. He had taken on a job he couldn't do, and he couldn't withdraw now without tarnishing his brand, so I'd be whipped one way or another. No amount of money was worth that.

Egon glanced at a large silver watch on his wrist. "I'm sorry, I'm really pressed for time now. We should meet again back in the city this week and talk."

He seemed unconcerned that the production was under tremendous time pressure.

"Well," I said, "are you happy with this meeting?"

"Oh, sure. I think we can work together."

Based on what? I was astounded he could even say that. He had no idea who I was, or what I could do. He just wanted someone, anyone, to wrestle this strange, emotionally wrenching piece of theater into a screenplay he could direct.

"Well, okay," I said, "so, if I decide to write the script –"

"If you write the script?" Icy eyes. "I was led to believe," he murmured, "you were on board."

"I had to meet you and hear your ideas –"

"Oh. So, what was this? My audition?"

"I came here to see if I could write the script that you want."

"Yeah? And?"

"I have to think it over." I hoped that was reassuring enough and I didn't just blow my chance. "Sometimes a director gives the writer a lot of notes, but you've left me with a lot of options."

There was a chilly silence.

"Oh." He stared at me, amazed, like he couldn't believe I got this so wrong. Didn't I know that everybody wanted to work with Egon Swift?

"So, I'll call Lenny and Juno once I decide," I said.

"Okay. Yeah. Do that."

He stood up and walked back into the house, shaking his head and mumbling. I stood there staring at my cellphone, pretending to send a text, so I wouldn't have to follow too closely behind him.

The kitchen was crowded with a white-jacketed catering crew. Meat smoke from the grill drifted on the dry afternoon breeze and ice cubes jingled, and from the front of the house came bursts of warm welcome and laughter. Egon, no longer sulking and quite the bon vivant, was greeting bronzed and well-dressed guests arriving for what appeared to be a barbecue for Hollywood people summering in The Hamptons. The aroma of food cooking, the prospect of drinks and food and conversation and meeting new people, lifted my spirits from where my worthless chat with Egon had dumped them. A party was just what I needed and might even give me a second chance to try to talk to Egon about the script.

But he turned to me.

"Sorry, but I have all these guests coming over."

That hurt more than it should have. Quickly, before my real feelings showed, I thanked him for making time to see me, and he escorted me toward the door past his guests, some of whom I knew. Going so soon, Adrienne? Yes, sorry, can't stay to party, work to do back in the city. Aw, too bad, I just knew they were thinking, unlike we insouciant and wealthy people of leisure, you have to work. Well, bravo to that good old blue-collar work ethic. From the front steps, Egon called out to his estate wagon driver to take me to the train station.

"So," he shrugged. "You think it over. And so will I." He looked at me for a moment, his eyes saying nothing, and turned back inside.

I stood in the cool shadow of the canopy over the platform beside the East Hampton station. I was hungry, thirsty, and my eyes and head hurt from the glaring sun in spite of my dark glasses. I was ready to go home and write off the day as a waste of time and try to forget about *"Lonely Sky."* My instincts were right when Marshall first called me. Egon was an inescapably sticky situation, and you might die before you got unstuck. My first instinct, which told me to say no, was right. But I came a long way to end up so disappointed, and now I was facing a long ride back to Manhattan, on a train so full of day-trippers from the south shore beaches they'd be standing in the aisles.

I kept the *"Lonely Sky"* play script in my shoulder bag. I didn't want to read it because I'd had enough disappointment for one day. I wanted to make the movie I'd been seeing in my head since I left the theater the night before, and that desire was clawing at me. My whole life I'd looked for stories that I just had to tell, only to find the perfect one clutched in the hands of a spoiled kid who didn't know what to do with it. Maybe the writing gig was still possible if I was willing to deal with Egon's dysfunction. Even then, the most I could hope for was to write the best script I could, hand it over to Egon and walk away, praying he wouldn't fuck it up too badly. But that wouldn't be enough. The impact *"Lonely Sky"* had on me and the passion to make the movie was the greatest creative excitement I'd felt in ten years. Every instinct told me this was the one. So why couldn't I call Lenny and Juno and commit to writing it? Because Egon was the wrong director and all the producers cared about was his brand name that got them the money so they could produce another movie.

The train from New York pulled in and the Victors got off, laughing and chatting with another couple. I backed out of sight around the corner of the station. No way was I ready to talk to them. They got into Egon's estate wagon to be whisked off to the barbecue. Thank God they didn't see me! Then I was struck by a depressing thought. At the party they'd certainly look for me and ask Egon about our meeting. Suppose he told them he didn't want to work with me? Suppose I was obsessing over a writing job that wasn't even available anymore?

I couldn't help but think of all the projects I'd believed in over the past ten years that never got a green light, that pile of screenplays on the shelf over my desk at home, rejected and unproduced, years of work that went nowhere. I realized then I was drifting into dangerous emotional territory and had to get tough with myself. Forget about *"Lonely Sky"*, Adrienne. Pack your bags and leave your sadness behind. Go hang out with your friends in Cherry Grove. Life there would be peaceful, quiet and green, the late summer seaside air would be fresh, the sunshine warm on the beach and the nights cool and sweet, life with the girls at The House of Red Roses would be an endless party, every meal would smell and taste wonderful, you could relax and enjoy life and maybe even meet someone new and sexy and exciting, and maybe you'd stop obsessing over one more film you didn't get to make.

Fuck it. It was time to shove in the knife. I composed an email on my phone:

"Hi Juno, hi Lenny. As I told you, I feel a deep connection to 'Lonely Sky'. The characters and stories have really gotten into my blood. I know it will make a wonderful film."

Should I tell them Egon was resisting the project and was creatively blocked? No, they signed Egon to direct because he brought the studio's money, and they ignored the gross incongruity of trusting this kind of movie to his kind of talent. Let them find out how much trouble they were in without my help. Of course at the back of my mind I hoped maybe the production would collapse and restart later without Egon and I would have a chance to direct it. So I simply wrote:

"But I need a vacation. Sorry to turn down your offer. Thanks for considering me. I wish you luck."

All of it bad! I decided to keep the email as a draft and waste more of their time. I'd send it late tonight when I got back to New York. By then, Lenny would be high and happy, the life of the party as his A-list director's latest producer, and Juno would be restless as a squirrel on meth waiting for my answer. I thought this was the best of many ways I could fuck them up, throwing them into a guilty panic while they were partying in the Hamptons. I imagined them reading my message and in desperation start working the party crowd looking for their next victim with a laptop.

Before the train to the city returned from Montauk, I needed coffee and a bottle of water for the trip home. Folded around my Amex card I found the cafe napkin with Jonathan Lehane's phone number from the night before. He looked down his nose at me, fondled my bare thigh, then practically dared me to call him.

I balled the napkin up, but my hand hovered over the trashcan. *I can tell you things about this play from the inside out*, he said. On second thought, suppose Egon didn't badmouth me to the Victors? Suppose he was as desperate for a savior as Lenny and Juno? If writing the script was all I could do, then at least it would keep me inside the production. Lehane might be my best chance to get an ally on a production run by otherwise shitty people. I saw hints last night that we both loved the play, thought the director was all wrong, and didn't trust the Victors. I've started business and creative relationships based on less. Then there was that other thing, that warm hand gripping my thigh under the table.

I dialed the number on the napkin, ready for him to be as boorish as he was the night before.

"Hey Lehane, it's Adrienne Monet."

"Who?" he demanded. "How'd you get this number?"

"You gave it to me last night when we were with Lenny and Juno."

"Oh, it's you. So, what's up?"

"I want to pick your brain about '*Lonely Sky*'."

There was a long pause. "You're going to write the script." He sounded unhappy.

"I don't know yet. We need to talk. Maybe you can help me decide."

"I might try to talk you out of it."

"Fair enough. I also want to straighten you out on a couple things."

"Oh yeah?" A soft, deep-in-the-throat chuckle.

"Yeah, so meet with me tonight. Dinner, drinks, whatever."

"Well, tonight's really not the best time."

"I have to make a decision fast. I just had a meeting with Egon."

"You did? A script meeting?"

"I'm in East Hampton waiting for the train. I won't be back in the city until tonight, can we meet later?"

"Yeah, listen, don't leave. I'm just up the road in Montauk." He gave me directions. "I'll see what I've got to eat around here. Can you cook?"

Fifteen minutes later my taxi turned into Jonathan Lehane's driveway. "Whoa!" the driver yelled.

I grabbed the armrest as we swerved to avoid a red Mustang speeding at us driven by a young blonde with her hand out the window and her middle finger raised.

Jonathan stood beside the house, in cut-off jeans, a white tee shirt, and loafers, with a grin on his face. He flinched when the Mustang's tires screeched onto the Old Montauk Highway.

He came over and opened the door for me.

"Wow!" he said. "She could've killed you guys!"

"Did you need more time?" I said as I got out.

"Nah!" he said. "It's cool." I paid the driver, and in the side mirror I caught Jonathan checking out my ass. I wiggled, and he grinned, like a kid caught being naughty.

"Okay Handsome. Do I get the tour?"

"Uh, yeah, sure."

His house was a classic two-story Cape Cod, with weathered brown shingles and white-trimmed windows and porches all around. Sprawled at the bottom of a hill of hardwoods and evergreens on a bluff overlooking the ocean, the place had an air of privacy and lonely contentment.

"What beautiful grounds!" I always thought one of the best things about having money was being able to afford people to keep your house spotless and the landscaping impeccable.

"Yeah, we're surrounded by the state park," he said. "C'mon, I'll show you."

The swimming pool in the back yard was surrounded by a tall evergreen hedge with a wooden gate. He led me through that gate, and we climbed a gravel path up a wooded slope past a small Japanese tea house – "Where I go to meditate" – and he showed me the guest cottage, a smaller version of the main house.

As we strolled back down, he said, "If the train to New York tonight is too much trouble, you're welcome to stay up here."

"Assuming you haven't kicked me out by then."

He chuckled as he opened the kitchen door.

The kitchen and dining room were at the back of the house. Their wide windows looked out on the back yard, pool and the woods. While Jonathan uncorked a bottle of pinot grigio and poured two glasses I wandered into the middle of the house. The floors, wide oak planks, gleamed with a honey glow. Worn and comfortable living room furniture was grouped around a large stone fireplace. The mantle and bookshelves were lined with framed photographs of Lehane from across his career: as a foxy teen model in sports clothes and suits; as Jimmy O'Neill, the foppish young detective from the *"Streets of Manhattan"* TV series that launched his screen career; in dark sunglasses as Dirk Dagger, the vigilante action hero he played in three 1980s films. There were no other people in the photos with him, except one picture of Jonathan and Delphine Tessier, the legendary French film star and chanteuse, both of them middle-aged and looking dangerously sexy, sitting at a sidewalk table very conspicuously in front of the Café Les Deux Magots in Paris in what looked like an ad for an aperitif.

We took our drinks to the front porch and sat in a pair of wicker armchairs. The August afternoon heat had begun to cool, the golden evening sun cast blue shadows, and soon the ocean and sky would merge into dusk.

"I wasn't sure I'd be welcome," I said, "after the way you treated me last night."

He made a face. "What way was that?"

"Kind of surly, I guess because you found me hanging out with such disreputable people."

"For all I knew you were one of them."

"You'd better be joking."

"It wasn't about you. Some nights the play leaves me kinda edgy."

"You seemed to make your mind up about me pretty fast. Like I was this chick out of left field trying to get her hands on your award-winning play. But you're a man, so I guess I should have expected that."

A tight grin. "Keep it up. I love being reduced to a stereotype." He took a sip of wine. "So why aren't you at Egon's party?"

I shrugged. "After our meeting, I was quickly shown the door."

"Hmm. Didn't go well?"

"Hard to say."

"Why, what happened?"

"Well, Egon was nice. He introduced me to his wife and kids. They were nice. Then we had kind of a nice chat about the script before the party got started."

"'Kind of' a chat about the script?" Jonathan said. "Kind of?"

"He's still finding his way."

"Jesus Christ," Jonathan muttered bitterly. "Joel's drafts aren't even worth talking about. I don't trust the producers, the hot shit director is 'still finding his way,' the script doctor may or may not take the job, and we start shooting in two weeks." He shook his head. "We all know it's a miracle whenever any movie ever gets made. This one's gonna need divine intervention."

"Egon didn't seem to be feeling any pressure."

"What is it with that kid? Is he cool, and thinks everything's under control, or is he oblivious, in which case we're in deep shit? We've never even talked about my role. Not that I'd expect anything useful from the director of *'Dangerous and Deranged'*."

"But you're still in the movie."

"I won an Obie for Best Actor. I own this role. I'm not letting it go to somebody else. This is a chance to act instead of just looking hot and hunky."

I got a glimpse then of who Jonathan Lehane was, and of his lifelong frustration. A woman knows what it's like to be wanted for reasons that have nothing to do with who you are inside.

"I can still feel Sawyer from last night," I said, opening what I hoped would be a substantive conversation. "His loneliness and desolation were almost unbearable to sit through."

"It's too much for some people." He shrugged and sighed. "Some nights it's too much for me."

"The play really says something about the impact of 9/11 on average people. One year later they're still coping with that morning. Take the East Village couple's story. He seems kind of nutty, but he's really acting out the fear that's still under everybody's skin."

"Yes. I think the flip side of that is the Muslim family's story. It's an emotional and political minefield. America torturing an Arab man? An American citizen? I think Joel was smart to keep the father silent for most of that story."

"I think so too," I said. "Better to experience his suffering through the reaction of the son and the mother and sister."

"I was sure we'd get some shit for showing a Muslim victim of American torture. But most of the reviews were great."

"In New York. Wait'll the whole country sees the film." I thought I was getting through. At least he was talking to me as one creative to another. "I think the suffering of David Sawyer will be the most emotionally powerful story for people."

He shrugged. "I love David Sawyer. And I'm scared of David Sawyer. He's powerful, all day he makes billion-dollar deals. Then at night he's helpless and haunted by the loss of a love he can't live without. He's got every material need met, but without his wife, his life is empty."

"So he creates a fantasy life with her."

He sighed. "Anyway, it's gratifying to get respect for my acting for once, instead of people getting all googly-eyed over my looks." He gave me a sideways glance. "Although you don't seem too googly-eyed."

I couldn't tell if he was relieved, or disappointed, or coming on to me.

"How do you know I'm not secretly googly-eyed?"

"Ah. Well, I've always said that a woman is only as interesting as her secrets."

"I could be googly-eyed in parts of me you don't even see."

"What parts are they?"

"If I tell you, it won't be my secret, then I might not be interesting anymore."

"Oh, I don't worry about that," he said. "You're shivering." The sun was down, and the salty air had taken on a chill. "Are you cold?"

"When I left the city this morning it was so hot." I picked at my shorts and lightweight blouse. "I didn't think I'd need warmer clothes."

"Aren't you hungry? Let's get dinner started."

He went upstairs and brought down a blue cashmere sweater. It fit like a minidress, smelled like musky cologne, and I had to roll up the sleeves, but it was warm.

"I'm glad I looked you up," I said. "After meeting with Egon I was really conflicted. But now I'm excited again. We can make a really powerful film out of these stories. The production, I guess it is what it is."

"It's not what I hoped for," he said. "But I'll know what to do, even if the director doesn't."

"And if I decide to write this, I'll need an ally above the line."

"Yes." He looked at me thoughtfully for a moment, then said, "You will." He held my attention a moment, then headed for the kitchen.

After I admitted I'd exaggerated my cooking skills, Jonathan took over. As he cooked, we talked about *"Lonely Sky"* and I think that's when we were sure we both wanted to make the same movie.

We sat down to dinner at a table in a corner of the kitchen. Jonathan flipped a switch and out in the backyard underwater lights illuminated the pool. He sipped the wine, set down his glass, and cleared his throat.

"Just so we're clear, okay?" he said. "I'm not sold on you as the writer."

"Well, I haven't decided to take the job, yet."

He reached to a sideboard for a sheaf of papers and started flipping through the pages.

"What's that?"

"Your Wikipedia bio," he said. "I printed it this morning. I also streamed your films."

"You must've been really worried I'd take the job."

"I'm still worried." He scanned the pages. "So how much of this is bull-shit?"

"As much or as little as you want."

"'*Lonely Sky*' isn't like anything you've ever done."

"You only saw what I could get produced."

"Fair enough. So, how much of this is true?"

I shrugged. "It's all true, one way or another." I brushed my hair back, swirled my wine in its glass, and prepared to discuss the last subject I ever want to talk about, myself.

He laughed quietly, then mocked my biography sentence-by-sentence.

"Adrienne Monet. Distant descendant of Claude Monet, the Impression-ist painter. The only child of a French diplomat assigned to the United Na-tions and his socialite wife. As a schoolgirl, her earliest films were storyboards she drew in her notebooks. While concentrating on English and History in high school in Manhattan, she also studied film scripts she bought mail-order from a company in Hollywood called Screenplay City, one of whose employ-ees sold her a bootleg set of cassettes of the Robert McKee story structure seminar."

"Uh oh. Sorry Bob. How did that get in there?"

"'She started writing and shooting movies on a video camera she got for her fifteenth birthday." He looked up at me, mock-impressed. "Was that your big Spielberg moment, when you decided to become a director?"

"No," I said in a flat controlled voice. "That was my big Adrienne Monet moment."

"Okay." He chuckled and put the pages aside. "So tell me what's not here."

"What more do you need to know?"

"When I think I know enough, I'll tell you."

I poured myself more wine, wondering what it would take to get him on my side and off this subject.

"Okay... That camera? My high school boyfriend shoplifted it for my birthday. I had to hide it from my parents. They wanted me to go to medical school and become a doctor. But as soon as I started playing with that little 8-millimeter camcorder, all I cared about was shooting everything in sight."

I didn't mention my first film, *"A Misfit's Adventures of the Flesh"*, personal porn I shot with my hidden camcorder as I had sex with my high school boy-friends and girlfriends, a collection that I still sometimes watched on lonely winter nights.

"In the school library I found a book of interviews with film directors by Andrew Sarris. Almost every major director of the 20th century was in there. So I stole it. I carried it around and read it night and day, cover to cover, again and again, 'til it fell apart. There wasn't a lot of technical learning in it, but it got me dreaming about becoming a filmmaker. The only thing wrong was all the interviews were with men, except for Leni Riefenstahl, for God's sake. Later I read another book by a man named John Gallagher. Again, mostly male directors, but at least he talked to Joan Micklin Silver and Susan Seidel-man. But no Elaine May? No Barbara Loden, Liliana Cavani, Lina Wertmul-ler, Ida Lupino, Shirley Clarke, Barbara Kopple, Gillian Armstrong, Amy Heckerling? In those days their films were even hard to find at Blockbuster."

"How did you even know who they were?"

"My high school had a very good art department, and our teacher had worked on film and a couple soap operas in the 1970s. She loved to screen movies for us, especially by female filmmakers. We'd analyze them afterwards. And she wasn't shy about warning the girls that women in the business had to learn how to survive in a man's world. There are more women directors now, but we're all skating on thin ice. You might get somewhere as long as you keep moving, but if you stop..."

"Yeah yeah," Jonathan said wearily, "and there's sexism and condescen-sion, and never being taken seriously or trusted with millions of dollars." He sighed. "I know what women go through."

"Well, that's very highly evolved of you, Jonathan. Far above the level of even the smartest lower primate."

"Whoa!" he said, laughing, "I knew there was a bitch in you somewhere." He looked at my bio again. "I don't see anything here about college. You never went? Don't be embarrassed, by the way, I didn't either. I barely made it out of Naperville High. Not because I was dumb. I started to do catalogue modeling when I was 14."

"Yeah, I saw the pictures. You were too cute for words. Anyway, college would have been a distraction for me. I knew what I wanted to do. So I moved to the East Village. This was the summer of '88, right after high school graduation. My parents disowned me, but I was in heaven. My roommates were students at NYU film school, and they had access to the school's cameras. I'd sit in on classes, too. We jammed ourselves into this grimy, roach-infested railroad flat on Avenue B. The place was like an oven. But all we cared about was movies. Not the usual Hollywood shit. Not 'Ferris Bueller's Day Off', okay? We ran all over New York to see stuff. The city used to have all those revival theaters, the Eighth Street Playhouse, Theater 80, The Regency, Cinema Studio, Bleecker Street Cinema, The Metro, The Thalia, 68th Street Playhouse. All gone now. I still have dreams about those theaters. They were my classrooms."

He got up and put on a kettle of water on the stove. "Coffee? Tea?"

"Nothing, thanks."

He sat down with a cup of coffee. "Okay, so when do we get to Lenny and Juno? Or would you rather not talk about it?"

"Yeah... I mean, no, I don't mind. They were important to my career. Not as much as they seem to think. But they gave me my start."

"I'd never heard of them until my agent told me they'd locked up the rights and signed Egon Fucking Swift to direct. I was literally sick to my stomach."

I kicked off my sandals and put my bare feet on the chair beside Jonathan.

"Juno was Juno Reilly, she was a script supervisor. My first movie jobs were working on set as a PA thanks to Lenny. They also made me their development person, reading and analyzing scripts for screen potential and writing coverage while they were hustling budget money. I found them the script for their first film. 'Blood of the Bayou'. Hillbilly Horror. They shot it in Louisiana the summer of 1989 and somehow nobody died of the heat. They offered me a job on it as a non-Guild AD. It would have been a big step up in my career, but I turned down the job. They were really pissed off."

"Well, of course. They were taking on their first production, and they wanted people they could count on working for them. They gave you your start, but when they wanted something back you let them down."

"They acted like they owned me. And I was depending on them too much. I decided I had to stay in New York and work on my career without their help. I freelanced as a set PA. I wrote coverage for studios and independent producers. From Day One, I hustled for budget money, but I didn't have a reel yet, just a couple of screenplays. The first things I directed for pay were low budget rock videos for a couple bands now forgotten. I only made about a hundred dollars a day, but it paid my bills, and I had a tiny place on East 7th Street. Those early videos got me a relationship with a producer who had a deal with a record label. She hired me to direct videos with bigger budgets. I shot them in the daytime and at night I used the cameras and short ends and a different crew to shoot scenes from one of my screenplays. I didn't sleep much in those days. I borrowed on my credit cards, I sent around a bunch of video dupes, held a couple showcase screenings, got some buzz going. It took almost a year, but I raised the money to make my first feature when I was twenty-two."

"The weird one about the coma patient."

"I was told a horror film was the way to get noticed, especially if you can shoot cheap. I came up with the idea to play a young pop star in the hospital after a car accident. She's totally paralyzed, but she can hear her family and entourage in the room around her, scheming to let her die and grab her money."

"You expect her to come out of the coma. But she never does."

"No, and that's a structural flaw, I admit. So to get around that we see her taking action in the revenge fantasies in her head. I made the characters around her so greedy and unscrupulous that they all eventually destroy each other. So in that sense, she's paralyzed, but she prevails, so it's an 'up' ending. I really didn't know how to make the story work until I read an article by a doctor who said you can be comatose and powerless to speak or move, and still be aware of what's happening around you. To me that would be the ultimate horror. I sent him the script for his opinion. He told me it was trash, but the medical science was basically correct."

"It reminded me of when I was a kid and went to the flicks by Roger Corman on Saturday matinees in Naperville. You got a creepiness very similar to his movies of Edgar Allan Poe stories."

"'*Coma*' still makes money. I get some checks off the DVD sales and streaming. I'm still cutting checks to pay the actors and crew who worked on spec. My share, by the way, is the same as everybody else's."

"What agent made that deal?"

"That was before I had an agent. I promised the crew if the film made money we'd all share equally and we do. Anyway, after '*Coma*', I turned down a lot of low budget horror things because I didn't want to repeat myself."

"Well that took guts, especially so early in your career."

"But if you don't keep trying new things you stop growing. That's why I moved to LA. I thought it was the place to be after '*Coma*' got me noticed. And I actually got married for a couple of years. You saw my documentary, '*Bust*'? That's about my ex-husband's rise and fall with his Internet startup. He lost billions. He was accused of fraud by his investors. Everybody sued him. By the time we were divorced he was dead broke, but the film was making money, so I increased his share of the profits."

"After getting divorced?"

"I didn't want to be unkind. He's not a bad guy. Just not the guy for me." Before the memories of that time began to replay in my mind, I changed the subject. "My best experience as a filmmaker was '*Girl in the City*', and that took seven years to get financed."

"Why'd you cast Willi Adams to play the lead instead of you?"

"She has that gamine kind of Holly Golightly thing, and I don't. She comes to New York to re-invent herself, and fails, and I didn't want to play a failure. I wanted to play the best-friend who tells her story. Originally, I wanted to film '*Breakfast at Tiffanys*', the right way, in period, the Upper East Side during World War II. I mean, let's face it, the Blake Edwards film sucks and it ought to be remade. But I was told the rights are out of reach. So I made my own version. A love affair with New York that didn't work, but a friendship that did."

He sang the first couple lines of "*Moon River*" surprisingly smooth and mellow. He must have been feeling the wine.

"I always liked that opening," he said, "that sweet soft New York early morning, the empty streets, with Holly gazing into Tiffany's windows."

"Yeah, but c'mon. Audrey Hepburn? As a girl who runs away from a Texas dirt farm and comes to New York to reinvent herself? I mean, really?"

"What are you talking about?"

"Too European. Too elegant."

"She was great."

"Until she opened her mouth. She didn't even try to sound Southern. And she wasn't great. She was great box office. Besides, I read that Capote didn't think she was so great. He wanted Marilyn Monroe, but he claimed Paramount double-crossed him. And what about that hokey happy ending with the cat? New York stories should never end cute."

"There are so many great young actresses today who could play Holly."

Jonathan poured me more wine. I didn't want anymore, but I didn't stop him.

"I had the number two box office gross in the U.S. in its opening weekend in the fall of 1999," I said. "One writer called 'Girl in the City' a lonelier version of 'Sex in The City', which came out on HBO while we were shooting. And for about five minutes I was the hot new actor-director of the moment – I mean, as hot as a thirty-year-old woman could be. Even then I couldn't get a call returned from Lenny and Juno even though we were all back in New York."

"Maybe they thought you didn't need them anymore."

"I didn't. But it still hurt. Even worse, I got no career bump at all after 'Girl in the City'. After being faceless in Hollywood, after being married and divorced, making 'Girl in the City' saved my life. But even though it was a modest hit, I was back at the beginning again, pitching and going up for jobs. Nothing worked out. I'd get offered things I didn't want to direct. I'd go after things I wanted to do, but they'd go to other directors. It felt somehow like I'd missed a step."

"Still, you got to make four films. You've had more luck than most."

"Which ran out when Lenny and Juno suddenly turned up and offered to produce 'Motherhood'. I had my doubts, but I felt grounded enough to take a chance with them. They had the financing I needed, and I thought we had a workable relationship. I was wrong. They were either condescending toward me or not around when I needed them. By the time production wrapped I hated them."

"Maybe they were still mad you turned down their job offer."

"My bad. I forgot how petty they can be."

"You think they undermined you on purpose?"

"Not Lenny. He's too disorganized, and he's basically a cokehead and a big baby. But Juno? Maybe. She's two faced, cold as ice, and totally capable of punishing disloyalty even years later. Decades later."

He was staring, nodding and listening. I hoped I was telling Jonathan what he needed to know.

"'Motherhood' was doomed when the studio got sold while we were in post-production. The new owners treated the projects produced by the old regime like stale leftovers. They kept cutting my post budget, demanding I deliver my cut sooner than planned, and they kept their promotion ideas a deep dark secret. And they were assholes, personally. I screened the film for the studio boss, and he said in front of his promotion team, "Sounds like paradise, a world where men aren't necessary. Is that your vision, Adrienne?' Basically calling me a dyke. And of course Lenny and Juno weren't around for that."

"Of course not. They weren't going to associate with a film the new bosses hated. They had future business to think of."

"The next thing I knew, 'Motherhood' was rebranded as the chick comedy 'Gimme Some Sperm'. They made that poster with my character leaning against a giant test tube. You saw the expression they Photoshopped on my face. In real life I couldn't look that insipid if I tried. I have no doubt the new boys running the studio were trying to make me look foolish. I called them and called them, but Lenny and Juno had moved on. They had produced the film, but they wouldn't help me fight the dumbed-down title and crass advertising. Then, fuckup of all fuckups, a film that should have opened at Christmas was dumped instead on Memorial Day weekend 2007 and was smothered by *Spider-Man 3, Shrek The Third,* and *Pirates of the Caribbean.* The reviews called it either an unfunny comedy or a weak drama. It opened to empty theaters. The distributors gave it two weeks then yanked it. And Lenny and Juno just went on producing films for different studios and got rich. They're the kind of people who think luck had nothing to do with their success. I kept reaching out to them for a while, but they ghosted me, and over time they became more and more evil in my mind. All I ever wanted to do for the Victors was lower them into their grave." I took one of his cigarettes and lit up. "Until I saw '*Lonely Sky*'."

I was getting vehement and bitter and Jonathan saw it.

"Let's take our wine to the porch and get a little air."

The view was spectacular, the night sky clear and the moon shining a path down the rolling ocean waves. After a few deep breaths, I calmed down.

"So after '*Motherhood*,' I slowed down and fell through the ice, and I've been swimming back upstream ever since. If you're a female director and your film flops, that's it. With the studio guys, even the big outside investors, you're finished. They don't even pretend to take you seriously. They know you've got a dream, and you're desperate. So they just sit back with a big grin and wait for the blowjob."

He looked eager to hear the salacious details, but I was overdoing it. I was beyond tired, and the wine had gone to my head.

"And they're still waiting. So," I sighed, "now all I've got is an embarrassing reality TV show."

"I saw it," he said. "It's so bad it just might be a hit."

"Unfortunately I know what you mean."

"But look at the upside. A hit proves you know how to deliver what a mass audience wants. It's good for the money people to see you that way."

"I suppose." I didn't want to talk about reality TV anymore. "Each time I read 'Lonely Sky' I get excited. I think we actually can recover that feeling that we're one people, at least for two hours."

"That's pretty idealistic, Adrienne."

"Probably. But that's the way I am. About movies, if nothing else."

"You really want to do this, don't you?"

"One thousand percent. I'd feel a lot better if I knew I had your support."

"Well, you're a good writer, you're passionate about 'Lonely Sky' and you've got Joel's play to work from. Time's running out. So do it."

"Is that a vote of confidence?"

"Let's just say I'll cross my fingers."

"But you'll be there if I need you?"

"I'll tell you after I read your script." He glanced at his wristwatch. "There's one more train to the city tonight, in case you want to go. You've got about thirty minutes."

"Are you kicking me out?"

"No, no, not at all."

After the fine meal and two glasses of wine I could barely keep my eyes open. A dull endless train ride with the alcohol dying in me, reaching Manhattan near midnight with a hangover coming on, would be torture.

"Can I use the guest house? I haven't slept much in the past three days. My brain's about to shut down. And it's so quiet and peaceful out here."

"Make yourself at home. Everything you need is up there."

We walked back through the house to the kitchen and left our glasses in the sink.

"You aren't going to come up in the middle of the night and try to molest me, are you?"

"I'd molest you right now, but you're drunk."

"Gallantry! I like that in a man. And I don't especially like men." I hoped by then he knew he was an exception. "When's that train in the morning?"

"Quarter to seven, and the next one's sometime in the afternoon."

"I'll be up at six o'clock. Will you be up, or can you give me the number for a cab company?"

"If I'm not up, the number to call a cab is next to the phone. There's breakfast things and coffee in the cabinets." He turned on the lights that lit the path up the hill. "Sweet dreams."

When I opened my eyes, birds were singing, the sun was shining on a beautiful day, and it was long past train time. I bathed, dressed in yesterday's clothes, and strolled down the path through the woods to Jonathan's house. As I got closer, brilliant sunlight sparkled off the waters of the pool where Jonathan was swimming laps. It took me a moment to realize he was nude. He ducked underwater and did a somersault, pushed off and swam in the other direction. His brown body slipped through the aquamarine water, lean and muscled, his hair slicked back on his head, a trail of bubbles streaming from his lips.

I was sitting at the edge of the pool when he surfaced and saw me.

"Hey! You're still here!" he said. He seemed unconcerned about being nude. "I thought you were taking the early train."

"I guess I needed the sleep."

"Come on in!"

I was tempted to stroll around the pool, slowly stripping, just to see if my teasing got him aroused. A naked plunge would be too perfect. I could glide through the cool water, press myself against his chest, reach down and explore the shadow between his legs. But I had more important priorities, so for now the more mystery the better.

"No thanks." I sat on the concrete apron of the pool and dangled my feet in the water. "I'll just sit here all googly-eyed."

Laughing, he pushed off from the side of the pool on his back, rolled over and swam away. He pulled himself up on an air mattress, lying on his stomach, bobbing on the water.

"It's going to be another gorgeous day," he said. "Why don't you hang around?"

"Suppose I do?" I leaned back. "What's there to do around here?" I kicked water on him as he floated past on the raft.

"Whatever comes naturally, I guess."

"That sounds dangerous."

"I'll bet you'd like that."

"Sounds tempting, anyway."

"So you'll stay, right?"

"No. I have work to do in New York."

"On a Sunday?"

"Every day's a workday."

"Well, okay," he sighed. "I'm being a poor host. I should be getting us something to eat." He climbed out of the water – no tan lines! – and wrapped himself in a robe.

He came back down to the kitchen wearing khaki slacks and a tee shirt and loafers. He made coffee and set out bread and fruit, and while we ate we passed sections of the Sunday *New York Times* back and forth. He got absorbed in the magazine, and I stared at him over the top of the newspaper. I had to stop myself from fantasizing about having him for dessert, like one of the biggest porn clichés, sex in the sunshine beside the pool on one of the lounge chairs, our sweaty bodies slippery in the summer heat.

When it was time for me to catch the train back to the city, he put on a tattered Harley Davidson baseball cap and horn-rimmed sunglasses, backed an old red Audi convertible out of the garage, and drove me to Montauk station.

"Well!" Jonathan said, as we parked next to the waiting train. "This was an unexpected pleasure."

"You're good company, Lehane." I held out my hand.

"That's it? A handshake?" He took off his hat and sunglasses. "Not even a kiss?"

"What kind of kiss?"

"The best you've got, of course."

"Oh." I chuckled. "One of those." I slid over and pulled him to me. I kissed him on the lips, a kiss, wet and eager, that was clearly an invitation. He kissed me back, and then his hands slid up from my waist and cupped my breasts.

I leaned back and looked at him. His grin dared me to resist. Instead, I left his hands where they were and kissed him again thinking, well, I've seen him stark naked, he knows I'm a great kisser, and that I'm a slut who lets him handle my breasts. Judging by that vertical stretch in his khakis, I had his attention. That was enough for now. I pushed him away.

"That's how I kiss those I like," I said, breathlessly. "And this is so you'll remember it."

I slapped his face, hard enough to sting. He fell back, his mouth open in astonishment. I backed out of the car, grinning. "Call me!"

As I walked toward the waiting train, swinging my hips for his amusement, he yelled after me with a laugh, "What the hell was that?"

Once the train was rolling, I deleted a half dozen urgent texts from Lenny and Juno asking if I'd made a decision yet. Apparently, the writing gig was still open. I found my draft email to them and did a quick revision.

Hi Juno, hi Lenny. As I told you, I feel a deep connection to "Lonely Sky". The characters and stories have really gotten into my blood. I know it will make a great film. Obviously, there are differences in taste between me and Egon, but I'm sure I can write a camera-ready script for a movie that will make us all proud. So, sign me up. I'm ready.

Send.

Once the train was rolling back toward New York, I gave in to the temptation to go online and see what people were saying about Friday night's pilot episode of *"Men R Dawgs"*. A Google search turned up a lot of posts on Lily Channel.com from viewers and from the critics, and most of them were excessive. The most frequent adjective was 'vicious,' either delightfully or appallingly, depending on whether the writer was male or female. One male writer whined, "If this kind of caustic bigotry were aimed towards women, you just know the world would be on fire." I checked my Alpha Bitch company email and found several dirty, violent, repellent threats. I ignored them, realizing I'd lost interest in *"Men R Dawgs"* and was already on to the next project. I pocketed my phone and sat staring out the window as town after Long Island town slid past.

D ay and night for the next week, I lived for the writing. I was under impossible pressure with a very tight deadline. I stopped only to eat, sleep, and work out at the gym to boost my energy and lower my stress level. I never read any of Joel Garner's attempts to write a screenplay. The play gave me enough great material to work with. The hardest decisions were what to leave out.

I checked in with Egon, of course, to ask if he had any notes for me. He sounded taken aback, as if I was trying to test him or something.

"Hey, Adrienne, what can I tell you that you don't already know?" Before I could say, "You can tell me what movie you want to make," he claimed he had to take another call and was gone.

So I was free to follow my heart. That was risky with no director's notes, but what choice did I have? I combined scenes, wrote new ones, deleted others, and toned down the stage speeches into more realistic dialogue for the screen. I searched my database of New York location photos from my earlier films looking for settings with the visual poetry the exterior scenes needed. All three stories had underdeveloped female roles, so that was the biggest change I made. The East Village hipster story "The Day Before Doomsday" became focused on the wife's efforts to cope with her husband's paranoia. The dramatic heart of "I'm A Stranger Here" was the anguished son's conflict between his wounded father and his American life, but in my version the son drew his stalwart mother and his runaway sister into his dilemma.

In the play, "Constant Companion," the love story of the investment banker David Sawyer and his wife's ghost was almost too despairing, too harrowing to bear. Alone on a black stage, Sawyer was a man adrift in a void, clinging to a fantasy, addressing the audience directly or speaking heartbreaking dialogues with a spirit only he could see. In his opening scene, he tells us that he'd decided if he was still suffering unbearable grief one year after his wife's death, he'd commit suicide. In the play, Sawyer's fate was left unresolved, letting each audience member decide for themself which fate Sawyer chose, life or death. But I wanted Sawyer to find a reason to go on living. So I put Josephine, his dead wife's ghost, on screen as an ironic, honest, and loving spirit from the afterworld, who tries to keep her shattered husband grounded as he struggles with his grief.

His crisis comes when Sawyer finally gets the courage to listen to the tape of his 9/11 experience that he recorded with his analyst's help, with instructions to keep replaying it and keep experiencing grief until it loses its power over him. But the listening intensifies his suffering until it is intolerable. Panicked, he tries to escape back into his fantasy marriage, calling into the void for the ghost of Josephine.

But she's gone. He's in the worst crisis of his life, trapped between unbearable suffering and its lost antidote, a fantasy he can no longer conjure. He is desperate for his life to mean something, but what? He needs to go on, but how? With Sawyer and Josephine's story now more intense than the stage version, and without an ending, I was also stuck, so I went to see Jonathan in the play again.

After the performance, I loitered at the curb as he stood outside the theater and posed for selfies with fans, signed some autographs, kissed some cheeks, then came over to me with a grin.

"Hey, look who's here!"

"Wow!" I cocked an eyebrow toward his fans, thinking I was being clever. "Nothing like stardom, huh?"

His grin vanished; apparently, he heard my harmless wisecrack as a put down.

"How could you say that Adrienne?" he muttered.

"Just kidding. Let's have a drink," I suggested. "I need to talk to you."

He stuck his thumbs in the pockets of his jeans and sulked as we strolled away from the theater.

"You know what a star is?" he grumbled.

"Sure. A star is an actor who got unlucky."

"*Unlucky?*"

"A star is an actor stuck in a tarpit called celebrity. Trapped by their image, created by handlers and publicists and surrounded by an entourage who promote their image because their livelihood depends on their stardom. Nobody loves them for themself. I've often thought movie stars are the loneliest people in the world, even though they can walk into a strange bar anywhere in America, any night of the week, and get laid in ten minutes."

"I'm not a star. I'm an actor."

"You're a fine actor. Of course, with your looks, I also had you pegged as a major male slut."

"Why?" Jonathan snorted. "Because when we kissed, I copped a feel?"

"Two feels." He just stared at me. "Don't tell me you don't remember."

"I remember. Vividly. You didn't seem to mind. You even slapped my face so I'd remember, so I don't want to hear any crap about injured dignity."

"It wasn't injured. Y'ever read a book by Camille Paglia called '*Sex, Art and American Culture*?' 'The unknown stranger is a wandering pagan god, keeping sex free from emotion, duty, family.'"

"That's not me."

"No? I can see you as a wandering pagan god. Maybe with an AARP card."

That broke the tension and he laughed. "Is this why you came tonight? To bust my balls?"

"No, I came to refresh my feeling for the play."

At the West Bank Café he ordered a beer, and I sipped my St. Germain Royale. He sat back and listened while I ranted about the women at the Lily

Channel bugging me to do more media to try to rescue the weak launch of "*Men R Dawgs*".

"I'm writing against a deadline, and I hate having to stop and shift into sales mode to do interviews. This woman freelancing for an arts magazine in Brooklyn said she was writing about the show as soft porn with a feminist edge. I didn't argue with that angle or endorse it. A creepy invasive guy from some Hollywood TV blog wanted to talk about my career and personal life, not the series. I got off that call as politely as I could. There was also a young woman named Cassandra St. George who insisted on doing an in-person interview, and we hit it off okay. Her story in *New York Magazine* was one of the better pieces."

Tired of hearing myself complain, I shrugged and brushed the subject aside.

"Y'know, I'm still buzzin' from that kiss," Jonathan said. We were on our second drink and I was glad he changed the subject. "Come home with me."

"Why should I?"

"You'll have a great experience."

"In your bed."

"Yes. And you won't need a slap in the face to remember it."

Now I laughed. "Do you always get what you want?"

"Not always."

"There are actually women who pass up the chance to fuck you?

"Believe it or not. Are you going to be one of those?"

I shrugged and waved for the waiter.

We got out of the car at a mammoth pre-war building on Central Park West near the Museum of Natural History. The doorman, a white-haired little guy named Jimmy, gave Jonathan a mock-formal salute.

I stepped into Jonathan's penthouse and fell immediately in love with the place, with its ten-foot ceilings and herringbone oak floors, tall casement windows looking east, the elegant, understated furniture and marble fireplace and antique mahogany bar beside the glass door to the terrace. He poured two glasses of wine and led me outside.

Lights from the buildings on Fifth Avenue far across the dark expanse of Central Park gleamed above the treetops. I leaned on the parapet and Jonathan lay back on a chaise under a yellow and white striped awning. We were ten floors above the city and the August night was still hot and I was damp under my clothes. Sitting with him in the back seat of the Uber on the way here, I'd smelled that same salty, tobacco-scented aroma from our first meeting, and it got me going all over again.

We flirted for a while, talking more for the pleasure of being together than about anything else. I could've fucked him that evening, but that would've complicated our potential working relationship and waste the energy I needed to finish the screenplay. I was looking for something that would suggest an ending to Sawyer's story, but I didn't want to talk to him about it too directly.

"So, how's the writing going?" he said.

"I think it's working. Don't ask me too much, though. I don't want to talk it all away."

"No problem," he said, setting down his glass and standing. "I didn't want to talk in the first place."

I let him kiss me, but as we neared the point of no return, I put my hand on his chest.

"Sorry, pal. Conversation is all I have to offer tonight."

"Adrienne, don't be a drag."

To disengage casually, I reached for my wine.

"I better get back to work while I'm still buzzing from the play."

"Well, I hope you got what you came for," he said. "From the play, at least."

"Thanks for the drink. And don't stop trying."

At the door he said, "Hey, I'm doing a performance at lunchtime tomorrow with some people I've been working with. Why don't you come?"

"What kind of performance?"

"A Shakespeare monologue, Macbeth's 'Tomorrow and tomorrow and tomorrow' speech, the one he delivers after hearing about the death of his wife. There'll be more performers doing various things, too. It's a benefit for a homeless shelter on the Lower East Side."

"You do that sort of thing?"

"Ever since I moved to New York to study acting."

"Text me the details. I'll still be writing, so please don't be disappointed if I don't show up."

"Well, I will be, but I get it. You're on a tight deadline."

I kissed him lightly on the lips. We hugged for a moment, then I reluctantly headed for home.

Downtown, entering my building, I thought about the ending of Sawyer's story. I sat at my kitchen table and scribbled some notes for a while, then I gave up and went to bed. My mind must have worked on the idea while I slept, because the next morning I woke up and wrote the whole thing out at breakfast. After Josephine's death and after losing the comfort of his hallucinated marriage to her ghost, Sawyer's story could have ended up or down. Joel Garner's play left Sawyer in bleak existential uncertainty. The playwright probably hated bankers – who didn't, these days? But what if Sawyer decided that to merely possess his enormous wealth was meaningless? What if he put most of his wealth into philanthropy, a foundation named after his beloved wife? Nothing could replace their marriage, but Sawyer discovers that improving life for people in need gives him a reason to go on living. It was an up ending, if banal. I hoped Jonathan would like it. I was sure the audience would want to see Sawyer go on living, so a life of generosity and compassion that could relieve his loneliness and bring him back to reality seemed the best way. In the end, his story would be a rebuke to both the terrorism that killed his wife, and to the gods of money and power worshipped by the Wall Street culture he was leaving behind.

In the dark hours of Friday morning, I read the screenplay for the final time then typed 'Fade Out,' emailed the draft to Egon and the producers, and collapsed gratefully into bed. That afternoon, as I was lying in luxurious half sleep, dreaming up excuses to stay in bed, my phone rang.

Lenny wailed, "We are so screwed!"

"Why?"

"Egon hates your script! He won't even let us send it to the cast or the crew! He says you didn't write what he wanted!"

I choked my immediate response: *Fuck Egon! Hire me!* and replied as calmly as I could.

"Did he, by any chance, tell you what he wanted?"

"No, but –"

"Me neither, Lenny."

"But you had a meeting –"

"Thirty minutes, mostly about what he hoped the film would do for his career. He had no ideas at all about the script. All he said was, 'Let's see what you come up with.'"

"I don't believe that."

"Believe whatever you want, Lenny," I said calmly. "My job is done." I hung up, immediately wishing I hadn't. It made me look weak.

He called right back.

"Your job is not done! Our deal is for a first draft, and 50 percent again if we need a set of changes."

"Read my contract, Lenny. Revisions to be performed after I get my first payment. You know, the one I was promised, and I'm still waiting for?"

"At a time like this you talk about money?"

"It's a language we both understand."

"You're gonna get paid. Everybody's gonna get paid. But if we don't get a script, nobody's getting paid for anything, because there won't be a movie."

"You have a script."

"Egon says it's no good."

"And I need to get paid."

"Adrienne –"

"Today."

"I'll talk to Juno –"

"Sure. Take your time. No reason to hurry, is there? Look, I've gotta go, I have weekend plans –"

"All right, damn it, you'll get your money. Is that what you want to hear?"

"No." In fact, I was eager to change the subject. "I want to hear your opinion of what I wrote."

There was a long pause, probably so he could calculate how much praise would be enough.

"You did a great job. You nailed it. You got the best of the play and the best of New York. Juno thinks so too. Is that what you want to hear?"

"Yes. Now go tell that to Egon. What's his problem?"

"We don't know. You need to get over here and find out. Egon wants us all to meet, like, now."

"He's had the script for one day. Tell him to sleep on it, we'll meet on Monday."

Wobbly-voiced worry: "You saw what he's like. He's an iceman. You can never tell what's in his head. He could turn on a dime and go back to L.A."

Worse things could happen. I almost let that slip.

"I thought we were all working together," he whined. "This is a fucking crisis."

"If you give Egon the support every director needs, I'm sure he'll calm down, and he'll shoot the script I wrote."

"We need you at Egon's office. Now."

"I just worked 24/7 for almost a week. I'm exhausted. I was exhausted before I took this job."

"Tough shit!" he hissed. "Get your ass to this meeting and finish the job!"

"As soon as my agent tells me I've been paid, I'll be there."

A long, disgusted groan, to which I hung up.

I dropped into the Eames lounge chair in my living room and started taking deep calming breaths. The whole time I was sweating out the first draft I expected there would be revisions. There always are. There always should be. That's the process. But Egon's total rejection wasn't really about the writing. He was postponing a confrontation with his own limitations. Nevertheless, I signed a contract, and I always lived up to a deal. I called Marshall, explained the situation, and made him promise to call me as soon as he got the payment the Victors owed me.

To keep my mind off things, I went through my email and cleaned my apartment, since I had let everything go while writing. Lenny called me two more times, but I let the calls go to voicemail and didn't listen. I set out a short sleeve white blouse and blue jeans and got dressed after I showered. I pulled on a distressed denim jacket and pinned my hair up. Finally, I got a text from Marshall. The Victor's assistant had brought over a certified check. But instead of feeling wealthier, I felt trapped. Now I had to rewrite a script I knew was the best I'd ever written. That was bad enough, but the thought of writing with Egon almost made me quit and forfeit the extra fee, except I needed the money, and more than that, I couldn't let go of *Lonely Sky*.

I sent Lenny a text telling him I was on my way, then left the apartment, bought a large dark roast coffee from Murrays Bagels on 8th Avenue, and drank it while strolling to Egon's offices on West 22nd Street, a tree-lined block of former warehouses rehabbed as condominium lofts and art galleries just off the West Side Highway near Chelsea Piers. Instead of boosting my energy, the coffee frazzled my nerves and left me feeling edgy and irritable, not the best mood to be in when Lenny and Juno burst from the lobby and held the door open for me.

"*Listen*," Lenny instructed me, jittering with anxiety. "Just listen to what he has to say."

"Lay off, Lenny," Juno said. "She knows what to do." They'd been fighting, I heard it in their voices.

"This is the most important meeting of your life."

I forced myself to smile, and to downshift to half speed, speaking slowly and thoughtfully and hopefully driving them mad

"Don't you mean our lives?" I patted him on the cheek, tempted to gouge out his worried eye with my thumbnail. "It'll be all right." We rose in the elevator to the top floor. "Egon and I have a great working relationship." My first big lie of the day.

The elevator opened right into Egon's office, one large room with a small galley kitchen and bathroom in the rear. The gray carpet, the filing cabinets and wide glass trestle desk, the leather sofa and chairs and coffee table looked like they'd just been unpacked, and they still stank of the factory.

Egon was leaning on his elbows on the desk behind a laptop. He was not the quietly insouciant, soft-spoken man of wealth and taste I met last weekend in his Hamptons mansion. He picked up a copy of my script from the desk and, his eyes shifty under an L.A. Lakers cap, flipped the pages as we spoke.

"Not what I was expecting, Adrienne," he murmured.

"Oh no." I pretended to be shocked. "I'm so sorry you feel that way, Egon. How can I help?" I sat down across from him, so we were eye to eye.

"It needs a lot of work, and you've wasted a lot of time. The schedule's really tight now."

Fighting the impulse to answer back, I took out a pocket notebook and pen, and got ready to take notes. He looked at the notebook as if I'd just pulled out a gun.

"I already told you what I need," he said, sulking. "But you didn't hear me."

"I thought I did. Very clearly." Poor boy. Someone ignored his precious needs. "Let's go over it again, shall we?" It was time for Lenny and Juno to see for themselves how empty he was. I could almost feel them trembling behind me.

"Well, now it's hard to put my finger on," he sighed. Apparently, products of his imagination had a short shelf life. Did Lenny and Juno see this, were they getting it? He stared away from us, and lapsed into a beleaguered, weight-of-the-world slump. "I'm more of a process person. That's how I work with writers. We've got to sit down and start again from page one."

Why didn't we do that a week ago? Suddenly he was ready to work with me, now that he felt the pressure. That wouldn't guarantee creativity, though, just constant anxiety. Contractually, I was only obligated to perform a rewrite, for a smaller additional fee, but Egon wanted to start over from page one.

I said, "What's the biggest issue we have to tackle?"

"This structural thing," he said, pushing the script away as if it was unclean. "It's all jumbled up." That was the same structure he once called intriguing.

"Weaving the stories together," I said, "is the play's structural metaphor for the interconnectedness of all human beings."

"Yeah, well I guess I don't see it in quite so elevated terms," he said with a sneer.

I sat there remaining calm and professional. Inside, I was raging: Don't sneer at me, you spoiled shit! You can't face the fact that you're not up to this project. You can't face the fact that you're nothing but an overrated maker of violent human cartoons. You can't face the fact that you don't know how the world works! You'd wreck Joel's play and my script rather than try to stretch your pathetic spoonful of talent!

He sat back and spread his hands, faux apologetically. "We'll start all over again, tomorrow at nine o'clock."

I was trapped. Just as I'd feared, I was going to write with Egon. I might be able to protect the characters and their stories, but what about myself? At what price in hour-by-hour anger management? I waited to hear Lenny and Juno defend my work. I turned to look at them, and they just stood there with bland half-smiles on their faces. I didn't ask their opinion of my writing. I couldn't trust what they'd say in front of Egon.

"I understand completely," I said, cool and cooperative. "You need a script you're comfortable with."

"That's what we'll write."

"I live nearby. I'll go get my computer and I'll come right back."

"Tomorrow's soon enough."

"Y'know Egon, Adrienne's right," Lenny said. "We have so little time —"

"When I want to hear from you, I'll ask." Egon turned to me. "Tomorrow. And now, I need to be alone to process this... this setback."

I gave him an upbeat, reassuring goodbye. "Already working on it," I said, tapping my temple.

Lenny and Juno tramped ahead of me, looking grim, and we marched into the elevator.

As we rode down, Lenny muttered, "So that's your great working relationship, Adrienne?" I just shrugged.

"He said it's 'hard to put his finger on' what he wants," Juno said.

Lenny said to her, "He actually said that, didn't he?"

"I'll like to tell him where to put his God damned finger."

"He's choked. He's blocked. He's scared. He's lost his mojo –"

"He's going to wreck a brilliant script to make it easier for him to direct," Juno muttered.

I couldn't believe that they were only now seeing Egon clearly. It took this crisis to force them to admit what they already knew. But they could afford to moan all they wanted. I actually had to work with him.

"It'll all be fine," I said. I shamelessly stretched out my bland, phony smile. "Kind of hard to argue with a nine hundred-million-dollar genius, isn't it?" I so wanted to savor their desperation. But I was already wondering how I would manage my own.

One week later on Friday morning, August 25, exhausted but too anxious to sleep, I shuffled through my dark apartment to the kitchen and made a cup of green tea, spilling some on the table as I sat down. To my weary eyes the red numbers on the microwave said 4 o'clock, a very lonesome hour of what I expected would be an awful day.

In a couple hours the cast and crew would be reading the brand-new Egon Swift draft of *"Lonely Sky"* on their computers, phones and tablets. I could anticipate their horror, because I had already gone through horror and worse as Egon's collaborator. I wanted to call Jonathan to warn him, but I was too tired for heavy conversation. Better he should read the script, then go to war himself with the producers and director. He would also be angry with me, but I would deal with that after I got some rest. I needed a long recovery from assisting Egon for the past week as he destroyed the best writing I'd ever done. At least my contract for *"Lonely Sky"* was completed. I would now force myself to take the vacation I'd postponed to some place far, far away.

On our first day of work at Egon's office he'd set our goals.

"I want to do something that'll get me serious cred as a writer."

My role, he said, would be to help him, the auteur, write the screenplay. And now that he was the writer, suddenly he had a lot of ideas. So for six days I faked enthusiasm for his creative process. It was more grueling than faking an orgasm over and over. I encouraged his ideas and contributed some ideas of my own, hoping the script would turn out so bad the studio would cancel the production and send Egon home to L.A.

First, he separated the three stories, so they played one after the other.

"Gotta do it," he said, "that story mashup bullshit, that's okay for a small New York theater with a hip crowd, but it won't go over in Pasadena or heartland America."

He thought it would be daring to present *"Lonely Sky"* as an anthology of three stand-alone short films. When I mentioned that format had been done many times before, he avoided my eye and said stubbornly, "Not by me." So, goodbye to our structural metaphor for the interconnectedness of all human beings. Goodbye to the audience's emotional journey and its deepening engagement with the film's themes as all three stories resonated with each other. Without the comic East Village hipster scenes to offset the stark loneliness of David Sawyer and the horror and fear of the tortured Muslim father's family, and without the interwoven structure to moderate the pacing, the stories unwound so fast that character development turned to caricature. When I pointed this out, Egon shrugged, said "Nah, nah, it'll be fine," and kept spinning out ideas that I had to try to work into the script every night.

Thus *"Lonely Sky"* devolved from a literate, deeply felt human drama into a shallow, denatured, new kind of Egon Swift film. He tried to soften the rushed characterizations with lame humor he called "character moments." He wrote two clichéd romantic comedy scenes for the East Village hipster survivalists that he insisted would deepen the audience's emotional involvement with the couple. He tried to satirize the husband's domination of his wife, but his rewrite didn't make Abel funny, just appallingly sexist. He cut a tender father-son scene from the Muslim story and replaced it with a gruesome torture flashback, violence he insisted was necessary to make the film politically "edgy."

I contributed the worst happy endings I could think of. So the survivalist couple join their East Village block association and the husband, inexplicably no longer paranoid, is elected to the City Council. The Muslim victim of CIA torture becomes a clichéd toxic father out of a pop psychology paperback, angry and unable to respond to his family's attempts to welcome him home, until his son confronts him and basically says hey, old man, get over it.

When it came to Sawyer the widower, Egon simply couldn't comprehend profound grief. We agreed we couldn't use Sawyer's stage speeches. But he was adamant that the spooky, amorous scenes between Sawyer and his widow's ghost would bog the movie down and depress the audience. He deleted the ghost wife that I had so painstakingly created. I retaliated by suggesting we hook up Sawyer instead with a chattering screwball named Chickie, who nicknames him Sourpuss, keeps nagging him to get over his lost wife, and, implausibly, wins his heart. I'll never forget the way Egon beamed at me after I'd gotten on his wavelength. He didn't need much help with that idea. He connected right away with his Inner Chickie and wrote those scenes with me cheering him on.

Each time Egon marveled at the awesome work he thought we were doing I wanted to vomit. With a fiendish effort I kept my cool through tedious days listening to his erratic, frothing-at-the-mouth stream of babble. I did what was necessary to get the ordeal over with. Finally the explosion of drivel reached the magic page number 120 and he declared that we were done.

After a series of sixteen-hour workdays we finished the writing in Egon's office on Thursday around lunch time. Before grabbing my backpack and heading out I graciously removed my name from the title page, telling him as the auteur he deserved all the writing credit. Egon got unusually quiet, stared at the floor collecting himself, then thanked me. He said he would put the finishing touches on the script alone but promised I would see every revision.

As soon as I hit the street, I called my former psychotherapist and begged for an emergency visit. During the Uber ride I called Marshall.

"Get my final payment from Lenny and Juno immediately. Hurry up before they read the script."

"Why?"

"I took my name off it."

"It's that bad?"

"Worse. And almost 100 percent Egon."

"Okay, no worries, A-Girl." It sounded like he was bouncing a ball against his office wall. "Good? Bad? The money's the same."

Therapy was a few minutes of reacquaintance, then smashing a tennis racket into the patient's chaise screaming "No! No! No!" climaxing in a snarling swearing demonic possession type eruption of obscenities, after which I collapsed, crying in the doctor's arms. When she suggested I start keeping regular appointments again, I stood up and wiped away my tears.

"I'll think about it."

After a quick hug I wrote her a check and left before my hour was up. I had learned long ago not to allow psychotherapy too far into my head. I only called her because I knew she had that tennis racket and she'd let me beat her couch and purge some of my rage.

I went to the sports center at the piers. I drove myself through a full body cross-training session and swaggered home feeling like a goddess. I poured a glass of Zinfandel and drank it straight down. I went back out and kept an appointment for a hair trim and a facial, then visited the Hell's Kitchen studio of Stieg, my favorite masseur, for a deep tissue massage and a hand job that sent me floating dreamily back home through the hot, crowded streets. I spent Thursday evening dusting and waxing and cleaning my apartment until it was immaculate, and I felt tired enough for a deep satisfying sleep. But it never came.

As I lay tossing in bed, Jonathan called.

"Are you all right?" He obviously hadn't read the script yet.

"Oh, sure."

I told him I needed to sleep, and I hung up wondering how much he would hate me in the morning.

I got a clue Friday around lunchtime. He'd left me a voicemail because I'd shut off my phone.

"It's me," he said. His voice dropped. "I've read it. Call me."

We met for drinks around 10 o'clock at his regular bar on Columbus Avenue. A public place was better than his apartment for the confrontation I was expecting. I asked the bartender to make me a St. Germain and champagne cocktail. Jonathan was sitting at a table in the back room with a glass of whiskey in his hand, coming down from tonight's performance.

He looked at me unhappily as I sat down. Seeing him, sympathy was impossible to avoid. But I also had to remind myself I had no reason to feel guilty.

He said, "Y'know, at first I thought, 'That has to be a joke, right? Is that really our script?'"

"Ask your director." I didn't mean to sound so cold. It just came out that way.

"My God, Adrienne. I supported you. How could I have been so wrong?" He shook his head, aghast. "Why'd you let Egon write such a, such a..?"

I emptied my glass and held it up for the waitress to bring another.

"I'm glad you realize none of it is my work."

"But you're the writer."

"Not anymore! I told you Egon gave me zero notes. That meant I had total freedom. I wrote an elegant adaptation of the play. The best writing I've ever done. And he tore it up. You can ask Lenny and Juno why, but they'll never criticize Egon. They're too happy basking in the glow of his nine hundred million dollar reputation. Bottom line, they forced me to work with him or they wouldn't pay me. He took over the writing. I did the typing. And you've read the results. Egon says it's the best writing he's ever done. Trust me, I'm sure that's true."

"Why didn't you tell me this was happening?"

"I'm sorry Jonathan. You're right to be disappointed. But the producers and the director had to see it first before distribution."

"Well, I thought we had a different kind of relationship."

"Not when it comes to the work."

Drawing that line made him pause, but he was still shaking his head and looking bewildered.

"Joel's drafts were clunky and static. But this new thing? It's insipid!"

"How do you think I feel?" I was actually on the brink of tears, sad that he was disappointed, and frustrated at being misunderstood. "Lenny and Juno sold me out. They just stood there and let Egon mock my work and me. But he's the A-list director, right? So he gets to have his way."

"But at least you could take your name off it." He glanced into his drink then downed it. "I either have to drop out of the film or perform what's written and look like an idiot. Send me your draft. Please?"

"You know I can't do that. Ask Lenny and Juno for it. Between you and me, they said they love it."

"But if it's better –"

"It won't matter. Staying in business with Egon and keeping him happy is what matters to them. So Egon gets to have his, uh, vision."

"It sounds to me like you lost control of the process." He brooded for a moment. "Why didn't you quit?"

"I couldn't. And not just because I was under contract. The characters, the stories, they're in my blood. We fought over every page, believe me."

"Fought and lost, you mean," he scoffed. "Even in post, I doubt there's a way to fix the damage you've done."

"Damage I've done?" I set my drink on the table carefully, though I wanted to throw it in his face. "Fuck you." I got up, walked out, and headed for the subway. I was off the movie, and now I was done with Jonathan Lehane.

Half a block later, he caught up with me.

"Where are you going?"

"Anywhere you're not. How could you say such a mean shitty thing?"

"Look, I'm sorry, okay?" he said. "But I'm in shock –"

"You're in shock." I whirled on him. My voice had dropped way low and shaky and I could feel my eyes brimming with tears. "What about me? My best work! *Trashed!*"

"How can I do my best work with that piece of shit?"

"I didn't expect you to share my feelings, but I expected you to hear them at least. Did you hear anything I said?"

"Of course I did." He saw he wasn't winning me back. "I'm sorry. I think I just insulted the one person who wants to make the same movie as I do. Adrienne, I'm sorry."

"I had no control over how it turned out. I did the best I could under impossible conditions."

He reached out, and I let him hug me. We turned onto Central Park West with our arms around each other. I felt his lips on my temple. My fingers tightened on his waist.

"I'm sorry," he said. "Can we start over?"

With my script ruined, my contract on the film fulfilled, and Jonathan desolate over the bad joke his award-winning role had become, there was only one good thing left to salvage.

"We're going to your place, right?"

He looked at me and said, "Yes. And I am sorry."

"And when we get to your place, are you going to keep apologizing?"

"No, no, sorry 'bout that... Oh, Jesus!"

We both laughed. "See? You can't help it."

"Blame my polite Midwestern upbringing."

We stood under the front awning of his building. I looked up into his eyes, large and shining and soft.

"It's been a rotten week for both of us," I said. "Let's go get liquored up and fuck."

I woke up throbbing and limp, the sheet beneath me warm and sticky, the bedroom shadowy and cool. The ceiling fan stirred the air and on the bedside table the lamp light glowed through two empty glasses. I lay half on top of him with my cheek resting on his shoulder, playing with my fingernails in the hair over his chest. He lay back with his eyes closed and a mild, contented grin, his arm around me, gripping my ass and holding me close. We'd gone right out of our clothes and straight to bed, and as we got busy, my mind orbited the bed like a camera, watching myself fucking and being fucked by a man of extreme beauty. Jonathan had been very gentlemanly: kisses and caresses, oral sex to heighten my excitement, and intercourse in all the classic positions. I was mildly disappointed the sex wasn't rougher, but Jonathan's exquisite timing made it very satisfying.

It would be uncouth to use his beautiful Pratesi bed linens to wipe my crotch. I pulled out the drawer of his bedside table and rummaged around

amongst a squeeze bottle of lube, condoms, a dildo, and a large chrome revolver and box of bullets, but no Kleenex.

"What do you need?" he said, yawning.

"Tissues."

"In the bathroom."

Cleaned up, I lay back down and wrapped myself around him, limp in the
afterglow.

"Why do you have a gun?"

"What gun?"

"The gun in your drawer with the sex toys and the Astro Glide."

"Oh, that thing. It's for home security."

"In a fancy building like this?"

"Sure. We've had robberies. We've had burglaries."

He reached over me and opened the drawer and held the gun up for me
to see.

"Are you trying to make me nervous?"

"Sorry."

"Is it loaded?"

"Of course. It wouldn't be very good protection if it wasn't. I should have
registered it and gotten a license a long time ago, but I never got around to it."

"Have you ever had to use it?"

"God no. I forgot I even had it."

"I wouldn't take you for a gun person."

"I'm really not. I got it as a gift from my co-star Burke Crawford after 'The
Streets of Manhattan' was cancelled. He was a card-carrying NRA member,
sort of a blue-collar conservative. He used to call me 'the liberal hippie of his
nightmares,' but we stayed friendly 'til he died. He had a farm upstate. We'd
drink whiskey and blast away at stuff in his cornfield."

"Doesn't keeping it around make you nervous?"

"Guns are not inherently bad, Adrienne. It's all in how you use them.
Here." He held out the ugly thing for me to take.

"Uh, no thanks. Put it back in the drawer, please?"

Monday morning, Megan poked her head into my office looking
apologetic.

"Lenny and Juno Victor on Line 1. Again."

I thought I was free of those two and their movie. To my astonishment,
they had promptly paid the balance of my writing fee, so I could afford to go

on vacation. Scattered across my desk were website printouts and magazine articles with vacation ideas. I wanted to get far away from New York and to get over a movie that I loved passionately and had crashed like a busted love affair. My night with Jonathan had been just the disruption I needed. Now I had to get away somewhere.

The light on Line 1 kept blinking. What more do they want from me? I'd already passed through three of the five stages of grief while Egon destroyed my screenplay, through denial (I'll just plow through this and do a fine professional job), anger (He's a fucking hack, he's murdering the story and characters, I feel like he's murdering me!) and bargaining (Please God, if I write an awful script will you make them cancel the production?). I was stuck now in depression (Now that I'm done self-harming, I just want the whole thing to go away). Maybe on vacation I would get to acceptance (I've moved on, I really have!)

Or maybe not. *"Lonely Sky"* was more than just another film I wouldn't get to direct. The characters, as they were before Egon Swift rewrote them and turned them to cardboard, had worked their way into my dreams.

I jabbed the button for Line 1.

"Hi guys," I sighed. "How's it going?"

"It's going," Juno intoned, as if announcing a funeral. "Somewhere."

"Forward, is where it's going!" Lenny grandly exclaimed. "Forward into the unknown!" He was high, I could hear it.

"You're working with an A-List director." I hoped my false cheer would feel like salt rubbed into their wound. "I, for one, feel privileged I got to work with him."

"Oh really?" Juno said acidly. "Is that why you took your name off the script?"

"Yeah," Lenny said. "That worried me before I even read it."

"Egon wrote that script. I didn't think sharing credit would be fair."

I could imagine Lenny and Juno exchanging incredulous looks. In the movie business, stealing credit was practically routine.

"It was an amazing experience! I watched Egon Swift become a true auteur, right before my eyes!"

"Adrienne? Cut the shit, okay?" Lenny growled.

Juno made a sound between a sigh and a groan.

"Maybe when shooting wraps it can be edited into something like the play."

Not a chance. The very thought gave me a painful throb where my emotional ties to the show had been cut. I wanted to tell the two of them to get out of my life, curl up in a dark corner, and die a slow painful death.

"So, why the call, guys?" I said breezily. "I'm kind of busy."

"We need you to stay on as the writer through shooting!" Lenny announced.

"Uh…" I never expected this. "I can't do that."

"Honey," Juno said, "if the movie turns out the way it's written, we'll be laughed out of the business. No offense."

"None taken. I told you, it's not my script." Thinking fast: "But I postponed a vacation to write for you in the first place. Now the job is done. I'm leaving tomorrow."

"Where are you going?"

I looked at the pictures on my computer screen.

"On a cruise to Antarctica. It's the hip place to go now. Before global warming ruins it. I'll be gone for about a month."

"No! No!" Lenny yelled. "Don't do that!"

"My plans are made. Everything's paid for. Non-refundable."

"We need you on set every day in case each scene needs a polish before it's shot."

Now they care about quality?

"I doubt Egon would agree to rewrites. We get along okay, but –"

"That's another reason we need you!" Lenny said. "He told us this morning you're the one person on the show who 'gets' him."

"Well," I paused, as if thoughtfully, "I'm just super-patient."

"Which is why we need you here to deal with him."

I can't tell if they want me to be the writer or to be their spy on the director. It felt like both.

Juno said, "He's already got an attitude toward the crew and we start shooting the day after tomorrow."

Returning to the show would be painful, yet it seemed inevitable. It wasn't Lenny and Juno calling, it was the film, beckoning me to return. Could I stand by and watch as Egon tried to direct that ruined script? I didn't know, but that didn't matter as much as the slim chance that by staying on the show, I'd be in the right place if something changed.

"You'll have to negotiate this with Marshall," I said. "And you'll have to reimburse my expenses for the trip I'll have to cancel." Squeeze, squeeze, and squeeze.

"Yeah, yeah," Lenny said. "We'll get the money from somewhere. We're overstaffed in a couple departments."

"No way! I'm not going to be the reason a crew member loses their job."

"We have no choice!" Lenny said. "The budget's tighter than a nun's cunt!"

Juno groaned. "Lenny —"

"So, all right," I said, with heavy reluctance, "call Marshall and work out the deal. But promise me: no crew member loses their job."

"C'mon Lenny," Juno said. "Let's talk to Marshall."

"Way cool!" Lenny exulted. "I feel like we just got our lucky charm back."

Heartache, dead ahead.

Egon began directing *"Lonely Sky"* at six o'clock on Wednesday morning on the Sawyer & Company investment bank set in a building on lower Broadway. Ordinarily a film shoot would begin with exterior locations, keeping the interior sets on reserve for cover in bad weather, but these offices were only available for a short time and were fully furnished so we were also able to save money on set dressing.

Every morning I powered up at the gym and reported to the set at crew call dressed in running shoes, jeans, tee shirt and a baseball cap, ready for anything. On Day 1, Egon came to work with a scowl and already looked tense, so I greeted him warmly, then stayed out of his way. I had no writing to do yet, so I hung around, explaining I was the New York script doctor, and hearing the predictable replies from crew members:

"Too late doc, the patient's terminal," "Doctor? I suggest euthanasia," and my personal favorite, "Sorry doc, no intelligent life here worth saving."

The first scene scheduled to shoot was the morning meeting of Sawyer's partners. In the play and my discarded script his graying debonair colleagues treat him tenderly on the one-year anniversary of 9/11 and his wife's death. In Egon's script, with the partners reimagined as brash young go-getters, they try to chase the old dude's blues away by sending him a strippergram.

Right away a nerve-wracking, time-consuming pattern was set. As the bankers, the crew, and the stripper stood around waiting, Jonathan and Egon bickered in hushed voices, Jonathan pressing for a revision, the director shaking his head, until the actor threw up his hands and cried, "But Sawyer wouldn't do that!" and Egon snarled, "He does now," turned away, and walked back to his chair at the video monitors.

Clark, Egon's 1st Assistant Director from Los Angeles – an officious martinet the crew was already calling Clark The Snark – yelled, "Let's go people, let's shoot this thing!"

"Whattya know," a set dresser muttered as she leaned on the doorjamb with her arms crossed. "He forgot and called us people."

The crew took Jonathan's side as the first two days ground on. They knew he'd won an Obie award playing Sawyer on stage every night, then came to the film set the next day, miserable, to play a vulgar distortion of the same character. They were appalled by the script and they detested Egon, a Hollywood creature who'd trashed a brilliant play about 9/11 and our city and was strutting around treating the crew like coolies rather than collaborators. He kept trying to lighten the mood with wisecracks but only drew blank stares from the crew, who'd already detected his insecurity in his shifty eyes and bluster. One of the set P.A.'s began tweeting bitchy remarks about the crew he'd overheard from Egon. No, they weren't imagining it – he really was an asshole.

"How can you stand to work with him?" Jonathan demanded of me on Thursday afternoon, Day 2 of shooting, in his trailer on Rector Street, around the corner from the location.

"Sheer professionalism."

"Admit it. You hate him as much as the rest of us."

"No, not really," I lied. "I was hurt that my script got tossed and working with him is like babysitting. But hate? Why do that to myself?"

"I refuse to give up this role to that God damned kid," Jonathan said. "I'll fight for every line –"

"You should."

"– and if it eats up time, too bad. I can just imagine what Clark is writing on the production report: 'Creative discussion with director requested by Lehane put company 10 minutes behind schedule.' Egon should be working with the other actors too. But he created this mess, not me."

That night I sat next to Egon watching dailies from Day 1 in a Tribeca projection room along with our director of photography, our production designer, and Clark. As I suffered silently through the footage, Egon spent most of the screening whispering to his editor. Done watching, he turned to me.

"What do you think?"

I said, just to him: "Jonathan's misery is working just fine for the character."

He burst out laughing for the first time since shooting began.

I woke up before dawn on Day 3, the Friday before Labor Day weekend. Out the windows it was dark and silent at 4 o'clock, the hour when the city seemed to catch its breath before a new day began. It was too early for the gym, so I curled up in the Eames chair in the living room and nearly fell asleep again when outside the cry of a sad and mournful horn frightened me wide awake.

Down on the sidewalk someone with a trumpet was playing Chet Baker's signature tune "Let's Get Lost," badly, the sour notes followed by spells of giggling. The music stopped, then got louder, the trumpeter aiming his horn up at the front of the building. I didn't need to look out the window. I'd know Aldo's playing anywhere.

The detective I talked to at the local police precinct took so long to get on the phone and complete the report that I had no time left for the gym. I called an Uber and dove right into the back seat, but I didn't see Aldo anywhere.

I got to the set just as the sky darkened and a thunderstorm blew in. Upstairs the crew was lighting the first scene. I took a cup of coffee from the urn. My cheerful greeting drew a frown from Egon across the craft service table, so I could see there was trouble ahead. He kept rolling restlessly from foot to foot. Usually dressed so fastidiously, he already had food stains on the front of his blue polo shirt. He glared at the crew as they worked, then turned to Clark and poked him in the chest.

"I want you to kick ass with these people today, Clark. We're way behind schedule and it's their fault."

Laying blame on the crew is what we called 'erecting a meat shield,' the heartless sacrifice of underlings when a director or star or a producer got into trouble. Egon scrutinized a piece of coffee cake, made a disgusted face, and flung it back on the table, missing the platter. When he walked away, I wrapped the cake in a napkin and tossed it in the trash, because Egon was red-eyed and sniffling and seemed to have a cold.

A set P.A. talking over a walkie talkie headset tapped me on the shoulder.

"*Yeah, she's here.* Adrienne?" she said. "Jonathan wants to speak with you. He's in his trailer. *Yeah, she got it.*"

I ran around the corner through pelting rain to Jonathan's trailer. I found him slumped at the table. He got up and tossed me a towel.

"I refuse to give up this role to that God damned kid."

He'd said that on Day 1 and I sympathized with his frustration. And when he'd said the same thing on Day 2, I tried to console him. But it was getting tiresome to keep hearing it and my impatience made me reckless.

"Maybe it's time for you to do something."

"Do what? Threaten to quit?"

"He'll just recast. It's easier for Egon to find a new actor than to write anything."

He sat there with his chin on his chest and his eyes downcast.

"Then I don't know what to do. I'm running on caffeine and anger. I haven't slept in two days, and I don't know how to fix the situation."

"Why don't you tell him what's on your mind? Heart to heart. One on one."

"I've been trying to. But we're both too angry."

"Maybe if you surprise him by being calm and reasonable, you'll catch him off guard. Maybe he'll listen."

He was so rattled his voice wavered.

"This is a nightmare."

I took his face in my hands.

"Jonathan, you'd better get all this off your chest. It's already hurting your performance. Next it'll be your health."

I sprinted back through the rain, went upstairs, and took my time drying myself off with handfuls of paper towels and the hair dryer in the lady's room. When I walked back to the set, I discovered work had stopped and everybody was in a bleak, frustrated mood. Jonathan had taken Lenny and Juno for a meeting with Egon in an empty office. I cooled my heels and crossed my fingers. I was sure urging Jonathan to talk with Egon had been the right thing to do. I started fantasizing an outcome in which Egon decided to shoot my script and Jonathan was happy. In this fantasy, I would be generous and would help the director any way I could.

Loud angry voices erupted down the hall. A door slammed open and we all heard Egon shout.

"Over! You hear me? Over! I don't care what it costs, I'll pay for it myself if I have to! You redo the schedule, I'll recast the role, just get him the fuck outa here!"

The news that Jonathan had been fired and three days of work would have to be shot again with an actor yet to be named spread through the crew like a case of food poisoning. In limbo, we hung around joking nervously about how big a hole the three wasted days would blow in the already tight budget and whose jobs might be sacrificed. Meanwhile, Jonathan was gone. I walkie-talkied the first team P.A. assigned to the dressing room trailers on the street, who said she hadn't seen him. He must've gone straight down in the elevator still in his wardrobe, hailed a cab, and gone home. Egon didn't return to the set either, having no actor to aim a camera or an insult at. I hung around, plugged into the electric air of crisis, while the assistant directors and production manager tried to salvage something to shoot and Lenny and Juno stood by, freaking out.

With no other choice, they finally cancelled the day's work, the crew locked down the equipment and the set, and everybody left for the Labor Day weekend with three whole days to worry whether we'd ever get back to shooting. I took the subway uptown to Alpha Bitch Productions. But once I got there I couldn't focus on editing "*Men R Dawgs.*" I called Jonathan twice, but he didn't answer. Instead he sent a text telling me to meet him tonight. Was he angry with me for pushing him to confront Egon? Did I go too far? On some level I must have wanted to blow things up. I couldn't say precisely how losing a lead actor and stalling production was a good thing, but even a full stop was better than the direction Egon was taking. I checked in with McPeek that the "*Dawgs*" editing was on schedule, then I went home to brood, my mind consumed with the day's fiasco.

I could see only one way forward. Would anybody have the nerve to say it out loud? For three days Egon proved he was impossible to work with and not even capable of shooting the shitty script he was so proud of. He'd never admit what we all could see, that he was foundering and sinking fast. Still, how to get him to withdraw without aborting the show? Without Egon, Lenny and Juno would lose the financing, the studio would pull the plug, and dozens of people would lose their jobs. Of course, the studio wouldn't suffer. Emerge International would either file an insurance claim for the three wasted days of shooting or hide the loss in the budget of Egon's next big production. Egon's team would manage the PR to make sure their prize asset didn't suffer from any negative press. They would blame it all on Lehane, a temperamental actor who slowed down production by arguing with the director.

Showered and dressed in Levis, a tight tee shirt and black linen jacket, I left my apartment around nine o'clock. Heading into an unpredictable evening with Jonathan, my mind still preoccupied with what had happened on set today, I stepped out my front door and found myself face to face with Aldo.

He was down on the sidewalk dressed in a dark suit without a tie and smoking a cigarette, his trumpet case at his feet. His eyes lit up when he saw me. With a suave gesture, he flicked his cigarette away, grinned, and opened his arms to me.

I backed up and got through the outer door and into the vestibule on trembling knees. I fumbled frantically for my keys, hearing his quick footsteps coming up the front steps. I got my key in the lock, swung through the inner door and got inside the lobby and almost got it shut, but Aldo shoved his shoulder against the door and stopped it from closing.

"C'mon Adrienne! Let me in!" His face was so close his breath fogged the window. His smile was huge, his voice weirdly jubilant, and his eyes gleamed with madness.

"Go away!" I pushed hard on the door. I couldn't make it close.

"Open the door baby!" he said, laughing. "What's the matter with you? Aren't you glad to see me?"

He pushed on the door and I pushed just as hard from inside. The door swayed, open, almost closed, open, almost closed, towards him, towards me. I braced my feet and pushed with my body as hard as I could, but I couldn't close it all the way.

"Come on, Adrienne! Didn't you get my messages? I'm different now! I'm a different man!"

"If you're so different, let go of this door!"

He shoved hard and gained a couple inches and wedged his shoe between the door and the jamb. I glanced behind me. The elevator waited. If anybody called it upstairs or needed to leave the building, I was dead.

"Adrienne!" He became stern, serious. "I did a whole thing in rehab for you! I got clean! They don't let you get away with shit in that place! I'm okay now! You need to open this door! Let me in so we can talk, damn it!"

I slammed my heel down on his foot wedged between the door and the jamb. He howled and cursed but kept his foot in the door. I gave up a couple inches then slammed the door on his foot. He cursed and pulled his foot out but still kept pushing hard and kept the door from closing. He was angry and that was making him stronger and I could feel I was going to lose this tug of war. Any moment now the elevator door would slide closed, but if I let go of the door and ran for it, he'd catch me, even with a bruised foot.

In the window his face was red and there were tears in his eyes. I heard him gasping, inches from me through the gap in the door.

"Open this fuckin' door, bitch! I swear when I get you, I'll fuckin' kill you! Open the fuckin' door! I'll kill your fuckin' ass, Adrienne, don't do this to me!"

A few steps into the lobby behind me, the elevator stood wide-open, waiting.

"You think you can do this to me?" Aldo screamed. "You think you can do this to me?"

I heaved on the door with my body, but I wasn't strong enough to close it. I reached into my jacket pocket and grabbed my can of jogger's pepper spray.

"When I get my hands on you, I'll fuckin' kill you, bitch! You hear me? I'll fuckin' –"

I gave up a couple inches and the gap between the door and the jamb widened. He reached through the gap and grabbed my hand holding the pepper spray. I pulled the trigger, and the spray went all over the vestibule, but mainly in his eyes.

"Fuck! Fuck! Fuck!"

He knocked the can out of my hand and it clattered on the floor at his feet. Blinded and cursing, he turned his back to me but kept his weight on the door, rubbing his face with his hands, gasping for air.

Behind me, the elevator door began to close.

I pulled the door inward with his weight on it and he stumbled and fell into the lobby. I ran and dived into the elevator. The door caught on my foot, knocking off a sandal. I pulled my foot free, and the door closed. I pushed the button for my floor.

Aldo staggered toward me, half-blinded.

"Adrienne! Adrienne!" His angry face appeared in the window in the elevator door. His nose was running, and his eyes were red and streaming with tears.

"Bitch!"

He pounded on the door with both fists. He punched the button furiously. His fingers scrabbled and scratched at the edge of the elevator door and tried to pull it back open, his face livid in the tiny window. The car lifted upward.

"You're dead, you hear me?!" His voice got smaller as the elevator rose. "You're fuckin' dead!"

I reached my floor and ran to my apartment. I didn't hear anyone coming up the stairs. I hoped he didn't know which apartment was mine. Like any sensible single woman I kept my name off the doorbell and the mailbox in the lobby. I got inside, threw all the locks, pulled the curtains closed and turned the lights off. My body was shaking uncontrollably. I leaned on the hallway wall, then slid down, sat on the floor, and started to cry. I loved every inch of my home, and I'd kill him before he forced me to move the way I'd had to move my offices. I pulled out my phone and angrily stabbed out 9-1-1. By the time the police arrived and began searching the neighborhood, Aldo was gone.

"Five curtain calls!" Jonathan sighed as we cuddled in bed. "And even that didn't take the sting out of getting fired."

He made intense love to me that night, but I couldn't relax into it. I didn't tell Jonathan what I'd just been through with Aldo. I just tried to give him all my attention. In one of my favorite positions, on my back, Jonathan holding my thighs open, bucking and fucking me again and again, I faked an orgasm and told him it had all been wonderful. He slid off me and soon began to snore.

But I couldn't sleep. The horror came right back to me. If Aldo had gotten ahold of me, he would have beaten me, strangled me, kicked me, tore me to pieces. My wrists and shoulders had been bruised in the fight and they ached. Such a sick boy. A sad, dangerous, violent, psychopathic... Stop, Adrienne, or you'll never get to sleep. It's over. Try to relax. Let it go.

I woke up with a jolt early Saturday morning. Jonathan's side of the bed was empty, and the sheet was cool. I found him sitting at the kitchen table, writing in a spiral-bound notebook. I poured a cup of coffee and sat across from him.

"I couldn't sleep," he said. "I thought I could dump this angst in my journal and go back to bed, but I've been at this since four o'clock." He riffled a bunch of freshly written pages, and heaved a deep sigh. "I do some of my best thinking this way." He read for a moment, then put down his pen. "I can't blame Joel for selling the rights to Lenny and Juno. I know he needed money, so he sold the film rights before the play even opened. And of course Lenny and Juno hooked up with Egon Swift. They only care about getting the money to keep working. What you had to go through over your script was outrageous. But there's nothing surprising about Egon firing me. He just behaved according to his nature."

"Don't you think you're being too understanding?"

"Bad luck, that's all this was. Story of my life. It's always been two steps up and one step back. Just when I'm on the verge of something great..."

He shook his head, and before his sadness became contagious, I came around to him and hugged him.

"I'm going downtown for a run along the river, then I have a little work to do from home." I kissed him and smoothed his hair off his forehead. "I'll come back for lunch."

"Will you?" He pulled me close. "Thank you for being here. It means a lot."

I took a soak in Jonathan's king-sized bathtub that didn't relax me, then got dressed. I needed exercise to compensate for skipping the gym yesterday, and I needed to get home to my computer to work on "*Men R Dawgs*" edits. But I kept imagining violent encounters with Aldo on the street. The police had come to my apartment the night before, wrote their worthless reports, told me they could do nothing else, and told me to protect myself. But how? Hire a bodyguard? Like, I could afford that. Pay a man to follow me everywhere? That would totally suck.

I dressed, then turned on my cell phone to check my voicemail.

Okay, bitch. Are you happy you made me crawl? Are you happy you made me beg you? Are you happy that while I was fighting with you – his voice broke into sobbing – somebody stole my trumpet? This is the kind of shit that brings out the bad Aldo, and you know it. So just remember one thing! I know where you live! One day when you don't expect it–

I quit listening, but I saved the message as evidence.

I glanced into the kitchen. Jonathan was still at the table, scribbling grimly, deep into whatever he was writing. I left him alone and went back to the bedroom and kicked my feet into my shoes. Then I sat on the edge of the bed to think. It was time to leave, but I couldn't get the deranged sob in Aldo's voice out of my head. *I know where you live... You're dead, you hear me?... You're fuckin' dead...*

On the edge of panic, I slid open the bedside table drawer and picked up Jonathan's gun. I was surprised at how heavy it was. It seemed to be fully loaded. Holding it scared me, and I put it back in the drawer. But what if Aldo was outside my building? Suppose he'd gotten inside? He could be waiting in the hallways or stairs. Should I ask to borrow the gun? Jonathan would never let me. It would be wrong to just take it. But I would only need it for a couple hours. I was sure I'd never need to fire it. If I pointed the gun at Aldo, he was such a sniveling coward he would run away. I'd return it at lunchtime and put it back when Jonathan wasn't looking. He would never know I took it. I decided I was safer with the gun than without it, so I picked it up again, and put it in my backpack.

I got home okay. I overdressed in black, tight leggings and a tee and hoodie, so I'd work up a drenching, purifying sweat, running along the Hudson in the blazing heat and humidity. I pinned my hair up under a baseball cap and put on my sunglasses, slung on my backpack, and was headed down the front steps when my phone rang, and I jumped. The screen said EGON SWIFT. I took a deep breath and whispered, Be calm and in control.

"Hi Egon! Beautiful day, huh?"

"Come to my office. We have to work on the script."

"Egon, it's Labor Day weekend."

"I'm aware of that Adrienne."

"Aren't you with your family?"

"They know my work comes first." This was a different Egon. Clipped, emphatic, pressured.

"It's been a rough three days. Don't you want to take some time–"?

"Adrienne, are you the writer on this show or not?"

That wrecked the day, maybe the whole weekend. Jonathan would be furious. The prospect of writing with Egon again twisted my stomach into knots. For just a second I almost told him I was out of town. But something stopped me, maybe professionalism, but I also sensed an opportunity.

"Okay, no problem. I'll be over as soon as I finish my morning run."

"Run? Where are you? I'll run with you."

"That's okay, I usually run alone."

Beep!

I stepped off the elevator into Egon's office. The air stank like rotten onions, the body odor of fear and frustration, even though the room was air-conditioned so cold that I began to shiver in my sweaty running clothes. Egon slouched behind his desk dressed in the same food-stained blue polo shirt, white tennis shorts, and spongy white sneakers he was wearing yesterday on the set. He looked exhausted. His face was taut and greasy and bristled with whiskers, dark smudges puffed under his eyes, and he chewed continuously on his lips. Script pages scrawled with notes lay scattered on the desk in front of him. Crumpled pages lay on the floor where they'd missed the wastebasket. He looked like a portrait in living color of a man in a dry-mouthed panic after crashing into personal limits as impassable as a stone wall.

His misery made me hopeful he'd be open to facing reality if I presented it the right way. I settled into a task chair across the desk from him.

"Egon! What's up?"

His normally soft murmuring voice now was taut with suppressed anger.

"I've been up all night, staring at this fucking thing." He flipped his hand across the desk and a few script pages fluttered to the floor. "None of this seems any good now. Who am I kidding, except maybe myself? I've written shit, and I know that's what people are saying behind my back."

Compassion and sympathy, even though I didn't feel it, seemed like the right approach.

"You're going through a temporary loss of faith in yourself, that's all. It happens to all writers. I've been there. It's a tough spot to be in."

"See?" He sighed a gust of coffee breath. "That's why I need my little muse."

It took me a moment to realize he meant me. Little Muse? I mean, what the fuck was that? In an ideal world, I might've helped him to overcome his fear, and to challenge himself by directing the complex script I'd written and he'd discarded. But this wasn't an ideal world. This was show business, a frantic, cutthroat, competitive men's world. Did he think it was my job, as his "little muse," to supply him with talent he didn't have?

"Thank you for coming," he said. "I was afraid you'd abandon me like everybody else."

"I wouldn't do that. Besides, I'm under contract." Then I asked quietly, "Why do you feel like you've been abandoned?"

"Adrienne?" He groaned as if I were clueless. "Weren't you on the set the last three days? The crew hates me."

I almost said he was only getting back what he'd put out. But I felt a gentler approach would be better.

"You seem frazzled. Are you sure you want to work today?"

His head snapped up as if he'd been caught at something.

"Yeah, yeah, we need to write. The script sucks, and we've gotta fix it. And for your information, I'm fine."

"I know how exhausting directing can be."

"I'm just hungry, that's all. Let's go to the diner for breakfast."

In his wastebasket I noticed an aluminum takeout dish crushed around a half-eaten omelet and a pile of French fries, and a large empty coffee cup, debris from stress eating that had been no comfort after an anxious night of creative frustration.

"I'm not hungry. Listen, Egon."

He heard my serious tone. "What?"

"We need to talk about something. I hope you'll hear it as coming from somebody who cares about you."

"I know, I know, I need a shower." He snickered. "You've been out running in this heat. Wanna take a shower with me?"

"It's not about how you smell."

He looked wary. "Okay..."

"We haven't been friends very long but it's hard to see you in such pain."

He grimaced. "Pain? What pain?"

I thought I'd better try to speak the truth and be persuasive.

"You're having a miserable experience with this film."

"C'mon. I need a cup of coffee." He half rose. I kept talking, so he sat back down.

"And after what happened yesterday, firing Jonathan, writing off three days of production –"

"No worries. If I have to, I'll pay the studio back out of my own pocket."

"I'm not talking about money."

"No?" His eyes narrowed. "Then what?"

"If what happened yesterday leaks to the media –"

"It better fucking not!"

"– they're gonna say your shoot has problems. Right or wrong, that's what people are going to think. People are not kind-hearted toward stars like you, Egon. They feed on your success, but they also can't wait to see you crash."

"Okay, so what? I should hire Lehane back? Is that what you're saying?"

"It's not about Jonathan. And you're wrong about the crew, they don't hate you. It's about you. You're not happy doing this. And everybody on set feels it."

He slouched back in his chair behind his desk, hiding behind a steeple of fingers.

"You're the reason the show's been funded. What if you become executive producer? They'll still promote the film off your name. 'Egon Swift Presents.' Let somebody else have the headache of directing this thing."

"The studio would never agree to that." He shook his head at such an absurd suggestion. "Besides, if I quit now the media will have me for lunch."

"The media can be handled."

"People think the only films I can make are those psycho thrillers." In a voice with a surprising note of pleading he said, "But this film is supposed to change all that, give me a new image, make people see me different."

I knew all about craving respect. But no way could I sympathize with him. He'd gotten the lucky breaks so many people hadn't, and how had he used them? To dumb down people's minds and coarsen their souls with his sick, amoral movies, getting rich and famous glamorizing violence against women.

I said, "I think you're in more trouble than you realize."

His face hardened. "'Let somebody else direct'?" An ugly grin, a flat voice. "Somebody like who? You?"

"I'm trying to help you out of a tough spot, Egon."

"Sure you are," he drawled in a soft, gravelly whisper. "Now I see. Whatta you think this is? One of your movies? Your little chick flicks where the men are stupid, and the bitches are always getting over on 'em?"

"I've never made a film like that. You're confusing me with somebody else."

"You're trying to run a number on me. And for a minute, I actually believed you cared." There was almost a sob in his voice. "I'll bet you're the one who's been tweeting that negative shit about me around the set."

"How can you say that? I've done everything I can to help you. I wrote a great script. And then I helped you rewrite it into what you wanted. How can you think I'm anything but supportive?"

"Oh yeah? Is that why you took your name off the script?" His eyes narrowed to angry slits. "You back-stabbing little bitch."

I could've gotten up and left, but I refused to back down from somebody like him. It was pointless to keep faking tenderness and concern.

"There's still time to save this movie, Egon."

"Save it? Save it from what?"

"From you."

He jerked to his feet behind the desk so abruptly his chair rolled back and struck the wall.

"Me? You're the loser. You haven't directed anything in years. The only way you'll direct another movie is to steal it. Or earn it on your knees."

"Egon," I said, pretending to laugh that off. "Take it easy."

"You're trying to undermine me."

"Why would I do that?"

"Because you want to steal my job. Because you're a bitch in a dog-eat-dog world. I know your type. You'll do anything to beat 'the man.'"

"I'm trying to help you."

Too far, Adrienne. You've pushed him too far.

"Help me? Yeah, right. Help me out of a fuckin' job!"

I tried sounding calm and business-like.

"It'll be better if you back out now. If the film comes out and everybody can see your limitations, that's when it'll really hurt."

His whole body stiffened.

"My limitations!? Who the fuck do you think you're talking to?"

He came around the desk and stood over me, bellowing.

"You're not stealing this movie from me!"

It took all my willpower to sit still, to stay too strong to be intimidated or provoked into fighting back. He jabbed my shoulder with his index finger, again and again. When he poked me, the energy and confidence I'd built up on my run along the river vanished.

"You got that bitch? You are not stealing this movie from me!"

I rolled my chair back out of reach and got on my feet. I knew if I stood up to him, I'd be hurt.

"It's time for me to leave." I picked up my backpack. "I can't work with you in this condition."

He stepped in my way, blocking the path to the elevator.

"I'm sick of trying to work with you New York fucks who don't get me at all!" he yelped, more to the world at large than to me. "Don't you know you're supposed to support the director, not undermine him, not gossip about him, not pull cute shit behind his back? If this was Hollywood —"

The phone in my backpack started ringing. I raised a hand for him to stop but he kept on yelling. Physically he was so much bigger, so much stronger than me. I was feeling battered without even being touched. My hand was shaking as I fumbled with the zipper and reached inside. I pulled out the phone. The Caller I.D. said JONATHAN LEHANE. As I put the phone back unanswered, my knuckles brushed Jonathan's revolver.

"Egon, I'm leaving. I'm sorry we didn't get any work done."

His face was contorted in indignation and rage.

"You're not leaving 'cause we're not done. You want out? Here's the way out!" He grabbed his crotch. "Get on your knees!"

"Egon —"

"Get on your fuckin' knees!"

How I sounded so calm, I don't know.

"C'mon, man –"

"No!" He spoke in a voice low and menacing. "You're gonna suck my dick. And if you do it good, maybe I'll let you leave. And if you don't, I'm gonna fuck you up big time."

I had pushed a stone off a dark hole. Out of it crawled a different man than the Egon Swift of the elegant East Hampton mansion with his soft hand-shake and monotonous murmuring voice. I was looking at the creature who made three movies in which women were so artfully, exuberantly abused. But that wasn't going to be me.

I reached into my backpack and pulled out Jonathan's gun. He looked at it, then at me, astonished.

"What the fuck is that?"

"I don't want any trouble."

"What the fuck is that?"

"Just let me leave, okay?"

"You pull a fuckin' piece on me?"

"Get out of my way, Egon."

"Don't you know who I am?" he screamed.

He grabbed my empty chair and shoved it at me. It hit me in the legs and the gun fired. The bang and recoil forced a sharp scream out of me, and the gun jerked out of my hand and bounced on the carpet between us.

My wrist ached from the recoil and my ears rang from the gun blast. Egon took a step back, his mouth open, blinking in astonishment. He stared at me then at the gun on the carpet. You just gave him the gun, Adrienne. If you reach for the gun, he'll grab you. But if you don't, he's gonna pick it up and shoot you.

He dropped straight down on his knees. I felt the impact on the floor through the soles of my shoes.

"Jesus Christ!" he moaned. He clutched at his chest.

He looked at his hands. They were bloody and a dark stain was spreading across the front of his shirt. The stain began dripping dark red onto his white shorts.

"Aw no! Look at me!" His mouth twisted, gasping curses. "What did you do to me Adrienne? What did you do?"

"Egon, I'm so sorry! It was an accident. I didn't mean to —"

"You bitch! You –" The words caught in his throat and he retched, and blood foamed between his gritted teeth and ran down his chin. Drops of blood fell onto his bare knees and the carpet.

"You bissssshh..."

He struggled to rise from his knees, then toppled over on his back. I swooped down and grabbed the gun. His cell phone slid out of his shirt pocket and landed on the carpet beside him.

Egon uttered a loud watery groan and blood gurgled from his lips and ran down his cheeks. Then he fell silent and still. His wide-open eyes, blank and dull, stared at the ceiling.

Oh my God, oh my God... I don't know how long I stood in shock, my mind blank, my feet stuck to the floor. Finally I began to move, very carefully and mindfully.

I pulled off a strip of paper towels from the roll over the kitchen counter. I wrapped the gun and pushed it deep down in my backpack. How long had I been here? A few minutes at most. What did I touch? The door, the elevator, and the chair I'd sat in. I wrapped my hand in paper towels and wiped down the leather upholstery and metal frame of the chair. What about old fingerprints from our writing sessions? That was too much to try to deal with now. I went behind Egon's desk and pulled the drawers out of his filing cabinets and left them hanging open like a burglar in a hurry might have.

I checked the bottoms of my running shoes. No blood. I carefully scanned the office. There was nothing more I could do. I had to get out of there. I covered my finger with the paper towel and pushed the button for the elevator. Then it occurred to me that if anybody knew Egon planned to work with me that morning, I'd immediately be the prime suspect. Suppose he'd told someone, like his wife?

I called his cell phone. It rang on the floor beside his body, a few bars of elevator jazz. His voicemail greeting in my ear felt uncomfortably intimate.

"Hey, this is Egon..."

"Hi, Egon, it's Adrienne." It was surprisingly easy to keep my voice light and casual. "Look, I'm sorry, I know we were supposed to meet this morning, but something urgent has come up and I have to cancel." The elevator arrived behind me. Time to go. "Call me if you need to, or call me later and we can reschedule, okay? And if I don't hear from you, have a great holiday."

I shut the door to my apartment and threw both locks. I put down my backpack, closed the venetian blinds, and stripped off everything I was wearing, sweat clothes, running shoes, underwear and socks, and stuffed it all into a trash bag. I was desperate to make sure I didn't bring any evidence from Egon's office home with me. Suddenly, I had to stop. I was trying to stay too busy to feel anything. Slowly, I sat down at the kitchen table, barefoot and nude. The summer heat and humidity in the kitchen should have been relaxing, but my whole body was trembling as if I was cold.

How did I get this so wrong? I thought I could convince Egon to stop directing our movie. I thought if I could arouse his insecurity and his fear of losing face and being judged inadequate, I could get him to accept reality and quit. But I misjudged the risk. He got insulted, he got violent, and now he was dead. Dead! I broke down inside, and I began to cry uncontrollably.

After a while, I forced myself to stand up and wipe away the tears. Drained, weakened, but forcing myself to function, I took a deep breath and tried to pull myself together. I had to go uptown to Jonathan's but there was a lot to do first. In the shower, I soaped up a loofah and scrubbed myself pink, as if mortifying my flesh would atone for what I'd done. I dressed in gym shorts, flip flops and a tee shirt. I hid Jonathan's gun, still wrapped in paper towels, in my dresser drawer. I carried the trash bag downstairs to the basement and put the sweat clothes and cap, backpack and underwear and even my running shoes through a hot water cycle in the washing machine with soap and lots of bleach.

Waiting for the wash to finish, I went back upstairs and drank a cup of coffee, booted up my iMac, and logged on to the editor's servers at Alpha Bitch Productions. I made myself focus on the latest edit of a "*Men R Dawgs*" episode and emailed my notes to McPeek. I was working, I assured myself, and also establishing an alibi. No, wait a minute – an alibi? For what? Criminals need alibis, not me. Other people might believe me or might not, but I better not start to doubt myself. I defended myself against sexual assault. Since when was that a crime?

When the spin cycle ended, I took the laundry out of the washing machine and groaned. The bleach had faded my black garments to an ugly mottled gray. What a dumb mistake! But wait – if careless washing ruined these things, wouldn't I throw them in the trash? To throw out perfectly good garments, that would look guilty. I bagged the whole soggy mess and took it out to the garbage cans behind my building. Hoping that nobody was looking out of the surrounding windows, I found an empty can, dropped everything in, and went upstairs.

Back at the kitchen table, I lit a cigarette and tried to think in between seizures of panic and brain freeze. What now, Adrienne? My mind detoured into useless whining and regret. If only I hadn't been terrorized by Aldo the night before. If only I hadn't known where Jonathan kept his gun. Did any security cameras on West 22nd Street catch me entering or leaving Egon's building? I was sure I didn't leave any evidence in his office or bring any home with me. In that way, at least, I was as clean as I could be, but I still had a lot to figure out. I calmed down enough to think through what had happened, and what to do now.

Fact number one: my well-meaning effort to solve a dilemma for the film company had backfired. Fact number two: I killed Egon Swift. Fact number three: I also killed the movie and maybe my future, too. But fact number four: I wasn't a murderer, for God's sake, I defended myself against a rapist. I took the gun, yes, I admit it, for protection against Aldo. I had multiple voicemails that proved he was a serious threat, so no problem there. And I really did forget that I still had Jonathan's gun in my backpack. When I pulled it out at Egon's office, I only meant to scare him. But it didn't stop him, did it? I tried to leave before things got out of control, but he stood in my way and threatened me. I didn't intend to pull the trigger. He threw a chair at me, it hit me in the legs, and the gun just went off. He got shot and that was a terrible thing, but if I hadn't stopped Egon, he might've done terrible things to me. It wasn't a "call 9-1-1" situation. So, should I call the police now? Or keep acting like a criminal? I was already guilty of destroying the clothing and shoes I wore. The longer I waited the guiltier I would look, even though the truth was on my side and justice ought to be.

But there was fact number five: nobody would believe me. I shot a man with a gun that I'd stolen from someone else. Nobody would believe that I'd never intended to shoot him, or that I'd had no choice. My victim was male, rich, and famous, and who was I? The man-hating madwoman who created "*Men R Dawgs.*" I wasn't even bruised where the chair hit me in the legs. Of course, as a decent law-abiding person it would be the right thing to call the police. But if I did, I was afraid everything would quickly go wrong.

Then there was fact number six. Because of me, Jonathan was in deep trouble and he didn't even know it. Any minute, the murder of Egon Swift would be breaking news. When I borrowed the gun, I was crazy with fear. The trouble I might cause Jonathan never occurred to me. But just like an episode of "*Law & Order*", the police, looking for suspects, would investigate any person Egon had trouble with. They'd believe that Jonathan shot Egon because he got fired. They'd search his apartment, find his gun, and match it to the bullet that killed Egon. Jonathan would be arrested, and I think we can be certain, I would be too. But what if I got rid of the gun, right now? The police wouldn't find it, but Jonathan would figure out that I took the gun and what I used it for. Would he believe me and protect me, or turn me over to the police to protect himself? After weighing the risks I could see I had no choice. I had to tell Jonathan what happened. My best chance was to put the gun back, tell him everything, and hope we could figure something out.

Rocking uptown on a clattering C train, I stared at my reflection in the window across the car. I looked like any girl heading for a holiday weekend at the beach with her man, freshly bathed, groomed and scented, and dressed in white: Vans, Levi's, a man's dress shirt and my mirrored shades. I began to feel better about myself until I lifted my bag to leave the train at West 81st and I felt the weight of the gun buried in my clothes. I couldn't wait to get rid of the thing.

When Jonathan opened the door, he gave me a quick kiss on my cheek, and walked off, muttering irritably into his cell phone.

"I'll tell you how you minimize the damage – you find me a new movie, and fast."

I strolled into the bedroom. I could hear his voice, he was still at the far end of the apartment. I had my next moves all thought out. I placed my bag on the bed. I opened the bedside table drawer. The box of bullets was about half full. Chances are he wouldn't notice one was missing. I took a bullet, wiped my fingerprints off the box and put it back where I'd found it. I unzipped my bag, dug out the gun, and locked myself in the bathroom.

I unwrapped the paper towels around the gun, took out the empty cartridge, wiped my fingerprints off the fresh bullet, and put it in the cylinder. I flushed the torn-up paper towels and the empty cartridge down the toilet, wiped the gun clean with another towel I also flushed, pulled the cuff of my shirt down over my hand and picked up the gun. All I had to do was put it back, then find the moment to tell Jonathan everything. I listened at the bathroom door. All was quiet. I stepped out and slid open the bedside table drawer.

Just then, Jonathan stepped into the bedroom and grabbed a pack of cigarettes off the dresser.

"Listen," he said, still talking on the phone, giving me an eye roll and shake of the head, "the play will be remembered long after the movie, which was a fiasco before it even started shooting." Then his eyes dropped to the gun in my hand. "Hold on."

I put the gun in the drawer and pushed it closed.

He looked puzzled. "Adrienne?" He shook a cigarette out of the pack and caught it between his lips. "What are you doing?"

"Looking for a tissue." Casually, I rolled my sleeve back up.

"They're in the bathroom." He raised his lighter, then stopped, looking at me in a way I didn't like. "Where they always are." He said into the phone, "I'll call you back," and hung up.

He walked over, putting the unlit cigarette in his shirt pocket, and pulled out the drawer while I stood there frozen.

"What were you doing with my gun?"

"I was just putting it back in the drawer." I tried to sound cool and casual but the tremor in my voice gave me away. "So! What's your pleasure today, Handsome?"

He would not be diverted.

"Why did you take it out of the drawer?"

"I need a tissue. I took it out to look in the back of the drawer."

He stared at me. I shrugged, silently praying for him to let it go.

He closed the drawer. I turned toward the bathroom, but he caught me by the arm.

"Just a minute," he said, looking at my open bag.

"What?"

"Did you take my gun out of here this morning?"

"Your gun?"

"Yes. My gun. Did you take it out of the apartment this morning?"

"What do you mean 'take it?'" I pulled my arm out of his grasp. "I was just looking for a tissue."

His worried eyes searched my face.

"You know where the tissues are."

He knew I was lying. He'd be insulted if I played innocent any longer.

"Okay," I sighed. "Okay. Yes."

"Yes, what?"

"I borrowed your gun."

He looked like he was going to faint.

"What the hell for?"

"Protection."

"Protection from what?"

"From a stalker. A guy named Aldo. He's been stalking me for months. He's threatened to kill me, more than once. I had to get an order of protection against him. He was on the sidewalk yesterday morning, harassing me. Last night he tried to break into my building. We had a huge tug of war over the front door. He was screaming and threatening to kill me. He almost did."

"That's a problem you take to the police. You don't pick up a gun. Especially one that doesn't belong to you."

"The police know all about him. They've known about him for over a year. There's nothing they can do."

"Why didn't you tell me about this?"

"Because you just got fired. I didn't want to add my problems to yours. Then I woke up this morning, and he'd left me a threatening voicemail."

I held up my phone and played it and watched his face change as he listened. At least we would not be debating whether Aldo was dangerous.

"I had to go home to change, and I was afraid he'd be waiting. So, I borrowed your gun."

"Without asking."

"I knew if I asked, you'd say 'No.'"

"But you took it anyway."

"The night before, he threatened to kill me, Jonathan. I was scared. I didn't know what else to do."

"If you'd told me about it, I would've come with you. I would've protected you. I get that you were afraid, he sounds like a lunatic, but you still should have asked."

"And have you say 'No'? And have no way to protect myself?"

"Get your own gun!"

"I tried! After he held a knife to my throat! I applied for a gun permit. And I was rejected."

"So you thought it was okay to take my gun?"

"Of course not! I knew it was totally not okay! But it was life or death! He's still out there! And he's insane!"

"All right, all right." He held his arms out and I stepped into his embrace. "My God, you're shaking all over."

"I'm scared. And I'm sorry Jonathan, really sorry."

He tightened his arms around me. And now, the worst part is... But I didn't have the courage at that moment to finish the story.

"The gun isn't legal," he said. "I never got around to getting a license. If I got caught, I'd be in trouble just for having it."

"I'll never touch it again, I swear."

"Okay." He lit the cigarette. "The hell with it, then. It's time for lunch. I have to finish talking to my agent and then I'll be ready. Okay?"

"Okay."

He hugged me, kissed me on the forehead, and left the room, dialing his phone with one hand and lighting his cigarette with the other.

I locked myself in the bathroom and sat on the floor, back against the tub, with my arms wrapped around my knees. Oh no! Oh God! Oh shit! Now what? I might as well shoot myself in the head. Two seconds too slow, and I blew the whole thing. If I'd put the gun back quicker this horrible morning would have had a perfect ending! Now, all I could do was wait, and worry about all the ways this would go wrong.

Any minute now Egon's death would hit the media and Jonathan would know I did it. My bad faith would be undeniable, and worse, it was toward someone who now could send me to prison with a phone call. I was the worst kind of screwed, the kind when trouble is coming and you don't know when, and you're gripped by a fear that can squeeze the life out of you.

I ran water in the sink until it was cold and splashed handfuls on my face. Jonathan knocked on the door and I jumped.

"Hey," he said. "The weather's supposed to be gorgeous tomorrow and Monday the theater's dark for Labor Day. Let's drive out to the beach tonight after I'm done working. You sound like you need a day off."

"Oh Jonathan," said the woman in white in the mirror. "That sounds wonderful."

I woke up Sunday morning alone in Jonathan's king-sized bed in Montauk, laid back listening to the distant crunch of the surf on the rocks below the cliff, and thought about last night. We'd drunk a bottle of Veuve Clicquot, skipped dinner, made love for hours, then fell into exhausted sleep. It was the third time we'd made love and this time we were in perfect harmony. Our first time, after our bitter argument over Egon's awful screenplay for "Lonely Sky," we were just finding out about each other, and he'd behaved like an urgent but thoughtful lover, aggressive, but attentive to my feelings. The second time, on Friday night after he'd been fired from the movie, he was angry, and I allowed myself to be the submissive bucket into which he dumped his deep hurt and anger after three traumatic days fighting with Egon, ramming away between my legs until he was exhausted. But last night we found the perfect rhythm, teasing and provoking each other, then I surrendered and gave myself to be possessed, again and again. After a disastrous week the candlelit hours of voluptuous sex were totally restorative, and I fell asleep hoping such a night would soften his anger with me in the morning when the news broke.

The news...Oh God...

I slid out of bed and wrapped myself in my silk robe. I sat on the edge of the bed and took a series of slow, deep breaths to try to stay calm and prepared. I came down the stairs and glanced into the library and immediately wished I hadn't. Jonathan was staring intensely at his computer, undoubtedly reading the morning's news. I went into the kitchen, took two cups down from the cabinet, and turned on the coffee maker.

I was gazing out the window over the pool and backyard when I sensed his presence. I turned, and he was in the doorway staring at me. I could tell by the look on his face that Egon had been found.

"Good morning, you beast," I said. "You look disturbed. What's wrong?"

"Somebody shot Egon."

"My God." I dropped into my seat at the table. I needed to.

"The *Times* says the police have no suspects."

"No? None?"

"He was found in his office by his wife."

"Oh my God. Poor Rita." I shook my head, hoping I looked wide-eyed and innocent. "Who could have done it?"

He took a long hard look at me.

"That's what the police are trying to find out." He took his seat at the table. He leaned toward me, his eyes watching my reaction. "Let's just hope he pulls through, so he can tell them."

I froze. "Pulls through?" I had to ask, terrified of the answer. "What do you mean?"

"He's in a coma."

"I thought he was dead." I immediately regretted saying that.

"Really? Now that's interesting. Why would you think that?"

"Well, when you said somebody shot him, I just assumed you meant somebody killed him, but they didn't, so that's good, I mean, maybe he'll live, maybe come out of it, out of the coma —"

I couldn't sit there with him staring at me. He knew. I stood up and walked out into the backyard. I stopped at the pool's edge and stood looking into the water. All day yesterday, repeating one ugly fact gave me hope: at least Egon was dead and could not point the finger at me. Now what if he recovered? The possibilities were too frightening to think about.

Beside my reflection in the pool, Jonathan appeared.

"This could have been such a beautiful day," he sighed.

I blurted out the first thing that came to mind.

"I was thinking about the research I did for my first film. For the family, coma is worse than having a loved one die. Waiting it out. Not knowing how it's going to end." I shook my head and let out a sigh. "I guess we just hope for the best."

That same stare, but harder. "You know what Adrienne?"

"What?"

He grabbed me by the shoulder.

"You're a really bad liar."

He shoved me off my feet. I heard myself yelp in shock, then I plunged into the pool. Breathing in and spitting out the cold water, my hair billowing around my face and tangling in my eyeglasses, I surfaced, blinded by the brilliant morning sun, paddling and coughing.

"Hey! Why the hell'd you do that?"

"Let's go. You may as well have breakfast before I call the police."

"The police?" I couldn't believe what he was saying. "What are you talking about?"

He sneered at me, shaking his head.

"Bad fucking liar."

I reached for his hand, but he wouldn't help me. I paddled to the shallow end and struggled out of the pool, my nose stinging from the chlorine, pulling my wet wrap away from my body, shaking water from my hands, and squeezing it out of my hair.

"My best robe, you bastard!"

"Don't worry," he said. "Where you're going, they'll give you a nice orange jumpsuit."

He turned and went into the house.

Dripping wet and too furious to speak, I passed him in the kitchen and fled upstairs. In the bathroom I peeled off my robe, rolled it into a towel, squeezed the water out and rolled it in a dry towel. I skipped the shower and got dressed in a hurry. I finished packing and came back downstairs.

He was sitting at the kitchen table eating a bowl of muesli for breakfast. I threw my bag with a crash on the floor and poured a cup of coffee.

"When's the next train?"

"Where are you going?"

"If I'm getting arrested, I'd rather be home. And as far away from you as possible." I leaned against the counter, sipped the coffee, and spit it into the sink. "This coffee's cold."

"I'll make more coffee," he said. "Have a seat."

"I'm not sitting here with you."

"Stand on your fucking head, for all I care."

He got up, and silently went about grinding the coffee beans and heating water in a copper kettle. I looked out the window, feeling almost sick with dread. The pool surface shimmered in the sunlight. Yes, it could have been a perfect summer day for us. He came over and stood beside me.

"You know," he said, "last night was wonderful. You really took me to another world. It felt like the start of something great. This morning, I woke up feeling like I was over the frustration of dealing with Egon and getting fired. I was really happy that you were here, that I could share this beautiful place and this beautiful day with you."

He sighed. "I hiked up the path through the woods to the tea house. The air was warm, the birds were singing in the trees, the surf was breaking down below the cliff. I meditated, I came back down and swam my usual fifty laps, then I came back in to read the news. And in the middle of the *New York Times* home page was a picture of Egon, wearing a tee shirt, baseball cap, and a pair of headphones around his neck. For a second, I was afraid the story was about me getting fired. Then I saw the headline: *Film director shot, police search for assailant*. And I went into shock."

His arm went around my shoulders.

"Right away, I knew you did it. But I hoped, I really hoped, that somehow I was wrong. Of course you were furious with Egon after what he did to your writing. Was that why you did it? C'mon, tell me."

Could I tell him? Could I give him that power over me?

He shrugged. "Or maybe it's better if you don't say anything. We'll eat breakfast and I'll call the police."

I walked away from him and went over and turned on the TV in the corner of the room to CNN to see if they were covering the story of Egon's shooting.

"You said you and Egon got along well."

When I didn't reply, he walked over and turned off the TV.

"Tell me what happened."

"Sounds like you have it all figured out."

"You stole my gun and you shot him."

"Yeah? Simple as that? Why would I shoot Egon?"

"I don't know. You tell me."

"I told you why I took the gun."

"You stole my gun to protect yourself from some guy named Aldo."

"That's right. A maniac who threatened my life. Taking the gun had nothing to do with Egon. I didn't even know I'd see him until after I left your place."

"So you did see him yesterday."

And, just like that, there was no going back.

"C'mon, tell me. You're gonna need to tell somebody."

My only chance was to tell Jonathan the truth and hope he believed me. Of course, he still might turn me in. And once I told him what happened, I'd have to learn to live with his power over me. I stared at him for a moment.

"Will you help me?"

"Will you tell me the truth?"

I closed my eyes, nodded, and despite myself exhaled with a soft involuntary moan.

"Promise you won't call the police?"

"I promise I'll listen."

I pulled a chair out from the table and sat down.

"Yesterday after I left your place, Egon called me. He said we had to work on the script. Right away, like, that minute. I knew it would be pointless. Three days in, the show was in trouble. Rewriting that terrible script was not going to help. But I went, because it's my job. When I got there, he was a mess. He'd been up all night, trying to work on the script, and got nothing done. He wasn't saying it, but I think he finally admitted to himself that he was in over his head." I lit one of his cigarettes and blew a plume of smoke. "He was scared. He was vulnerable. I thought it was the right moment to try to get him to quit."

"What? You thought he'd listen to you?"

"Three days into shooting, he was wrecking the show. He knew he was making everyone miserable and he didn't care. He said, 'I'm the director, I can do whatever I want, and everybody else has to suck it up and live with it.' The production was in a crisis. But to him that wasn't his fault."

The coffee was ready, and he took care of serving it. He put a cup in front of me.

"I tried to get him to see the damage he was causing. But he wouldn't listen. He accused me of trying to steal the movie from him. He flipped out. Screaming, yelling at me."

I pulled my knees up, heels on the chair, and wrapped my arms around my shins.

"He mocked my whole career, Jonathan. Calling me horrible names, trying to belittle me. He said the only way I'd ever direct another movie is if I fucked somebody to get it. And he got violent. He threatened to beat me up. He wouldn't let me leave the office unless I sucked his cock. Then my phone rang. It was you, but at that moment I couldn't answer."

I closed my eyes and took a deep breath.

"I was putting the phone in my backpack and, I swear, that was the first time I realized I still had the gun." I looked up at him, blurry through my tears. "He told me he was going to hurt me. He seemed much bigger than me. And I was terrified. So I pointed the gun at him, and I told him to leave me alone." I cringed at the sound of my voice, so high and shrill. "I was just trying to scare him. I just wanted to get out of there. But he flipped out and threw a chair at me. It hit me and I flinched, and the gun, it just went off."

"All by itself."

"I didn't decide to pull the trigger. He threw a chair at me and the shot was, like, a reflex. He threatened to rape me. To put me in my place. I couldn't let that happen."

"I'm not saying you should've. So then what?"

I reached over to the ashtray and flicked the ash off my cigarette.

"Then he left me alone."

"And you didn't call the police."

"I only pulled out the gun to scare him, that's all. I just wanted to get out of there without getting hurt. And in a way it was lucky that I still had the gun. I don't want to think about what he might have done to me..." I brushed the tears off my cheeks. "That's what happened. I swear it's the truth."

"Why didn't you tell me this yesterday?"

"When? After you caught me with the gun? You were already angry with me. I was afraid you'd call the police."

"You should have told me everything."

"I was in shock, Jonathan. I thought I'd killed him, and I knew nobody would believe me. And see? You don't."

"You say Egon threatened to rape you. And I believe you. He's a bully and a spoiled brat. And the way you describe the shooting, I can see it happening that way. But now I don't know what to do."

I'd groveled, I'd almost begged, but he still wouldn't partner with me even though he was in trouble too.

"Go ahead..." I slid his cell phone toward him across the table. "Call the police. Have me arrested."

He didn't like that. He picked up the phone, staring at me.

He dialed a number. I froze.

"Hello, it's Jon Lehane. Very well thank you, happy Labor Day. I'd like to order some wine." He put his hand over the phone.

"Have some breakfast," he said.

While we ate, I told him again how sorry I was that I shot Egon, and that I was afraid of what could happen now to the film, to him, and to myself. Jonathan listened, then was silent for a time. Finally he said what I hoped he'd say.

"We'll have to get our story straight, and maybe I should get rid of the gun."

We immediately agreed on two things. Nobody would believe that I shot Egon in self-defense because by throwing away the clothes I wore and not calling the police I looked guilty. We also decided to get rid of the gun and say and do nothing, but if we were forced to, we'd tell the police the truth about how we each spent yesterday, only leaving out my short visit to Egon's office.

After breakfast, alone by the pool, I reminded myself life could have been a lot worse. I could have been handcuffed in the back seat of a police car or in a New York city jail, instead of sunbathing nude beside a sparkling blue swimming pool in Montauk at the seaside home of my handsome lover. I'd told him the truth and he didn't call the police, and he promised he would help me. I was no longer in trouble all alone. I should've felt better, but being forced to trust him made me realize how little I knew him.

All morning he was distant. I tried to not let that worry me. He sat at his computer for a while, went jogging, drove over to Montauk to do some shopping, then sat in the kitchen and wrote in his journal. I let him have his space. I had to believe I could trust him to keep our secret, but I was very aware that our secret was a leash around my neck Jonathan could jerk at any time.

We had a quiet lunch together without much conversation. Afterward, I cooled off in the pool, then lay down and let the sun have me. He came out, disrobed, laid on a chaise next to me, and, amazingly, fell asleep.

There was no such relief for me. I felt awful that I'd caused such pain to Egon's sweet children and his wife. And what about the one hundred crew members I'd put out of work? I believed passionately in *"Lonely Sky"* and yet thanks to me our film might never get made. I thought about my situation from every conceivable angle and I could see only one way to try to redeem myself and fix the damage I'd caused to so many people. It was extremely risky, but I had to try.

I picked up my phone and made the call.

"Hey," Lenny said.

"My God! Such horrible news!"

"It's a nightmare," he muttered.

"Any change in his condition?"

"They say he's in a deep coma. The bullet's too close to his spinal cord. They may not be able to remove it."

"So you think it's all over?"

"It's too soon to tell. He may pull through."

"I mean the show."

"Oh. Yeah, of course. Allwether's gonna pull the plug."

"Did he say that?"

"Trust me, I know how studios react to —"

"We can't let that happen, Lenny."

"No worries. All of us above the line will get paid."

"The crew will lose their jobs."

"Production in the city's busy right now. They'll find jobs."

"We can't let that happen."

"Adrienne, are you listening to me? It's out of our hands."

"Not yet. But if we don't do something, an important film might never get made."

"Well," he said, exasperated, "what do you want us to do?"

"Egon may live, or not. That's up to God. One thing he won't do is direct our film."

"There isn't gonna be a film, Adrienne. I know how much you care, and I know this is hard to accept, but the reality is —"

"I can't accept it. And shame on you. You're giving up 'way too easy."

"Oh bullshit," he snarled.

"It's the same thing you two did to me on 'Motherhood'. I begged you to rescue our movie from those studio hacks and you abandoned me. And you did it again two weeks ago when you forced me to help Egon destroy my script."

"You're taking this too personally, Adrienne."

"You know me. When I'm committed, it's one hundred percent."

"Yeah, okay, so what are you saying?"

"We have to fight for this movie, Lenny."

"How?"

"I'll take over and direct it."

"What?!" Lenny said, and started laughing.

On the chaise next to me, Jonathan sat up as if he'd just heard something crash nearby.

"If you and Juno will partner with me, I'll take over and direct 'Lonely Sky'," I said, hoping he heard me through his laughter. "Is that such a strange idea?"

"Strange? Fuckin'ay —"

"You know I can do it."

Jonathan came over and sat at the foot of my chaise, trying to catch my attention, but I ignored him.

"If I were a man," I told Lenny, "you wouldn't be laughing at me."

"Don't start that shit with me, Adrienne."

"Tuesday we'll have a crew ready to work and no director."

"Adrienne, this is not a girl's film."

"Now who's starting some shit?!"

Lenny scoffed, "No director in his right mind would take the job under these conditions."

"Maybe I'm not in my right mind. But I know how to make this film the right way. You liked the script I wrote. And you know I'm a good director."

"Yeah, and now you want to be the hero."

"It's an important film. It could be a great film. It deserves to be made. And I know how to do it."

"They're gonna close the show."

"You'd let the production shut down –"

"Blame whoever shot Egon, not me."

"– rather than fight to keep it going?"

"No," he said. "But you, as an option..."

Of course he never thought of me, only the buyout check he'd get from the insurance settlement. Money for nothing.

"I'm here and I'm ready. And you know I'm super-functional under pressure."

"Hold on, hold on, I've got another call... It's Whit Allwether."

"Tell him you talked to me about taking over."

"Don't tell me what to do."

"At least buy us some time."

He hung up, muttering, "Fuckin' women..."

I put my phone on the poolside table. No turning back now. I lay back and sighed. No director in his right mind, he said. Well, I hadn't been in my right mind for the past 24 hours. But at least I was taking action and I no longer felt so powerless.

Jonathan was staring at me in disbelief.

"Are you crazy? Yesterday you shot the director. Today you're after his job?"

"Yesterday I fucked everything up. Today I'm trying to fix it."

"People will think you shot Egon to take his job."

"What people?"

"The police, for one."

"You're still going to call them?"

He shook his head.

"No, now that I know what happened. Besides, I can't tell anybody. You used my gun."

"I can't make Egon better, and I can't heal the pain I've caused Rita and the kids. But I can try to straighten out the mess I made for everybody else. This way, maybe we can all keep working. And it doesn't help, you being so cynical."

"You could get us both arrested."

"I think it's worth the risk."

"It won't work. The studio financed the film as Egon's passion project."

"Well, maybe you're right." I got up and strolled to the pool and stretched, loving his eyes on me. "But maybe you're not."

I stepped to the concrete lip of the pool, saw myself in the water, and liked what I saw. I turned around, blew him a kiss, and dove into my reflection.

A while later, Juno called. "All right, Adrienne," she sighed, like she was already weary of me. "What're you trying to do?"

"If the studio pulls the plug," I said, "the whole crew gets put out of work."

"Don't you think we care about that too?" she said. "Our crews are like family to us, you know that."

"A film that deserves to be made, won't."

"You and your emotional blackmail. That was the problem the last time we worked together."

"Don't even go there, Juno. Let's talk about now. Do you want to make a movie or collect an insurance check?"

"How dare you even ask that!"

"This can still turn out all right, as long as you accept me as the director and you straighten out your caveman of a husband."

"Huh," Juno said. It was a laugh, but not a funny one.

"Where are you?"

"We're in the city," Juno said. "We came in from the beach when we heard about Egon."

"Let's meet tonight and put our heads together. Seven o'clock. Text me the name of a restaurant."

I hung up before Juno could refuse. I waited, but she didn't call back. So they were either talking about it, or ignoring me.

Her text came when we were drinking coffee out on the cliff with the surf breaking below. Jonathan offered to drive me to New York.

"The train will be faster."

"Traffic going into the city will be light. The holiday isn't over until tomorrow. If you're leaving, I may as well go too."

I wanted to be alone to think about how to handle the meeting with the Victors. But maybe now it was better to keep him close.

On the Long Island Expressway he kept trying to talk to me about *Lonely Sky.* I deflected him as gently as I could.

"Jonathan, please. I need to think."

He sat back, brooding and driving faster. Just past the Dix Hills exit, I got a conference call from Lenny and Juno.

"We just got off the phone with Whit Allwether," Juno announced. "The studio has definitely decided to pull the plug and start an insurance claim. But they can't officially take action until Tuesday, so if we're going to change their mind, we have to do it tomorrow."

We, she said. Maybe that was progress.

"I'm on my way in."

"Y'know," Lenny said, "we're already rolling. We can't start all over again." I knew what he meant: casting, schedule, budget and key crew members, director of photography, production designer, location deals, and a hundred more moving parts in the organism that is a film crew.

"I'll work with what we've got, except for one thing: we have to shoot the script I wrote."

"We can't prep all over again," Lenny said.

"There won't be that much. I'll explain when I see you. So, my script or not?"

Juno said, "We admire your writing. Why do you think we hired you?"

Yeah. They admired my script so much they forced me to help Egon trash it.

"Also, Jonathan Lehane. We have to make a special effort to heal that situation and bring him back. Nobody else plays Sawyer, right?"

"Of course, of course," Juno said. "We never agreed with his firing anyway."

Jonathan reached out and gripped my knee. I took his hand and slid it higher up my thigh.

He dropped me off in the city at 23rd and 7th a couple blocks from the restaurant.

"Can we get together later?" he said.

"I'll see how this meeting goes."

"Are you okay?"

"Sure. Why not?" The question irritated me because it forced me to lie. "I'll call you later."

Walking to the restaurant, a comfortable northern Italian place called Le Zie, I phoned Tawana Barber, my friend, my roommate in the early days in New York, and the 1st Assistant Director who worked with me on *"Motherhood"* and *"Men R Dawgs"*. She was on a family visit to Louisiana, had heard the news about Egon Swift, and was surprised when I told her I was working with Lenny and Juno.

"How'd y'all get yourself involved with them again?"

"I've never been afraid to suffer for my art." We didn't quite laugh. "I emailed you the script. I need you to read it and tell me what you think. I also sent you a cast list and a crew list."

"Just a minute, let me look... Yeah, okay, I got all that."

"The investment bank sets are still standing downtown. We can shoot there for a couple days until we get our feet under us."

"You go girl! Go on up and put your tongue in their ear!" Tawana liked to tease me about that, because one night after a party, fully aware that she had a husband and two daughters, I put my tongue in Tawana's ear and was firmly turned down.

"I need your help, T. I want to do this movie more than anything I've ever done. When you read it, you'll see why."

Despite the holiday weekend, Le Zie was busy with people eating Sunday dinner. Lenny and Juno were waiting at a table in the back room. They were sunburned red in their weekend clothes, Juno in a baggy linen shift and Lenny in tennis whites. Juno looked calm, she was even grinning slightly, but Lenny looked disgruntled, and I sensed trouble, or, looked at another way, opportunity.

"Well," Juno said, "the situation has taken an interesting twist."

"Allwether's not going to pull the plug?"

"He's agreed to listen," Juno said.

"What changed his mind?"

"Nothing, really," Lenny said abruptly. "It's just that they have to wait until after the holiday to put in a claim, so —"

"I talked to Whit about you," Juno said, overriding her husband. Lenny shot her an irritable look.

It was unusual for Lenny and Juno to let anyone see that they disagreed with each other. When I worked in their home office years ago, they always took their fights out on the balcony. Maybe Egon getting shot had shaken up things between them. Juno said Whit Allwether had tried to fly to New York but heavy fog on Martha's Vineyard had grounded all aircraft, so he'd been calling for updates.

"He still wants to file an insurance claim," Juno said. "But we told him we would see you tonight and call him afterward."

"So this is it," I said. "At least you got me through the door."

"Don't get your hopes up," Lenny said. "Without the Egon brand to put the asses in the seats they're gonna shut us down."

Lenny's pessimism clearly annoyed Juno. She ordered a double Johnny Walker Black, she who rarely drank anything but white wine. Lenny was sipping Sambuca in a snifter. I just shook my head at the waiter.

"I think Emerge is a lost cause at this point," Lenny said to Juno. "Let's be smart and look for backers all over again. We've got Adrienne and an excellent script as a package. There's an upside to Egon getting shot. It's made the project high-profile. So if we act fast –"

"That's a God damned cold-blooded thing to say," Juno hissed.

"No it isn't," Lenny shot back, "it's just the business, something you've never understood."

"Well maybe if I'd done business with as many drug dealers as you –"

While they bickered, I tuned them out to do a fast reality check. If I were those two, I'd negotiate with Emerge International to get the rights to the script back, and fast. They'd be able to shop a director and the script while

Egon's shooting was still news. About that upside, Lenny, who could always be counted on to list the ugly realities, had been right.

But I was a realist too. If my script got any buzz going in Hollywood, Lenny and Juno would dump me and try to hook up with a new director, male, with the power to get a bigger budget and stars. If only I had the money to buy the rights. What a perfect career redirection that could be, after "*Men R Dawgs*"! But what studio would greenlight a director like me, whose last film flopped 10 years ago, to make a painful, politically controversial movie in a world where 3D, superhero thrillers, IMAX and comic book movies and sequels were Hollywood's best ideas for saving its desperate ass?

"I think Emerge is the best chance we've got," I said, cutting into their squabbling. "If our momentum stops now, the show's over. We've got to make this work with them somehow."

My enthusiasm irritated Lenny.

"You really want to do this?"

"With my script? And with Jonathan?"

"Yes, of course," Juno said.

"I'll salvage this production and I'll make an unforgettable movie."

"If you say so," Lenny shrugged, tired of arguing with Juno, and probably hoping that I'd fall on my face.

"Okay. So tell Allwether I'm committed. Email him a copy of my script and get him to read it tonight. Get me a meeting with him tomorrow on Martha's Vineyard. I'll fly up on the early plane in the morning."

"Call the airline," Lenny told Juno. "Reserve three seats."

I said, "I'm going alone."

"No fucking way!" Lenny said.

"Not negotiable."

"Why not us too?" Juno demanded. "What's the problem? Let's get it out in the open."

"It's my job interview."

"Oh, come on –"

"You can always take your buyout and forget the whole thing. Maybe you'd rather do that."

"Here we go again," Juno said. "Emotional blackmail."

I hoped I hadn't pushed too far. But I couldn't risk that Lenny might undermine me and angle for the script rights and a buyout. He'd sabotage any chance of continuing with me if he could.

"It'll be easier to sell myself without you two involved. I've got to talk with Allwether one-on-one without any distractions."

"Distractions?" Juno said. "We're not a distraction. We're the producers."

"Our best chance is for me to show Allwether my passion for the project."

"What about our passion?" Lenny said.

I almost laughed in his face.

"This afternoon you were ready to let him close the show," I said. "You had your chance. Now let me have mine."

Whit Allwether's house in Chilmark, a rural town of ponds and meadows and rolling hills on Martha's Vineyard, was at the end of a one lane dirt trail through oak and pine forest. The taxi from the airport swayed and crawled over tree roots and rocks and under overhanging tree limbs until it came to the back yard of a two-story house overlooking a sunny, secluded cove. A cheerful Latina maid in a gray uniform and white apron came out the kitchen door, greeted me, and escorted me around to the front.

I'd researched Allwether on the flight up, but I didn't learn more than you'd find in an official company bio. He grew up in Colorado, graduated with an MBA from Harvard, and had held production executive positions at two of the major Hollywood studios, including overseeing two Oscar contenders for Best Picture. Now he was a partner in a private equity company and president of Emerge International, the boutique studio that Egon Swift had made rich with his films.

He was sitting reading on his iPhone at a table for six on a wooden deck shaded by a wide awning, a blonde, bearded man in his 50s, lean and tanned as a mountain climber. He was wearing khaki cargo shorts and Timberland work boots, and a blue chambray shirt with the Emerge International logo on the pocket. I was dressed for business in a black pants suit and had my hair tucked under one of the *"Lonely Sky"* baseball caps Lenny had handed out to the crew.

Allwether greeted me with a tight-lipped smile, a quizzical look, and a strong handshake, and asked the maid to serve coffee. I took the seat across from him.

"Thank you for seeing me on such short notice."

"You've come a long way to have this talk in person," he said, in a voice that seemed to warn me I might not like the conversation.

"So what does that tell you?"

"It tells me you really want to make the film."

"I believe creative partnerships should start face to face."

"Ideally, yes. But didn't Lenny and Juno tell you? I'm canceling production and cutting our losses."

"They told me. With Egon in a coma, pulling the plug certainly makes financial sense. But they also said you were willing to listen."

"I'm willing to listen." Just don't expect much, he seemed to say.

"I assume you've read my adaptation of the play. The draft before Egon's."

"I did. It's very smart, subtle writing. It's also plotless, with too many POV characters, and it's too left wing. And why's the Arab torture story still in there? I told Lenny and Juno I hated that."

"Oh, come on. That's hardly violent at all, compared to Egon Swift's misogynistic porn."

He did the smallest of double takes.

"I believe, Whit, that these days real escapism means telling the truth, and showing the drama in the lives of ordinary people."

"What truth? That the country's fucked up? That the American people are angry and scared, and captive to crazy fantasies? You want them to pay money to be told that?"

"For their money they'll get the truth, artfully presented." I cringed inwardly, but that was the best I could come up with.

"The truth? Yeah, okay," he said gazing out over waters of the cove. "Of course, that's a very different film from what we usually do."

I couldn't help myself. "I'm well aware of that."

"You think people want to be reminded of 9/11? Isn't the country sort of past it?"

"Yes. Now it's history. And 'Lonely Sky' is the most original treatment of that tragedy I've ever seen. That's why I'm so passionate about it. And it resonates very strongly with the current—"

Allwether's cell phone rang and he took a Face Time call.

"She's here, we've just started."

He propped the phone up on the table where we both could see it and sat back.

"Jude Harper is my v.p. for production. Jude, say hello to Adrienne Monet."

"Adrienne, it's a pleasure," said a chipper, handsome young guy on the screen. "I know and respect your work." Oh shit. When they start like that...

"Hello, Jude. I'm here to persuade Mister Allwether to let us keep making what will be a very successful film for the studio."

"And we talked about that a lot Adrienne, we really did. But 'Lonely Sky' was a risky project from the start. The pre-sell was limited to audiences who'd seen the play in a small theater in New York, and we had no stars. At least after Egon's reworking of the eccentric play structure the material was less dark and painful. It came to us as a passion project from our most successful director, so we greenlighted it with a strict limit on cost."

"Without stars, and even with a low budget," said Allwether, "we'd need the kind of opening weekend gross we'd get off Egon's name."

"Before people tell their friends what a downer the story is," Jude added. "All due respect."

Respect? Was that a joke? The only thing these studio exec bots respected was profit.

"Even though it explores the wounds of 9/11," I said, "our film will be a feel-good picture. You'll walk out feeling more human, more compassionate, more connected to your fellow human beings. Is that what you call a 'downer'?"

"Well, do we want to do anything quite so artsy?" Allwether said.

"Ultimately, what do we want from any movie?" I said. "To experience our common humanity. Also, financing a drama like this will be a signal to the creative community that Emerge International isn't only about violent movies for boys."

"Boys buy a lot of movie tickets," Allwether said with a chill.

"So do we girls."

"Statistically untrue. And then we have that other issue."

On cue, Jude said, "Adrienne, as a feature film director, you haven't worked in, what's it been, like, ten years? These days you're an unknown quantity. It just makes sense for us to cut our losses rather than to invest in you. But we did promise Lenny and Juno we'd give you a hearing."

"And there's a lot more I want to say –"

"I'm sure there is, Adrienne," Allwether said, with a gentleness I found condescending, "and we do appreciate you coming all this way. I'm sorry we couldn't work it out. But this is how we see it." These bastards were bored and dismissing me before my coffee was cool enough to drink. "But by all means try us again with another project sometime, because you're a talented woman. Your TV show certainly proves that."

Allwether stopped talking, looked past me, and frowned. I turned to see a silver Escalade pull into the gravel car park at the end of the house. From the back seat hopped a slim, longhaired Asian woman in white tennis linens, who glided across the lawn grinning cheerfully, and reached out her hand.

"Adrienne Monet," Allwether said. "Meet Nikki Xiu." I recognized her name. Who wouldn't? She was more than a successful producer of Hong Kong action films and Emerge's principal financier out of Chinese sovereign wealth funds. She was known worldwide as the most powerful female film executive in Asia.

"Very pleased to meet *you*," she said, as if she'd been looking forward to this meeting. Her handshake was weightless. "I hope I'm not interrupting."

"We were just getting started," I said.

"Well, by all means, join us," Allwether said, a little too heartily. Nikki sat at the table and said hello to Jude on the phone.

Allwether told her I flew up from New York that morning to pitch myself to take over for Egon. She never stopped looking at me, curiously, but kindly.

She said, "Egon Swift has made us a lot of money. We agreed to finance '*Lonely Sky*' to keep him happy."

"So you don't represent fresh hope we can keep shooting?"

"I represent an open mind. My government has entrusted me with some of the wealth of the People's Republic to bankroll films however I see fit. I don't always know what stories I'm going to like, but I know talent when I see it."

That was an opening, and I dove for it, as if my conversation with All-wether had never happened.

"Well, let's start by getting you a copy of the script I originally wrote."

"I've read your script. I read every draft of every script for every film we make. I was taken by your deep empathy and insight into the characters."

"Nikki," Allwether said, "had I known you were coming I could have saved you the trip. I just told Miss Monet –" She held up a finger and he fell silent.

"I saw on our calendar you had a meeting scheduled, Whit, so I flew down from Kennebunkport. I am impressed that Adrienne came here to make her case in person," she turned to me, "under what must be difficult emotional circumstances."

"I worked very closely with Egon," I said. "I got to know and to like him. My film will be quite different from what he had in mind, but I consider finishing what Egon started my duty to our friendship and to Emerge International."

A beatific grin. "A beautiful gesture, to be sure," she said.

"Nikki," said Jude from Allwether's phone in a weary, irritable voice, "we've already explained our decision to her." She picked up the phone, ended the call, and shoved it at Allwether across the table.

"Adrienne," Nikki said. "Commitment as strong and sincere as yours deserves a hearing."

"That's why I took this meeting," Allwether said a bit defensively. "But we can't go forward without the insurance of a brand name actor or director."

"I know I'm not a big draw like Egon Swift," I said. "But my first three films made money. Not the zillions that Egon's made, but I'll compare my reviews to his any day. 'Lonely Sky' is a serious drama on an event that changed America forever. But it's also three intimate family stories that people all over the world will recognize. I think you'll be able to count on foreign revenues even though it's not a boy movie."

"You keep talking about 'boy movies,'" Allwether said. "But your most recent film was over ten years ago, and it flopped."

"The new studio owners were getting rid of any projects approved by the previous executives. And their marketing was all wrong, which was written about extensively at the time."

Nikki said, "But it was with the same producers. I'm sure you understand why that concerns us."

"Lenny and Juno and I are a very functional production team."

"We hear there's a lot of friction in that relationship," Allwether said.

"You're referring to the shooting of what became 'Gimme Some Sperm'. I haven't had any fights with them lately. But you know, we've all worked on movie shoots where everything was cool, everybody worked in perfect harmony. Invariably, the final product was dull. The best work happens when people fight for their ideas. Energy like that sometimes has a way of permeating the film."

"And it keeps things on the set from getting boring," Nikki said, and all three of us laughed, at least two of us sincerely. "What have you done lately?"

"I've done a lot of writing and script doctoring, and I created a reality TV show called 'Men R Dawgs' –"

She sat back grinning.

"My most favorite new show! Such a simple idea, so well done! How many episodes did you direct?"

"All of them. Twenty-four 30-minute episodes."

"I smell money," she sang.

"A steady paycheck is always nice. But my medium, my real passion, is the two-hour feature film."

"You're a very versatile talent. I'm impressed that you did such risqué TV, then turned around and wrote a film script so nuanced for 'Lonely Sky'."

Nikki turned to Allwether and startled me by speaking in rapid Chinese. Allwether replied in Chinese, dismissively, and turned to me.

"Adrienne, I'm sorry, but we're going to pull the plug. Everything you've said may be true, but it's too big a financial risk, even at low cost."

Nikki was closely watching my conversation with Allwether.

"I've directed four films and I've never gone over budget. In fact, on my last film there was enough money left at the end of principal to pay for the reshoots."

"But that was how long ago?"

"A month ago I finished 24 episodes of reality TV. Directing actors without a script. I work fast and I work cheap."

"Our actors were cast by Egon," he said, as if that was a major problem.

"I'll work with what we've got."

That was disingenuous and we all knew it. Once production was rolling and the money was burning, I'd have more leverage to get what I wanted.

"Crew, budget, schedule. I'll replace 35-millimeter film with my ultra-hi-res video cameras and operators. That'll save time and money. My editors will cost you less, too. I'll throw in the editing equipment rent-free because it's already up and working in my offices."

Nikki said something in Chinese, and Allwether took a deep breath and issued a torrent of words, glancing at me once or twice. Finally, out of patience, I cut in.

"Listen, I'll put up my revenues from 'Men R Dawgs' as collateral against budget overruns. With the savings from Camera and Editing you'll risk less than the low budget you gave Egon, any overruns will be paid for by me, and you'll get a better, more prestigious film. This'll also expand Emerge's brand image to include quality, literate drama."

During the Chinese palaver that followed Nikki stared at me. What she thought she was seeing, I couldn't even imagine. I kept a smile on my face and didn't show how I felt about them speaking Chinese in front of me. Instead, I pushed my luck.

"And one more thing Whit," I cut in. "For the guarantee I'm giving you, I need to be an executive producer on the same line as you and Ms. Xiu."

"Why do you need that?" Allwether said, already irritated by the intervention of Nikki Xiu and my refusal to take no for an answer. Nikki, in the corner of my eye, was smiling. "You're not asking for points, are you?"

"I'll need the leverage the title will give me with Lenny and Juno. I want a vote on any decisions that could impact my collateral. That's only fair."

They talked some more in Chinese. Nikki tried persuasion, Allwether grew resistant. I didn't understand a word, but it was clear Allwether wasn't budging, which only made her laugh and try harder.

Then she leaned forward and spoke quietly, intensely to him. This made him glance at me, looking a bit startled. Laughing nervously, he asked her a couple questions. Nikki nodded both times, after which Allwether shook his head and shrugged.

"Okay, okay."

He turned to me, and more respectfully than before, he nodded.

"We'll fund you to shoot 'Lonely Sky' if you put up your reality TV revenues as our security against overages. You can have your executive producer title. But you've got to shoot in the forty-five-day schedule we gave Egon."

"How many prep days?"

"The meter's running," Allwether said, leaning back, the deal done.

"None?"

"We'll give you tomorrow to prep. That's all we can afford."

"Shooting must resume on Wednesday," Nikki said.

"Then it will." It was impossible, but somehow, I would do it. It was going to be that kind of show. "It is what it is."

It is what it is: time pressure, money pressure, personnel pressure, weather pressure, dozens of decisions, and little time for calm, careful thinking. But I'd done that kind of filmmaking before, so I knew what I was facing. And if I had to pay for overruns, then the revenue from the TV show, my sole income, would have to serve a higher purpose, some trash to burn to get my real career cooking again.

Nikki sat back with a smile as Allwether called Lenny and Juno.

"Okay folks, you're still in business. Adrienne will direct 'Lonely Sky'. She's got one prep day tomorrow to turn it around and forty-five shooting days starting Wednesday... Yeah, I know, but it can't be helped. We've also agreed to make her an executive producer." He grinned at Nikki and winked at me. "Well, *get* comfortable with that."

I remained calm and composed even though I was dancing inside. There would be plenty of time to gloat after I returned to New York as the savior of our film and as one of Lenny and Juno's three bosses.

Allwether handed me the phone. Lenny was muttering.

"I knew we shouldn't have let her go alone."

"Hello, Lenny."

His voice brightened. "Wow, you pulled it off! I can't wait to hear the whole story."

"Would you get us a reservation for dinner? Loop Marshall in, too. We've got lots to talk about."

"Got yourself a promotion, too, I see."

I saved your production, asshole. The least you could do is thank me. "I'll call you when I land. Bye!"

I gave Marshall's name and phone number to Allwether so they could revise my contract. After handshakes with Allwether, Nikki and I left the table together and strolled off across the lawn.

"So, what else can Emerge International do for its newest director?" Nikki Xiu said cheerfully.

"How about lunch? I mean, I'll pay of course—"

"I'd love to, but another day. I have family waiting for me in Maine."

"How about a ride to the airport? I've got to get back to New York and get to work."

"Yes. You've got a lot to do. And very little time."

"Like every other film I've made."

"When you were hired to adapt the play, I watched your films," she said. "I found quite an original voice. You're a talented writer and director. Also," she glanced back with a smirk casually dismissive of Allwether, "very resourceful." She sighed. "It's really sad, what happened to Egon. New York is a great city, the capitol of the world, but it can also be dangerous if you get involved with the wrong kind of people."

"Much like anywhere else."

"Much like our industry. And by the way?" She glanced back at the house. "You should've asked for points."

In the Escalade she handed me a card. On the back she'd written her name and phone number in a small but vivid longhand.

Before my plane took off, I called Tawana. Her post "*Men R Dawgs*" vacation with her family was over and she was at the gate at Louis Armstrong International Airport in New Orleans waiting to board a plane back to New York.

"Let's make a movie," I said.

"It's a go?"

"It's a go."

"O-kay!"

"You read the script?"

"Yeah. It's gonna be tough to schedule three different stories."

"I'd love to shoot them one at a time, but we can't afford it. I haven't even met the location manager yet, but he'll have to find hub locations where we can park for days at a time and shoot scenes from all three stories."

"We've got exteriors in Brooklyn, the Upper East Side, Wall Street, and the East Village. Where are the sets?"

"The Piers."

"It's gonna be a real workout for the director and A.D.'s. You really want to location-hub like that?"

"I don't see how we can avoid it. We're working with very little money. Plus, this is going to take more than the usual fiendish attention to detail because I want different looks for each story. Like, for the Muslim father story, furtive, intrusive, like surveillance footage. The survivalist East Village thing I want to do rough, jump cuts, hand-held, almost documentary. Then for 'Constant Companion,' smooth, elegant, like Sawyer's world, with opticals that allow the ghost of his wife to appear and disappear."

She laughed. "Wow. Don't make it easy on yourself or nothin'."

"If this was easy, I wouldn't have bored you with it. Starting Wednesday, we've got 45 days."

Those days would be long and maddeningly complex, even if they went like clockwork. And they never do.

"So, tell me everything you need." That's Tawana. The heart of a lioness.

"Get the office coordinator, whatever her name is, to email my script to the cast and crew, like now. Tomorrow, six A.M. production meeting at the Pier. All department heads and their seconds. Days 1 and 2 we'll be on the Wall Street set. The gear has been frozen there since Friday. Tomorrow after the meeting we'll scout locations for Day 3 and 4. After that I want to do a read through with the whole cast in one room. I need to hear the script spoken from beginning to end. So we'll do that at four o'clock with everybody on one of the stages. Get the production office to pull all that together. Call

Gabriella and tell her to do camera tests and get the Redcam kit and her crew ready for tomorrow, 6 p.m. call. I want a two-camera setup on Stage A ready at six o'clock to shoot an improv with Jonathan. I'll announce which set at the meeting tomorrow."

"Got it," said Tawana.

I found Lenny and Juno waiting for me with Marshall in a restaurant on the Upper East Side named Charlie's, a wooden furniture and plastic tablecloth neighborhood trattoria.

While Lenny and Juno got us a table, Marshall, looking troubled, waved me over to the bar.

"Why'd you put up your TV money?"

"I had to." I told the bartender how to make a St. Germain Royale.

"A-Girl, you should call me before you make deals like that."

"There was no time. Besides, what would you have said?"

"Don't give away so much."

"Nothing less would've worked."

"I coulda negotiated something better for you."

"I had to close the deal before I left the Vineyard."

The bartender set the drink in front of me, and I drained it in two swallows. I could hardly wait to sit down, not for the meal, because I was running on excitement, but to reset my relationship with the Victors.

"Well, I hope they don't have to take any of that TV money. That's your life raft."

"That'll only happen if I'm not a good director."

When we joined Lenny and Juno at the table, the waiter was uncorking an expensive Barolo, their idea to celebrate my rescue of the show. I sipped enough to appraise the flavor and bouquet.

I told them the basics of my dealings with Allwether. I didn't mention Nikki Xiu because I didn't want them to know I had that relationship. They would hear about it eventually. I had saved *"Lonely Sky"* from cancellation and put my own money at risk, and it was time to have a serious talk.

"The last time we worked together, I was betrayed and abandoned by you two," I said. "Now I want to hear you say, in front of Marshall, you'll give me your one hundred per cent support."

Lenny shot Marshall a hurt look. He got back an expectant stare that said, Well?

"Let's not forget you got this far with our help," Lenny said.

I refused to be distracted.

"One hundred percent."

"But that's our job," Juno said. "We would support and protect you anyway."

"We all know that hasn't been my experience."

"Oh, so that's what you're here for?" Lenny said. "Payback for –"

"I'm here," I overrode Lenny, "because I can direct a movie and you can't. And Executive Producer isn't a gift I got out of the goodness of Whit Allwether's heart. I'm risking my own money, way beyond any investment you have. That's why I need to hear it, not some petty desire for payback. Okay? One hundred percent?"

"Of course," Juno said.

I didn't literally have Lenny by the balls, but you wouldn't know that from the pain on his face.

"Yeah, of course."

"Now we know where we all stand. Now, some details. My A.D. Tawana Barber replaces Clark. Send him back to L.A."

"The crew will love you for that," Juno said.

"Send Egon's camera crew and editor back and get all that equipment off rental. I'm using my reality TV camera crew, my hi-res digital cameras, and my editing operation. We won't need a lab, or to digitize film, that'll save money."

"I'll hide the money somewhere else in the budget," Lenny said, "in case we need to move funds around."

"The spitball budget for your script was already lower than Egon's," Juno said.

"Did he cast an actress to play 'Chickie'?"

"No."

"Good. We won't need one. Okay, here's our one day prep schedule. Tawana is revising the shooting schedule and getting the office to set up a production meeting for 6 a.m. at the Pier. After the meeting we're scouting locations for Days 3 and 4. I'm doing a full cast read through at four o'clock. I'm shooting an improv scene with Jonathan onstage at six. Wednesday morning, six o'clock call, we're back to work, Day 1 at the Wall Street set."

Lenny looked at Juno, sat back and drained his glass, and reached for the bottle.

After such a day, I should have gone home to bed. But there was one more thing I had to be sure of. I got to Jonathan's penthouse around nine o'clock. He was barefoot, in boxer shorts and a tee shirt, and practically dancing around the room.

"I've been reading your script," he said, as he led me into the living room. "Man!" He held it up. "Brilliant! It's the best of the play, taken out into the world. I can't believe they let Egon reject this for that piece of shit, that —"

"Going forward..." No time, no patience, no looking back. "Four o'clock tomorrow, cast readthrough at the stages. After that, I want to shoot an improv with you."

"An improv?"

"Remember the grief tape Sawyer's therapist got him to record? He's supposed to keep replaying it, day after day, getting control over his feelings?"

"But he can never bring himself to replay it. And when he does, it's a crisis."

"Right. I want you to improvise Sawyer recording that tape. That scene is the heart of Sawyer's story."

"Ah... That's, yeah yeah, that's... an interesting idea."

"I think we'll do it on the Sawyer Townhouse set, in the library."

"Okay. I think that's where it would be."

"Can your understudy step in for you tomorrow night at the theatre? I'll also need you to waive your 12-hour turnaround so we can start Wednesday at six o'clock."

"No problem."

I kicked off my shoes.

He said, "The Sawyer and Josephine relationship is so much richer, now that you've put her onscreen. Who do you want to play the part?"

"I don't know. We won't start shooting those scenes for a while. We'll find the right actor."

I took off my suit jacket, then my bra, and dropped them on the couch.

Jonathan looked puzzled, but he was also smiling.

"Good, yeah, Josephine, okay, let's uh, talk about that. At some point."

"At some point. For now, just the improv. Go deep. Deep as you want."

While he watched me with that quizzical grin, I peeled off my slacks, maintaining eye contact with him, then my panties. I tossed them on the couch, and took a slow stroll around the room, dressed in nothing but a *Lonely Sky"* baseball cap, strutting for my audience of one.

"Oh, I'll be ready," he said. "You know I'll be ready."

"I love the cool smoky air of this apartment," I said, sweeping my hands up my belly and chest so my nipples popped. "I feel like rubbing it into my skin."

"Adrienne," he said, laughing helplessly, "have I ever told you –"

I raised a Nikki Xiu-like finger that silenced him. "First rule of filmmaking." I strolled to a comfortable armchair, slouched back, and draped my legs over the arms. "Show. Don't tell."

He nodded his head and knelt before me, rubbing his hands together.

"Wet your lips."

He did as he was told. I took off my baseball cap and put it backwards on his head. He slipped his warm hands under my ass and leaned into his task like a hungry man tucking into a fine meal.

TWO *The night of January 9, 2018*

Now I sit in that same armchair, staring at the dead men on the floor. Down the entry hall a heavy hand pounds on the front door and deep male voices holler, "NYPD! Open up!" The doorbell rings and rings. It is bad strategy to antagonize the police. But this is the last moment I'll have Jonathan and A.J. to myself, the man who loved me, and the man I hated at first but came, to my surprise, to love.

I get up and raise the living room lights to full brightness and kneel next to Jonathan. He sprawls face up, in jeans and a blue cashmere sweater. One leg is bent under the other, his arms have fallen to the side, and the gun is in his hand. Under his chin is a bloody, burnt wound. The bullet entered there and came out the top of his skull and painted the ceiling in blood and gore. His face is bloodless, gray as ash, his mouth half-open, his eyes dull as nickels. Beneath his head his blood has blackened the carpet. The rank smell of his body, sweet from too much whiskey and the smoky brassy smell of spattered blood and burnt flesh, makes me wretch. But nothing comes up because I already vomited after he slapped me. My swollen cheek still stings.

This didn't have to happen to us, Jonathan. What kind of man did you become? What kind of woman did you think I was? How did the love we had come to this? We knew what the future could have been. We could have been happy people. As your director I gave you everything I had, but as a woman, my need for you had its limits. Why couldn't you accept that?

"Police! Open up!" Bam bam bam!

I crawl across the floor to A.J. Upton, the notorious conservative writer, the man who was the greatest love and biggest mistake of my life. One expensive slip-on is twisted half off his bare foot. He hadn't stopped to put on socks before he jammed his feet into his shoes and rushed here to rescue me from his father's fury. Such gallantry! I want to cry, but it's more of a thought than a feeling.

"NYPD! Open up!" Bam bam bam!

A.J., my miracle, my fiancé, my fascinating partner, sexy, brilliant, rich, awkward, and so contemptuous of all the wrong things. I want to wrap myself around you, breathe life back into you, rewind life back to an hour ago when we had a beautiful future. Look at your poor face, bronzed from our idyllic Christmas in Palm Beach, a face so familiar to America from your appearances on the political talk shows, and so beautiful except for the bullet wound in the middle of your forehead.

"Police! Open up!" Bam! Bam! Bam! Bam! The telephone on the bar rings and rings. It barely intrudes on my thoughts.

How long was I here before A.J. intervened? From the fragments littering the floor of my memory like outtakes of film, I splice together a sequence of events. I tried to reason with Jonathan, but he was drunk and threatening and he slapped my face. A.J. arrived and got between us. A lifetime of bitterness between father and son rose to where there was no going back. The gun in Jonathan's trembling hand was pointing at me even as I tried to reason with them both. Then came a horror I will never forget. Two gunshots. Two lives extinguished in one awful moment. Fade to black.

The doorbell and telephone keep ringing. The fists pounding on the front door get louder. "NYPD, open the fucking door!" I'm making things worse for myself the longer I make them wait. But I'm not ready to give up the last privacy and peace I may ever have.

I pick up my cigarette from the ashtray on the bar, and go back out on the cold, windy terrace. I inhale a lungful of smoke and let it drift from my nose and lips into the wind. The door pounding, the angry voices, the telephone ringing fade deep into the background. I crush the butt under the toe of my cowboy boot of black alligator skin and, staring at my feet, an absurd image out of nowhere stops me cold. I picture a jet-black alligator on a jungle riverbank, snoozing under a palm tree in the heat. His rows of sharp teeth open in a wide grin, and his eyes open, glittering with hunger, as he slowly turns toward me.

Labor Day weekend was over and department heads from the *"Lonely Sky"* crew were back to work with me in the location scout van.

We were trying to get downtown to the investment bank sets and were stuck in traffic beside City Hall Park, surrounded by an orchestra of angry blaring horns from cars and trucks, trying to squeeze around a giant construction crane blocking one lane of Broadway.

I sat in the front passenger seat with a tablet on my lap scrolling through photos and video clips of possible locations for Days 3 and 4. They had to be near each other so we could park the trucks and trailers in one place for several days and not burn up time and gasoline moving from place to place through city traffic. We had already spent hours in the van on an itinerary mapped by our location manager, a wired, thirtyish guy named Hal with a stuffed shoulder bag and a perpetually hassled and nervous personality.

I was in combat mode and ready to blast through any obstacles that got in our way. But so far, on our one day of prep, work was going okay. The crew members in the seats behind me were on their phones talking to their assistants and vendors, using every precious minute to prepare to start shooting again tomorrow. Lenny and Juno were murmuring in each other's ears. Beside them Tawana was poring over her laptop. Anxious to keep the scout moving, Hal kept leaning forward over the front seat and suggesting alternate routes to the Teamster at the wheel, who listened calmly, nodded, and ignored him.

Earlier that morning around the production meeting table the key crew members breathed a collective sigh of relief that we were back to work. My script, thumbs up all around, seemed to energize everybody. Of course, a woman director with a mostly male crew could lose that respect quicker than a man, so I kept to the same rules I'd learned the hard way on every film I'd directed. Don't push too hard or be too arrogant, they'll think you're overcompensating or hiding insecurity. Don't try to be one of the guys, you're not, you're a woman, and they'll always remind you of that. Everybody would be testing me and Tawana. It was rare to find a Black female 1st Assistant Director running a film set, even in New York. Some male crew members would never trust or respect us but if they did their jobs I didn't care. The women on the crew would be more supportive, but not if I screwed up. No doubt the whole crew saw me as the producers' desperate solution, brought in to save the show. They were glad they still had their jobs, but I'd still have to prove my right to mine every day.

After lunch we climbed back into the van and I turned to my chief electrician and key grip.

"You guys will love my camera crew. They run between setups."

"Why's that?" Terry the electrician said. He wiggled his eyebrows. "Do you crack the whip?"

"No, they just know I expect it." I was looking back at them between Juno and Tawana's heads.

"I hope you don't expect me to run," Daly the key grip said, sitting back and crossing his arms. He looked like a Russian weightlifter with a gray goatee, and he was not going to be pussy whipped.

"Please don't," I said. "A big guy like you would only knock over the furniture." That got a laugh from everybody but Daly, who had to take a beat first. Tawana grinned at me, rolled her eyes, and bent back to her work.

The final stop on the scout was the investment bank set, standing silent since Friday on a vacant floor in a lower Broadway office high rise, the camera dolly and lights still locked down in place. We'd already spent two twelve-hour days here and everybody quickly understood the shots I described.

While we were waiting for the elevator to go down to the van and return to the Piers, Annie Levy called.

"They got him!" she said.

"Who got who?"

"Your guy Aldo! The police caught him trying to get inside your building last night. They're holding him for breaking and entering and violating the order of protection."

"He's better off behind bars."

That's because by now I wanted to kill him. If he hadn't terrorized me by trying to force his way into my building, I'd have never borrowed Jonathan's gun, and Egon would never have been shot.

"Aren't you relieved?"

"Sorry, I'm just incredibly busy now."

"The assistant D.A. needs you to testify Friday morning at his hearing."

"Friday morning? Are they out of their minds? I'm working."

"You have to be there."

"That's impossible!"

"If you don't testify, they might let him out on bail. Do you want that?"

Aldo! Even from a jail cell he was fucking up my life.

I met the rest of the cast that afternoon, reading their lines and playing off each other. It was exciting to be an audience for the characters who had taken over my imagination. The damage Egon's script had done to them went unmentioned by everyone, especially Jonathan. That afternoon they were re-born, taking human form in front of my eyes. With nobody cast yet to play Sawyer's ghost wife, I read the part myself.

Egon and his casting director had made excellent choices in the actors playing the Muslim family in "I'm A Stranger Here." Hussein Harari was Palestinian, in his late 50s, an archetypal family patriarch, short and thick-set, salt and pepper hair and beard, with a deep chesty voice. His wife Niesha was played by tall, elegant Abeela Noor, beautifully poised, hair the color of ice, playing a woman of strong spirit who rolled up her sleeves when her husband disappeared and kept the family business going. Their son, played by young Indian actor Sonny Banerjee, had just the perfect thin and intense, worried demeanor for a young man of high ethical and moral scruples trying to reconcile the torture of his father by the country he'd come to love. They performed so smoothly and with such chemistry and warmth you could believe they were a family.

But I had a problem with the twenty-somethings cast as East Village hipsters in "The Day Before Doomsday," who met each other for the first time today. Ruthie the wife was played by Brooke Kirby, a skinny, clever blonde gamine in cat's eyeglasses. In the role of Abel her husband, Egon had cast Lee Jeffries, sexy, handsome, but not especially talented without a large gun in his hand. He'd played supporting roles in all three of Egon's thrillers and I wondered if he'd been comfort casting so Egon would have a bro to hang out with in New York. He was impressive, six feet and buffed, with chiseled features, bronzed skin, well-coiffed curly brown hair and dreamy green eyes. But he was so poker-faced he'd make Clint Eastwood seem Italian. In the readthrough, to make up for his lack of skill and emotional nuance, he tried too hard to act out Abel's post-9/11 worries about all the disasters he saw coming, talking too fast, too loud. Sitting beside him, Brooke, who had far fewer lines, was relaxed, vivacious, nuanced – alive!

While we were having an impromptu party after the reading I strolled over to Brooke and Lee so I could check out their chemistry off book.

"Have you guys seen the tenement set we've built for Ruthie and Abel's story?"

"No, is it ready?" Brooke said, in a wow-so-cool voice.

"Sure. C'mon."

Lee cast a sleepy-eyed glance at the time on his phone then trudged after us.

I lit the overhead stage lights, and we were in a tenement flat, lower East Side bathtub-in-the-kitchen variety, a table and chairs in the middle, a loft bed off to stage left and the bathroom on stage right. While Brooke whirled in an excited orbit around Lee, he sat at the table, tapping his rolled-up script against his thigh and looking lazily around.

"It's pretty small," he said.

"Yeah, but honey," Brooke said, and Lee frowned at her as she danced around the space, "this is our love cave in the city. Don't you think it's kind of cozy?" Her vivacity clearly got under his skin.

"This is your life raft on an unpredictable sea," I said. His silent look at me said So lame. I understood, of course. With his buddy Egon off the picture, he was already unhappy, and we hadn't even started filming.

The more we chatted the more I was certain this casting would not work. Before I could tell them, Lee shook his head.

"Adrienne, I don't know," Lee drawled. "This new script. I mean, this is really a curve ball, y'know?"

"Why's that Lee?"

"Well, the original script was, like, a comedy, and I's like, 'Okay I can play this,' but now this thing is like, heavy, y'know?"

He preferred Egon's script to mine. I nearly laughed. "Have you seen the play?"

"Nah, I had to hurry up and catch a red-eye from L.A. I haven't even un-packed yet, and now I've got, like, all these lines to learn in a hurry."

He was already getting on my nerves. To work with me, Lee needed to get over the disappointment of not working with Egon, get over himself, and lively up. I had to work fast, with actors who could do the same. Abel on the page was anxious, needy, and dominating, and Lee seemed to think overplay-ing him was acting. We could get another actor, but unless he withdrew vol-untarily, we'd have to pay Lee anyway, which we couldn't afford. Recasting would eat up time looking at video or sitting through auditions and would throw Tawana a new scheduling problem on a show already hard to organize. I wasn't confident I could direct my way out of the problem, either. Then I thought of the one really radical thing I could try.

"Come with me, you guys."

I told the production coordinator no calls and no interruptions and closed my office door. We all sat down, and I asked Brooke and Lee to read their first scene, which introduces Abel's paranoia and Ruthie's response. They looked at me, then at each other, nervously.

"What are we, back to auditioning?" Lee said.

"No. I want you to switch roles. Forget about male and female. Just read each other's lines."

Lee did a double take so violent it almost rearranged his hairdo. Then he sighed and shook his head, deciding to humor silly little me.

I switched my iPhone to record on Voice Memo.

"Okay, action."

Brooke slipped right into the paranoid, aggressive speeches. Lee's sullen, tentative reading, which he basically shrugged off, had potential as a husband exasperated by his wife who needs to get a grip on his impatience.

"Hey," Brooke said when we finished. "How was that?"

"Lee?"

He looked worried. "You like that?"

"Let's do another scene. Scene 32. Just read the lines."

Lee sighed and went along. Two more scenes later, I felt the switch had a chance of working. I was also sure Lee would be unhappy, which could work at times for the character of Abel if he could keep it under control.

"So?" he said.

"At the table reading," I told them, "I heard two actors reading two characters. But just now, I heard a duet."

"A duet? I don't know what that means," he said.

"A marriage under stress. The relationship is essentially the same, isn't it? One character is aggressively paranoid and controlling, the other is trying not to get caught up in that."

"But these lines were written for a woman." Lee looked incredulous. "Why are we doing this?" At least he said "we" instead of challenging me directly.

"Your energy level, strong and quiet, works better for the character who has to deal with the other character's mania. The audience will be startled by Ruthie's paranoia, but their hearts will be with Abel, the strong patient husband trying to cope with her. He's kind of a quiet hero."

He nodded and swallowed. "So I've got a new part to learn."

"I'll get you the rewritten pages ASAP, but for now, just learn the lines as they are. You've got time, you don't work for a couple of days."

"I'm not good with time pressure."

"Lee honey," Brooke said eagerly, "sometimes we do our best work when we don't over-think it."

Lee recoiled like she'd just elbowed him.

"Besides, man," Brooke said cheerfully. "You're good. You're this guy. You don't need to try so hard."

"Hey," his face reddened, "who's the director here?"

"I'm just sayin'—"

That was the friction between them that I could use. The switch was already working.

A half hour later as I was rewriting the scenes, Lenny called. He'd just heard from Lee Jeffries' agent.

"Lee is unhappy with some script changes you made. He thinks you're giving Brooke all the best lines."

My fingers froze over the keyboard. "Is he quitting?"

"No, no. He burned his agent's ear for fifteen minutes, but his guy talked him into staying."

"So where do we stand?"

"His guy told him he'd have to get comfortable dealing with 'pussy power.'"

"Works for me. Gotta go."

That evening I stood beside the camera as Jonathan improvised David Sawyer recording his grief tape, sitting at the desk in the bookcase-lined library of the Sawyer Townhouse set. Unhinged by grief and trying to maintain his dignity, he told the story of how he learned his wife had been killed. Gripping a digital recorder, he poured out memories and feelings in heartbreaking detail, ranging through horror, disbelief, desperate hope, sorrow, the loneliness where a great love once had thrived, and the desolation of living without her. He wept, he laughed, and Jonathan never once backed up, restarted, rewrote himself, or held back any riches.

Finally, he reached a moment of silence, then sat back staring at the recorder in his hand. He looked up at me and nodded.

"Cut!" I called, exultant, and the crew broke into a rare moment of applause. It was the first time they'd seen the real David Sawyer in front of a camera. I was already thinking of places in the film where I could use his voiceover or clips of the scene.

The lights went down, and the set dressers stepped in and began to wrap. He came over to me with a weary grin and I gave him a hug.

Jonathan was exuberant as he walked with me to the elevator.

"Come on, I'll buy you dinner," he said.

"I need to go to bed."

"Okay. I'm all for that."

"My bed. I need sleep."

"Is any sleep sweeter than after *le petit mort*?" he said. "Let's go to your apartment this time."

"Jonathan..." Before this went any further, I plunged ahead with the risk I decided I had to take. "Actually, I want to stop sleeping together."

His face fell and he stopped short. "What?"

"For a while anyway," I added. "While we're shooting."

He was dumbfounded. "Did I do something wrong?"

"No. I just need to detach a little to work with you. And I definitely don't want to take a chance we'll become gossip." I kept walking and he had to hustle to keep up with me. "Nobody thinks twice about a male director sleeping with his female star. But I can't be seen as a woman who's loose with boundaries."

"Adrienne..."

I pushed the elevator button.

"I have to go, Jonathan. I've had two very busy days and I need a solid night's sleep before we start shooting tomorrow. So do you."

We had the elevator to ourselves on the way down. "At least let me come over and tuck you in."

I sighed at this sweet, unserious retreat.

"You were brilliant tonight. Go home. Sleep. You're in every scene for the next two days."

He cleared his throat and said, a little too lightly, "I think it would be interesting if we live together while making this film. Think of the conversations we could have about the project. Wouldn't that be helpful to you?"

"I can't direct you and live with you too. You know how complicated this job is going to be for us," I softened my voice, "considering our other situation."

He was about to reply but we stopped at the ground floor and the doors opened. Two young women and an older man were waiting to get on. The women gave Jonathan lingering yum-yum looks as we passed.

We walked to the exit down a corridor lined with movie star posters.

He said, "I was just thinking it might potentially enrich the creative process."

This was getting annoying.

"For you, maybe, but there are other actors I have to work with. And if I lose my perspective on your work, what good would I be to you?"

"Hmm, yeah, okay," he said, the words dropping like a dirge as he held the door for me.

In the drive outside Pier 62 we each had a car waiting.

I hugged him. "It won't be forever."

"Just not what I expected. Considering our other situation, as you called it."

That was a none-too-subtle tug on the leash, just the hint of a threat.

"Oh really?" I stepped in front of him. "What was it you expected, considering our other situation?"

He just stood there looking at me. "I guess I thought we were closer than this." Finally he shook his head. "All right. Sorry."

"It doesn't mean I don't want you," I said. "It'll be hard to give it up. But I have to keep my priorities straight. A lot is at stake. For both of us."

"Yeah. Right. Got it." He waved me away. "Gotta go. Big day tomorrow." He walked around me without a backward glance, got in his car, and slammed the door.

The next morning, my Day 1 of shooting, Jonathan walked onto the Investment Bank set prepped, dressed, and ready. He was warm toward everyone; with me, he was cool and strictly about the work.

We blocked the first scene and did one rehearsal, then rolled camera. I saw immediately that improvising the grief tape had had the desired impact. Just like on stage at night, Jonathan was deep in the heart of David Sawyer. The two scenes we shot were crucial because they showed Sawyer returning to work at the investment bank after 9/11, a man working through profound grief but determined to do his job. Jonathan played Sawyer with such utter authenticity that I just kept out of his way. When I called "Cut" and gave him the nod, he turned and left the set without a word.

In the first scene on the morning of Day 2, Sawyer is hit on in his office by a frisky young associate, played by a blonde with a wry grin named Jody that Egon had originally cast for the strippergram scene. I gave her a quick reading, then cast her to play a character I'd created to emphasize Sawyer's loneliness, a girl to whom any man would say "Yeah, let's go," but Sawyer says, "No thanks." He tells her he's still terribly lonely for his late wife.

"Your heart may not be into me David," she says, "but your cock can be, any time you like."

Startled by her boldness, Jonathan froze on the line with which he gently deflects her. Finally I called, "Cut."

"Sorry," Jonathan said, sheepishly. "I forgot the line."

"It's okay. Stunned and speechless works."

"So we don't know whether he goes with her or not?"

"Let the audience decide for themselves." I turned to the actress. "That was great Jody, thank you."

He said, "So we're not going again?"

"We can if you want to. It works with or without the line. The look on your face says it all."

Jonathan nodded and smiled for the first time all day. He walked with me to the video monitor tent and slumped into his chair beside me. He leaned back and closed his eyes.

"I've decided on who I want to cast as Josephine," I said.

"Who?"

"Me."

His eyes opened and he sat up and stared at me.

"The other night, during the improv, looking at me as you were addressing her, didn't you feel it?"

"You want to work with our relationship?"

"We were doing that Tuesday night. Don't you think me and you, our chemistry, would work for this?"

He leaned over and whispered.

"First, you stop sleeping with me. And now you want to burn up what we have left to make a movie?"

"Don't make it sound so crass. It's not some game I'm playing with you."

"It's a lot riskier than a game."

"Well, if you don't like the idea –"

"I'm just saying, you're asking me to trust you with a lot."

"What about my feelings for you?"

"Well, okay. Just so you know what you're in for."

"Don't you think I know that?"

"Okay," he said, with a searching look, then sat back. "I'll take the ride."

That night as the crew wrapped, I met with Tawana, Lenny and Juno, and our production manager Moe Sperling, and we talked through the next few days until we were pretty sure we could stay on schedule. When we were done, I slung my backpack over my shoulder and rode the elevator with Tawana to the street, just in time to see Jonathan holding his SUV door open for Jody.

He got in after her, and his Teamster driver turned at the corner to head up-town.

Tawana made a funny sound.

"Mmmm... Time for some fringe benefits?" We both laughed.

"Oh, why not?"

"Men, as we say so eloquently every Friday night, are such dogs." A weary high five, and Tawana headed for the subway to Brooklyn.

After my Teamster dropped me off at my apartment, I took out my phone, debating whether to call Jonathan. I couldn't afford a random move with him now with shooting about to resume in a few hours. He knew too much that he'd promised not to tell. But promises are fragile, easily broken, and I'd made him unhappy by chilling the sex. So wasn't the poor guy entitled to a hookup? Maybe he was making a declaration of independence from me. I should either endorse that or leave him alone.

"Hi," I said. "I missed you at the wrap."

"Sorry. I had to leave in a hurry. I've got a thing to take care of."

"Oh. A thing. Well, I guess you'd better go take care of your thing. I hope your thing takes good care of you."

A nervous chuckle. "We'll see."

"Too bad we took a vow, or I'd join you two, and we could all get kinky."

"You took a vow, not me."

"That's right. So, go wild. Woof woof woof."

He laughed, and I'd made my point.

I hurried down to the courthouse on Foley Square on Friday morning for Aldo's hearing, hoping I could get it over with quickly and make it to the set for an 11 a.m. crew call for Day 3 of shooting. Annie Levy was waiting in the corridor. She gave me the big Earth Mama hug and pinched the shoulder of the conservative gray suit I'd borrowed from Wardrobe.

"Look at you, so elegant!"

In the hot stuffy courtroom we sat down at a table next to the assistant D.A., a short dark-haired woman with a permanent scowl who said her name was Sybil.

"His lawyer made a motion to get him released," Sybil said.

"I don't mean to be melodramatic, but if he gets loose again, I'm dead."

"Relax," Annie said. "When it's time, just tell the truth."

The judge was male, fiftyish and grave, with narrow eyeglasses he kept adjusting as he typed notes into a laptop computer. Two court officers brought Aldo to the defense table and stood by. He was wearing one of his cool jazz suits without a tie and was obviously going through a rough time without drugs. His head hung and his whole body seemed deflated. As his female lawyer whispered in his ear, Aldo scanned the courtroom, saw me, and glared. When I testified, he slouched back and crossed his arms and legs, enjoying my discomfort.

Sybil led me through my history with Aldo and played the recording of his threatening phone call. Aldo stared at me with a crooked sneer. But when I described our struggle in the vestibule of my building, his smirk vanished, and he shook his head. His eyes seemed to burn through me.

"At that point I pepper-sprayed him, and that gave me enough time to get into the elevator, get up to my apartment, and call the police."

"And during this incident you had no doubt you were in danger of bodily harm?" Sybil asked.

"He threatened to kill me. Two or three times."

Aldo's lawyer was a young woman in a pants suit and horn rim glasses, a blonde with a cool haughty manner. I didn't care if Aldo had her fooled, or if she was just doing the best job she could for her client. She was the enemy.

"Miss Monet, you had an intimate relationship with Mr. Hassell before this alleged harassment, is that correct?" his lawyer said.

"It's not alleged, it's real. Didn't you hear my testimony?"

"You had an intimate relationship, is that correct?"

"We had sex once in a while."

"Until you dumped him, is that correct?"

"He has mental problems and a drug habit." Aldo squirmed at the defense table.

"Again, I'll ask, you dumped him, isn't that correct?"

"Wouldn't you?"

"Your Honor, please direct the witness—"

"I told him I couldn't see him anymore."

"And that was because —"

"His drug habit. It scared me. What if he shared a needle and got HIV, had sex with me and made me sick too?"

"Miss Monet —"

"He also tried to control what I could do and with who, even before he attacked me."

I glanced over at Annie, who nodded, satisfied I was handling myself well. Beside her, Sybil the assistant D.A. was making notes on a legal pad. Aldo sat motionless, staring at me and looking hurt.

"Isn't it true he reacted that way after you told him you were done with him sexually?"

"I never said it that way."

"Isn't that why you broke up with him? You no longer had any use for him as a sexual partner?"

"I broke up with him to protect myself. His crazy behavior proves I made the right decision. It's all there in the police reports —"

"Which are only what you say happened."

"— including the day he attacked me with a knife."

Aldo's voice, low and quavering, cut across the room. "You lying, fucking cunt!" His lawyer closed her eyes and sighed.

The judge rapped his gavel once. "Counselor, control your client."

Aldo jumped up and with a sob in his voice cried out, "The bitch is lying, judge!" The judge ordered Aldo removed from the courtroom.

"I'm 'onna get you, bitch!" he yelled as the court officers dragged him through a side door. "You're fuckin' dead!"

"Motion denied." The judge rapped his gavel. I left the witness stand. Annie looked at me and shuddered. She'd never seen Aldo in person before today.

"This means he stays locked up, right?"

"My office will always know where he is. And so will you."

The judge ordered Aldo to remain in custody for a psychiatric evaluation. As I left the courtroom, I didn't feel any safer. If anything, I'd just given Aldo more reasons to be obsessed with me while he rotted in jail.

After returning the suit I borrowed to Wardrobe, I sat back and watched in the mirror as our hair and makeup artists turned me into Josephine Sawyer, an elegantly coiffed brunette. I got dressed in a white silk cocktail dress with a gold choker.

I was scheduled to be Josephine's ghost for the first time that afternoon and I was worried. In the two days since I decided I'd play her I hadn't found time to do more than learn my lines. I walked onto the set feeling very unsure of myself, trying to imagine how it might feel to exist suffering eternal loneliness, and how to comfort a grief-stricken husband. Part of me was ashamed to be so unprepared, but I'd written the role from a pained and soulful place in me and I hoped I could find that again once Jonathan and I got to work.

When Jonathan walked on the set his eyes sought me out, and he smiled slightly and nodded. As we began to rehearse, I realized I didn't have to work so hard. Josephine was a spirit, conjured up by Sawyer to cope with his unbearable grief, so a certain calm and coolness would be natural.

We shot the master, then close-ups on each of us.

"Action."

INTERIOR. SAWYER'S HOME — LIBRARY — NIGHT — From his bookshelf Sawyer, alone, takes down the *New York Times* book titled *"Portraits 9/11/01,"* with profiles of the victims of September 11 in alphabetical order.

CLOSE-UP ON BOOK — He turns to the 'S' section, where Josephine Sawyer should appear. There's no entry because his wife was never found. No last-minute cell phone call or beeper message. No email, no voicemail. No remains. Just missing.

Josephine appears to him across the room, seated on the arm of the sofa facing his desk.

JOSEPHINE

Why do you do this to yourself, David?

Sawyer peers at her, uncertainly, then lets down and bares his soul.

SAWYER

Every day I have to start life over again without you, without a single reason to go on. I mean, literally, I get out of bed, I clean myself, I feed myself, I to go to work. All the while asking myself, What for?

                              JOSEPHINE

What for? Because you have a life to live. That's a
gift. Don't waste it.

                               SAWYER

What good is a life like this?

She gets up and slowly crosses the room to his desk,
her hand combing her hair back. His eyes devour her.
He's breathless, they're about to touch. But she stops.

                              JOSEPHINE

It's still a life, my love. It's filled with
possibility for all sorts of things, including
happiness. Take it from me, it's better than the
alternative. My world is empty, and it's forever.

                               SAWYER

I'll come with you now —

                              JOSEPHINE

No David. Don't ever think that way.

She sits on the corner of the desk, inches away from
Sawyer. He starts to reach for her, but stops before
they touch, frustrated because they can't.

                              JOSEPHINE

You're alive. You have everything. I have nothing.

SAWYER

You have me. We still have each other.

All Josephine can offer is a sad smile.

Over the time it took to shoot, I relaxed. It was The Walk, as the crew nicknamed it afterward, that made it my scene, when she stands up and moves toward David, both of them feeling unbearably lonely. By the third take I began to feel a consuming compassion for his suffering. We shot my close ups last, when I was immersed in her sadness, unable to sooth her husband's anguish. When we finished, Jonathan put his arm around my shoulders and whispered "Okay," and walked off the set.

I needed time to be alone, so I stole it. I found a quiet corner of the stage and sat there on an apple box. I'd acted in all my movies with no formal training, and never had any confusion between real and make believe because I basically played myself. But now I was feeling too vulnerable and unable to control my mind, and I slipped into worry about Egon's family. I remembered a day working with Egon at his family apartment when I'd sat and played with his daughter Ricki, so sweet, so innocent, and so adoring of her father, and a flood of guilt and sorrow gushed through a crack in my psyche. Oh my God, the worry, the suffering that little girl must be going through, all because of what I did to her father.

I couldn't stand to be with myself, and I didn't want to talk to anyone. I left the stage and hurried down the back stairwell, through the cavernous Pier 62 parking garage and out to the end over the river. I stood at the railing under the vast gray sky. The Hudson flowed smoothly downriver below my feet. Raindrops made rings on the gray waters that mirrored the sky. Upstairs they'd be looking for me to rehearse the next scene. But I needed this time by myself. I stood staring down at the water, one moment feeling illegitimate, another feeling how unfair it was that an ugly twist of fate had brought me here and enabled me to practice the art that I lived for.

That evening Jonathan was leaning on the wall in the corridor, waiting as I locked my office to go out shooting on location. We spoke as crew members crowded into the elevators.

"I saw the playback," I said. "It works. You can see there's a lot going on."

"A lot going unsaid."

"We don't need much rehearsal for that."

"I'm not working tomorrow," he said, almost sorrowfully. "So I guess we won't see each other."

I put my arms around him for a quick, collegial hug. "I'll call you when I can."

"Come over after wrap," he said. "I'll take you for a nice dinner someplace."

"I'll need to go home and sleep."

"What about Sunday?" he said. "Let's catch an early train out to Montauk. You can sleep on the way out."

"Sleep on a train seat? Not very restful. Sunday I'll have four days of dailies to look at. But once that's done maybe we can get together for dinner if you're around."

"Oh, I see," he said, stiffly. "Well, fit me in, if you can, okay?" With a dismissive wave, he walked off.

On a cool gray Saturday morning in Chinatown shooting got off to a rough start. First up, on Canal Street, we shot a scene in which Ruthie and Abel buy a large inflatable life raft at a sporting goods store. They can only afford the scuffed-up floor model, and it's inflated, so they bitch and strain as they haul the awkward thing through the crowds on the sidewalk. We lost ten minutes because two Asian store owners were angry that we'd steered pedestrians away from their establishments and the NYPD movie unit cops had to get things under control. Lee got annoyed by the delay, pacing around muttering racist stuff about the Chinese and embarrassing everyone, until Tawana got in his face and told him to cool it.

But that was just before we started shooting again. Lee got rattled from being reprimanded, and once we rolled the cameras, he kept blowing his lines, forcing us to keep lugging the raft back and starting the scene over again. He finally got so frustrated he went off script and hoisted the heavy raft over his head and marched off up the sidewalk, with our Steadicam operator keeping pace alongside him and Brooke trailing after him ad-libbing. Talk about talent on demand – she segued out of that into her lines, Lee miraculously remembered all of his dialog, and in the playback the Steadicam footage looked so perfect that I ordered a safety copy duped right away and moved on to the next shot. When I praised his improvisation, Lee strolled away looking very full of himself.

Once that scene wrapped, we rolled the equipment around the corner to a coffee shop where Khalil, the teenage son of the tortured father in "I'm a Stranger Here," is having lunch with his younger sister, Katya. The scene had been pre-lit to save time, we rehearsed, and the actors were set to go. Khalil angrily criticizes his sister for staying aloof from their father since he came home. She begs him to understand how frightening she finds life with their broken-spirited patriarch. The young actors played the scene beautifully, with such withheld anger and hurt in their hushed voices, and although we were a little behind schedule it felt like the day was back on track.

It was a relief to be free for a day of Jonathan and his gloom and hypersensitivity. But that evening at camera wrap after an intense first week of shooting, I was facing a depressing night of solo dining, inevitable masturbation, and exhausted sleep, so I called him.

"Too late to go out and eat?"

"Never!"

Over dinner at a Thai place on Columbus Avenue not far from where he lived, Jonathan was in a relaxed and flirtatious mood.

I couldn't resist. "How did it go with Jody?"

"What about her?"

"Was she good in bed?"

"Oh, you," he said, twirling a forkful of Pad Thai noodles. He shrugged. "She was all right, I guess."

"You guess?"

"Once she stopped talking about acting."

"Details!"

"Oh come on," he said. "Why do you want to hear that?"

"I'm a voyeur."

"Who isn't these days?"

"Were you hot for her? Or did you just do it to get under my skin?"

"Were you jealous?"

"Maybe a little bit. Of course I've got a lot more on my mind than who you're having sex with."

"Had sex with."

"She didn't live up to expectations?"

"What she lacked in experience she more than made up for in beauty and enthusiasm."

"Beautiful bodies are their own reward."

"Yeah, but at my age I need intelligent conversation, too. Young people these days don't know anything. I couldn't wait to get out of there."

"You didn't bring her home?"

"God no. We went to her place. Adrienne, I want you to know something, in case you don't already see it."

"What?"

"My feelings for you. They're evolving."

Oh God. Next, he'll tell me he's falling in love.

"I know what you mean," I said. "I'm kind of in that same space." I hated lying about that, but he softened a little when I said it. "I've just been trying to keep the personal and professional separate so I can be at my best for both."

When we left the restaurant, he slipped his arm around my waist and seemed content. I put on a show of feeling the same, but in a world where everybody has a camera in their pocket, I was uncomfortable with his arm around me in public.

Those words "my feelings for you," spoken to me by a man, always made me uncomfortable. According to the cliché, women in bed want a romance novel and men want a porn movie. But for me, freak that I am, I liked both, hairy muscular domination by a man and the spiritual sensual sharing of love with a woman. I'd probably be called bisexual, but when it comes to sex, I think of myself more as an opportunist. At heart, I think I'm still a lonely, insecure teenager who wants everything but can't trust anyone. I've always treated sex with men the way boys treated girls, like it was a game, thrills with no obligation, more satisfying than masturbation but a lot less than love. The more aggressive a man treats me, the more intense the fear and the thrill, and the better the sex. Just so you don't think I'm a cold-hearted player, I know men have feelings. But unlike most women, I don't mind if they're unfaithful, because I don't want them to get too attached. I've never felt like I needed a man to complete my life. Lots of girls let themselves be heartbroken over the way men are led around by their cocks. But I grew into womanhood expecting nothing more. When I find a playful hound, I keep him around as long as he stays playful. But when my heart opens, it's always for a woman, and then it's usually me whose heart gets broken.

We strolled to the corner of Central Park West. "Listen, I won't be available tomorrow after all. I've got too much work to do. I'm sorry, I hope you understand."

He lit a cigarette. "I thought this felt like a consolation dinner. How about a consolation fuck for dessert?"

"Let's not end a lovely night like this. Please?"

"Okay." He sighed a breath of smoke. "I'm glad you could find a couple hours for me."

He kissed me at the West 81st Street subway entrance, and said in my ear, "And I meant what I said about my feelings for you." He stepped away from me, stuck his hands in his pockets, and walked off, sullen and alone.

On Wednesday morning, Day 7, shooting was on schedule on the Sawyer Townhouse set onstage at the Pier. The crew was lighting the second scene listed on the Call Sheet. I took a cup of coffee to the director's chair in the video monitor tent and checked my email on my phone. I had a Google alert linking to a story about Egon on the September 13 *New York Post* website under the startling headline: DRUG DEALER HELD IN DIRECTOR'S SHOOTING. The police had lifted a suspect's fingerprints off a bag of crystal meth they found in Egon's pocket and taken a known drug dealer into custody. The story quoted an anonymous NYPD source, who said toxicology tests turned up methamphetamine in Egon's blood.

Juno eased down into her chair beside me, read the story on her phone, and sighed with disgust.

"Although," she said, "maybe in a crazy way this is the best thing that could happen. Overall, I mean. If Egon was on drugs, that could've caused us a real problem in the middle of shooting. I hope they put this dealer, whoever this scum is, in prison for the rest of his scummy fucking life."

After years of marriage to a gluttonous drug abuser, I figured Juno was entitled to let her usual poise slip on that subject.

So Egon was on meth when he assaulted me. That's why he was so disheveled and volatile that morning. So maybe his vision for *"Lonely Sky"* was nothing more than a tweaker's fantasy and when he couldn't make it real, he choked, and he tried to overcome his deficiency with even more speed. It gave him the chemical courage to write but all he produced was an inane script, a fight with Jonathan, and bad feelings with the crew. The *Post* story quoted the doctors who said his coma might be irreversible. Terrible thing to admit, but that gave me hope. I didn't want Egon to die but if he recovered and talked my life would be over. The situation had a nasty irony: the meth dealer in custody, who had undoubtedly committed other crimes and never got caught, might go to jail because of my necessary act of self-defense.

That night the crew moved from the stages to a street in the East Village, where the set P.A.'s had to wrangle a large mob of curious onlookers, possibly attracted by the fact that our production, of the many shooting in the city, was now a news story. The scene was Ruthie and Abel walking and arguing on the sidewalk approaching their building. The dolly shot of them walking lasted about a half a block, and it was hard for the sound recordist and camera operator to get clean sound and footage with spectators taking flash photos and talking behind the blue NYPD sawhorses. After some friendly begging from Tawana, the NYPD movie unit cops moved the crowd off the block to the avenues and kept passers-by quickly moving past the set.

All night I was operating at high function: hunched in my chair under the video tent replaying takes on the monitor, taking Brooke and Lee aside to direct their performances, arguing about a scheduling decision with Lenny and Juno on my way back to the monitor, answering a series of emails and texts, then turning my total concentration to the moment when real time turned to filmic time and the actors became their characters. As I'd feared, Lee Jeffries had become difficult to work with but with my careful stroking and Brooke's cheerful patience and professionalism, his sullen personality was working fine, though without much subtlety, for the way Abel copes with Ruthie's paranoia. Luckily, Brooke's performance was brilliant, her fears heartbreakingly familiar, the post-9/11 paranoia none of us wanted to admit or could escape.

Traffic rushed by on the avenues at the far ends of the block. We had a permit from the city to film on the street until daybreak. On a clear September night the air held the chill of autumn approaching and the crew was hustling, all of them agents of my creative will, like the truckloads and hampers filled with equipment and the brilliant lights on high stands and the cameras, all of it the tools I needed to capture my vision.

It was autumn in New York. I was directing a movie. I was in love with life again.

On Thursday afternoon Jonathan was fighting off a cold but he insisted he was able to work. So we kept to our schedule and shot two scenes between Sawyer and Josephine. This time playing a ghost in a Gothic romance, with an actor I was having an affair with, didn't leave me feeling as vulnerable as the first time. After we finished, I said good night to Jonathan and moved with the company to the East Village to do more night shooting with Lee and Brooke. When we got to the location Tawana marched over to me with her phone to her ear and a worried look on her face.

"Yeah, yeah, she's here now," she said into her phone. "I'll tell her." She lowered her voice. "That was the production office. After we left the stages two cops showed up. They talked to Jonathan in his dressing room."

I managed to say, "Police? What'd they want?"

"Nobody knows. Or nobody's saying."

But of course I knew. The police must've found out Jonathan had been fired by Egon and they drew the obvious conclusion. Now they were investigating him, which meant they'd soon be on to me. While the crew pulled equipment from the trucks to set up the first shot, I called Jonathan. It was about 7:30 and if he wasn't under arrest, he'd be in his dressing room at the theater.

"How are you feeling?"

"Oh just great." He sounded anything but.

"I hear the police came to talk to you."

"Yeah. They were really fucked up about it, too."

"You're angry. What was it about?"

"Egon. What else?"

"What'd they say?"

"I can't talk now."

"Just give me the short version."

"I'm preparing to go on."

"Please?"

"Come over later if you're interested." He hung up.

If you're interested?

I had to force myself to stay focused on work. I shot a scene with Brooke and Lee and two establishing shots of their building. We wrapped fifteen minutes late. I released my Teamster driver because the subway up to Jonathan's would be quicker.

He was barefoot, his robe was tied crookedly, he was red and damp from the shower, and his hair lay flat on his forehead. He was pacing the living room in front of the TV screen, watching a CNN report about a terrorist attack in the London Underground.

He clicked off the TV.

"Are you okay?"

"Are you serious?" he snapped. His eyes, red and shining, glared at me. "The cops treated me like a fucking criminal!"

"Yesterday the *Post* said they arrested a drug dealer."

"The cops said he had an alibi, so they had to release him. Now they suspect me of shooting Egon."

"Why would they even think that?"

"The found out Egon fired me. The next day he got shot, therefore, I must've done it!"

"That's it?"

"No, that wasn't it," he said irritably. "But that's their theory. They asked me a lot of questions."

"Questions, like what?"

"Why did he fire me?"

"Well, if I were them, that's what I'd ask."

"I told them the truth. Creative differences. It wasn't personal. He was making a terrible movie out of a play I'd won an award for. The male cop, he kept trying to antagonize me. He actually said, 'I guess you're happy somebody put Swift in his place, right?' And they made me account for everything I did that day."

"From what you told me it was just another day."

"Like every day. Breakfast at the coffee shop, I spent the morning here reading, I made a few calls. I went out to lunch, and I spent the rest of the day here. After the theater I went out to my house in Montauk and I was there the rest of the weekend. They wanted someone to verify all this, so I told them to talk to you."

My hope for anonymity died. "What did you tell them?"

"The truth, just like we agreed. I said we were together all afternoon and all weekend out in Montauk. They already knew about somebody named Adrienne anyway. They had a voicemail from her on Egon's phone, canceling a meeting."

"I left that message after he got shot in case anyone knew he was meeting me."

"Well, that was fast thinking," he sneered.

He turned to the bar and poured himself a glass of whiskey.

"How did you describe me? As your director or your girlfriend?"

"Both." He gulped the whiskey, wincing as it went down. "They asked me how you and Egon got along. I said very well. They asked if I knew what you did that morning. I said you left here to go jogging and came back at lunchtime."

"So I'm your alibi."

"Hey." That irritated him. "You're the one who needs an alibi, not me."

"So they want to talk to me?"

"That's why I'm telling you all this. Our stories have to match."

"It sounds like you did okay."

"Yeah, until they asked me if I owned a gun. And I lied."

"I would've too. Give me the gun, I'll throw it in the river."

"I don't trust you with it. I'll take care of the gun."

"Will you? Please? You'd be taking a huge weight off my mind."

"What about the weight on my mind?" He wrung his hands, breathing hard. "The weight that you put there?"

I didn't answer. After four 12-hour workdays I was too tired to take up that subject.

"Well, it sounds like you didn't say anything that'll get me in trouble."

"You're welcome," he said bitterly.

"I'm sorry. That was a selfish thing to say."

"I told you I wouldn't talk. I just hope you've told me everything."

"I swear I did. The only way we'll make it through this is for our stories to match."

I needed a good night's sleep. Tomorrow I had to play a scene with him and direct the rest of the day on location, and now maybe I'd have to deal with the police, too.

"It's quarter to eleven and my Teamster pickup tomorrow is at ten. There's no sense in me going back to my place. I'll go down in the morning. Can I stay?"

"I don't want you to catch what I have," he sighed. "Take the guest room."

Slump-shouldered and droopy-eyed, he shuffled off to sleep. In the guest room I got undressed and climbed into bed. But I was too restless and worried to sleep. So the police had found their way to us. We were in deep trouble. I lay there staring into the darkness. My mind wouldn't stop racing and I couldn't lay there with Jonathan in the next bedroom, so I got dressed and left. I walked down Central Park West until I was almost asleep on my feet, then I caught a cab the rest of the way home.

S aturday morning, Day 10 of *"Lonely Sky"*, as my car was pulling into Chelsea Piers, my cell phone rang. Lenny groaned. "Did you see today's *Post*?"

"Now what?"

"Jonathan's picture is on Page 3. Big headline: ACTOR GRILLED IN DI-RECTOR'S SHOOTING."

More trouble for Jonathan, and the day hadn't even begun. More reason for him to be angry with me for the trouble I'd put him in.

"Do we know if Jonathan has seen it?"

"He's not here yet."

"No, he's on a Will Call for after lunch. Has anyone talked to him?"

"He's not answering his phone."

"So what does the story say?"

"It quotes NYPD sources, anonymous, of course. They're saying Jonathan is suspected of shooting Egon," Lenny said. "It says he and Egon fought constantly. They've got Egon firing him and getting shot the next day all tied together like it proves Jonathan did it."

"They wrote that Jonathan got fired?"

"Yeah."

"Get that studio publicist we met to immediately put out a statement saying Jonathan Lehane is not fired, he's working in the movie during the day and onstage every night and doing brilliant work."

"Should we run that by Jonathan?"

"We don't need to. I'm sure he'll appreciate the support."

"This sucks," Lenny groaned. "Big time."

That afternoon Jonathan strolled into the Hair and Makeup room without a hint that he was feeling any pressure. He joked and laughed with our hair stylist and our makeup artist while they prepped us. After Wardrobe he was relaxed, strolling with me to the Sawyer Townhouse set on the stage.

Cautiously, I said, "Are you okay?"

"Preparation, my love. You hold the work inside in a place nobody can touch. Not even the tabloids."

We worked through three lighting setups, a master shot and close ups on Jonathan and me. It was hard going. Once we were close up on me, I didn't like how tense I looked in the playbacks. My voice was flat, so I kept ordering more takes. Jonathan could've gone to his dressing room and left me to run my lines with our script supervisor reading his, but he stayed and played every take with me, holding back nothing, until I was relaxed and could perform with real feeling.

Hours later, as the crew set the camera and lights for Jonathan's close up, Tawana strolled over and directed my attention to two well-dressed people in the shadows at the entrance to the stage.

"Cops," she whispered. "They're asking for you."

"Who the fuck let them in here?"

"The P.A. at the door couldn't stop them."

"And they asked for me?"

I knew sooner or later the police would show up, but did it have to be today? We were about to shoot Jonathan's close up. Now my set felt like a danger zone. I couldn't imagine how Jonathan would play this scene with two cops watching, but he seemed oblivious to everything but my presence. I decided the only way to deal with this was to take a deep breath, walk over and take charge.

"I'm Adrienne Monet. Is there something I can do for you?"

The male detective was stocky, like a boxer, and swarthy.

"Detective Ferino," the cop said. He had a gruff, staccato way of talking, very t'rough de uppa lip Brooklyn. "NYPD Homicide." He was my age, in his forties, and I just knew he'd been a hoodlum in high school. His hard eyes were creased with expressive wrinkles, his thick black hair in a blunt cut, his goatee flecked with silver. He wore a perfectly tailored silver suit and tie. Beside him was a tall slim Black woman.

"My partner, Detective Peavey."

She was thirtyish, wearing a gray pants suit and white blouse with her badge and gun on the belt and long beaded braids. I said hello, but she looked right past me, taking in the set with a confident, appraising gaze.

Ferino's hooded, deep-set eyes were cold and predatory.

"We need to talk to you," he said. "Where can we go?"

"We'll go to my office." He turned to go. "Just one thing, though."

He stopped, annoyed. "What?"

"We have one shot left in this scene. It'll only take a couple minutes."

"No, let's go."

I stood my ground. "After that we pack up to move out on location, so I'll be free until I have to go down to the van. We can talk then."

"No," he said. "Let's go."

"We don't have time to wait," Detective Peavey said.

"It'll cost us a lot of money for the crew to wait around for me. And I'll be in a hurry to get back to work."

Peavey turned to Ferino, but he was looking me up and down.

"If we have to talk now," I said, "my answers will be brief."

"Okay," he said, probably calculating how much control he was letting me have. "Yeah. Okay."

"Let me have somebody get you a cup of coffee –"

"Just hurry up." He glanced at his watch, a digital on a plastic strap. "We'll be here."

They weren't leaving the set and I couldn't make them. I assumed they were the same cops who questioned Jonathan and drove him into a fury, but if he knew they were there he didn't show it.

I put them out of my mind and concentrated on the anguish of Mr. and Mrs. David Sawyer. We'd already done numerous takes and I could feel us getting tired. The camera was on Jonathan, who was full of the romantic melancholy and heartbreak I'd tried to get into the writing.

When he was seated at the desk, I said, "Action."

INT. — SAWYER TOWNHOUSE — LIBRARY

Early morning before dawn. Sawyer is at his desk. He is relaxed, composed, anticipating. He engages the speaker phone on his desk and dials a number. After several rings, we hear Josephine's warm, friendly voice.

JOSEPHINE'S VOICE

Hello, you've reached the cellphone of Josephine Sawyer. I can't come to the phone right now, but if you leave me a message I'll call you back as soon as I can. So, start talking at the beep, and have a lovely day.

BEEP

SAWYER

Good morning, my darling. Did you sleep well? I had a dream last night. I dreamt it was Labor Day weekend and we were spending it in the cottage in Amagansett like we always do. We were on the beach and it was a glorious late summer day. You looked so beautiful, the way the sun had made your body so tan and warm and the breeze ruffled up your hair. We lay there for hours, just talking about things, like we always do. Then we made a wonderful dinner together, and afterward we went to bed. And —

His voice breaks. He begins breathing hard and can't continue. After a moment, he continues.

                    SAWYER

Do you know how precious you are to me? Do you know the greatest gift this life has ever given me is the chance to love you the way that I do —

He stops as the ghost of Josephine enters.

                    JOSEPHINE

David.

                    SAWYER

I was just leaving you a message.

                    JOSEPHINE (gently)

Why haven't you canceled my cellphone, David?

                    SAWYER

It's the only way I can still hear your voice, from... before.

                    JOSEPHINE

I can't check my messages anymore, darling.

                    SAWYER

I can't bring myself to cancel it. I just can't.

(He starts to cry.)

                    JOSEPHINE

David —

                    SAWYER

Don't, please. Don't ask me to cancel it. I have so
little that's left of you. Your clothes are still in
our closet. Your place at the breakfast table is still
set exactly as it was... that day. I wake up in the
morning and —

He can't continue.

                    JOSEPHINE

I don't know what to say.

                    SAWYER

Say you'll always be here. In my life.

                    JOSEPHINE

But I'm not.

                    SAWYER

Just like this. Like you are now. That you'll always
come back to me this way. Please.

They stare at each other. Then, without answering,
[OPTICAL EFFECT] Josephine fades before his eyes and
disappears.

```
                    JOSEPHINE (as she fades)

You know as well as I do. Nothing's guaranteed.

Sawyer falls back in his chair, desolate. Then he
lunges at the phone and dials the number again. As
Josephine's message starts to play we...
```

"Cut."

I was in awe of how Jonathan acted after she vanished, leaning over the phone, longing to hear her voice again, still caught in the fantasy, with an urgency both heartbreaking and scary.

I stepped over and gripped his shoulder. "Another?" He looked up and shook his head.

I turned to Sally our script supervisor. "Okay, that's the one."

"Company move!" Tawana announced over the walkie.

Jonathan stood up, hugged me and walked silently off the set.

I told Tawana, "I'll take the cops to my office."

She whispered, "You want somebody with you?"

"I'll be okay. Give me a five-minute warning when it's time to go down to the van."

I led the detectives off the stage and down the hall to my office. The work had left me too sensitized for what was coming, and I needed time to get my guard back up. I left the cops standing by in the corridor while I changed out of my costume and into my street clothes. I went to the lady's room and removed my make-up. Forcing the police to wait made me feel better. I stared at myself in the mirror and repeated a simple mantra that I must've remembered from a cop show somewhere: "Listen carefully, don't try to make them like you, and say as little as possible."

I came back to where the detectives were waiting.

"I'm all yours."

In my office, I took a drink from a large bottle of Evian, checked my iPhone, then put it on the desk in front of me. I leaned back in my chair and twisted my legs under me into a lotus position, took a deep breath, and prepared to act helpful. Detective Peavey stood with her back to the door at one end of the room. At the other end Detective Ferino sat on the sofa. I couldn't see them both at the same time. Did they bracket me on purpose? Did cops use tricks like that, and if they did, what for?

Ferino sat back, scrutinizing me with a frown, and nodded to Peavey.

"You know why we're here, Miss Monet," Peavey said. "We're investigating the shooting of Mister Swift."

"God help him. We try to keep in touch with the hospital, but they won't tell us anything. How is he?"

"Critical?" she said, dramatically. She had a clear, crisp voice. Every sentence sounded like a question, and a veiled accusation. "Com-a-tose?"

"His poor family. How can I help?"

Ferino said from his corner, "You can answer our questions."

"I couldn't believe what I read in the papers this morning. You don't really suspect Jonathan Lehane, do you?"

Peavey ignored that. "Mister Lehane said he had a fight with Mister Swift and got fired. Can you tell us what that was about?"

"A disagreement over the script."

"What kind of disagreement?"

I shrugged. "Creative differences."

Peavey said, "Can you be more specific?"

"Jonathan didn't like Egon's version of the script. He didn't want to play what was written. The arguments were holding up shooting and putting Egon behind schedule."

"Mister Lehane told us you were the writer."

"Originally, yes."

Ferino said, "What happened? You got fired too?"

"No. I adapted the play into a screenplay. Then Egon wrote the final shooting script."

Peavey said, "On the morning of Saturday, Labor Day weekend, you were at Mister Lehane's apartment?"

I felt their interest shift from Jonathan to me. Carefully, I answered.

"I was there, yes."

"You must know Mister Lehane very well."

"We're in a relationship."

Ferino said, "What kind of relationship?"

"Professional and –" since Jonathan had already told them – "personal."

Ferino lightened and sounded intrigued.

"That scene you just did? What was that?"

"That was acting."

"Yeah, of course... I'm just curious. What was goin' on there?"

"He's playing a grieving husband who lost his wife on September 11. They were very much in love. He can't let her go, so he hallucinates her as a ghost. That way, she never dies."

"Oh," Ferino says, nodding. "Interesting." He glanced at his partner. "You could see that she and Lehane have a..." he spun a finger and came up with the word. "Rapport." He looked back at me. "Right?"

I knew what he was trying to do, and I wasn't falling for it.

"Acting is rapport."

That brought a dull stare.

Peavey said, "How long have you known Mister Lehane?"

"A couple of months. We met on this film."

"How well do you know Mister Swift?"

"Pretty well. We worked together on the writing."

"How would you describe your relationship with Mister Swift?"

"It's a good working relationship. Do you have any idea who really shot him?"

"We're working on that," Ferino said.

"In other words you don't know." I stared at him a moment. "You've already been at this for a couple weeks, haven't you?"

Instead of answering, he nodded to Peavey and she continued.

"Tell us more about your relationship with Mister Swift."

"He needed a writer. The producers knew me and put us together."

"How did you get along?"

"Fine. We got the writing done against a very tight deadline. Egon's a talented man. And he treated me respectfully, which is not always the case."

"For women?" Peavey said.

"And writers."

Ferino said, "You know of any problems he was having with anyone?"

"None that I saw. None that he mentioned."

"We heard the crew didn't like him."

"Did Jonathan say that?"

Peavey said, "His wife said Swift came home frustrated every night. We also called his assistant, Clark, in Los Angeles. He said the crew had an attitude toward Mister Swift. Like he was some kind of Hollywood smartass, is how he put it."

It must've been Clark who told them about Jonathan fighting on the set with Egon.

"The crew was respectful and professional with Egon. But, you know, nobody likes their boss. Do you like yours?"

That got a slight smirk from Peavey. Ferino didn't find it funny.

"So, you're in a relationship with Lehane," he said, "and you're getting along fine with Swift. How'd you feel about them fighting?"

"On a film shoot, fights over creative differences happen every day."

"Lehane didn't know you canceled a meeting with Swift the morning he got shot. What happened, you forget to tell your boyfriend about it?"

"No, Egon called me after I left Jonathan's. But I wouldn't have told him anyway. Egon had just fired him."

"What were you doing the day Swift got shot?"

"You mean, like, what I did, where I went?"

"Yeah. The day Swift got shot. What'd you do? Where'd you go?"

"Wait a minute. Am I a suspect in this?"

"Just answer the question."

I shrugged; if he suspected me, well, that was his problem.

"I left Jonathan's early. I took the C train down to my apartment on West 20th. Put on my running clothes to go over to the river to jog. That's when Egon called. I said I'd work with him as soon as I got cleaned up after jogging. But then I changed my mind."

"Why's that?"

"Jonathan needed me. The scenes Egon wanted to work on weren't scheduled to shoot for a few days so there was time. Besides, it was Labor Day weekend. So I went jogging, and when I got home, I called Egon back. He didn't answer, so I left the message."

"Your message said something was urgent."

"Like I said, Jonathan needed me more. I did a little work at home, then I went back up to his place."

Peavey said, "So when you and Lehane got back together what'd you do?"

"We had lunch. We took a walk around Central Park. We spent some time hanging out at his apartment. That night after the theater, we drove out to Montauk."

Peavey said, "And during all this, how was Mister Lehane?"

"Moody. Depressed about getting fired."

"Angry?"

"No, he was sad. You know, he won an award for the play —"

Ferino said, "Where were you when you heard Swift got shot?"

"Jonathan's house in Montauk. He saw the story online on Sunday morning and he told me about it."

"And how was he then?"

"Shocked. Sad for Egon's family."

"Even though Swift fired him the day before?"

"That's what I'm trying to tell you. He's not the type for revenge. He's a very compassionate man."

Peavey said, "So you were with Lehane the rest of the weekend?"

"Yes. We came back Sunday night so I could meet with the producers."

"Is that when you took over as director?"

"Yes."

Ferino said, "Tell us how that happened."

"I've directed four films. The producers thought I could save this one from being cancelled."

"So, what, they asked you to step in?"

"I offered to. Egon put a lot of work into this movie. I thought it would be a shame if it didn't get made. Also, the crew would lose their jobs. I felt like I had to try to help."

"Of course. The show must go on, right?"

"Always."

Peavey said, "Where do you live?" As she wrote my address down, Ferino looked like he'd just thought of something.

"Which way did you walk to the river to go jogging?" he said.

"Across 20th Street."

"You're sure about that?"

"I always go that way." In pointed out my office window to that intersection. "There's a stop light at the West Side Highway and 20th Street. You can go right onto the jogging path."

"Swift's office is on 22nd Street."

"I've been there."

"So, you were two blocks away around the time he could've been shot."

I stared back at him. My face got warm and my eyes teared up.

"That's a frightening thought," I said.

"Yeah? Why?"

"If I hadn't cancelled the meeting I might've been shot too."

"You were in the neighborhood," Ferino said. "Why didn't you stop in and tell Swift you couldn't work?"

"Why didn't I go there, to tell him I couldn't go there?" I turned to Peavey and said, "I don't know how to answer that." I saw Ferino's jaw tighten. "Anything else?" Ask me something, lady detective, anything to shut this guy up.

Peavey said, "You took over as director and Lehane got his job back. Was that your decision?"

"We all wanted him back."

Ferino said, "How did Lehane feel about getting his job back?"

"He was happy, of course."

"And no complaints about the script?"

"We're shooting the version that I wrote."

"Oh. Interesting."

A knock came on the door and a female voice announced, "Adrienne, we're ready to leave for location."

"I'll be right there," I called back. "Anything else?"

"That's all for now?" Peavey said to her partner.

Ferino stood up and stretched. "For now."

Ferino handed me his NYPD card. "If you think of anything else that might help us, call me."

"I will. Here's my card, too, it's got all my numbers on it."

He read it. "Alpha Bitch Productions?" He chuckled and handed my card to Peavey. But when he looked back at me from the doorway, there was no humor in his eyes.

Those cold eyes worried me. When I was alone, I locked the door and crash landed on the sofa. Breathe, Adrienne, just breathe. Ferino's peppery aftershave stunk up my office. Worst of all, he was really stinking up my mind.

He was 'way too curious about me and Jonathan. He called it our rapport, but he meant co-conspirators. When I revealed that I offered to take over from Egon he was like a shark swerving toward the smell of blood. He did it again when I said I was near Egon's office around the time he might've been shot. He treated me like a witness, but I had to assume Ferino thought I shot Egon to steal his job and to get Jonathan his role back.

I opened the window, found the pack of unfiltered Camels I kept in my desk drawer for emergencies, shook one out and lit it, and blew a thick plume of smoke out toward the West Side Highway outside. I stubbed it out after a couple puffs. The nicotine cleared my mind. I needed to get down to the director van. But first I had to check something.

I plugged in my earbuds and replayed my talk with the police on my iPhone. When it ended, I took a huge breath and relaxed. Certain facts had made Ferino suspicious: that Jonathan and I were lovers, that Jonathan and Egon fought, that I became director, that Jonathan got his role in the movie back, even that we were shooting my script. But I hadn't done as badly as I feared. I'd told the detectives the truth except for a few minutes I left out. I also admitted I was near Egon's office around the time he got shot. From a cop's point of view only an innocent person would admit to that. My jogging timeline was so open that unless they had proof that I visited Egon's office they'd never know about the few minutes when I met with him, shot him, and got away.

That night the weather turned sharply colder. We filmed a scene between Sawyer and Josephine using a fog effect and eerie lighting in a small park near the Sawyer Townhouse exterior in the East 80s. Jonathan played his part so tenderly, trying to comfort Josephine's loneliness in eternity, and the scene aroused such sadness in me, that after the last time I called "Cut," I had to sit silently on a park bench in Josephine's cashmere overcoat and come back to myself, while the crew hustled around me, wrapping the equipment for our Sunday off.

Once I was out of makeup and back into my street clothes, I decided to work off the tension of another week of shooting by walking all the way home. It was more than 75 city blocks, but I didn't care. A long walk would let me forget about filmmaking for a while. I could wander like Garbo did in her old age, down through the lights and shadows of the city streets on a Saturday night, alone in the crowd in Times Square, reading the stories in the passing faces, humming Rogers and Hart songs in harmony with the harsh night music of New York, a city steeped in history while each day carrying its millions of souls headlong into the future. A long exhausting walk through the autumn streets in the cold would settle me down so that when I got home, I could crawl into bed and sleep late into Sunday morning.

Jonathan was waiting for me in his trailer.

"Twenty-nine more days of this," he said. "Are you going to make it?"

"Why? Is something wrong?"

"Lately, you just seem, I don't know, fragile or something."

"I'm okay. It's been a rough week. That's all."

"Have a drink with me. Let's talk."

I dropped my hat, backpack, and jacket on the sofa, and sat down to the glass of red wine he set on the table. Outside the street echoed with shouts and staticky walkie-talkie voices as the crew hurried to load the trucks so they could head home for their one day of rest.

I sat back and sipped while Jonathan changed out of his three-piece suit. Dressed in corduroy trousers, sweater, Barbour waxed coat and newsboy cap, he sat across from me.

"Why didn't you tell me those detectives questioned you this morning?" he said.

"I didn't want to distract you while we were working."

"I warned you they'd get to you, didn't I?"

"Yes, but don't worry, it was actually cool."

"Oh yeah? What was so 'actually cool' about it?"

"I don't mean I enjoyed it. I mean they asked questions that I expected. How well do I know you? How well do I know Egon? Why did you guys argue?"

"What did you say?"

"Creative differences. Everything I told them was true."

"I see," he said. "Just a nice friendly chat with the NYPD."

I refused to respond to that. "They were kind of uptight, that's all. They've been at this too long and they still have nothing."

"They think they've got me," he said gloomily. "Any day now I'll get arrested just so the God damned police have something to show." I swirled the wine, annoyed by his hurt, put-upon pout.

"You won't be arrested. They won't find what they're looking for, and they'll move on."

"The sooner the better."

"The sooner you calm down, the better."

"Calm down? I'm suspected of shooting a man."

"Yes, but you didn't. So chill out."

"'Chill out'? Is that what you advise? You, the person who got me in this trouble in the first place?"

He was about to play the blame game with me again and I refused to go there.

"Whatever trouble you're in, mine is ten times worse."

"You think they suspect you too?"

"I know they do. I asked them."

"What did they say?"

"'Just answer the questions, Miss'. I have a bad feeling about the male cop."

"So what'd you tell them?"

"I told them I went jogging then I went home. I left Egon a message saying I wasn't coming. Did some work at home. I went back to your place around lunch time, and we were together the rest of the weekend, in the city and out on the Island. Simple. And except for a few minutes on Saturday morning, one hundred percent true."

"Well, at least I'm not the only suspect."

"I'm sorry you're involved at all." I thought I'd say that, then get out of there. Things were getting strained. I drank my wine and stood up, put on my jacket and hat and picked up my backpack.

"Adrienne," he said, softening, "I know it's late and tomorrow's our day off, but stay with me tonight." He stood up. "We won't talk about this anymore."

I wanted to be alone. But now with both of us under suspicion, I was afraid to let too much space grow between us. After the tension of the last two days and sensing that Jonathan was no longer one hundred percent on my side, a night together might help.

"Okay, let's go. Just so you know up front, I have to look at dailies when I get up."

"I'll set the clock for whatever time you need."

"Promise not to be so angry?"

"It's a deal."

I turned off the lights so nobody could see us through the Winnebago's window curtains, took his face in my hands, and kissed him.

We spent that night together, happily, and Sunday morning too, until I had to go to work. When I headed downtown, I felt those hours had brought us closer together, at least for now.

A few days later I got a call while I was in my trailer office at our Lower East Side location eating a vegetarian burrito for lunch. I had just enough time to finish eating before I had to go back to the set, so I glanced at the screen, let the call go to voicemail, ate the rest of my burrito, then listened to the message walking up the street to the location. It was Marshall, at his most irritating.

"*Yo, A-Girl, it's me. Listen, I get that you're busy with the film and all that and I'm sorry but I gotta give ya the heads-up. 'Men R Dawgs' is fading. It started strong but the numbers have been dropping since episode three. It's got the girls at Lily worried, but the thing is, sooner or later, Allwether's gonna find out and worry about whether your TV money is still good collateral. That means he, or somebody like him, will be on your ass. Uh, I mean, on your case. So, keep it together, okay? And uh, have a great day."*

My phone ringing woke me up on Saturday morning. I had forgotten to turn it off when I crawled onto my bed exhausted in my clothes last night and fell asleep. Outside my window it was still dark. Who could be calling me? Tawana? Lenny and Juno? Let me sleep! Thank God today was the last workday of the week. My screen said RON HARDING and 4:57 A.M. The name was vaguely familiar.

"Hello?" I croaked. After a fifty-hour work week I had hardly any voice left.

"Adrienne Monet, please." The voice was familiar, but I was barely awake and couldn't place it.

"Who's this?"

"Ron Harding at The *New York Times.*"

"Ron Harding? Oh, Ron, yes, of course." I'd done an interview with him when '*Men R Dawgs*' dropped, and the piece was positive despite the usual *New York Times* condescension.

"Sorry if I woke you."

"Yeah. We filmed 'til about three o'clock."

"I'm sorry to be calling so early –"

"Uh huh. So what's up?"

"– but I've got to get the story on our website ASAP."

"What story?"

"Egon Swift. He died this morning."

My heart did a drum roll. "Died?"

"I just got confirmation from the hospital and the detectives on the investigation."

"What'd they say?"

"He regained consciousness briefly. Then he died."

"Did he say anything? I mean, anything that would help with the investigation?"

"According to the police, he did."

Adrienne! Stop talking, pack a suitcase, grab your passport, jump in a cab to JFK, get on a plane...

"What'd they say, exactly?"

"'Information pertinent to the investigation.' But they wouldn't say what."

"No, of course not."

"I'd like to ask a couple questions."

In the mirror on the wall I saw myself sitting at the foot of my bed and I didn't know how I got there. My mind was floating free from my body while my stomach was dropping down through my guts.

"Uh, Ron, are we on the record?"

"You haven't said we aren't."

"Okay. Well... This is sad news for everybody on the show. Obviously, we all hoped Egon would recover."

"The police have interviewed people on the production, right?"

"They came to the set a couple times."

"They interviewed Jonathan Lehane?"

"They did. You'll have to ask Jonathan how that went."

"Have they interviewed you?"

"They did. I couldn't tell them much." Danger ahead! Get off the phone! "Ron, I'm sorry to cut this short, but now I've got phone calls to make. I just want to say my heart goes out to his parents and his wife and children."

Stuck with nothing elegiac to say, shameless hypocrisy was all I had to offer.

"Millions of Egon's fans around the world will be heartbroken, but at least they'll have his films to remember him by. This tragedy cuts short what would have been a long and illustrious career." Before I got too disgusted with my-self, I ended the call.

I had caused the death of another human being. Oh my God. Never had nothing, absence, loss, emptiness, felt so real. I called Jonathan but he didn't answer. I didn't want to leave him a message with such awful news. He had been given the weekend off and would either be asleep or on an early train going out to his place in Montauk.

So Egon woke, he gave information pertinent to the investigation, then he died. The police might be coming for me at that very moment. But this would be the worst possible day for me to be arrested. We were going to shoot one of the most emotionally complex scenes of the film, Ibrahim's re-entry into his community at a Brooklyn Islamic center. Six Middle Eastern actors, a dozen Muslim extras from the community, a mostly white male American crew, and torture the unspoken subtext. I might have to work through social tensions on the set on top of the crew's reaction to the news that Egon had died.

I found the TV remote and clicked on *NY1*. Their reporter said Egon had died in the hospital a couple hours ago. The segment flashed through interview excerpts with Egon, candid shots, and clips from his movies. How did they put it together so fast? I turned it off and took refuge in the Eames chair in the corner of the living room, but I couldn't sit still.

I stripped off my moist wrinkled clothes, ran a bath, lowered myself down, and let the heat relax my body. Just as I was slipping into drowsiness, sadness surged up in a huge rush and I came all undone. Was I sobbing over Egon? More than once I'd fantasized what a relief it would be if he died, but now that he had, I was ashamed I'd ever had that thought. He was dead and I'd caused it and I felt terrible about it, even though it had been an accident. Tears for his family? I felt sorry for them, but they would mourn with plenty of support from everyone who wanted to get in on the public circus of grief. No, my bitter tears were for me and my art. Would the world please stop fucking with me and let me make my movie?

That was Day 22, and crew call was 12 noon. While we were lighting for the first shot, I finally reached Jonathan on the phone. He was changing trains at Babylon station.

"You heard the news?"

"Yes."

"Can you talk?"

"Yes. The train's almost empty."

"You're not in Montauk yet?"

"I'm coming back. There were satellite trucks outside my house."

"Oh shit."

"Well, I'm the prime suspect, aren't I? How are you?"

"A lot of media at the location but the movie cops are keeping them away."

"I asked about you."

"What do you think? I just got hit with a huge karmic debt. One day the bill will come due."

"Don't dwell on it."

"According to the police he said something before he died. 'Information pertinent to the investigation,' according to a reporter who called me."

"Well," he was silent for a moment before he continued, "you better just focus on work."

"Do I have a choice?"

"Can I see you later?"

"I'll call you when we wrap. It'll be late."

"I'll wait up for you. You shouldn't be alone tonight."

"Jonathan?"

"Yes?"

"Thank you. For everything."

"Everything?"

"You know what I mean."

E gon's death was front page news, and every story emphasized the lack of progress at finding his killer. After that, nothing happened for several anxious days, until Tuesday evening. I was walking with the shooting crew down Atlantic Avenue in Brooklyn near the Barclay Center to the next location, a storefront we'd dressed as Ibrahim Salaam's travel agency. We were about to film a flashback, the evening he was arrested by the FBI. I checked my messages as I walked.

I found a text from Detective Buddy Ferino asking me to call him. It took a moment before I could calm down and return the call.

"Sorry you lost a friend the other day," he said.

"A bad day for everyone on the show."

"We've got new evidence we want you to look at. Can you come by the precinct? Maybe you can help."

"Tonight?"

"Can you manage it?"

"It'll be late."

"That's all right, I'll be here."

Egon must have named me before he died and Ferino was inviting me to walk into his handcuffs. No, if that was true, the police would have come for me by now. I tried to concentrate on work, but I was on autopilot while my mind was distracted by worry. The only way to stop worrying was to find out what the police knew.

I got to the precinct after midnight. A uniformed officer brought me up to the detective squad room. Ferino was at his desk in shirtsleeves, his tie loosened. He was twirling a pen nervously, and when he saw me, he nodded and tossed it on a folder on the desk blotter. I took off my backpack and coat and dumped them on the chair of an adjoining desk. I tried to appear relaxed and ready to help, but I was so nervous I could hardly stand still.

He looked at his watch. "You people work unbelievable hours."

"It takes time to make anything good."

"We've got some security camera video. I want to get your opinion, since film is your thing."

"What do you want me to do?"

"Just look at it. Tell me what you think."

"Video?" The clock on the precinct wall said 12:08. "How long is it?"

"A few seconds. Less than a minute."

"Oh. So where is it?"

"Right here. On my computer." He rolled another chair around so I could sit next to him. The monitor on his desk was paused on a low-resolution image of a street and building.

"What are we looking at?"

"The camera is on the ground floor of an art gallery on 22nd Street. But in the front window," he put his finger on the screen, "you can see across the street. He tapped his finger. "That's the entrance to Swift's building."

Oh shit. "When's this from?"

"The morning Swift got shot."

I took off my glasses, wiped them and fitted them back on, prepared for a nasty surprise. "Okay."

He fast-forwarded the video. After a couple seconds a shadow jumped back and forth across the screen. He rewound the video past that, then played it again at normal speed.

There I was, in running clothes, backpack, a baseball cap and sunglasses, arriving at Egon's building. I was turned toward the door and there was no chance my face could be recognized. Ferino fast forwarded, and there I was again, coming out of the door. This time I was hurrying, my face was a feature-less blur, and suddenly the video stopped in a freeze frame.

I turned to him. "What happened?"

"The end of the tape," he said, scowling.

"There's not much to go on. Can you play it again?"

"Yeah, sure."

I watched the video again, very aware that Ferino was watching me. Out of all the security cam tape he and Peavey must have looked at he chose this snippet to show me. He obviously thought it was me. So why not say so?

"Hmmm," I said, and shook my head.

"We posted fliers in the neighborhood and witnesses came forward saying they saw this person. But we still don't know who it is."

Witnesses... I asked him to play it again, and I forced myself to stay cool.

"We think it's a female."

I said, "Based on size, on the way they move, it could be a woman, or a small man. Do you know where they went in the building?"

"We're working on that. You said you jogged in the area. Does this person look familiar?"

He was trying to make me sweat.

"I don't remember seeing anybody over-dressed like that. It was really hot that morning."

"I remember. What were you wearing?"

"Why do you ask?" If I was only a witness, why would that be important?

He shrugged. "In case you show up on any of the security videos, I'll know it's you."

Since he'd got me here to mess with my head, I gave it right back to him.

"I was all in white. Shorts, tee shirt. Baseball cap. Sports bra. Little thong sorta thing, y'know?"

He watched my hands at my crotch tracing a 'V'.

"Uh huh. White?"

"Yeah. It was really too hot for jogging that morning."

"Brutal."

"I could've been nude. It still would've been too hot."

I avoided his eye, so he'd feel free to look at me in whatever way he needed.

"But sometimes I need to work up a drenching sweat. It's a purification thing."

He had to drag his eyes back up to meet mine. He turned back to his computer.

"Well, I've gotta go get some sleep," I said. "I hope I've been helpful. Sorry I can't tell you more."

"You look exhausted."

I shrugged, like, why complain?

"Exhausted doing what I love. What could be better?"

Ferino quit out of the video app then swiveled around to face me. "I know what you mean."

"Can I ask you something?"

This was risky, but I couldn't resist.

"What?"

"Before Egon died, did he say anything helpful?"

"He said something we're investigating."

"I won't repeat it."

"No. Can't do it."

I was desperate to know, but I forced myself to drop it.

"Is it hard to watch a person die?"

He considered this, then shrugged. "You've never lost anybody?"

"I've been lucky, I guess. How do you cops do it?"

"Do what?"

"Process violence. The horrible things people do to each other. How do you sleep?"

He picked up the pen and tapped out a beat on the case file on the desk.

"That's what my ex-wife always wanted to know. She thought police work deadens the soul. But it doesn't have to."

"No? What's your secret?"

"Don't get personally involved."

"How is that even possible?"

"Training. If you get involved, you're no longer an effective investigator. Take this case. I have a hunch the answer is right in front of me. I just haven't seen it yet." He stared at me silently for a moment, then at the monitor, and smiled thinly. "But I will. I always do."

That was a bad moment, and I was trying not to show it. Ferino obviously thought he had me figured out. His game playing pissed me off. I got up, tugged on my coat and picked up my backpack.

"If you need my help again, call me."

Before things had a chance to go any further, I said good night. As I left the precinct, I could feel his eyes on my back.

One morning about a week later, a story in the *New York Times* about Harvey Weinstein totally ruined my breakfast. Women ranging from employees of Miramax and the Weinstein Company to some of the biggest female movie stars in the world were coming forward to call Harvey a rapist and a bully. I put the newspaper down, my whole body pounding with each angry heartbeat.

The rage I thought I had under control, the doubts about myself I thought I'd settled, came boiling back, and suddenly I was 18 years old again. I'd already been a sexual opportunist and adventuress for a few years, but the sordid and exciting thing that happened between me and Lenny Victor was on another level entirely. My feelings about it changed from day to day, sometimes hour to hour. At times I was disgusted with myself for letting him fuck me when I found him so physically repulsive. Other times I believed it

mentally toughened me, and to submit to him meant I was daring and sophisticated. At times I felt lucky to be the mistress of such a powerful man
and told myself this was an initiation into a very tough, very exclusive industry. He had the power to help or ruin the career in filmmaking I hungered for.
I thought I'd give him what he wanted, he'd help me, and eventually I'd be out
on my own.

And Lenny did live up to his side of the deal, mostly. He never physically
forced me to do anything. He just made sure I knew what I could gain or lose.
So I kept working for him and having sex with him, telling myself it was a
trade-off, it was just a very adult game, rather than office rape.

But that morning a flood of questions came back. Why didn't I report
him? Report? To whom? I was sure that nobody would listen or care. Or was
it because I felt I owed him something for the jobs he gave me? I was in the
movie business. I was living my dream. I admit it was kind of exciting to be
so secretive and decadent, hiding what I was doing even from Juno, and
maybe that made it so seductive.

Over the six months or so that I was Lenny's hot little secret, I developed
a twisted pride in my ability to be tough, telling myself as I let the hairy beast
fuck me that I had him by the balls, that it was actually me who had the power.
I told myself this was one way a girl with no connections and no training
could get ahead in show business. That all ended long ago, and yet I was still
surprised at the rage I sometimes felt. I restrained the impulse to email the
Weinstein story to Lenny. Just being near him today was going to make it hard
to work.

I was running late. I kicked into my shoes and pulled on my leather jacket.
Ready to pour every ounce of my energy into making a movie, I rushed out
of my apartment building into a frosty October dawn. I looked for the SUV
and my Teamster and production assistant waiting to take me to work.

Instead, I found two squad cars with their lights flashing parked at the
curb behind an unmarked detective sedan. On the sidewalk, four uniformed
cops were standing around talking with Detectives Ferino and Peavey, who
noticed me and started coming over.

Oh my God. My arrest. Here it comes. Janey my PA got to me first, looking indignant.

"Those cops made us park up the block."

"What for?"

Ferino stepped up with Peavey, who held up a piece of paper.

"Good morning officers," I said. "What's up?"

"We have a warrant to search your residence, Miss Monet," Ferino said.

He was all business now. No coy games like video night at the precinct. What a fool I'd been. I should have seen it coming.

Since there was no evidence in my place, I had no reason to be cooperative or polite.

"Why do you want to search my apartment?" I demanded.

"It says why on the warrant. 'Evidence in the murder of Egon Swift.'"

"Oh. So I am a suspect. You've been very evasive on that point, Buddy. What is this —"

Peavey said, "Here's the list –"

I spun on her. "Don't you fucking interrupt me!"

Her face froze. Then I got in her partner's face.

"What is this, Buddy? A fuck you for the help I gave you?"

"This?" Ferino looked me with a self-satisfied gleam in his eyes. "This is us doing our job."

"Your job? What have you been doing for the past six weeks? Big celebrity murder, all this media attention. I'll bet your bosses are screaming for results. And here's poor old Buddy, just trying to do his job."

He chuckled, refusing to be insulted by the likes of me.

Peavey waved the warrant, her voice hard.

"If you have anything on this list and you turn it over, we won't have to mess up your apartment."

"This isn't an investigation," I said to Peavey. "You're using your power as cops to harass me." I turned to him. "Y'know Buddy, maybe if you got laid more often you wouldn't be on such a power trip."

He laughed, or pretended to. Peavey scoffed in disbelief.

"You want to fuck me for real, Buddy? Be a man about it and say so."

That made him angry. "You think this is personal? Go ahead, flatter yourself. Now let us into your place, or we'll kick the fucking door down."

"I'll let you in. After I read the warrant."

It was all there, the running clothes, cap, and sunglasses that I'd worn, my backpack and sneakers, and the gun. When he showed me that video at the precinct, he knew it was me. By now, everything but the gun was probably in a New Jersey landfill or dumped at sea. The search would not turn up what they wanted, but they would wreck my home anyway, and I was already late for work.

"You really think I could have killed Egon?"

Ferino stood there breathing steam in the cold and said nothing. I gave the warrant back to Peavey.

"I don't have a single thing on that list."

I let the police into my apartment. I reached into my shoulder bag, pulled out the mini high-def camcorder I always carried, and gave it to Janey.

"My assistant is going to video the search."

"No she's not," Ferino said.

"Yes, she is."

"The hell she is!"

"Janey, are you getting all this?"

The red light went on. "Rolling," Janey said, holding the camera at shoulder level.

"You," Ferino said. "Stop right now." Janey stepped out of reach and ignored him.

"You can't stop her from filming," I said. "It's legal to video cops doing their job. And you're on my property."

"Okay," he said. "You were warned."

Janey trailed the police, shooting video of the search and ignoring their hostility. I called Tawana and told her I'd be delayed and why. Work on the set was at a standstill without me and money was going up in smoke. But I was afraid that if I left, the cops would plant evidence or copy my computer drives. They tramped around in their heavy shoes, going through my desk and my clothes drawers, emptying my laundry on the bed. I felt violated and furious. But I finally forced myself to let go and leave, because if I didn't, I knew I'd lose it and say or do something to get me in worse trouble and my crew was already falling behind schedule.

I gave Janey my keys and told her to lock up when the police left.

"Watch closely and record anything they take." I hurried down to the street and found my driver. When I got in the car, I called Annie Levy, who flipped out.

"You've been questioned by the police two times already?" Levy said. "They're searching your apartment? For God's sake, why didn't you call me?"

"I don't know what to do in these situations. They've been treating me like a witness. Now it turns out they think I killed Egon."

"You need a criminal defense attorney. I'll make some calls."

"Is that necessary? I'm not guilty of anything."

"I'm giving your cell phone number to an attorney. I know you won't call, so he'll call you."

We were shooting that morning on location on the Upper East Side near Hunter College. The first scene was a walk and talk between Khalil and an American buddy on the sidewalk near Lexington and 68th Street. Then we went around the corner to a coffee shop for a scene with Khalil and his American girlfriend and two classmates. They were important scenes that showed how painfully Khalil was caught between his Muslim identity, the senseless torture that has scarred his father's psyche, and his idealism toward America.

As we trooped over to the coffee shop, I got a text from Janey. "Srch over. Kind of a mess. Nothing taken but your cam. Sorry. C U soon."

We completed the master shot of the coffee shop scene in four takes. Lenny wanted me to break the crew for lunch as scheduled. But the actors were working together beautifully and if I delayed shooting their closeups for a meal break I might lose that chemistry. So I insisted on racking up meal penalty payments to the crew every 15 minutes to finish getting the shots I needed. It also allowed us to start again at the next location after lunch. Just as we broke, my phone rang. The screen said BRUCE BERGER, whoever that was.

"Yeah, Miss Monet, please," a man said, adding, "uh, Adrienne Monet?"

"Who's this?"

"Bruce Berger. Annie Levy says you need a lawyer."

"I didn't think so, but the police searched my apartment this morning."

"She said they already questioned you twice. Is that true?"

"Yes."

"What's the matter with you? Did you not get that you're a suspect? Did they ever treat you like a suspect? Before today, I mean."

"No. Never."

"Ever read you your rights?"

"No. They've been pretty friendly."

"Of course they were friendly. The whole time they were setting you up."

"Yeah okay, I get it. Stupid me, right? Look man, are you gonna help me or keep up this condescending bullshit? I need a lawyer, not a fucking lecture, and I need to find out what happened with the search."

"What did the warrant say? You did read the warrant I hope."

"'Evidence in the death of Egon Swift.' My assistant said they didn't take anything. So maybe they'll leave me alone."

"Don't count on that."

"All right. I guess you're my lawyer. Just don't be this way, okay?"

"I'll make some calls. I can find out how the search turned out. And just so you know, my retainer is fifty thousand dollars," he said. I could hear what was left of my director's fee jingling like so many silver dollars down the drain.

"I'll need time to arrange that."

"I understand. I'll call you later."

I called Marshall, told him what was happening, gave him Berger's phone number, and told him to wire him the retainer.

Berger called back as I was eating lunch with the crew.

"Okay. They searched, and as near as I can tell they got *bupkis*, so you can relax about that," Berger said. "Now listen. Very important. No conversations with the police. They wanna talk to you, they go through me. Got that?"

"This is a very scary situation."

"I'll get you out of it as soon as I can. Oh, and by the way. Somebody named Jonathan Lehane is also a suspect. You know Lehane?"

"We're in a relationship."

"What kind of relationship?"

"Personal and professional."

"What's that mean?"

"We're making a movie. The rest is none of your business."

"I can only work in your behalf with what you give me. Lehane? I know that name from somewhere."

"Off-Broadway."

"Oh really? Well, they've got a warrant to search his place, too."

I tried to warn him, but his voicemail picked up, and "Call me" was my only message. Jonathan was waiting to come to work to play David Sawyer delivering a talk on finance in a lecture hall we'd rented from Hunter College. So, where was he? Were the police already searching his apartment? Had they found the gun? Was he under arrest? Would he show up for work or not? Every five minutes I kept glancing down Lexington Avenue where his dressing room trailer was parked.

I was watching a video playback of the coffee shop scene when the first team P.A. said over the walkie talkie that Jonathan had arrived. I radioed Tawana and told her where I'd be and hurried down the block. His Teamster driver was settling into a folding chair on the sidewalk with the *Daily News* open to the sports pages and Jonathan was letting a pair of middle-aged women take selfies. He seemed cheerful and untroubled.

I followed him into his trailer. He dropped his backpack and turned to me with a smile and appeared to be relaxed, open-hearted, and ready to work. It killed me to have to spoil that.

"Hey there beautiful," he said.

I took him by the hand and pulled him back through the motor home to the bedroom in the rear with him laughing "Hey! Hey! Hey!" I shut the door and went around checking that the windows were closed. Amused, he slouched back on the bed.

Quietly I said, "Did the cops search your place today?"

"What?" He looked at me like I was crazy. "No, nobody searched –"

"Did you get rid of the gun?"

Now he was stressed, tense. "Why? What's wrong?"

"Did you get rid of the gun?"

"Why are you asking me that?"

"The police have a warrant to search your apartment."

He stood up abruptly. "Who says they have a warrant?"

"My lawyer."

"Why do you have a lawyer?"

"Because they searched my place this morning."

He blinked. "Oh shit."

"Did you get rid of the gun?"

I could see he didn't want to talk about it. But he really had to.

"No."

"What? You said you would!"

"I'm keeping the gun."

"Jesus Christ, Jonathan, why?"

He backed away from me and stood against the wall, hands in his pockets.

"I'm not going to destroy evidence. That's a line I refuse to cross. And you need to know that."

"But you already lied to them."

"I lied to them to protect us. But now I have to keep the gun whether I want to or not."

"Because you lied, you – that doesn't make any sense."

I hated the way I sounded, like a perplexed adult scolding a child, but I couldn't help it.

"The gun is well-hidden. They'll never find it."

"What are you talking about? Jonathan –"

"Suppose they arrest you? Suppose your lawyer talks you into telling them the truth? If they come to me for the gun and I tell them I lied to them, then I threw it away, I could go to jail."

He'd thought about the situation and now we had new boundaries. That scared me worse than anything else that had happened that morning.

"So where is it?"

"Stop asking me about the gun."

I was making him angry and killing the relaxation he needed for work, but I couldn't stop myself.

"I'm trying to help you. You're a murder suspect."

"Thanks to you. And now you are, too."

"Yeah, but I'm not the one who lied about owning a gun."

"No, you're the one who actually killed somebody with it."

"If the police find it, they'll think you lied about everything. They'll think you shot Egon."

"But I didn't, did I?" I didn't want to think about what he was implying.

"The police have the bullet from Egon's body by now. If they search your place and they find the gun they'll match the bullet to it."

"Yeah, I watch television too. I know how that works."

"So will you please go home and get rid of the gun?"

"Shut up about the gun!"

"Ssshh!"

"They're not going to find it!"

"That notebook you're always writing in. What about that?"

"What about it?"

"Where is it?"

"It's here in my backpack."

"Did you write about any of this?"

"I write when I need to make sense of things," he said, his voice telling me to mind my own business.

He pulled out his phone and dialed.

"Who are you calling?"

"My lawyer." On the phone he said, "It's Jonathan, hi, is he in? It's important." I grabbed his hand holding the phone.

"Please don't tell anyone what I did." I hadn't begged for anything in a long time and I hated the way I sounded.

He pulled his hand away. "I told you I won't. Go back to the set. I need privacy."

"Maybe your lawyer can go there and remove the gun."

"Oh sure. Then he can be guilty of hiding evidence, too."

He stared at me for a long moment, weighing his loyalty to me against his self-interest.

"Go back to the set, Adrienne."

I left him alone. When the time came, we shot his scene in a lecture hall, four angles and a few reaction shots of the students. As he spoke, the one or two times he faltered, seemingly confused about what he wanted to say, might've been caused by the distress I'd caused him.

As the crew set up lighting for the final shot of the lecture scene, I went to see him in his trailer. I was clearly not welcome, but I couldn't stay away.

"Did you talk to your lawyer?"

"Yes. They sent an associate to babysit the search."

"What were they looking for?"

"A gun."

"Really?"

"Yes."

"Was that all?"

"Just a gun."

"Did they find it?"

"No. He said it was an intense search and they made a huge mess, but they left empty-handed."

I was hit by a wave of relief so powerful I had to sit down. He stared at me and offered me no comfort at all.

That night he called me while I was still shooting. He was hurt and furious.

"They wrecked the place!"

"I'm so sorry."

"Come over after wrap. We need to talk."

"Why?" That worried me. "Why? What happened?"

"Not now." He hung up.

When I got there, he was standing in his bathrobe in the middle of an apartment that had been hit by a tornado.

He looked like he needed a hug.

"Are you okay?"

He ignored my outstretched arms, lifted a stack of books off the carpet, and put them back one by one on the shelves. He didn't want me there to talk, he wanted me to see the damage. He mocked me, muttering, "Are you okay?

Are you okay?" I stepped back and walked through the apartment, appalled at the mess.

Thank God he'd ignored me and hadn't come here when the police were ransacking the place. He would have lost it. Piles of his belongings were dumped everywhere. Furniture cushions were stacked in the middle of the floor. In the bedrooms, closets hung open, clothes lay in heaps all over, dresser drawers were pulled out and left open. In the kitchen, food from the refrigerator had been left out to spoil, food in boxes and cans and china from his kitchen cabinets sat on the counters, the floor, and the island, and all the lights had been left blazing. The glass door to the wine cabinet had been left open a few inches and a broken wineglass lay in the sink.

"What a mess. Jonathan, I'm so sorry –"

"They couldn't find the gun. So they took it out on my beautiful home."

"I'm so sorry." I put a hand on his shoulder, but he shrugged it off. "So where's the gun?"

He gave me a furious look.

"They didn't find it. That means we can still get rid of it."

"I already told you why I can't."

"Is it too much to ask for a little peace of mind?"

"What?" He turned and glared at me. "How dare you ask me for that? I'm a murder suspect! To the police! To the world! Thanks to you!"

"Jonathan..." I sat on the arm of a sofa, deflated. "This is not the relationship I want to have with you. When do we get back to normal?"

At first it felt like an anxious attempt at sexual healing. I didn't resist when he led me to the bedroom, pushed me onto his bed, and pulled off my jeans and underwear. I peeled off the rest of my clothes, then his bathrobe and pants. He was already aroused. He held me by my head, fucked my mouth, lowered me on my back, and rammed his anger into me, pushing me over the edge into terror and ecstasy. I was scared and I was turned on, all at once, excited by my power to provoke such aggression from this ordinarily gentle man. Just as my adrenaline peaked, as I was swept by orgasm and running with tears and sweat, he seized my hips and threw me on my belly and pushed my legs apart with his knees. He spit noisily, warm wetness dripped between my butt cheeks and I felt a slippery finger shoved roughly up my ass.

"No!" I yelled, my face in the pillow. "No way!"

His hand on my back pressed me down, pinning me to the bed. My arms were free, and I flailed backward, but he wouldn't let me up. He had his cock in his hand and he was trying to push it into me and tightening my ass made it hurt even worse. For a moment I was paralyzed by fear. The gun! The bedside table drawer was just out of reach.

He raised himself up to push harder. I swung back wildly with my elbow into his belly and knocked the wind out of him.

"Ow, Jesus Christ!" he gasped, and rolled back, enough for me to squirm free and pull myself out from under him. He grabbed me by the forearm. I kicked him in the chest and twisted away. He lost his grip and I rolled off and fell on the carpet.

I lunged for the bedside table and tore open the drawer. There was no gun.

He looked at the drawer, then at me, in disbelief.

"You're lucky it's not there."

He was speechless. Maybe he was thinking about what happened to the last man who tried to assault me. I grabbed my clothes up off the floor and started dressing hurriedly, shaking.

"You bastard! How dare you treat me like that?" He was kneeling on the bed, doubled over like he was going to be sick. I stood over him, fists clenched, and screamed. "How dare you? How fucking dare you?"

"I'm sorry," he said, rubbing his chest.

"Not good enough."

"Would you have shot me?"

I was outraged. Nothing mattered, not even a movie that was only half finished. I hissed in his face.

"If you were me, what would you do?"

"You once said you like to be forced a little. You said it excites you."

I couldn't believe what I was hearing.

"You don't see the difference?" I backed up to the doorway.

He stared at me, bewildered and speechless.

"Forcing me to give you pleasure, that's one thing," I said. "It's not the same as trying to degrade me because you're angry."

He shook his head. "I wish I'd never met you."

"You fucking ingrate! Thanks to me, you got your role of a lifetime back!" I kicked on my shoes. "And this is how you thank me!?"

I grabbed my coat and backpack on my way out of the apartment. He kept calling me to come back, each time sounding weaker and more contrite. I went home and found that the police had also left my apartment a shambles.

Then with 12 days of shooting left I hit the wall, energy overdrawn. I knew I was in trouble one morning on Stage A, when it was time to rehearse a scene between Ibrahim and his wife Niesha in the Salaam Apartment kitchen set. I sat in the video monitor tent, quietly panicking, because I could not comprehend my handwritten notes in the margins of my script. My best ideas about subtext, character intention, camera placement, all in my neat handwriting, may as well have been graffiti. I was literally too beat to read or remember my own ideas. Did my mind need to shut down that badly? Apparently, yes. I closed my eyes and tried to imagine my way back into the character's hearts and minds. But my brain was a muscle pushed beyond its limit, and I almost fell asleep. Before crew call, I'd gone to the gym and tried to power myself out of my weariness and I exercised too hard. I burned up all my physical and mental energy. I dragged myself to work feeling weak and empty inside. Now my script notes to myself were just scribbles. Who wrote this? What did that mean?

On the brink of becoming too crazed to sit still, I finally told myself to stop worrying about how to hide my inadequacy. I had two fine actors, Hussein Hirari and Abdeela Nor, who would play the scene as it should be played. Trust, Adrienne, trust! Still, for celestial insurance, I was just about to ask God for the strength to get through the day when a gentle hand touched my shoulder.

"Adrienne?" It was my set assistant Janey, looking concerned. "Those cops are back, and they're looking for you."

"Tell them I'm not available."

I tried to go back to mental preparation. Janey turned around to deliver the message, but the detectives walked right past her to get to me.

"Let's go, Miss Monet," Detective Ferino said brusquely.

"Go where?"

"To the precinct for questioning."

"My lawyer's name is Bruce Berger. You're supposed to call –"

"We're not making an appointment with your social secretary. Let's go."

"I can't leave now. I'm working."

"Not our problem."

"We break for lunch in three hours. I can talk to you then. Or you can ask me your questions now."

"I said, let's go."

"Come back in three hours."

I turned back to my reading.

"Now Miss Monet."

"If I leave, production stops. Every day of shooting costs more than you make in a year."

"Not our problem."

"Eight thousand three hundred thirty-three dollars an hour. One hundred thirty-eight dollars a minute. That's what it costs to shoot this film."

"Never mind the math lesson. Let's go."

"Why are you harassing me, Buddy?"

"My name is Detective Ferino. We have questions. They can't wait."

"Can't we talk in my office?"

"Detective Peavey, put the cuffs on Miss Monet." Peavey held her handcuffs up and stood there waiting. I glanced behind her; flashing the handcuffs caused several crew members to whip out their phone cameras.

"You can't cut me three hours slack, so all these people don't have to stand around waiting for me?"

"No."

"I have to call my lawyer."

"From the car. Let's go."

I stood up and put the script down on my chair.

"Janey, tell Tawana and Lenny and Juno about this, please." Then I said, as level and calm as possible, "Okay, let's get this over with."

Berger took over an hour to arrive, $8,333 worth of my time. My legal savior, five foot eight and slim, looked like a fortyish assassin of Mediterranean heritage with thinning black hair and a thick moustache, dressed in an impeccably cut blue suit, white shirt, and black and gold striped tie.

In the precinct corridor, he listened to me, nodding, his mouth pursed tight.

"I've already answered their questions. I've been totally cooperative."

"Yeah, that was a big mistake," he said. "Of course you didn't know you were making a mistake. They count on that."

"They asked me for my help."

He grimaced in disbelief. "Why would you want to help them?"

"They're investigating the killing of my friend."

"You mean the killing they're trying to put you in jail for? Okay, alright, you didn't know that at the time. By the way, when did you realize you were a suspect?"

If I said it was from the start, he'd think I was an even bigger fool.

"I guess when they searched my apartment."

"And up 'til then, did the police read you your rights, or give you any indication you were a suspect?"

"Never."

"Did they say you could refuse to talk?"

"No."

"Or that you could have a lawyer present?"

"No. And now they just pulled me off the set and put my crew behind schedule. We're bleeding money. What they're doing is harassment. Watch the male detective. He's got a weird thing for me."

"Okay. Let's see what they've got."

The green walls of the small interrogation room smelled from a recent paint job. The cold glare from the fluorescent lights and the stench of plaster dust and drying paint irritated my eyes and nose. A large mirror, which I assumed was a one-way window, took up part of one wall. It creeped me out, not knowing how many people were behind it watching me. A video camera on a wall mount was pointing straight at me, red light blinking. It wasn't the camera angle I would have chosen. Was I in close-up? What did the camera see in my face?

"Interview of Adrienne Monet," Ferino recited for the benefit of the video. "Present are Detectives Artemis Peavey and Buddy Ferino, and Miss Monet's attorney Bruce Berger."

Ferino read the Miranda card.

"Do you understand these rights as I have explained them to you, Miss Monet?"

"Yes."

"With these rights in mind as I've explained them to you, are you willing to talk to us at this time?"

I looked at my attorney and Berger nodded.

"Yes." Peavey gave me a card and I signed it.

The way Berger stood up to the detectives was encouraging.

"Let's get a couple things on the record," he told them. "In your prior interviews with Miss Monet you misled her into thinking she was only a witness."

"Nobody was misled," Ferino replied. "At that time that's all she was."

"Since you never informed her of her rights, none of what she said is admissible, so just forget about anything she told you."

Peavey scoffed, "We don't need you to tell us that."

"There's been so much deceit and bad faith from you people I'm tempted to advise her to say nothing. But taking her away from work is causing her a financial hardship, which I know you're well aware of. So, if answering any new questions will help catch whoever shot Mister Swift, and get her back to work, let's get on with it."

"That's what we're trying to do."

Ferino leaned forward, his palms up, as if they held the simple truth.

"We know Swift and your boyfriend Lehane had issues. Swift fired Lehane. Next day Swift got shot. Couple days later, you've got Swift's job and your boyfriend is back in the movie."

He paused, but he got nothing from me.

Peavey said, "Can you see where that might catch our attention, Miss Monet?"

"No."

"Lehane says he never went near Swift's office that morning. But you told us you were a couple blocks away. We have a video of a person entering and leaving the building that could be you."

"Whoa whoa, wait wait," Berger said, looking at me aghast. "What video?"

"It's on You Tube," Peavey said, handing him her phone.

Berger watched it, then nodded and smirked.

"Yeah, okay. This is bullshit. You can't even tell if they're male or female."

Ferino said, "No signs of forcible entry at the crime scene. That tells me Swift let somebody into his office. Somebody he knew, somebody he felt safe with. Maybe somebody he worked with. He was found on the floor near the elevator. It looks like he was shot trying to stop somebody from leaving. We think that somebody was you."

"I didn't hear a question," Berger said.

"Miss Monet?"

"I didn't hear a question."

"If I'm right," Ferino laced his fingers together on the table, "Lehane gave you a gun and you went there to kill Swift and get you and Lehane back on the movie shoot. The fact that you didn't, and you were trying to leave, tells me you couldn't go through with it. That's in your favor. That doesn't surprise me, either. I don't believe you're a cold-blooded killer."

"Still no question," Berger said.

"I can think of other possibilities," Ferino said. "We know Swift was loaded on crystal meth. So maybe this wasn't your fault. What happened? Did he get violent with you?"

"I wasn't there."

"Maybe you had an argument," Ferino continued. "More of those famous 'creative differences.' But he was cranked up on meth, and he got out of hand. You felt threatened. You protected yourself."

"I wasn't there."

"Detective, Miss Monet is telling you she wasn't there. If you have evidence she was, let's hear it."

"Where'd you get the gun?" Ferino said.

"What gun?" Berger said.

"We know you got it from your boyfriend Lehane. He already confirmed that for us."

I couldn't stop myself.

"Bullshit."

"Oh no it's not. He told us a lot about you. He's scared. Scared of you."

"Miss Monet," Berger said. "Don't let him in your head."

"You think you've got this thing sewed up tight," Ferino said. "You even covered yourself with a voicemail in case anybody knew you were gonna see Swift that morning."

He was so right about so much of what happened it was scary. I could believe he was an investigator with special gifts.

"What's the question, detective?" Berger said.

"I can't get over the fact that you've got Swift's job."

"I told you how that happened."

"What I mean is, I'm surprised you're in the movie business at all," he said, reading his notes in a folder of paperwork on the table in front of him. "I think you know what I mean, Bobbie Jean. Bobbie Jean Blivka? From South Brunswick, New Jersey? Daughter of a New Brunswick city cop and a nurse at Middlesex General Hospital. Bobbie Jean Blivka. That's your real name, isn't it? Blivka?"

A cold feeling spread inside me. I closed my eyes, took a deep breath.

"My name is Adrienne Monet."

"Well, it wasn't Adrienne Monet who got raped when she was seventeen, was it? Had a baby girl at Middlesex General Hospital and gave it up for adoption?"

"Detective Ferino," Berger cut in angrily. Ferino ignored him. It took everything I had to contain myself. Peavey avoided my eye.

"According to something called the IMDB, Adrienne Monet, supposedly the daughter of a French diplomat, used to be a hot filmmaker. But then you didn't direct a movie in like ten years. Must've been a real comedown for a talent like you. I mean, you used to be a star. Lately all you've done is a little crappy reality TV. Then along comes Egon Swift, and whatta you know, he gets shot, and you get his job."

"I earned that job, motherfucker!"

Ferino reeled backward, feigning shock. He looked at Berger as if to say, better put a muzzle on this mad dog before she bites someone. Berger leaned in to say something to me, but I waved him away.

"After the producers hired me to take over directing the film, I went to the head of the studio. I convinced him to let us keep shooting. I saved a lot of jobs. The production was on time and on budget. Until you showed up today to harass me."

"Poor you," Ferino said.

"Fuck you." I came half out of my chair, but Berger gripped my arm and I sat back down.

"Detective Ferino," Berger said, "if you can't control your personal animus towards my client —"

"It's a professional animus. Toward murderers."

"She's done talking," Berger said. "Charge her with a crime or let her go."

A female uniformed officer came to the door and nodded to Ferino.

"We're not done yet," Ferino said. "A witness has come forward. He can identify the person of interest in the video I showed you. We need you to stand in a line-up."

"Forget that," Berger said.

So that was why they'd brought me to the precinct. Somebody must've seen me on West 22nd Street that morning. I was careful not to show how much I wanted to get up and run out of there.

Ferino ignored my lawyer. "Look Bobbie Jean —"

"My name is Adrienne Monet."

He spoke softly, with an intimacy that was creepy.

"You say you have nothing to hide. Prove it."

I said, "When you showed me that video, you couldn't even tell if it was a man or a woman."

Peavey said, "Before Swift died, he said the person who shot him was female."

Maybe they were lying, maybe not.

"Did he name Miss Monet?" Berger demanded.

"We'll get to that," Ferino said.

"I didn't think so."

"Our witness says the person in the video walked past him while he was out walking his dog."

"A dog walker? Totally unreliable," Berger said. "Their attention is on their pet, not their surroundings."

"We think he's a solid witness. So Bobbie Jean, how about it? If you pass, we'll have no reason to investigate you any longer."

"You have no reason to investigate me now."

"You'll be home free." He sat back and shrugged. "Or, we can question you all day. All night, if necessary."

I wished I hadn't told the police what a delay in shooting would cost.

"I have to get back to work," I said to Berger. "And I want this thing over with."

"Wrong I.D.'s happen all the time. So do wrongful convictions."

"I'll risk it."

"I advise against it, Miss Monet."

"I'll pass, I promise. Let's just do this and get out of here, Bruce. Please?"

He sighed and shook his head.

"I can't lose a whole day of shooting. We're on a low budget. It would be a financial disaster."

"They know that, and they're playing you," Berger said.

Berger was right, I should refuse. Did I see a dog walker that morning? I couldn't remember. If the witness identified me the police might arrest me, based on an iffy match to the video and the assumption that I went to Egon's office that morning. But if the witness didn't identify me, maybe the police would leave me alone. One thing was for sure. I was wearing a black and white polka dot mid-thigh jersey shift, under a knee-length black cotton jacket with low heels on my feet, I was definitely not dressed for jail. I missed my chance earlier. I should've prayed for an easy day.

"How long will this take?"

Nobody answered me. Berger just shrugged, resigned to watching me make a big mistake.

A policewoman took my jacket and my necklace of large black beads and helped me pin up my hair. She gave me a hoodie to pull on. The sunglasses and cap I put on were also like those I wore that morning. I shuffled into the room with four other women. I was shocked to see they all were either taller or heavier than me. We faced a large wall mirror in which I looked very different than the others, and I realized the line-up had been rigged so that I'd stand out. I began to wish I'd listened to my lawyer. Breathe, I reminded myself. Breathe and relax, believe in your innocence, and everything will be fine.

From a speaker on the wall came Ferino's voice. "Turn left," then "Turn right." He asked one of the women to step forward, then back. Then he asked number three to step forward, and it took a couple seconds for me to realize that was me. I did as I was asked. I turned left and right when asked, then stood still, waiting. What was happening behind that mirror? He didn't make the first woman stand out so long, and he never told me to get back in line.

The door at the end of the room opened. I closed my eyes, expecting to feel my arms seized and handcuffs snapped on my wrists. But a policewoman walked us out and collected our sweatshirts and hats and glasses and gave me my necklace. I went back to the interrogation room, expecting the worst.

Sitting silent at the conference table, Peavey was closing the file. Beside her, Ferino had his head down, quietly frustrated.

"You're free to go, Miss Monet," Peavey said.

"What'd the witness say?"

Berger, standing in front of me holding his attaché case, grinned down at Ferino.

"I believe he said, 'Sorry, they all look the same.'"

Ferino stood up and leaned across the table toward me.

"Either you were after his job, or else you argued, it got out of hand, and you shot him. Either way, the man is dead." Peavey looked up at him, surprised at this outburst. "You shot Egon Swift. And then you hooked back up with your boyfriend and went on with life like nothing ever happened."

"Enough, detective," Berger said. "We're outa here Miss Monet."

But Ferino and I had locked eyes.

"I don't need to kill anybody to get a job."

"You're not what you seem, Bobbie Jean."

"Takes one to know one, Buddy."

"The name is Detective Ferino."

"Detective Ferino, you've got a very vivid imagination," I said as Berger pulled me toward the exit. "You ought to be writing movies."

I hurried out of the precinct. All I wanted to do was get back to work. My Teamster had the SUV idling at the curb and my assistant Janey was in the back seat.

"Thanks for everything," I said to Berger.

"You might be okay for the moment. If they had enough evidence to arrest you, they would've."

"Let's hope this is the end of it," I said, putting on my sunglasses against the brilliant autumn sunshine.

"Not likely. High profile case, celebrity victim, celebrity suspect. They're under a lot of pressure."

"Speaking of pressure, I have to get back to work. This downtime is gonna cost me personally almost twenty thousand dollars."

"Then I'll make this brief. I will no longer act as your attorney, Miss Monet," Berger said.

"What? You're quitting?"

"I'll return what's left of your retainer after I bill for today's work."

"Why?"

"Because you didn't listen to me."

"Who knows better than me what I did and didn't do?"

"That's not the point! You're enmeshed in the justice system now. On the best of days, unfair and illogical things happen in that system and innocent people get hurt. You're in deep shit Adrienne, and you need a lifeguard. But the greatest attorney in New York can't help you if you don't listen."

"I've never been in a mess like this."

"All the more reason to listen to your attorney. When you find one."

"I want you."

"Sorry."

"I didn't get how serious this is until now. Stay as my lawyer, Bruce. Please? I'll listen to you. I promise."

A black Mercedes driven by a burly chauffeur pulled up and stopped. Traffic behind it stalled. Angry horns blew.

"Find another lawyer." His mouth pursed in a sour twist. "But if they come after you again, and you don't have anybody yet, call me."

He got in his car, nodded to the driver, and took off.

Once I was in the SUV and we were zipping through the streets of Chelsea toward the Piers, I called Tawana and told her I was coming. A few minutes later we pulled into the parking garage and I ran up the back stairway to our sound stages two steps at a time. When I called out a hey-hey, I got a lot of grins and finger wags from the crew – the neighborhood bad girl was back. Lenny and Juno greeted me with raised eyebrows and came towards me, but I waved them away.

"Don't worry! Everything's okay!"

I told Tawana to give me ten minutes then bring the actors to the set for rehearsal. I made my way out of the soundstage area and down the corridor.

I locked myself in my office. I lit a cigarette from the pack in my desk and smoked it, pacing.

Bobbie Jean Blivka! Nobody had called me that in thirty years, except once when I went down the Shore for the funeral of a favorite cousin. Ferino's sneer when he said that name unlocked my worst memories, like soiled clothes spilling out of a cheap plastic suitcase: frightening mass at the Slovak Catholic church on winter Sundays, followed by suffocating afternoons trapped in my grandparents' tiny house in New Brunswick, jammed with overstuffed furniture and stinking of fried schnitzel and cigarette smoke, Grandma Blivka hollering from the kitchen in a guttural incomprehensible language, my Slovakian grandfather ignoring her, sitting drunk with my father silently staring at a football game on the television, while my mother sat silently in a corner drinking herself blotto.

I'd always known somebody would dig up my past someday. The reality was that Bobbie Jean Blivka died at eighteen years old when I left the dead-end town where, through some cosmic mistake, I endured childhood and youth as the oddball daughter of two useless parents. The day after high school graduation I escaped to New York and started life over again. I became Adrienne Monet, filmmaker, New Yorker, a citizen of the world, now and forever. I'd done everything I could to become an artist and a person of substance and style. So what if some macho cop found out about my past? In his mind he probably thought my ability to recreate myself in a new identity meant that I was a phony, a role-player, a liar, certainly guilty of something.

The cops might track down my parents and my brother. But none of them knew anything about my life since I left home. Without his Army or police uniform, my father was a spineless nobody, a petty dictator too lifeless to hold my mother's interest, who finally quit being so Catholic and divorced her for her flagrant adulteries. He was living in Sarasota on his cop's pension, working as a security guard at an apartment building and waiting for his hard, frightened heart to fail.

I always thought my mother was the one who was headed for tragedy. She'd been a beautiful, brilliant, adventurous girl eager to escape her suffocating South Jersey town and see the world. She thought her marriage to the handsome Army lieutenant she met at a Fort Dix Christmas dance would free her from a boring life in the Pine Barrens. But life with my father became one dreary Army base after another, crummy housing and the company of dull Army wives, and she got pregnant before she could escape. By the time my brother and I were in high school she'd turned into a castrating, promiscuous drunk who deserted my father and took me to live with her and a series of worthless boyfriends that she wore out and discarded. I spent my teen years either listening to her whine about my father's shortcomings or criticizing and ridiculing me. I finally gave up on her forever the day I woke up in the hospital after being beaten up and raped by one of her boyfriends. As I came out of the drugs, there she was, standing over me in her nurse's scrubs with a twisted rueful grin, chewing mint gum to hide the booze on her breath, gripping my hand and shaking her head.

"Johnny wants you to know he's so sorry for what he did," she cooed. "He's going to rehab to straighten himself out. I doubt he'll be around much anymore."

I cut her out of my life and out of my heart. I was sure she'd come to ruin, probably in some cocktail lounge on Route 9 so dimly-lit her age wouldn't show right away to whoever she picked up for a cheap thrill, and she'd die at the hands of some loser in a by-the-hour motel. But no — instead, she embraced AA, stayed sober, and was living comfortably with her Jewish psychoanalyst husband in Highland Park across the river from New Brunswick. She'd reached out to me many times and tried to run the repentant parent number on me, making amends and asking for forgiveness, especially after I became famous. But Mom sober was just as dangerous as Mom drunk, so I stayed a ghost.

The one I really missed was my brother Kent, who'd changed his name from Blivka to Butler, married his boyfriend, and was teaching literature at San Francisco State. I resisted the occasional urge to call him for fear we would drag each other down the rathole to our past and wallow in a swamp of shame. I had his address and his phone numbers and email address, and he had mine. I just hoped he was happy.

I stubbed out the cigarette. Desperate to vanquish those memories, I took off my glasses and did a brief victory dance, then dropped to my knees, pounded the sofa with my fists, and wept with relief. I beat Ferino in his interrogation, I beat him in the lineup, and I got the last word. Emptied of pain, at peace, I got up and put my glasses on, checked the time, and headed back to the stage, newly energized.

The crew worked hard but we still wrapped two hours behind schedule. We would make that up before Day 45, but it still pissed me off that the police could do what they did. Love me or hate me, that's all fair, but don't fuck with my work. When I got home that night, instead of going to bed I sat brooding in my living room. What gave the police the right to waste $16,000 of my time? Was it just me, or didn't Ferino let it get weirdly personal when it ended in embarrassment for him? He couldn't arrest me, and I hoped he was so frustrated that he couldn't sleep.

I couldn't resist. I had to hit him back somehow. I dialed his cell phone.

"Hello?"

"Hello, Buddy." I kept my voice warm, languid. "Was today as good for you as it was for me?"

An incredulous grumble.

"What are you callin' me for?"

I laughed, low, intimate, like pillow-talk.

"The interrogation? The line up? The little tiff we had? I thoroughly enjoyed all that. And I know you did, too."

"You don't know anything about me."

"I know you're desperate to put handcuffs on me. Is that how you like your women, Buddy? In handcuffs?"

"Were you listening? You don't know me."

"That's why I'm calling. Help me understand this obsession you have with me."

"That's easy, Bobbie Jean. I'm a cop. You're a killer."

"Then why aren't I under arrest?"

"I'll take your confession any time you're ready."

"There's nothing to confess, except how much I pity you."

A chuckle, tinged with acid.

"You were undressing me with your eyes the whole time I was there. You've got a thing for me. Everybody else saw it too."

"What thing? I'm gonna put you in jail. That's the thing."

"Oh Buddy... you can lie to yourself, but you can't lie to me. I know what you want. In fact, right now I'm lying in bed with my legs wide open, and my hand on it."

"And of all people, you called me. I'm honored."

"Mmm, this feels so good."

"I'll bet it does."

"C'mon man," I said, between a laugh and a moan. "Talk dirty to me. You know you want to."

"Get some therapy, Bobbie Jean." Under his breath, I just barely heard him mutter, "Bitch!" as he hung up.

After that I worked for a while without fear of arrest. My energy was back, and I was relaxed and patient and looking forward to the shooting days ahead. One night when we wrapped early, I released my driver and traded a precious hour's sleep for a glass of wine and a few laughs with Tawana at a bar off Broadway near the 72nd Street subway station. Just one glass, but when we hugged and parted company I was feeling bold. Strolling toward the subway station, I gave in to the urge to call Detective Ferino.

"You again?" Traffic and street sounds echoed behind him. "What's the matter, Bobbi Jean? You just can't stay away?"

"I got my camcorder back today. The video'll be part of my assistant's NYU law thesis in unconstitutional police tactics, and of course if I ever decide to sue for invasion of privacy, it'll come in handy. So thank you for giving it back, especially since you had no right to take it in the first place."

"I had every right," he said, bored and impatient.

"Not according to the law."

No reply.

"But I think you're that kind of cop, Buddy. A real boundary jumper. A cop who thinks he can ignore the rules. You haven't hung up on me yet. Does that mean you recovered from getting told off? No hard feelings?"

"I have no feelings for you at all, Bobbie Jean."

"Did you see yourself in the video? Searching my apartment?"

"What're you talking about?"

"You have real screen presence. Has anybody ever told you that?"

"Oh yeah. I was just talking about that with Al Pacino."

"Real charisma."

"Why do you keep calling me?"

"Because you're bungling the investigation into the murder of my friend Egon Swift."

"We're making steady progress."

"What kind of progress?"

"No comment."

"Oh Buddy. Why are you so afraid to make real contact with me? All I want is information. Is that too much to ask?"

Silence.

"I tried to help you catch whoever killed my friend, and what did I get? You treated me like a criminal, searching my apartment, accusing me of murder, for God's sake. You need to work on better self-control."

Silence.

"Well Buddy, if you ever get any actual evidence, you know where I am."

"I always know where you are." He hung up.

I put away my phone, laughing to myself at the risky head games I was playing with this cop. Then at the subway steps I saw him, sitting in his car parked across Broadway, staring at me.

Production of *"Lonely Sky"* was a few days away from finishing when an email from Marshall popped up in my Inbox marked "Urgent! Important '*Men R Dawgs*' Request."

I knew right away what it would say. The Lily girls had been worried about the series after its weak start, so I'd tried to help and did some more interviews. Then in the past couple weeks the show began to pick up a lot more viewers, but not because of my help. The social and cultural climate had radically shifted, influenced by #MeToo, and turned my trashy little TV show into a hit. Entertainment writers were saying the show was "of the moment." Writers and bloggers, Tweeters and talking heads all over America attacked, praised, analyzed, and spun think pieces on the show's place in the Zeitgeist. I sat for a profile in the *Times* Style Section that had the irritating headline, "Is Adrienne Monet a feminist, or does she just hate men?" Viewers wrote comments on the web pages for the series, the Lily Channel, and Alpha Bitch Productions, saying they liked the show's vulgar, guilty-pleasure, thumb-in-your-eye comedy, which was what I'd aimed for.

Most important, the sudden eruption of stories about my show of the moment brought an avalanche of subscribers to the Lily Channel. Despite this welcome windfall to my sisters and co-conspirators at the network, their promo people kept bugging me to do even more media. I kept telling Marshall to remind them I was shooting a movie, but he was no help, he kept nagging me to keep them happy. According to him, the Lily girls complained I was standoffish and hard to work with.

So after I read his email, I called him.

"Remind them that I raised Lily's brand recognition, brought in a lot of new subscribers, and got everybody writing about the show. Tell them I want to help, but I don't have the time."

"*Men R Dawgs*" was having an unexpected cultural moment. *Schadenfreude*-loving viewers enjoyed the weekly cuckolding and shaming of two mortified husbands. News junkies were drawn to the social media trash fire. Oddly enough, a certain kind of twisted male viewer who hated the show watched it to further inflame his misogyny. My ridicule of the male libido had inspired a barrage of troll emails from men who talked crazy and threatened violence, including a bomb threat to the Lily Channel headquarters in Manhattan from a group calling itself the Incel Justice Brigade. I'd seen stories about the group, but I just couldn't imagine any man being so hopeless that he'd publicly blame women because he couldn't get laid.

All that controversy really boosted the show. But to have my face back in the media and to be known as 'The *Men R Dawgs* Bitch' made me nervous. I didn't like being talked and speculated about by so many people who thought they could read my mind. I had no desire to be trolled, threatened, doxxed, stalked, harassed, cursed, or to find a mail bomb on my desk one day. One essayist gushed over me for producing a show that had "perfectly caught the Zeitgeist," which was ridiculous, because it was the eruption of female indignation and reckoning that turned my vulgar TV show into a guilty pleasure for enough people to pull it back from a premature death in the ratings.

Thursday night after we wrapped shooting at the Piers, I was packing to leave. I was eager to go home and sleep, when Jonathan came knocking at my office door.

"I need to speak with you."

Since the night I'd fought him off he'd kept away from me except on the set. No calls, no flirts, no dates, no attempts at make-up sex. He came to work, performed brilliantly, and went quietly away. All my scenes as Josephine had been shot so I would no longer perform with him. His work was as rich and moving as ever, but he was aloof and that worried me. In the distance that had opened up between us I was no longer sure I could trust him or know where his head was at. Was he contrite? Or still angry with me? I couldn't tell. We'd never talked about what had happened. Now, leaning on my office doorjamb, he wasn't looking me in the eye.

"It's urgent."

We walked to a deserted seating area in the public park at the river end of Pier 62 and took a table. A chill rose from the swirling waters of the Hudson as we huddled in our coats. I was focused on his every twitch or shift of the eyes, wondering what was so urgent. Had he done something drastic? Had I done something wrong? He just stared out over the river, hesitating, until I couldn't wait any longer.

"Jonathan? Talk, please. It's cold out here."

"You know how deep my feelings are for you."

"I do," I said. "Because I have much the same feelings for you." I hated lying about that more than ever. "Why? What's wrong?"

He shrugged.

"Is this about that night?"

"No, no. I said I was sorry. I was angry and out of my mind. I blamed you. That was wrong. It's just that, the police wrecked my place, and..."

"Jonathan please, let's not relive that night."

"It's not about that night."

I reached out and gripped his hands on the tabletop. "C'mon man, it's cold out here."

"Tell me the truth this time." He sighed. "What really happened between you and Egon?"

This Time? Did he think I've been lying up to now?

Calmly, I said, "Self-defense. Like I told you."

"And I believed what you told me. But then you went after his job –"

"I tried to salvage the film. And I have. Was I wrong? Has this all been a mistake?"

"You're sure self-defense is all it was?"

"Why would you think it was anything else?" I was tired and getting irritated. I had to end this. "I wouldn't murder somebody, certainly not for a job. Being attacked by him was the last thing I expected."

"So you're saying nothing else was involved."

He wasn't hearing me, because he didn't want to.

"Well, actually," I said, too angry to be patient any longer, "I was having a real bad PMS day, okay? You know, one of those funky female hormone things?" I shoved his hands away from me, and sat back. "You know, you're the second person, the second *man*, to accuse me of shooting Egon to get his job. You and that cop."

"I wasn't accusing –"

"No, you didn't come right out and say it. You just wondered whether I was self-aware enough to know the real reason why I shot him. Why won't you believe me? I forgot to take the gun out of my backpack. He threatened me. I pulled the gun to try and scare him. He threw a chair at me and the gun just went off. Egon got shot by accident. It wouldn't have happened if he hadn't attacked me."

"Or if you hadn't stolen the gun."

"Or if he hadn't threatened to degrade me." I let him think about that for a moment. "If I can't get the benefit of the doubt, even from you —"

"I've been giving you that. But there are limits."

"What limits?" I said, afraid to say anything else.

"And this is really screwing me up," he said. "Here I am, in love with you —"

He shook his head, like I was an impossible, existential problem for him. But I wasn't his problem, his problem was with himself. I had upset the balance and the purity of his precious conscience. How tragic it was that he, Jonathan Lehane, a humanist, an artist, and law-abiding citizen, had fallen in love with a killer.

"You think this is easy for me?" I asked.

"I'm sure it's not."

"So why are you bringing this up?"

"Because I've been thinking lately," he said. "How beautiful it would be for our future to be clear. No trouble ahead. No issues. Nothing to worry about."

Our future? "Yes, that would be nice." I mean, what else could I say?

"I think once the show's done shooting, we should both go together, with the gun, and our lawyers, and tell the police what happened."

I was expecting and dreading a little romantic neediness, or even a fresh marriage proposal. Now I'd trade that for this lunacy any day. I fully grasped how dangerous he'd become.

"Are you insane? Are you that out of touch with reality? Tomorrow is the last day of shooting. Do you expect me to get up on Saturday and throw myself on the mercy of the police? Because I'm not going to do that, Jonathan. What can you be thinking?"

"Well, how do you think we should do the right thing here?"

The smug moralism behind that question infuriated me.

"Leave it alone."

"I don't know if I can do that, Adrienne. A man is dead. Egon was a messed-up guy, but his family doesn't deserve to suffer. And like you said, it was self-defense —"

"No, Jonathan. First it was kidnapping. He refused to let me leave. Then it was a verbal assault that got more and more violent and frightening. He ordered me to suck his cock. I refused. He threatened to beat me up. He threatened to rape me. All because he got insulted when I told him the truth, that he didn't have the talent to direct our film. I took the gun out to scare him, hoping he'd let me get out of there. But he threw a chair at me and the gun went off and he got shot. It was a reflex. I didn't mean to shoot him. Do you think the cops are going to believe that story from me and let me go? Especially since I stole the gun?"

"We won't know unless we try. A man is dead. And thanks to you, I'm involved." He sounded disappointed that I was resisting his perfectly noble solution.

"If I could change that –"

"You'd do what?" he muttered. "Use somebody else's gun?"

That did it. No matter how many gooey-eyed times he said he loved me I could see his anger with me was deeper than I'd feared. How I wished that the end of shooting tomorrow could mean I'd never see him again. But now if I dumped him, he might give in to the better angels of his unctuous nature and turn me in just so he could sleep better.

"Leave it alone, Jonathan. Please?"

"I've wrestled with this for weeks," he said, shaking his head. "I'm ready to face the consequences for having an illegal gun. And lying about it."

"Well, aren't you admirable." I had to fight hard not to scream at him. "And you think I should risk going to prison for what everybody will call murder, even though it was far from it."

"Egon was on drugs when he got shot. That's been in the news. And I'll back you up. If you tell the police what you told me, they won't hold you responsible."

"Jonathan, you're dreaming. My God, what is happening to you?"

He sighed dramatically. "Look, I know this has been horrible for you –"

"Horrible?" I hated him for making me do this. "I'll tell you what's horrible. You want to know why I reacted to Egon like I did? Or to you? I was tied up and raped when I was seventeen. For hours. And when it was over -" I couldn't hold back the tears "- the only way to deal with it was to promise myself never again. Understand?"

That stopped him, shocked and confused.

"I'm so sorry." He gripped my hands again. "I can just imagine the struggle."

I hated the way he said that. Jonathan had no idea what a woman's life was like. He'd say Hey, I understand, I empathize, then turn around and sell me out to the police so he could feel better about himself.

"Well, if you can imagine my struggle, as you put it, why do you want me to spend my life in prison? You'll get probation and you'll be enjoying your life free of bad vibes, and I'll be one more rat in a cage."

"You have a valid case for self-defense," he said. But I sensed he was weakening. He gave me a pained look and shrugged. "At least, that's what you said."

"See? Even you don't believe me. Just promise me something. You say you love me? Prove it. Promise me you won't say anything to anybody."

"All right." He sighed. "I promise. Again."

"No police. No lawyer. Nobody."

"I said yes."

"And promise me something else."

"What?"

"Promise me you're not punishing me for taking your gun and getting you in trouble."

"Of course not," he said, indignant. "I'm 'way past that."

"And one more thing." I grabbed his coat lapels and pulled him face to face with me. "Swear to me you haven't already gone to the police and that you're not wearing a wire."

He tore my hands off him and fell back, offended.

"You watch too much TV." He pushed himself back from the table.

I got up and started walking away. But I turned and said what I knew I had to say.

"You're a dear, dear man, Jonathan, and I'm going to continue to trust you. I believe you when you say you love me. And we should talk about the future of our love," inwardly, I shuddered, "soon."

As we strolled arm-in-arm to the parking lot, I told myself this was no longer an affair, it was an ultimatum: either I accept his icky-sticky love, or risk arrest for murder if I broke his icky-sticky loving heart.

Once I got home, I sat in my living room in the glow of the streetlight through the front windows. On the night I should have been anticipating my biggest triumph in ten years all I could think of is how my circumstances hung in such precarious balance. I'm making a film after ten years, I've become a force in lowbrow TV, and that's something, right? But my good luck came at a price. One thing was now sure: Jonathan Lehane would always be a threat to my freedom. Somehow, I would have to keep him close, but not too close. When he suggested we go to the police, for one bright, shining moment I felt how much lighter my burden would be if I confessed and by some miracle I was absolved. But that was wishful thinking, bordering on insanity.

We finished shooting *"Lonely Sky"* on Friday evening, October 27, 2017 on our main soundstage at Chelsea Piers, on schedule and slightly under budget, with an intense scene between Ibrahim and his son. It's February 2002, and Khalil, suffering a crisis of faith in both Islam and America, resists going to the mosque with his father to offer prayers at the end of Eid al-Adha, the Feast of Sacrifice honoring Abraham's willingness to obey God's command to sacrifice his son. Khalil's refusal upsets Ibrahim, who tells his son that while he was imprisoned and being tortured by American soldiers only his own trust in God and the dream of returning home to America and his family kept him from going mad.

Everybody working on the show, from cast members, office staffers, craft service people and even the parking P.A.s and location scouts, crowded around the shooting crew on the set to be present for the end of principal photography.

When I called "Cut" for the last time I turned to the camera operator.

"Keep rolling." I stepped onto the set, surrounded by my actors and my crew, my people, with my voice at a high, breathless pitch.

"Thank you, everybody, thank you! I am so proud to have made this film with a crew that worked as hard as all of you have. We've made a movie that shows some very good people trying to recover from a horrible tragedy, done with total respect and compassion for the characters and a deep love for our city and our country. When this film comes out, people will love it and people will hate it, and that'll be proof that we did an honest job. So I thank you from the bottom of my heart for all your hard work and your great spirits, and I love you all!" I threw my head back, shook my fists at the heavens, and yelled, "That's a wrap!"

The popping of champagne corks, the laughter and relief, went on for half an hour. I actually hugged and kissed Juno who, with a huge grin, kissed me back. Lenny, roaring drunk and clutching a bottle, careened around refilling everybody's glasses, except those of Hussein Harari and Sonny Banerjee, who didn't drink alcohol.

I held my arms out to them.

"I don't know your customs, but I want to hug you both to death!"

They looked at each other and laughed and all three of us embraced.

"I hope we get the chance to work again. If you're ever back in New York, please let me know, we'll get together."

I worked my way around the edges of the crowd, avoiding Jonathan in the center taking selfies with Brook Kirby and Lee Jeffries. Their last scene had wrapped two days ago, but they kept their hotel rooms so they could stick around, Brooke to celebrate the end of shooting with the rest of the company and Lee because he was having a thing with one of Gabriella's camera assistants.

I gazed around at my company of filmmakers and I began to feel like I always do at the end of shooting. The daily rhythm and stress are what drive me and give my days meaning and when that ends, when we sadly go our separate ways, it's the loneliest feeling I ever have, making me feel so lost I'm practically mute. So after everybody said their goodbyes, and the crew members began drifting off to workshops and offices to start preparing to wrap the show, I said good night to my driver and slipped down the back stairway to the garage.

I trotted across the West Side Highway and strolled home, getting drunk on deep breaths of cool autumn air. I locked myself in my apartment and opened the front and rear windows to let the cool October night wind flow through my home, lifting car horns and voices and sirens and music up from the street, the sounds of the city, my city. I poured a large splash of tequila in a glass, turned on a couple of small lamps, and settled into blessed silence and solitude.

I did it! I wanted to yell out my window to the world. *I'm back!*

My phone rang. The call was from Jonathan, probably hoping to come over, and I ignored it. Instead, I called Detective Ferino.

"This is gettin' to be a habit Bobbie Jean."

I felt so good I didn't care what name he called me. I heard traffic and voices behind him.

"It's over," I said.

"What's over?"

"I finished shooting."

"Shooting who?"

"Not who, my movie."

"So soon?"

"Soon? Are you kidding? Forty-five days. Twelve to sixteen hours a day."

"What do you want me to say, congratulations?"

"I just want you to know I can't be stopped."

"I'm not trying to stop you. I'm not even trying to figure you out. I'm trying to arrest you for murder. And I will."

"My movie will be in the theaters next year. When we have the premiere, maybe you can come as my date."

That made him laugh.

"Bobbie Jean," he said. "What are you, drunk?"

"Well, I should be, but no, I'm just glad to be done."

"I won't have time to go to the movies. And you'll be in jail."

I chuckled. What was this strange intimacy I shared with this edgy, macho cop?

"You probably wonder, why do I call you like this?"

"Do you even know?"

"It's because I enjoy bothering you. And the weird thing is, I think you enjoy being bothered by me."

"No bother, Bobbie Jean," Ferino said. "Call me any time. I always like to hear from killers when they're in a talkative mood." He hung up.

The wrap party for the cast and crew of "Lonely Sky" took place on Saturday night at a club just east of Times Square, with everybody in Halloween costume. I knew if I declined Jonathan's invitation, he'd be obnoxious and pissy all night, so I agreed to go as his date. He texted me a picture of himself in costume, a swallowtail tuxedo, white shirt with wingtip collar, silver vest and bow tie. The finishing touch was a realistic, horrifying werewolf's head mask with shaggy black fur and a snarling mouth full of sharp teeth and long canines and burning red eyes. The costume party idea dreamed up by Lenny and Juno was pretty corny, but I tried to have fun with it. I rented a matching swallowtail tux and white shirt with a wingtip collar with silver bow tie and spats over patent leather shoes. I pomaded my glistening hair flat from a sharp part that accented my cheekbones and pretty ears, set a top hat rakishly on my head, and wore a monocle, transforming myself into an elegant androgynous Berlin sophisticate of the 1920s to accompany Jonathan's wolfman. He picked me up in a chauffeur-driven town car. In the back seat, the wolfman turned and looked at me.

"Wow," he growled.

At midnight my monocle lay at the bottom of a half glass of warm champagne. I'd lost my top hat, and my tuxedo jacket, shoes, and cummerbund lay in a heap on our table. I danced in shirt, suspenders and trousers with anyone and everyone, male, female, old, young, whomever. Half the time I didn't know who I danced with, the costumes and makeup were so well done, and I was so high. Jonathan kept up with me for a while, and then fell back on the banquette out of breath.

We left the party around two in the morning. Out on the sidewalk a sparkling drizzle fell through the streetlights on a warm autumn night. In the back seat of the car, he hooked an arm around me and we kissed. We went to his place, too drunk and too flush with success to care about anything but getting our rocks off. We left a trail of our evening clothes from the front door to the bedroom. We made love with the windows open as rain pattered on the terrace. At one moment when Jonathan was standing beside the bed and I was down on all fours sucking his cock he growled deep in his throat, and I looked up into the snarling face of the werewolf. The fright was exquisite, a full-body shock. I turned around and watched in the mirror on the wall as the beast took me from behind.

Two days later I was forced into bed by the sickness I call The Vacation Flu, a bug that lurks and waits inside when you're working so willfully that you refuse to be sick, and then strikes when you finally relax. I woke up shivering uncontrollably. I bundled up against the cold wind whipping down the street and dragged myself to a neighborhood clinic in Chelsea. A nurse checked my blood pressure and took my temperature. It was 102F, and I ached all over. The young doctor breezed in. She was peppy and clever and said she was a fan of "*Men R Dawgs*". She examined me and made notes on a computer rig bolted to the wall. She gave me a shot of B-12, a prescription for an upper respiratory antibiotic, and said I should go home and rest, as if I needed to be told.

For the next two weeks I shuffled around my apartment, weighted down by deep fatigue and prone to sudden crying jags for no apparent reason, except maybe because I missed cigarettes, alcohol and caffeine. I kept nodding off at odd moments like a cat or a narcoleptic. I spent the early days of November in a delirium, laying in my bedroom gazing out the window at the bare tree branches swaying in the cold wind against the gray sky, suffering with a high fever, a nagging headache, a dry hacking cough and constant shivering and nausea. I accepted the sickness as my body healing itself from the stress of the past year, but I still felt trapped and miserable.

I lived on hot, heavily-garlicked chicken egg drop soup delivered by my favorite Chinese place on Ninth Avenue, liberally doused with cayenne pepper. I web-surfed and feasted on pictures of properties for sale in France and daydreamed of owning a fine apartment in Montmartre, a discreet chateau in the Loire valley, or a farmhouse in Normandy. Every morning I did my living room rug exercise routine, sweating and stinking up rotating pairs of pajamas. I sat for sessions of silent meditation every morning and evening. I propped myself in front of the TV and had my own film festival, streaming movies by Lina Wertmuller, Jonathan Demme, Jane Campion, Gillian Armstrong, Todd Haynes, Paul Thomas Anderson, and Elaine May. While winter held New York in its gray frigid grip outside my windows, I booted up Netflix and traveled to many *"Parts Unknown"* with Anthony Bourdain. I got off caffeine, sipped cups of holy basil tea, and did restorative yoga. I soaked in a hot Epsom salts bath every night before bed.

Once a day I answered email and checked in with the office and kept up with McPeek's editing progress by remote accessing the Alpha Bitch servers. I watched the latest edits to *"Lonely Sky"* every afternoon, excited as the movie, piece by piece, was coming to life.

After a week, Tawana called to check on how I was doing.

"I've been crying a lot," I said, "and I've been having a lot of weird dreams. I don't know, it's probably just the flu."

"Yeah, well, let me tell ya, flu, #MeToo, I don't know, but something has brought up a buncha my shit big time."

She brought lunch over the next day. I was weak, but my fever had broken, and I was happy to have her company. Tawana breezed in, put the bags down on the kitchen table and opened her arms.

"I'd love a hug, but I might still be contagious."

"I had my shots," Tawana said, hugging me tightly.

"And this is better than any medicine."

I sat at the kitchen table while Tawana laid out lunch.

"You said you've been living on nothing but tea and soup. So I brought some vegetable pad thai, moo ping (which is basically grilled pork on a stick), steamed dumplings, and nice easy-going down Tom Juad soup." She caught the look on my face. "Girl, what's the matter?"

"I just spent a week puking and starving."

"You don't feel like eating?"

"It's not that. It's just that, I look, y'know, really slim."

"Ha!" Tawana was one of the only people who could laugh in my face and get away with it.

She unpacked the food on the table and passed me the chopsticks. I ate slowly, absorbing every bit of flavor from the first solid food I'd eaten in over a week.

"How about the Ridley Scott reshoots?" Tawana said. "You hear about that?"

"I don't watch or read the news lately. I'm depressed enough. What reshoots?"

"He has a movie coming out at Christmas. He's got Kevin Spacey as that billionaire guy Getty whose nephew got kidnapped. Except he's cuttin' Spacey out of the movie because of his sexual assault thing and he's gonna reshoot all his scenes with Christopher Plummer."

"And still open at Christmas?"

"He says he's gonna do it."

"How? It's already the middle of November."

"He says he's gonna do it."

We shook our heads just thinking about the amount of work it would take to shoot, not to mention edit, mix, strike prints and distribute them to the theaters in time. "I mean, has anybody ever done that? Replaced the star of a finished film?"

"Woody Allen shot a movie once, didn't like it, then shot it all over again."

"Well, even that ain't risky like shooting twenty scenes that have to fit into what's already done."

"How'd you like to A.D. that job?"

"I could pull that off," Tawana said.

"I know you could."

"Tough break for Spacey," I said. "He's a brilliant actor."

Tawana shot me a surprised look. "Yeah, and a fucking sexual predator."

"Sometimes very talented people do very bad things."

"Yeah, and you know what? They always get away with it."

I'd used my illness as an excuse to avoid him, and Jonathan was feeling left out and angry with me again. By the end of the second week I felt better, so I went to see him for a reality check. We spent most of it in bed, having a night of colossal sex. He was beaming afterward, but for me this felt like a relapse. I tried to keep him at arm's length emotionally, but he was so sweet and considerate of me that in the morning I felt sad when breakfast was over. I stepped out into the frigid sunshine on Central Park West and walked downtown through the park to the office, feeling like I'd fully recovered my health, and Jonathan's loyalty.

A couple days later Marshall took me to lunch and surprised me with a deal he'd made for a paperback book of my screenplay with production photos scheduled to drop when *"Lonely Sky"* was released. The advance, after taxes, was barely enough to pay a couple months of rent on my apartment, but he said the publishers, MetroTerraNova Books, were sophisticated and cutting-edge.

"They're in an old building off Union Square," Marshall said. "They do a cool combination of literary fiction and high-quality art books. Your editor, um, associate editor, her name is Evangeline Barksdale."

Associate? On a film crew that's a fancy title for an entry level job. Did they give my book to an intern with the name of a spinster librarian? I decided to show up at their offices, catch them off guard, and check out the situation. The offices were bright and airy with cubicles down one wall and the executive offices along the windows, and a motley crew of young people – tattoos, piercings, one or two florescent hairdos – working earnestly. The receptionist brought me back through the cubicles and introduced me to a thirtyish woman peering at her computer screen. Her office window looked across the street to a cycling gym in a former firehouse and had a view of Union Square East and a tiny slice of the park.

"Oh, hi, come on in!" She waved me to a chair facing her desk. "I'm taking another look at the memo."

Her eyes went back to the screen. She wore a tight black blouse and slacks, and she had bright blue eyes, a thick pile of reddish-brown hair and ivory skin, and a lush pout of lips the color of dark cherries.

"Screenplay and pictures." She sat back, nodding. "Looks interesting. I've heard about the play, but I haven't seen it. We wanted to put the play in the book too, but we couldn't reach a deal. Business Affairs dropped the idea because the playwright was a difficult negotiation."

"Joel? Difficult?"

The way I said it made her laugh.

"And of course, I've read the news about Egon Swift and, y'know, all that."

"Which of course we'll leave out of the book."

"Oh no!" She looked at me like I was crazy. "Why would we do that?"

"Dredging all that up again would be tacky, don't you think? Sort of tabloidish? Unless that's what you really want."

A chilly stare.

"The book will be tastefully done," she said curtly. Was she offended on behalf of the company, or herself? "Our publisher loved the play. When the film was announced he immediately made a deal with the studio for this spin off book. That was before Egon Swift was killed and the production became a news story, and we held our breath as one scandal after another piled on."

"Scandals starring me."

"My point is, this was supposed to be a typical 'making of' book and then the circumstances changed. There are other values in play now."

"Yeah. Murder. Drugs. Lead actor and director suspected. That's a gigabyte of juicy gossip right there."

"You may not like them, and for that matter I may not like them, but they are what we'd call a marketplace reality. Those values will help sell the book. The notoriety alone will be a promotional bonanza. Everybody will want you on their show."

"I just don't want the beauty and importance of what we've created buried under the salacious bullshit."

She frowned. "It feels like we're getting off on the wrong foot here."

"Just so you understand where I'm coming from. I was trying to direct the film while the police were all around me investigating Egon's killing. They were a huge distraction. I'm afraid with too much of that in the book it'll distract readers from the screenplay."

"Key words: too much." I was taking too long to get it and she was impatient. "Too much violence and scandal, some people who love the play will be turned off. Leave it out entirely, and other readers will be disappointed. The reality is, Swift's killing is part of this story and readers will expect it to be addressed." She let that sink in a moment. "I don't know anything about Egon's movies. They have a big following, don't they?"

"I doubt if his fans would buy a book and actually read it."

That got her, and she laughed.

"Well, then let 'em look at the pictures."

"How about if I dedicate the book to him?"

"No, it's got to be more than that. How about this? An introductory essay is basic to this genre of book. How about if you write about Swift in the intro? You're the logical person to tell that story. So you address it, then get on with the rest."

Marshall never told me I'd have to write anything, much less relive an experience I hoped was behind me. On the other hand, it was my chance to get the story of Egon's death on the record, and I had no doubt that would help sell books, especially if we could place the essay in a magazine before publication.

"All right, I'll try it."

"But I'll expect more than just a mention."

To relax things, I told her a couple stories from the making of the film that she found amusing. I could see that fast work would be necessary to get her up to speed. She surprised me by canceling a date for that evening so I could take her to see the play.

When the lights came up, she was stunned. She said, looking around at the audience, "Do they know what hit them? I'm not even sure I do."

"Wait'll you see the film. It's gonna have an even greater impact."

We met Jonathan afterward for drinks. He was polite, but his mind was elsewhere, perhaps brooding over tonight's performance. He didn't flirt, and he left after one drink. Ms. Barksdale seemed intrigued.

"Gorgeous," she said. "Probably gay, right?"

I non-answered with a shrug.

Seeing the play fired up Ms. Barksdale's passion for our book, just as I'd hoped. The next time we met she had design concepts, photos, and fonts for me spread out on her desk.

"I don't want this to be just another promo book," she said. "In its own way, I want the book to be an artwork up to the level of the play and the movie."

That evening we relaxed a while after work in her office.

"I wanted to be on the literary side of the company, editing fiction, but they stuck me in the picture book division."

"I'm glad they did."

"Yeah well, I don't get projects like yours every day." She was still recovering from her last assignment, a photo memoir by a boho photographer. "She was this tedious East Village burnout, sort of a left over from the Punk Rock days. She made herself difficult to work with just so she'd feel important. She hated the publisher for no good reason, just rebellious bohemian bullshit. Her ideas for the book, which I had to listen to at length every time we met, changed every time we met."

"Maybe that's why they gave you the 'Men R Dawgs' bitch to work with."

"Yeah. I'm the difficult bitch specialist."

She emailed me a link and a password so I could log on to the publisher's servers and follow progress on the book from home. But I much preferred to work with her in her office, sitting at the monitor shoulder to shoulder, laying out pages, debating each decision. I found myself yearning for each time I could sit down and get deep into work with Ms. Barksdale, or 'Barky,' as I secretly nicknamed her.

I tried to make her aware of my attraction, trying to see how forward I could be without turning her off.

"I never knew making a book could be so much fun," I told her one afternoon.

"Depends on the author," Barky said, obviously hearing what I meant but not showing it. "Not everybody is as easy to work with as you. Or as talented."

Her colleagues called her Evangeline, and her intern called her Ms. Barksdale. When I slipped and called her Barky, she laughed, then decided she didn't like it, and said so, profanely. Nevertheless, but never around others, I often called her Barky, teasing her. It was the quickest way to get her going.

"Don't call me that, damn it!"

She seemed at times to be uncomfortable with her beauty. When people called on her, I could see that her cool response to unwelcome attention protected a sensitive, tender nature. During one of our work sessions, I sat watching and quietly lusting as Barky deflected two guys who phoned and a drop-in visit from a man in the company who wanted to date her. I figured the odds of me getting her into bed were slim, considering the competition, beginning with a fiancé named Garth.

"He's a regular kind of guy," she said, "with a nice apartment over in Hoboken. He makes a lot of money working at an investment bank downtown. He spends his Sunday afternoons with his buddies in this sports bar in Hoboken, drinking beer and watching football. Kind of a new experience for me, but he's kind of fun. He's a whiz with numbers. He's sort of naïve about everything else. But at least he's not crude and obvious, like these men who are after my ass all the time."

On her computer desktop was a photo montage of a foxy, dark-haired young man. In a couple of pictures, he wore a sports jersey of some kind. Garth had a nice even smile, and he was definitely younger than Barky's mid-30s. Looking at him, she came into clearer focus. Her biological and social and professional clocks were ticking, and she wanted financial security, to rise in her company to where the more prestigious work was being done, to get married, and to have children. My sympathy for her was just as strong as my pleasure at working with her, but mostly I felt the finest purest lust whenever I was near her.

Walking home after being with her one afternoon, I was struck by a piercing kind of loneliness, and I realized I wanted more from her than sex. I paused at Fifth Avenue and 20th Street, debating whether to keep walking or go back to her office with some excuse to spend more time with her. I took out my phone but stopped with my fingertip over her number. No, not yet.

One frigid evening not much later we were walking through Union Square Park after a meeting and I invited Barky over for dinner.

"But the evening doesn't have to end there," I said.

She slowed down and looked at me, her eyes practically ordering me to explain myself. I shrugged and smiled.

"It's just that lately, whenever I'm with you, I can't stop undressing you with my eyes."

"Oh God. You too? I thought I was getting a certain vibe from you."

"If you don't like it, tell me now."

"It's just strange." And then, afraid she'd insulted me, she added, "I mean, it's okay, it's just that I usually get that kind of attention from men. And I just automatically flip 'em off, y'know?"

"Well, so what about me? Should I stop fantasizing about you?"

She looked at me a moment.

"Adrienne... that's up to you." Then she laughed nervously. "I think I'd better go." She gave me a long curious look, then we hugged, we hesitated, she kissed me quickly on the cheek, then turned and hurried off.

So Barky knew how I felt. My innuendoes intrigued her, or at least she paused for a moment before she shrugged them off. Then one afternoon she called me out of the blue, offering to bring the proofs of the book to my apartment after work so she could show me some new ideas over a takeout dinner. Dinner and a bottle of wine turned into a flirtatious talk that lasted late into the evening, until it was time for her to get up and say good night.

"So, I've been thinking about what you said to me that day in the park."

"Oh?"

"How'd you like to undress me for real?"

"Can we leave the lights on?"

I kneeled on the bed and she let me take off her clothes. The sight of her in the raw left me momentarily speechless. I thought it might be her first time with a woman, which turned out to be not completely true. She was very uninhibited; when we both were naked, she took my head in her hands and kissed me, so deep, so long, I was ready to fall over, which I did, taking her with me.

Afterwards as we cuddled, Barky couldn't stop talking. She told me about her determination to get ahead in publishing by discovering writers of color and other marginalized artists, and her love affair with weed. She told me all about her "horror movie" Catholic childhood and her rebellious college years at Fairfield University. She'd had one experience with a girl back then, a freezing winter night at college when she and her roommate returned drunk to their dorm room from a party, and feeling both horny and lonely, got into bed together. She said her roommate's bodily hygiene was horrible, but the sex was thrilling, and all the more exciting for being 'off-line.' The next morning, though, her roommate was mortified and begged her not to tell anyone. Their friendship became strained and when the semesters changed, her roommate moved to another dorm, leaving Barky in the room by herself for the rest of her freshman year. The experience left Barky feeling very daring and sophisticated for a while, until she found out sex between college girls wasn't that rare.

Despite the 10-year difference in our ages, it felt like one of those passionate friendships I'd had with girls in middle school but without the possessiveness and intrigues. Cool and intellectualized though she was, Barky was a surprisingly eager lover. Out of bed, though, she was the most unromantic person I had ever dated.

"Doing this with you was amazing," she said that night as she was getting dressed to go home. "I knew it would be."

"For me, it's about more than sex."

"Well, I have feelings for you, too," she said. "The company has a strict rule about editors dating authors. So we need to keep this very private."

"*This*? So there's really a *this*?"

"Yeah," she said briskly. "Somehow I knew—" She thought for a moment, then shrugged.

"Is the company the only reason we have to hide?"

"Well, like I said, there's also my fiancé, and I might still have a few molecules of Catholicism left, I don't know." She turned apologetic. "But I don't want to mislead you, Adrienne. I plan to marry Garth. You need to remember that."

"Oh for sure," I said, despite my sinking hopes. "Whatever makes you happy."

I was eating lunch with Jonathan at a crowded Applebee's in Times Square. "I've been thinking about that vacation you want to take," he said, looking at me over the rim of his dark glasses as I munched my grilled chicken Caesar salad. "How about a canal barge trip through France?"

This again, I thought.

"It's the middle of winter."

"The barges are heated and they're very comfortable. They stop in villages where the cooking is regional and authentic."

"And we'll both put on about ten pounds. Anyway, better in summer when the countryside is green, don't you think?"

"Okay, then. Paris. No hotels. We'll rent an apartment."

"It's December. How about someplace warm?"

"I know some beautiful places in Mexico."

I shook my head. "Narco violence. Bugs in the water."

"Miami, then."

"Been there a lot. Also been to the Bahamas, been baked in Jamaica, scuba'd in Aruba, been to St. Bart's, been to the Virgins –"

"What about New Orleans?"

"Maybe someday, but not now."

"I thought you said you need to get away."

"I do."

"Well, I'm trying, but I feel like I'm wasting my time."

I knew then there would be no happy ending to this. Only anxiety, only the fear of saying or doing the wrong thing, only the fear of betrayal, and the constant chafe of that leash around my neck. He was calling and texting me every day about his vacation fixation. Too bad I couldn't tell him the vacation I needed was from him.

THREE *The night of January 9, 2018*

I step back into the living room and close the glass door to the terrace. Down the entry hall fists keep pounding on the door and voices roar. "NYPD! Open up!" My journey to the front door seems to happen in slow motion, passing over the bodies of Jonathan and A.J. sprawled on the floor.

I try to take a deep breath. It catches in my throat and I can't fill my lungs. I gasp, and try again, and breathe.

"Open the fucking door! Now!"

I can't delay the rest of my life any longer.

"Okay! Okay!"

I snap the lock with a shaking hand. The door bursts open forcing me back and two large policemen in uniform come crashing in. One of them, Black and tall and very angry, points a gun at me. I stumble back with my hands up.

"Thank God you're here," I say.

"What took you so long?" he yells in my face.

"I'm sorry, I'm sorry, I'm upset, okay?"

"A neighbor said shots were fired!"

"They're... they're in the living room."

"Who?" the Black cop demands. "Who's in the living room?"

I can't find the right words. Finally I just say, "They're on the floor."

Mickey the doorman is right behind the second cop. "Miss Monet!" he says. "Are you all right?"

The Black cop brushes past me and goes deeper into the apartment with Mickey on his heels. The second cop, a short Latino built like a weightlifter, holsters his gun, takes me by the elbow, turns me to face the wall, and cuffs my hands behind my back.

"Nunez!" the Black cop yells from the living room. "We got two down in here!"

"Oh my God!" Mickey staggers backward from the living room. "Miss Monet!" Mickey gapes at me. His face is brilliant red and he's gassing me with vodka fumes. "What the hell happened?"

"You!" Nunez grabs him by the arm. "Get outside!" He pushes him toward the open door to the corridor. "Go on!"

"I'm gonna be sick," Mickey mutters, "I'm gonna be sick –"

"Don't go away!" Nunez closes the door.

"Nunez!" the Black cop yells from the living room. "You copy that?"

"Copy that!"

He takes my arm, brings me to the bench in the entry hall, and makes me sit. The steel bracelets on my wrists are tight and ice cold.

"Are these necessary?"

"Yeah. Sit still." He draws his gun back out. "Anybody else here?"

"No. Just me."

"She says she's alone!" he calls out.

He marches into the living room, his leather belt full of gear squeaking.

A walkie talkie squawks down the hall. I hear the Black cop, calling himself Officer Harris.

"Two adult males... gunshot wounds to the head... EMS and Homicide respond, over." A staticky radio voice replies, harsh noise that cuts through the air of the plush, silent apartment.

The cops prowl through the place checking out the rooms. I hear them shouting "Clear!" to each other. Nunez comes back and takes hold of my elbow.

"Okay, stand up."

With him gripping my elbow, I obey. He spreads open my jacket. I guess he's looking for weapons.

"What's your name?"

"Adrienne Monet."

"Do you live here?"

"No."

"Where's your I.D.?"

"Inside pocket of my jacket, left side." His hand brushes my breast and I flinch angrily.

"Hey, watch it!"

He smirks with one corner of his mouth.

"Sorry."

He takes my wallet from my jacket pocket and flips it open. He looks at my New York driver's license, then at my face, and slips the wallet back in my pocket, carefully this time.

"You saw it all?" he says.

"Yes."

"Nobody else was here?"

"No."

"Are you okay?"

"Is that a real question?"

"I mean are you hurt?"

"No. Not physically."

"All right, sit down."

Things will go better if I obey the police and don't complicate things. I need the situation to stay calm so I can think. I should be all right if I just stay in the moment, go with events as they happen, and don't show what I'm really thinking and feeling.

Harris comes back from the living room. "Who's that guy again?"

"What guy?" Nunez says.

"The old guy with the gun."

Nunez shrugs. "The doorman said he was an actor."

"He looks familiar," Harris says. "Didn't he used to be a cop on TV?" He looks down at me. "What's that guy's name again?"

"Jonathan Lehane."

"And who's the other guy?"

"His son. A.J. Upton."

"His son?" Nunez says. "Jesus."

"Upton," Harris mutters. "Him, I seen on *Fox News*. He's the one got that congressman killed, right?"

"It was suicide," I say, "but yeah, he had something to do with it."

It was the week after Thanksgiving, and it was time to assign one of the kids on my staff to produce the Alpha Bitch Productions Christmas party. Three of them were begging me for the honor, each with their own ideas on how we should celebrate 2017, the most successful year for our company. The decision was a delicate matter for office morale. Those I didn't choose would feel unloved. Their generation took everything personally, especially when they didn't hear the Good job Buddy! they'd been hearing since they were toddlers. Last Christmas, I divided the party tasks between them, but it led to bickering I had to constantly referee. Finally, I put the decision out of my mind and left the office to go eat lunch.

Down on the sidewalk the weather was so cold and wintry I almost decided to go back to my office and order lunch delivered. But I wanted to be away from the office for a while, so I hunched down into my leather jacket with my scarf wrapped up to my cheekbones. Squinting into the wind and sleet and trying not to slip on a sidewalk bumpy with frozen slush, I trudged down West 49th Street over to a small Pret A Manger on 8th Avenue.

I took a large cup of steaming Moroccan lentil soup to a table in the crowded back room. The astonished chatter of the three young women at the table next to mine intruded on my thoughts. *Oh my God! Matt Lauer too! Can you believe it?* I plugged in my earbuds and was about to turn up the music on my iPhone when I got a text from Barky – DID YOU SEE THIS SHIT!? – linking to a YouTube video with the headline, "Jonathan Lehane's Son Blasts His 9/11 Movie."

I tapped the link and there he was, A.J. Upton, the arrogant contrarian you either loved or hated, chuckling and sneering about his father and my movie.

"His new film, from what I've heard, is pure Victim Chic."

Lehane once told me he had a son from his failed first marriage who hated and publicly ridiculed him every chance he could, mocking his work, his politics, and even his closest friends. I knew A. J. Upton like the rest of America knew him, as a writer and political provocateur on the far right and a big booster of Donald Trump. I'd read his columns years ago and I'd seen him once or twice on talk shows and I laughed him off as a political exhibitionist with nothing to offer but over-the-top personal attacks. He had a gift for invective, but not much else. He stank of white male belligerence, Ivy League variety.

Also, watching him close up on YouTube, I realized A.J. was even more handsome than his father. A dirty-blond Adonis somewhere in his late thirties, his looks made him perfect TV bait. He was dressed classically Ivy League, khakis, navy blue blazer with gold buttons, striped rep tie and button-down blue shirt. He sat across a glass table on the *Fox News* set from a bleached blonde interviewer who grinned like a she-wolf and looked eager to lick him from head to foot. Clutching and waving a pen, he drawled on, his high sandy voice tripping off the tongue with the precise diction of the East Coast upper class, in the compound sentences of someone who had watched too many videos of William F. Buckley Jr. He spoke in the tone of a privileged Eastern prep school kid, his chin thrust forward, in love with the sound of his own voice.

"From what I've read and heard, this film '*Lonely Sky*' is just the kind of thing that Jonathan Lehane, a Hollywood liberal deep in his copiously bleeding heart, would consider important," he said. "People are saying the filmmakers have twisted 9/11 and made a real tearjerker out of it." I couldn't help but notice as he played "*Fox's*" standard outraged "real American" he had a broad smile and perfect gleaming teeth.

It really pissed me off, the way he swooped down from right-wing cuckoo land to mock his father and a film he'd never even seen. *People are saying.* He was playing that Donald Trump trick of quoting something everyone supposedly was saying without saying it himself, thus protecting himself from disagreement.

"Of course, Lehane's got to make a living, so he can afford to support all the worthy causes he no doubt contributes his big Hollywood salaries to, since he's a real believer in the engaged artiste, you know, on the barricades like a good radical, fighting for the masses. When the film opens, maybe they should hand out hankies at the door so everybody can have a big pity party.

But I think I'll save my pennies for the DVD of the film based on *'Atlas Shrugged'."* Chuckle, chuckle, chuckle.

As I sat there gathering myself for a fight, Barky texted again to tell me A.J. Upton would be promoting his new memoir that afternoon on "The Combat Zone," conservative deejay Gunner Crockett's call-in talk radio show. I asked Megan to contact Crockett's booker and tell them I would call in.

"Then drop whatever you're doing and get me all the research you can find on this guy. I'll be there in a few minutes." I tossed the soup and bought a large coffee to go.

I paced my office scrolling on a tablet and reading everything I could about A.J. Upton. I was appalled but not surprised to learn that in 1985, according to a *Salon.com* profile, Jonathan Lehane abandoned his wife, the former Rosa Lee Prentice, and his five-year-old son Andrew Jonathan, for a new life in Paris with the French film star and chanteuse Delphine Tessier. Well, woof, woof, woof. An angry divorce followed, following which Rosa Lee married Royal Upton, a billionaire investment banker and devout Catholic of ultra-conservative views who got sent to prison for stock manipulation, putting a strain on the marriage. In his Wikipedia bio, A.J. gave Roy Upton credit for mentoring him in the spirit of conservatism and encouraging his writing, setting him on the path to become a notorious social and political commentator and author of caustic hit pieces that targeted liberal politicians and celebrities.

It was the kind of writing that made me dismiss him as an irritating publicity-hungry gnat, buzzing around the national political media theater, a genre of TV even lower than reality television, but where A.J. nevertheless was a star. I could picture him and Ann Coulter playing a couple in a *Fox* TV sitcom, the blonde and beautiful Mister and Mrs. Archibald Bunker Jr., gleefully tag teaming and destroying clueless well-meaning liberals.

His media profile had exploded a few years earlier due to an ugly scandal that lifted him from right-wing gnat to media star and prominent Christian convert. He wrote an excoriating expose of a liberal Democratic congressman on corruption charges, a Gingrich-style takedown that led to the congressman's conviction. Widely condemned for his extreme viciousness, at first A.J. acted like he welcomed the uproar, then after the congressman blew his brains out and his family revealed the man had been bipolar, he abruptly announced he had suspended all TV appearances to immerse himself in "prayer and reflection." He emerged a suspiciously brief time later, announcing his soul had been saved by Christ. Megan had found several reviews of his memoir of spiritual salvation published by Comitatus Press titled *"Nearer My God To Thee."* The reviews from the political and religious right gushed with admiration, while one leftist reviewer insisted that God would never embarrass himself by conferring salvation on A.J. Upton.

I had no time to buy his book and read it, but there were numerous YouTube video clips of his appearances promoting it on *Meet The Press*, Charlie Rose, Gunner Crockett, and with the *Fox* opinion hosts, most often ridiculing Hillary Clinton and Nancy Pelosi and using that "pity party" slur to mock the Women's March in DC the day after the Trump inauguration. On an audio clip he gloated with Rush Limbaugh over the ways the Republican majority in Congress had made life hell for Barack Hussein Obama, and chuckled over how they shrugged off the misbehavior of President Trump. So – an absurdly handsome rich boy and pseudo-intellectual bully, with no scruples or taste to inhibit his wit and with zero respect for facts, who had everyone holding their breath waiting for his next outrage. He was so smug and smooth I couldn't wait for the fight he'd just picked with me.

I stared at A.J. Upton's shiny grin in freeze-frame on my tablet.

"You stuck-up bastard," I said to his picture. "You clueless fucking brat. Do you even know how dishonest you are, attacking a movie you haven't even seen? How dare you use my work as a platform for your neurotic issues with your father, fucking around with the way I make my living! Smear your father all you want but leave me and my work alone! If that label 'pity party' gets stuck on my movie, which is obviously what you hope, I'll rip out your fucking tongue!"

I spun around and had to restrain myself from smashing the tablet on the corner of the desk.

"Our friend A.J. Upton is here!" Gunner Crockett bellowed, sitting behind his microphone, loudly tanned and muscled. "And he's gonna talk about his new book, it's called 'Nearer My God To Thee', just like the old hymn, right? Hey, weren't they playing that the night the Titanic went down? No? Well, I guess my history's kind of hazy. Anyway, we're gonna talk about that book, and A.J.'s spiritual journey and rebirth through Christ, which I know many of you want to hear about, I know I do..."

I was at my computer, connected to the show and on standby, my image in a window on my screen, waiting to join the web simulcast of the show. I was not one of the five million listeners who tuned in every afternoon because even a small taste of Gunner Crockett was for me like eating spoiled meat. He was hugely buffed and yoked, his biceps bursting the short sleeves on his polo shirt, tanned a burnt orange all the way up his thick neck and shaved head. He had small intense eyes, huge lips, a thin moustache, and a hoarse voice always edging on hysteria.

Crockett and Upton had close-up cameras on them. Across the broadcast desk from Crockett, Upton looked like a college kid with his neatly coiffed hair and his jacket and tie. His camera angle was not flattering, just a three-quarter profile, and there was nothing I could read in his face. Before I linked in, I'd adjusted the lighting in my office, brushed my hair and applied a rose lip gloss, and positioned myself where the light on my face was flattering, with posters of my films behind me.

"...but first we have a special guest joining us now. She's the creator of a reality TV series called, get this, '*Men R Dawgs*', in case you didn't already know! And she's the director of a new film that just wrapped up shooting here in New York, starring A.J.'s father Jonathan Lehane, one of the real classic Hollywood libs that A.J. talked about on *Fox News*. So, welcome Adrienne Monet! You're in The Combat Zone!"

Then I was on a split screen with Crockett. In a corner of my screen was a small Post It note reminder:

FIVE MILLION PEOPLE.

"Thank you for having me on, Gunner. It's great to be with you and uh – " I lowered my voice to a husky, suggestive whisper – "hullo, A.J."

All I got from Upton was silence as we went to a three-face split screen. He looked calm, composed, a pleasant, meaningless smile on his face. Crockett must have told him I'd be calling. Where was his famous verbal prowess now? Did he think I was too insignificant to deserve a response?

"So as I understand it," Crockett said, "your film is about the aftermath of 9/11."

"That's right. Its impact on everyday people."

"Okay, and the film follows three stories, about three groups of characters?"

"The film explores their struggles to cope with the impact of 9/11 on their lives on the first anniversary of the attacks. I adapted it from a play running Off Broadway that's been playing to packed houses and getting sensational reviews, mainly because Jonathan Lehane's performance is so powerful. As I'm sure you know, he was given the Obie award for Best Actor."

"So, your film takes us back into the pain of the nation. We go back and relive 9/11's effects on people and how they've coped?"

I sensed with his next breath he was going to describe *"Lonely Sky"* as a downer, but I was ready.

"How heroically they've coped. These are three stories anyone in the world could take to heart and be encouraged by. It's definitely a 'feel-good' movie."

"How could three painful stories add up to a 'feel-good' movie?"

"By showing us their courage, and reminding us of the ties that bind us, Gunner. I think that's something we need now, especially with Donald Trump being so divisive —"

Upton, who'd seemed frozen, lunged forward looking directly into the camera, grinning, eyes bright, attacking.

"Why is it you liberals," he said, in a tone suggesting I was a laughable fool, "always resort to suffering when you're trying to tell a story? What's this obsession you liberals have with pain?"

The split screen became Upton and me just in time for my reply.

"What's your obsession with inflicting it?" That smirk again. That smirk hid a lot, I was to discover. "There's an awful lot of pain in this world, A.J. I'm sure you've had your share of psychotherapy, right?"

"Nice try." A private chuckle, all for himself.

"No? So many people love you, hate you, talk about you all the time. That must be hard to bear without professional help."

"No," he said in a condescending singsong, "I'm doing just fine."

"Well, it doesn't seem like it. You went on TV and attacked a movie you haven't even seen. I'll bet you haven't seen the play either, because you'd be too scared to run into your father."

"Too bad Miss Monet." He and Crockett chuckled, but you could hear that he was getting nervous. "I'll stand on what I said about my father, and your movie."

"You haven't seen my movie. So you know nothing about it. Which makes your views on the subject worth nothing."

"Oh really? You think you know a lot about my views?"

"Views? That's not what I saw on *Fox News*. I saw a kid who hates his father throwing a tantrum."

Upton sat back, raised an eyebrow and crossed his arms over his chest, trying to appear unaffected.

"Like I said, nice try. But the fact is, my father hasn't been part of my life for most of my life."

"Maybe that's why you're so lonely and filled with anger."

"My father..." He stalled, took a breath, then laughed scornfully. "He's just not relevant to anything —"

"You just made him relevant. You attacked a movie you've never even seen just because he's in it. Your father is like an unwelcome guest living in your head."

"He's been out of my life since I was young." He apparently thought that fact made further mention of Jonathan unnecessary.

"I know. We can hear the pain of that loss in your voice, can't we Gunner? Don't you think it would be good for A.J. to talk about this?"

"Look." Upton's voice got hard. "I'm not here to discuss my upbringing."

"But that's exactly what you did by mocking your father. Don't you get that?"

Crockett cut in. "Weren't we talking about your movie?"

"Yes, Gunner, thank you. Look A.J., don't call me a liberal, okay? Just because you don't understand me, don't try to reduce me to a bumper sticker."

The men laughed, despite themselves.

"My film is apolitical. Unless you think compassion for suffering people is a political statement."

Split-screen, Upton and me. He'd loosened up with the laughter, leaned on his elbows with his hands clasped.

"Well," he said, "in case you haven't noticed, these days everything is political." He glanced offscreen for support from Crockett.

"Only for guys like you, obsessed with politics, probably to make up for something you lack."

"No no no," he said, chuckling at my cluelessness. "I lack for nothing, I assure you."

"Yeah. You and the president with the little fingers –"

"Oh, that's so petty. Do you really want to go there?"

"—whose entire vocabulary could fit on one side of a matchbook cover. Isn't that who you identify with? Not the non-MAGA other 99 percent of humanity. No wonder you don't want to see my film. The regular people in it don't matter to you."

"I just think there's a thin line between exploring a subject and exploiting it. 9/11 should not be the excuse for a tearjerker. We should be strengthening our country for the challenges of the future, not weeping over the past."

"You're missing the point A.J.," I said, with exaggerated kindliness, "obviously because you haven't wept enough over your own past."

He shrugged, trying to look deadpan.

"Which only means I'm just like most people."

"And so are the characters in my movie. You really ought to see it before you criticize it. Why don't you go see the play, at least?"

"Because I have no interest in my father's life, or work."

"Except when you feel like taking cheap shots at a hard-working actor." He looked unsure of what to say next.

A sudden, irresistible impulse came over me.

"Tell you what. I'll pick you up at seven o'clock tonight. We'll go see the play."

That made them both laugh again.

"Wait a minute. Are you asking me out on a date?"

"C'mon, we'll sit in the back row. Your father won't even know you're in the theater. You're not afraid to sit in the back row with me, are you?" That got another burst of laughter. "I'll keep my hands to myself."

Not quite laughing again: "I am so not interested."

"I promise not to tell anyone if the play makes you cry."

"Oh, please." He jumped half out of his seat then realized he was out of mike range and sat down. "Y'know Gunner, this is getting –"

"I'll reserve a comp ticket for you at the box office every night. Then if you ever get up the nerve –"

"Don't bother."

"Okay. Two tickets. Just in case you're able to find a date, which seems doubtful. You're a good-looking guy, but you're not much fun."

"Well, you're no day at the fucking beach, either."

Gunner yelped, "Hey, hey, we're on the radio!"

"Sorry."

"Okay, how about this: I'll show you the latest edit of my film. Then if you want to keep putting it down, at least you'll know what you're talking about."

A weary sigh, and a glance off-screen to Crockett, like, Hasn't she said enough?

"I'm more interested in whether America is moving on."

On that weak note, Crockett said, "All right, we're gonna move on" – the three of us again in split-screen – "and talk about our guest A.J. Upton's new book 'Nearer My God To Thee'. But before we do, I want to thank Adrienne Monet for joining us."

"And thank you, Gunner, for the chance to clear up the misinformation about my movie being spread by Mister Upton."

"Yeah," Upton said, with a sarcastic pout. "So nice to meet you, Miss Monet."

"I'm going to haunt you, A.J., until you agree to watch my film."

"Better beware of my security," he said. "They're trained to shoot first and ask questions later."

"Of course," I laughed. "A squad of premature ejaculators."

Cheers and laughter erupted down the corridor where my Alpha Bitch troops were listening. Gunner Crockett was trying not to laugh, but A.J. Upton's face twisted into a sneer.

"And if you see me coming up the sidewalk," he said, his voice shaking and low, his face reddening, "do yourself a favor? Cross over to the other side. I'll have more to say to you that I can't say on the radio."

"I can't wait to hear it," I said, mimicking his upper-class lockjaw. "Good luck with your Jesus book. Thanks again, Gunner. Seeya 'round, *Uptown*."

I called Megan into my office.

"You get the webcast?"

"Got it. We also put a copy on the archive server. You totally owned him," Megan said, "but I wish you'd said more about his shitty politics."

"I wanted to talk about the movie. And about him."

"'Seeya round, Uptown.' That was cool."

"Five million people heard it. Theoretically."

"Awesome!"

"I want to keep this going."

"We'll go to full blast. You want me to put the webcast on our website?"

"We can't. Crockett'll sue us. What we can do, until his lawyers tell us to take it down, is post the audio on YouTube with headshots of Upton and me. Make sure I'm smiling and he's not. When it's available, post the link to CombatZone.com and post it on Twitter and our Facebook page. Tell everybody in the company to repost it on their personal social media."

"Got it."

"And close the door, please? DND for a while."

I turned off my phone ringer. I lay back on the couch, thinking about what I'd just done. I hadn't rehearsed at all, yet when I talked to Upton the scorn came so easily, so naturally. It was the first erotic excitement I'd felt with a man since last summer when I met his father. I'd only seen A.J. on TV, but after our skirmish on the radio I couldn't stop thinking about him. Winning the argument was sweet. Now I wanted to pull off his public mask and wipe that rich kid smirk off his face, by sitting on it, stark naked, gripping fistfuls of his golden wavy hair.

The talk show smackdown of A.J. Upton by the madwoman creator of "*Men R Dawgs*" quickly went viral. My office people were buzzing all afternoon, high on all the attention we were getting. We got texts and emails and calls from friends and crew members, but hundreds more from the public came through our website. Lenny and Juno texted their praise. Whit Allwether called, thanked me for defending the film, and reminded me to clear press contacts with studio publicity in advance.

Barky called and exulted at how I had put A.J. in his place.

"You're the new hero around this office," she said, "and I'm editing our coolest author! Challenging him to see the play was awesome!"

"It just popped out. But I couldn't let him get away with what he said on *Fox*. It's so easy now for bullshit to become reality."

"I'm sure nobody remembers that stuff he said on TV," Barky said. "Your radio thing is a 'way bigger story."

When my editors and I took a break for coffee they replayed the Crockett webcast for comic relief and laughed themselves silly. To my employees I was a verbal ninja who destroyed A.J.'s defenses and forced him to limp away from the fight. But when he muttered that weak goodbye, *Yeah, so nice to meet you, Miss Monet*, his dejected voice and his downcast face tugged at my heart in a surprising way. I caught a glimpse of someone else behind that mask of superiority, someone dispirited, disappointed, and more than a little bit like me. Maybe he wasn't happy, even though his life of comfort and privilege turned out just as he'd been promised. And then, strange as it may seem, I felt sad for him. Sad?! For him? What was wrong with me? Compassion for a man who had none for anyone else? I told myself I'd better get over that. As things turned out, though, it wasn't that simple.

Megan announced that Jonathan was calling. Reluctantly, I picked up the phone, knowing I'd have to talk to him sooner or later.

"A total demolition!" he crowed. "Exactly what the little shit deserved!"

"I defended our movie, that's all."

"I was surprised when you offered to take him to see the play."

"I knew he'd refuse."

"Have dinner with me," Jonathan said eagerly. "I want to hear the whole story, from the beginning."

"Sorry. Can't do it tonight. We're behind schedule and I have to work late. I've got to go. My editors are waiting."

"Well, okay," Jonathan said, peeved, "but tell me: how much begging do I have to do to get a date with you these days?"

"Jonathan, don't start this again, okay?"

"No, really. I think it's time we sat and talked about our relationship."

I resisted the urge to scoff or slam the phone down. "Okay. Whatever you need."

"I just need to be clear on what our deal is."

Was he trying to make me worry? "Yeah. Me too."

"We're overdue for that talk."

"Then let's make it soon." But then I, with the most to lose, weakened. "Jonathan?"

"Yeah?"

"Are you okay?" There was a pause. "I mean, are we okay?"

"How many times do I have to tell you? You've got nothing to worry about," he muttered, and hung up.

I got to the Alpha Bitch offices early the next morning, and found I was either famous, or infamous.

So many people wanted to hear me put down A.J. Upton that the Alpha Bitch website server kept freezing and crashing. We got over two thousand comments overnight. Many of them were supportive, but a lot were violent, obscene, and sexist, threatening "The 'Men R Dawgs' Bitch" with everything from rape to dismemberment. *Fox News* absurdly called the "debate" a win for A.J. and replayed his mockery of his father and my as-yet-unseen film. The *New York Daily News* ran the story with my picture under the headline "'Dawgs' Director Bites MAGA Magpie." Nobody from the Left said much about the play or the movie, but there was a lot of mockery of A.J., and one writer proposed that I "emasculated" him. What A.J. must've thought about this emasculation theme, I didn't know, but in the pictures of him in various media he looked scrumptious. The picture of me on *Slate* was pretty good, and both *Fox News* and *MSNBC* replayed the moment when I offered to take him to see the play. Some commenters called me bold, and others, a predator. I got a text from Jonathan saying demand for tickets to see the play had shot 'way up. Requests for interviews kept coming in but I had Marshall politely decline them and I kept editing *"Lonely Sky"*.

At mid-morning, Megan's voice came out of my phone's speaker.

"Hey, guess what? That guy's on Line 1."

"What guy?"

"That guy from yesterday. Uptown."

"He is?" Was I ready for more combat? I'd had that inexplicable moment of sympathy for him, but that was yesterday. I opened Line 1, and said cheerfully, "Hello!"

His voice was low, velvety, amused. "Miss Monet?"

"No, this is Hillary, would you like to donate to the Clinton Global Initiative?"

He laughed. "I'm calling to follow up on yesterday. We seem to be having a media moment."

"Was it as good for you as it was for me?"

"I thoroughly enjoyed the whole thing."

"You enjoyed being whipped by a woman?"

"'Whipped'?"

"And in public."

"Who said I was 'whipped'?"

"Seems to be the consensus, A.J."

"According to what, some liberal poll?"

"Polls are your world, not mine. Why are you calling?"

"We need to do a rematch."

"The last time I looked at my list of needs a rematch with you wasn't on it."

"Reconsider. There's value to be had in this moment for us both."

"So you admit you were whipped."

"What show would you like to do?" he said. "They're all asking."

"I know, we're getting calls too."

"They all want us to do another debate."

"That wasn't a debate. You lied about my movie. I straightened you out and corrected the public impression you caused."

"Well, in any event, let's do it again. Let's put American pop culture under a magnifying glass. But we have to move fast or else —"

"No, I'm too busy." I felt it was my social duty to keep baby fascists him out of the media as much as I could. Plus, I liked fucking with his head. He was frustrated and trying to be cool about it.

"You can't find 20-minutes?"

"You're lucky I have time for this call."

His voice tightened. "This is not very sporting of you, Adrienne."

"It wasn't very sporting of you to mock a film you hadn't even seen."

"Oh, will you get over that!?"

"A lot of people worked hard on that film. You disrespected their work."

"Oh well, excuse me. Will I be hearing a formal complaint from their unions?"

"They have more important things to do."

"You're not giving me a chance to reply to the things you said."

"I'll give you my email address."

"In public."

"You want to set me up on a talk show with one of your right-wing buddies so the two of you can cut me up."

"We'll do MSNBC, if you're more comfortable with them. I'm not afraid of that pack of dribbling libs. I just want a chance to even the score."

"The score is even. You took cheap shots at my movie, I fired back."

"You're missing the point. Another debate –"

"It wasn't a debate."

"– another appearance with me would be good for your brand. We're the hot story of the moment. Let's take advantage of it."

"My film will be released next year. That's when I'll need publicity. You're just trying to use me to sell your Jesus book."

He laughed, a goofy giggle that didn't quite go with his nose-in-the-air. "It's too bad you don't have the nerve to face me again. We could have fun with this."

"It's too bad you don't have the nerve to see the play."

"I checked you out on the Internet Movie Database. I read your Wiki bio. You're a worthy adversary."

"Gee, I'm flattered. After all, you're much more famous than me."

He apparently didn't hear the sarcasm.

"I'm giving you a chance to get a piece of that. I see you wasted no time getting our little scuffle online."

"We're expecting a call from the Crockett show telling us to take it down."

"No worries. It's staying up. Gunnar's favor to me."

"You actually asked them not to squelch it?"

"Sure, why not?"

"You don't come off too well, Uptown."

"I call it 'feeding the beast,' Adrienne. Sometimes you get the fist pump. Sometimes they want to see you with your pants down. It's just part of being famous."

"I don't want to be famous because of a tiff in the media."

"Too late for that, I'm afraid."

"I want my work to be famous."

"Well, okay –" a glum pause – "I've got to take another call. But can we continue this, maybe over dinner tonight?" Whoa, wait a minute... "I think we need to finish what we started. Even though I usually don't date know-it-all liberals."

"Really?" He clearly enjoyed needling me as much as I liked antagonizing him. My God, did that mean he was attracted to me? "How would you like to finish it?"

"Dinner tonight. Come on, I promise to go easy on you."

"Go easy? After I kicked your ass all over the radio you should be begging me for mercy."

"Let's get together and see who kicks what."

"Let's go see the play."

"Dinner first."

I made him wait while I pretended to check my schedule. We chose a restaurant and a time to meet and exchanged cell phone numbers and email addresses.

"Okay, but just be aware, postproduction can be unpredictable. Last minute problems come up all the time." That was my escape hatch. "And no telling anybody about it, okay?"

"Of course not," he said. "That wouldn't be sporting at all."

Just to test him, I called him an hour later and cancelled.

"Why?" he said, annoyed. So he passed the test. A low chagrin threshold often meant genuine interest.

"I have to work tonight."

"Oh, don't be such a drudge."

"Straightening you out yesterday put me behind schedule."

"I think you're afraid of me."

I dismissed that with a laugh. "Friday's better for me. How about you?"

"If we make it early, say six o'clock? Same place?"

So that's how we began. It was clear from the start we were totally unlike each other. I wanted to drag his golden ass to bed and fuck him to the brink of death, and he wanted to use me to promote his book about being saved by the Savior. And yet the longer we played with an unlikely attraction that puzzled us both, the more we were likely to give in to it.

Friday morning, eating breakfast at my gym's café, I got a Google alert saying a book signing and reading by A. J. Upton was scheduled at the Barnes & Noble on Union Square at seven thirty that night. He was obviously going to squeeze in an early dinner with me, so he could tell his book-signing audience we'd met, or worse, try to drag me along to sex up the reading. I called him around lunchtime.

"I've got to reschedule again."

"I knew you'd try to wiggle out," he said, sounding like he'd won something.

"I'm not wiggling. I just can't make an early dinner. How about later?"

"I'll be free after nine."

"Okay. Or should I come down and make a scene at your book signing? Give your fans something to blog and tweet about?"

"I prefer they blog and tweet about my book."

"Of course. So call me when you're free."

Around nine thirty, I was home and getting hungry when he called.

"Adrienne?"

"Uptown?"

"One second."

Quiet and intense against the crowd noise, I heard him snarl to someone, "Because he's a complete asshole, that's why!" Then he came back to me.

"Are we still on tonight?" he said. "Because I'd really like to have your clever, ball-busting company."

We met at a country French restaurant on Tenth Avenue in Chelsea near the High Line, in a gentrifying old industrial neighborhood. As soon as I entered, there he was, leaning on the bar, a golden-haired blue-eyed devil, taller than his father, wearing a gray three-piece herringbone suit and silver tie, thumbing out a text on his phone.

I sidled past him, bumped his elbow messing up his text as if by accident, and acted surprised.

"Oh, hey! It's you! Jonathan Lehane's kid, right? What's your name again?"

That got me a suave lift of the eyebrow.

"Pleased to finally meet you, Miss Monet." As he shook my hand he leaned back and looked me over from head to foot. I hoped those ice-blue eyes were seeing through my clothes. It wasn't too soon to start heating up his caged animal impulses. "Very pleased, actually."

"We'll see how long that lasts. The name is Adrienne, remember? Like what you see?" The second I asked that, I cringed inwardly.

"Do I like what I see?" A close-mouthed, chuckled version of his goofy giggle. "Well, the wardrobe is a little," he wobbled a hand, "I guess... transgressive." I had on jeans and Chelsea boots, my well-worn motorcycle jacket and a knit cap, and I was purposely bra-less under a blouse so sheer it barely hid my nipples.

In return, I mocked the way he looked me up and down.

"Taller than anticipated," I said, note-taking out loud. "Sort of Brooks Brothers tweedy, Ivy Leaguey. Looks, not too shabby. Maybe a little too pretty. Inflicts a shameless visual appraisal on new female acquaintances."

He was charmed. "Ha! Advantage Monet!"

The hostess brought us to a corner table. Nobody looked twice at us, but A.J. still wanted to sit with his back to the crowd.

"That's okay," I said. "I like the gangster seat, back to the wall. If I see any liberals about to attack, I'll grab my knife and fork."

"Really? You'd defend me?"

"If anybody gets to attack you tonight, it's gonna be me."

We ordered drinks and dinner: for him, endive and Roquefort salad, grilled lamb sausages with sautéed apples and a dark beer, and for me, chilled avocado and cucumber soup, skate wing with lemon butter and capers, and a glass of white Burgundy.

Then I attacked. I'd waited all day to slam him for his blog post that morning making excuses for the recent police killing of a young black man and ridiculing those in the Black Lives Matter movement for their "grievance-mongering."

"That was heartless. You should be ashamed."

"He got shot committing a crime!" he yelped. "The kid had a gun!"

"You'd think he pointed it at you personally."

"Well, thanks to the police, he'll never get the chance, will he?"

"The police didn't have to kill him. The bodycam video shows he was surrendering. The gun was in his waistband. It wasn't even in his hand."

"Not yet." He shook his head. "Y'know, you liberals, you're hopeless."

"Suppose that was your brother dead in the street?"

"No brother of mine would rob a bodega."

"No, but if your brother and that black kid both went to court for the same crime, who do you think would get better treatment?"

He slumped back as if I was being terribly unfair. "Are you going to keep identifying me with everything you think is wrong with America?"

"You mean the way you did with me and my movie?"

"Man! People call me unbearable."

"I can't imagine why."

The drinks arrived, Stoli on the rocks for him, Campari and soda for me. His cell phone rang. He took it from his pocket, checked the screen, pushed a button and pocketed it. "Off. Okay?"

"Thank you. So –" I smiled sweetly. "Are you pissed off at me?"

"Not yet," he said.

I took a sip of Campari and soda, tart and fizzy. "So, how was your book signing?"

"Just great, until Lehane showed up, drunk, and took over the microphone. He told everyone he laughed when he heard me slag him on TV and, get this, he didn't hold it against me."

"He crashed your reading. He's a bigger drama queen than I thought."

"He grabbed me in this maudlin, staggering hug, kissing my cheek, telling me he loved me, and he got the biggest applause of the evening. I should have slugged him."

"I'm sure that's what Jesus would have done."

He ignored that, fulminating. "I was too shocked to react. I just stood there, looking like a complete fool. The whole thing made me ill. In fact, I think I still am, a little. But this should help." He raised his glass and drank half his vodka. "I'm sure somebody's already posted a cell phone video. So, for the second or third day in a row the media will have an embarrassing incident involving the notorious A.J. Upton, and his so-called real father. My mother wanted to kill him."

"She was there?"

"Oh yes. Mummy's very supportive."

"Did she confront Lehane?"

"God no," he said. "They don't speak, not even to insult each other."

"And who's 'Upton'?" I knew the answer, but I wanted to hear his version.

"My stepfather. He lives in Palm Beach, except for the 18 months the government put him in the gulag on a politically-motivated insider trading charge." A.J. was clearly proud of him. "We get along very well. He's been a better father to me than Lehane could ever be."

"So tell me A.J. How do you feel about all this?"

"About what?"

"Us. Here. Like this."

"Oh God." He gave me an anguished, disappointed look. "Don't tell me you're one of those types."

"What types?"

"The type of woman who wants to know what I'm feeling every two minutes." A chuckle of extreme discomfort. "I'm warning you. I'm not the emotional type."

"It's funny how men think they can keep their feelings hidden. You're really only hiding them from yourself."

"Adrienne, don't you think amateur psychotherapy is kind of off-putting on a first date?"

"Scares you, doesn't it? That I can read you like a book?"

"No, it doesn't, because no, you can't."

"Then why are you so nervous?"

"Oh please. Nothing makes me nervous anymore. Surviving an ugly scandal was a big help with that. I'll get blowback from that on my book tour but with the Lord's help, I'll handle it."

"Something you wrote destroyed a man's career and he killed himself. I think you can expect some 'blowback.'"

"Look," he said, putting down his drink. "I refuse to pull punches when I expose corruption, decadence, or malfeasance in public office. You accused of me of having a thing about inflicting pain? Well, sometimes it's unavoidable if you're trying to do the right thing. The congressman had other issues too, like a female intern who withdrew a sexual harassment complaint and left his office with a large severance secretly paid by one of his donors. He also had a nasty gambling addiction, which is why he needed the slush fund. I was right about the corruption. That's what everybody forgets. He was found guilty. That said, I'm not okay with him killing himself. It put me through a painful period of soul-searching, questioning the way I was doing things. Ultimately, I decided the only thing we can do is put ourselves in God's hands, see everything in our lives as a manifestation of His will."

"Does that include this get-together?"

"Actually, I was surprised you accepted my invitation."

"I admit I hesitated. But then this deep commanding voice came down from Heaven..." He was not amused. "You know, I really enjoy antagonizing you."

"I feel the same about you. Kind of interesting, isn't it?"

"Are you married?"

"No."

"Me neither. Girlfriend?"

"Not lately. Boyfriend?"

"Nobody who has what I'm looking for."

"Which is what?"

"I'll know when I find it."

"By the way, don't hold your breath waiting for me to see the play."

"I think we should smoke a joint, go sit in the front row, and make our presence felt."

"My God!" He laughed, horrified. "Despite my reputation," he said, "I generally don't like drama."

"Like it or not, you got some tonight, A.J. Thanks to Jonathan, the coverage will be bigger. More people will hear about your book."

"It doesn't mean they'll buy it."

"Should've thought of that before you started this feud."

"I started it?! It started when that bastard ran off and left me without a father."

Again, I felt that twinge of sympathy for him. His hatred of Jonathan was right under the skin. The poor kid was still fighting the war that his father carelessly started when he was five years old.

"Why stop there?" I said. "Why not blame his evil seed for causing you to be born in the first place? After all, you've had such a rough life up there on Park Avenue." He scoffed, and his eyes took on a glazed defensiveness. "Or, instead of staying stuck in the past, it might be healthier for you to forgive him for not being perfect. I get that you hate him, and you have a right to. But what good does that do you now?" He leaned forward, listening to me intently. "Think about that. Maybe you can become a person of generous and compassionate spirit. Develop an open and loving heart, beginning with gratitude and compassion toward your father."

He stared at me, then his eyebrows formed an imperious arch.

"Fuck that," he said, and laughed. For some reason, when he was appalling and obnoxious, I was even more attracted to him.

"Oh well. Not everybody wants to be happy."

"I'll be happy when we get off this and into some food."

But I kept at him before he could change the subject.

"We don't get to choose our parents," I said. "My mother was a socialite, self-involved and neglectful, and we haven't had any contact for years. My father was a cold fish who died years ago. But I've forgiven them. They did their best with what they had. It just wasn't enough."

A.J. cocked an eyebrow and looked worried, perhaps anticipating an unwelcome appearance by my suffering inner child.

"People raise their kids as imperfectly as they do everything else," I said. "We all need love, and we never get enough. Our parents probably didn't either and that's why they fell short."

He was getting restless, but he held back as the waiters placed dinner on the table.

"I'm okay with imperfection," he said. "That has to be forgivable, or we're all in trouble. But not selfishness and irresponsibility."

"Let's make a deal." I sniffed the wine in my glass. "I spent all summer working with your father, and that definitely had its ups and downs. Let's not have him here at the dinner table with us. Okay?"

He nodded, and we ate quietly for a while. "So – Monet? I guess you're French."

"Sounds like that's a problem for you." Given that his father abandoned him and his mother for a French film star, that wouldn't be surprising.

"Well... Don't get me started on the French."

"Why do all you right wingers hate the French?"

"I think contempt is a better word."

"Y'ever hear the old saying, 'Contempt is the mask of envy'?"

"Oh, please."

"Why don't you look at your own life the same way you criticize other people? You might learn something."

"Oh really?" he said with a disdainful smirk. "Go ahead. Teach me."

"Politics isn't everything. It just seems that way, because we're drowning in media thanks to people like you."

"I provide information and insight in a free marketplace of ideas."

"You exploit anger, self-pity, resentment and envy," I scoffed, "which sets people up to be manipulated by a con man like Donald Trump. Thanks to people like you, they're so emotionally revved up they don't notice their pockets are being picked by the rich."

"The Number One Liberal Delusion."

"That's not delusion. That's reality."

"It's tiresome class warfare, Adrienne. Without the so-called 1 percent with their power to create wealth and jobs, the other 99 percent would be broke, naked, living in caves, and with nothing to eat but each other."

"Wow." I had to laugh. "Who's deluded now?"

"It's not deluded to see that power and wealth are the essential values in life. For me, writing about politics is fascinating. I write about people who pursue power, and the things they do with it."

"How about the damage they do?"

"I cover that too. All I'm saying is, politics is a respectable news beat."

"And writing and arguing about it is how you get your own power fix, right?"

"You bet. Millions of people hear me on the radio, see me on TV, read my blog and my essays. I influence the way they see their country and their government. That's power, and I won't deny that I enjoy having it."

"Because you're an exhibitionist, looking for attention."

"The trouble with you liberals is, whenever you get power, you use it as an excuse to punish success and force a decadent European morality on the American people."

"A decadent European morality?" Such piety was an irresistible target. "Tell you what, A.J. Go ahead, call me a liberal. Better yet, 'left wing liberal eco-feminist humanist Godless half-queer bohemian filmmaker.' How's that?" I wrapped my calves around his under the table and leaned in closer. "Will that make it more exciting for you to fuck me tonight?"

He surprised me. He turned red, from his smooth and noble forehead all the way to his fingertips. He stared into his drink.

"I, uh, heh-heh, well," he said with an embarrassed chuckle. "Tonight's too soon for me."

I tried to not let my disappointment show. He was so full of anger and aggression that I was sure we could give each other a wild time in bed. Damn! Of all people, he's shy with women!? He couldn't even look me in the eye.

"Of course, A.J., I wouldn't want you to do anything that would violate any of your moral convictions. Especially not on the night you promoted the story of your redemption through Christ." He sighed, to him I was impossible. "But since you called me for this date, and you slap labels on everything, I thought you might have an appetite for a little secular-humanist-liberal-bohemian pussy." He rolled his eyes.

He laughed. "You're too much!"

I almost said I'm even better in bed. I waited for an answer, but he kept laughing.

"Pussy, A.J. Right here. It's calling you, can't you hear it? A.J! A.J! Please!"

He was laughing, and too flustered to say anything. He told me later no woman in his life had ever come on to him like that. I wanted to keep attacking his smug righteousness with promises of raw sex for the asking, but A.J. was more than a few years younger than me, so I shut up before he thought I was just an old cougar in heat.

We talked about safer topics while we finished dinner, and he offered to walk me home. As we left the restaurant, he waved to an SUV and the smoked window on the passenger side went down. As he spoke to the driver, I got a glimpse of the man at the wheel, shaved head, dark shirt and jacket, wraparound dark glasses, even at night. He nodded, then rolled up the window.

"Who's that?" I said.

"Him? That's Billy. He's my shadow. There have been some threats."

Billy followed in the SUV about a car length behind us. We entered my building vestibule, both of us a bit drunk, and I slung my arm around his waist.

"Well, A.J.?"

He leaned down and kissed me, his cold hand on my cheek, a clumsy kiss tasting of beer and coffee, but it lasted, and it lasted. He didn't hold me in his arms, he crushed my body between his body and the wall. And I liked it – holy shit, I liked it a lot. The kiss ended, and he leaned back, looking astonished, and both of us were, like, Whoa!

He shook his head. "You drive me out of my mind. I'm not sure it's in a good way, either."

"That's okay. I don't know what the hell I'm doing with you either."

"You realize," he said, looking around warily, "if we're going to see each other, we have to be absolutely discreet."

"You mean, like, not making out in my building vestibule?"

"If my friends saw me doing this, they wouldn't believe it."

"If my friends caught me kissing you, they'd have me committed."

"But we are seeing each other," he said. "Right?"

I grinned, stood on the balls of my feet, and kissed him, another lingering kiss.

"So right."

He trotted down the front steps to the SUV, climbed in, and he was gone.

Upstairs, I paced up and down the hallway of my apartment, too aroused to sit down. I had an urge to masturbate to take the edge off, but I wanted to hold the excitement inside, even if I lost a night's sleep. I was looking forward to shocking A.J. out of his protective piety. More than ever, I was eager to corrupt him, and I had a feeling that deep down he'd enjoy it. Not that it would be an affair made in anybody's idea of heaven. It would be love, or war, or maybe both.

Around midnight, I was in bed when Barky called from an Uber coming in from Newark airport after a business trip to LA. Her shabby railroad flat on the Upper East Side would be cold and lonely after such a long trip and she missed me. I was thrilled; she was going to bypass Hoboken and Garth's cozy apartment to come stay with me.

She set down her luggage and shook off her coat, and after a hug and a warm kiss, I made us tea while she smoked a joint she'd bought legally in LA.

"I didn't have time to chill out before the plane," she said, exhaling the smoke into the range hood exhaust fan over my stove. "I've been waiting to do this for five boring hours. Whoosh!"

Once she was relaxed and giggly, I surprised her with a DVD screening of the first time we made love, secretly filmed with the three-camera hidden setup in my bedroom.

"You sneaky bitch!" Barky gasped, shocked. "You didn't tell me you were filming us!"

I hit the Pause button.

"I didn't want to make you self-conscious."

"I'd never let some guy do this."

"I hope not!"

"He might say he loves me, but if I ever dump him you just know the video'll be online."

My surprise was backfiring.

"If that worries you, I'll delete the whole thing."

"Well," she shrugged. "First let's watch."

She curled up on the couch beside me, bashful and fascinated. She flushed red with embarrassment as she watched me eat her pussy, and as she saw herself in the throes of orgasm, gasping, gripping handfuls of the sheet and moaning, she shook her head, amazed.

"Oh my God," she whispered. "I've never seen myself like that!"

"You've never made a sex tape?"

"Never! God no!"

"I think we look we look great together."

"So hot!" She turned to me, awed and surprised. "Where's my copy?"

The video faded out with us in each other's arms. Tossing her hair back, her eyes bright with mischief, Barky straddled my lap and began kissing me. That night was the second time Barky and I made love. Compared to such sweetness, having sex with a man, no matter how physically perfect or exciting, shriveled to a lesser thrill. But as hot as we were together, I couldn't forget that Barky had a fiancé that she wasn't willing to dump. So I didn't see any need to tell her about my plans for the notorious A.J. Upton.

The next morning eating breakfast at a place on 8th Avenue, she handed me The *New York Times* folded to an advertisement headlined "Who killed Egon Swift?" taking up the entire back page of the first section. Under a heroic picture of Egon, a long list of people from his personal and professional lives had co-signed a letter from Rita Swift addressed to the mayor of New York, blasting the NYPD's failure to catch his killer.

"We demand a commitment of greater resources to the investigation to get justice for a stellar member of America's creative community." Among the signatories were Egon's parents, his agent, publicist, manager, and his personal assistant in L.A.

"I don't see your name here," Barky said.

"I would've signed if I'd been asked."

But it made me wonder. If I were ever murdered, how many people would pressure the police with a full-page ad in the *Times* to catch my killer? I guess to find out, I'd have to grow a penis and a pair of testicles, do $900 million worth of business, and thus become a stellar member of the creative community.

On Monday morning I tried to concentrate on work, but I kept getting distracted thinking about that first date with A.J. Upton. I needed to find out if he could understand me and the film he shamelessly slandered, so I messengered him a DVD of the most recent cut of *"Lonely Sky"*. To my surprise the messenger returned with an autographed copy of *"Nearer My God to Thee"*, luckily in a plain manila envelope. He'd written on the title page, "To Adrienne Monet, my sexiest antagonist." I took a look inside, expecting a cynical public relations effort to repair his image after he drove a Congressman to suicide.

But he took me by surprise. I recognized his voice immediately, but it wasn't in his sneering TV or blog tone. On the page he was soft and sincere. His apology to the dead congressman's family – "I deeply regret the unfortunate way some people felt about what was for me an act of patriotism and investigative journalism" – was clumsy and inadequate, but it sounded like the man I'd just met. He wanted to be believed, so there was none of the vitriol and caustic wit he inflicted on the decadent world he saw around him. Instead, he shared the insight that he said changed his life.

"Each of us plays our small part in the Divine Plan. We may not understand the plan, but it is our job as humans created by God in His image to live in its light."

I'd never been drawn to religion and often wavered in my belief in God. But the more I read, the more intrigued I became with A.J. Upton's spirituality. He was trying to change the world's view of him as a bully and political provocateur, and my gut instinct was that his story, like any fall and redemption story, would be convincing to many. But I read a different story beneath the voice on the page. I sensed a vulnerable, sad, fatherless boy, frightened by a world that was changing all around him and desperate to hold on to his place in it, a boyish man with a deep feeling of inadequacy that he covered up with anger and hubris. In some ways, he was a lot like me. We'd both been abandoned young, and we'd both created personas to protect that damaged, unfinished self. It was clear from what I read that A.J. had sincerely embraced Christianity, which was good news for me. Trying to corrupt a cynic would be no challenge at all.

I read his book all evening and finished it the next morning on the subway and in my office. At noon, I peeled off my work jeans and tee shirt and put on the party outfit I'd brought with me: a knee length black leather skirt and white chenille blouse, low heels, and a string of fake pearls. I brushed out my hair and freshened my makeup, then bundled up in my overcoat and walked over to the Hilton for the annual Muse Awards luncheon of the New York Women in Film and Television.

Heads turned as I strolled into the ballroom. I even got a pattering of applause. Women I didn't know high-fived me, maybe for my performance on the Crockett show a few days earlier, or maybe because they liked "*Men R Dawgs*". The women at my table unanimously toasted my takedown of A.J. Upton and assured me that they all loathed him, too.

I loved the applause, but I also loved the irony. My knowledge of A.J. had deepened far beyond what they thought they knew. He needed a woman, one he could fight with and fuck with, to break him out of the prison of his mind, an Alpha Bitch to free his crushed sexuality and put all that passion he wasted on politics and religion to better use. I was anticipating an exciting night in bed, hopefully soon. Sitting amidst a couple hundred New York women in film, all of us drinking and ignoring the inedible food, I knew I couldn't announce it to my lady friends around the table, but I'd already promised myself that soon I'd have A.J. Upton fucking me on a crate of Bibles and begging God to forgive him.

For the next week he flew to nine cities in seven days to promote his memoir. He gave readings in towns and colleges across America, leaving a noxious trail of news stories and YouTube videos. A tense supercilious debate with a Black female book chat host. Looking foolishly excited being interviewed by Pat Robertson. Sparring with progressive college audiences. Getting such loving attention from the *Fox* affiliate in each city you'd think he was a candidate for beatitude. I followed his antics through his website and on Twitter and YouTube, which left me laughing and shaking my head. I was surprised that I missed him as much as I did. During the day when he did TV and radio interviews, I never got a callback or a text from him. He called late at night when he was in his hotel room, when he was either too exhausted to talk or so pumped up from the turmoil of his appearances that he couldn't stop talking. He emailed me a couple snarky vignettes and cell phone videos of protesters at his appearances. He called me from California, indignant because a Black student protest forced a college administration to cancel his appearance. He emailed me the rough draft of a vitriolic blog post about Left Fascism and the suppression of free speech, gloating that the cancellation would only prove to conservatives that the Left was out to get them. I didn't take the time to criticize the piece and I knew he'd ignore me anyway.

When he came home to New York he called from the airport and asked me to dinner. I had no time to change, so I headed uptown in my work clothes. As we ate chicken wings and salad and drank beer at a hole-in-the-wall bar on Lexington Avenue, I was aware that his townhouse was just around the corner, and I was trying to guess the odds for a memorable evening.

He was glum and weary after all the traveling and squabbling with protestors. He apologized because he hadn't had time to watch *"Lonely Sky"*. He asked how the editing was going, but I could tell he wasn't interested. I wondered if he was losing the thrill of our passionate antagonism.

Then he asked, "Uh, by the way, when you were making your movie, you never slept with Lehane, did you?"

I wasn't ready for this, but I answered quickly, before I told a lie that might turn on me later.

"Of course I did." Telling the truth is always better if you can afford it, and I was glad he asked. It gave me a chance to see how much truth A.J. could handle. He reached for his beer.

"This is one of your jokes, right?" He gulped down the beer and held up the bottle for another.

"No. Would you rather I lied about it?"

"I don't know." He gave me a hurt stare. He picked up a wing and poked it into the pot of melted blue cheese on the table between us. "I really don't know."

The only thing I could do was mix true and false and hope that it wouldn't backfire on me later.

"All during shooting, we had a strictly professional relationship. It was a demanding schedule, long hours, a lot of work together, getting on each other's nerves. And then, one night..." I shrugged. "And then, like, the next day, I found out he was hooking up with an actress who'd played a bit part. There was also a sultry little extra who kept showing up on set and bugging him until the producers had security drag her away. That was it for me. I chalked it up to experience and moved on."

He stared at me and said nothing, poking the cheese with the wing.

"A.J.? Is this a problem for you?"

"Well, yeah. Of course. My father? Of all people? What the hell, Adrienne?"

If he was too immature to handle this, there was nothing I could do.

"Are you sorry you asked?"

"I don't know."

"It was long before I met you. There's nothing between me and Lehane now but work, and that's almost over."

"Yeah," A.J. said. "Lehane sticks around just long enough to get what he wants, then he's gone."

He kept jabbing the cheese with the chicken wing until it ran down the sides of the pot. "You show business types are always jumping in and out of bed anyway, right?"

"I'm not a type. I actually lead a very quiet life."

He nodded, but I couldn't tell if he believed me.

"You know," he muttered, "the whole time I was traveling, I was thinking of you."

"I missed you too."

He dropped the wing on his plate uneaten and began wiping his hands with the napkin. I hoped the talk would lead away from Lehane.

"I suspect that beneath this ballsy feminist thing of yours, dark and interesting depths await the explorer."

"I've never had my depths explored by a Republican."

"But I don't want to explore any deeper. At least not tonight." Before I could reply he just shrugged and waved for the check.

On the sidewalk, he brushed a quick kiss by my cheek, said "It's been nice," and waved at the black SUV at the curb, which pulled out and followed him home. Devastated, I watched him walk away. I didn't know what else I could say or do.

That night I sat up at my kitchen table drinking beer. I'd only told him a small part of the truth about his father and me and he couldn't even handle that. I'd just been getting to know him, hadn't even had sex with him, and yet I felt like something I had just died.

Winter arrived, cold blustery December days under damp gray skies that turned Manhattan into a black and white movie.

I got out of bed at five o'clock each morning, worked out at the gym for an hour, and walked home. I talked to Barky on FaceTime while I ate my breakfast of oatmeal with honey, raisins and walnuts, chewy, gooey, hot and delicious on a cold winter morning. I dressed in my work clothes, jeans and tee shirt and hoodie, black leather jacket, a wool knit cap pulled down over my hair and ears, and waterproof boots. I walked out to Eighth Avenue, stopped at Starbuck's for a large dark roast with half and half, and rode the C train up to the Alpha Bitch offices. I was on the stairway coming up to 49th Street when Barky texted me a link to a story on the *Village Voice* home page. "Egon Swift: The Man, the Career, and his Murder," with the startling sub-head, "Meet the cop who's bungling the investigation."

I held my breath. The reporter's angle was 'the paradox of Detective Buddy Ferino', a respected veteran detective with numerous citations for bravery who was bringing criticism down on the NYPD because he couldn't solve the murder of a Hollywood celebrity. The story confirmed a couple things I'd read about Ferino on the Web. He had recently been cleared in the killing of a teenage drug dealer and the crippling of his accomplice. The victims were Black, and the incident had caused a furor. The reporter also quoted an anonymous NYPD source who said the department brass were concerned about an affair Ferino had had with his sister-in-law, which had caused his brother to divorce his wife and sue Ferino for damages. Perhaps that was distracting him from the investigation.

Neither my name or Jonathan's was mentioned. I thought Ferino's scandalous cuckolding of his own brother was amusing, trashy gossip. I quit being so amused when I thought of how he might react to his dirty laundry being aired in public. The scandal might make him work harder to arrest me to redeem himself. I hopped over the pool of slush beside the news kiosk at 49th and Broadway and marched to work past the sparkly Christmas decorations in the Cinema Arts Building lobby, reminding myself that my first job was to stay out of jail.

A few days later, as I was pulling on my jacket ready to leave the office and go home for the evening, A.J. texted.

Okay, I watched your movie. Let's talk.

An hour later, he was bringing me a glass of wine in a woody old bar in the East 70s. He put my glass on the table then sat opposite me, leaning back in his chair with his arms crossed.

"You didn't tell me you played the ghost of Lehane's dead wife. Those husband and wife scenes made me very uncomfortable."

He still had feelings for me, much to my relief.

"We were playing characters, A.J. Off-screen, our relationship was nothing like that."

"Yeah, except for that one night."

"There was nothing romantic about that. It was just animal lust—"

"Yeah okay, I don't need to hear more."

"What did you think of the movie?"

"Well, I understand that the film isn't finished."

"That's right."

"But I think I saw all I needed to see."

Uh oh.

"You're not going to like what I have to say."

"I'm a big girl, I can handle it."

Which wasn't true. I wanted him to like my movie. And he didn't, I could feel it coming. I'd foolishly set myself up, hoping the meanest Republican wit in the blogosphere wouldn't attack me.

"I stand by my original opinion."

"You mean the one you gave on *Fox*? Before you even saw the movie?"

He ignored that and cleared his throat like a teacher quieting an unruly student.

"I was merely being prescient, and it turned out I was right. The country has moved on from 9/11, Adrienne. Your movie will drag America back to wallow in victimization and self-pity."

"Then I'm no better than your hero Donald Trump. He's good at wallowing in victimization and self-pity and dragging half the country down with him."

That went right past him. He shook his head.

"I think you've just directed another box office flop."

He took the DVD from his jacket pocket and handed it to me.

"Okay. Well, thank you for watching, and for being so honest."

I was disappointed in him, repeating the same meaningless opinion he spun out on *Fox News*. He was getting me back for my fling with Jonathan, that's all.

"Do me a favor, okay?" I said. "If you write about it, wait until it's released."

"No problem. That's when people will need a warning."

I had to laugh at that.

"Your readers wouldn't go to a film like mine anyway. They're too busy stocking up on guns and ammunition."

He liked that, and he chuckled. He pulled open his suit jacket.

"I'm unarmed, I swear."

"So, what's with this 'victimization and self-pity' shit you keep saying?"

"It's a year later, but your characters are still stuck in the aftermath of 9/11. All that'll do is make your audience feel stuck in the horror again themselves, and what for?" He stopped to think for a moment, and his voice lowered. "Can I ask you something?"

"Ask."

"Were you even in New York on 9/11?"

"Of course. That morning I flew into Newark from L.A. with my friend Jill on a red eye. I had meetings scheduled."

I took a slow drink of wine while I considered how much to tell him.

"We were in a cab, headed for the Holland Tunnel, when the first plane hit. It happened right in front of us. Traffic stopped dead. People got out of their cars. I thought I'd seen one of the worst plane crashes in history and I was furious because my camera was in my luggage in the trunk with a dead battery. And then, the second plane."

Across from me, A.J. listened, expressionless.

"They closed the tunnel. The cab driver got us to Hoboken, but the PATH train was shut down too. We were standing on one of the piers in a huge crowd of people when the buildings fell. It was a perfect disaster shot, from across the river you could see it in scale with the rest of the city. We dragged our luggage to the dock uptown in Hoboken and got a ferry across the river to Manhattan. The bus up to Jill's apartment on the Upper West Side was standing room only. The driver let everyone ride for free."

He sat back and raked back his hair with both hands.

"And now you want to put people through all that again."

"The film takes place a year later."

"Well," he dropped his hands, "it felt the same."

"I could take that as a 'thumbs up', y'know."

He drained his wine glass.

"People are going to hate you for dragging them back into all that."

"Do you hate me?"

"No, but it was painful to watch. I mean, okay, you don't show planes crashing into buildings and all that, but the aftermath is what was so devastating."

"For everyone. Like my characters."

"Like me, Adrienne," he said. "That damned movie, I just —" He shook his head.

"What?"

He thought for a moment, then waved me away.

"Never mind."

"It's okay, A.J." I said, "I'll just listen."

He hesitated. I reached for his hand, but he sat back.

"No. Never mind."

"You're sure?"

"Yeah." While I sat there, disappointed that he didn't open up to me, he looked around the bar, at people drinking and eating. "I think I've had enough of this place. Let's go." He called for the check.

We walked outside into a light snow, A.J. with his chin tucked into the collar of his overcoat. Outside we strolled toward the black SUV, parked up the street. It felt again like he was breaking up with me, and I didn't want to prolong the pain.

"Well A.J., I guess I'll say good night."

"No, no, wait." He looked confused. "Come home with me."

Now I was confused. First, he trashes my work, and now... "Do you want me to?"

"Well, isn't that what you want?"

"Well, yeah. I *have* invited you to fuck me. More than once."

"In fact," he said, mock-appalled, "on our first date!"

"The invitation still stands."

"It's cold out here." He sighed and looked around. The traffic on Lexington Avenue hissed past, fluffy snowflakes had started to fall on a huddle of people waiting to get into a nearby comedy club. Finally, he shrugged.

"I just want to be with you tonight. Maybe just to talk, or something, I don't know."

"Okay. Although sinful and unimaginable things could still happen."

He waved to his driver, and the SUV pulled away.

"I'm sure my moral foundations will survive the Adrienne Monet experience."

"If that's true," I said, "I'll be so disappointed."

A.J.'s bedroom on the top floor of his townhouse was luxuriously quiet. I could imagine him coming home after a long day provoking the anger and resentment and self-pity of his fans and sleeping peacefully in that cool blue room, swaddled like a baby in linens and soft lighting, the clamor of the city muffled by charcoal gray floor-to-ceiling curtains and thick carpet. When he woke up each morning in his king-size bed, the first thing he would see on the wall were silver-framed magazine covers with his face on them, hung alongside a wide screen TV tuned to *Fox News*. His bed was neatly made, but his clothes were tossed over an armchair in the corner, and a set of golf clubs, a lacrosse racket, and a large canvas gym bag lay on the floor between the furniture.

Getting us into bed was the easiest part. Both of us were sort of drunk, we kissed and groped our way upstairs, tore off each other's clothes, and slipped between the sheets so quickly we had to breathe on each other's cold hands to warm them. I was pleased with his response to my naked body, and I was excited by his thick muscles and the fine golden hair coating him from head to foot.

"I love this," I said, running my hand through the hair over his pecs and down his impressively cobbled abs. "So animalistic."

He laughed, kind of bashfully. He kept kissing me for a long time, until I got the feeling he was kissing so he didn't have to talk. He held me in his arms but showed no curiosity about the erogenous zones of my body. I reached down and took his hard cock in one hand and lightly brushed it with the other as one might admire a precious work of art. He frowned and exhaled a long wine-scented sigh. He seemed oddly conflicted, his expression seemed to say Wow, what am I doing?

He pulled his arm out from under me. He laid on his back, his eyes roaming, looking for something on the ceiling with an anguished expression. That alarmed me, and I was ready to climb on top of him when, without looking at me, he started talking, softly at first.

"Okay so, that morning? I was downtown on Foley Square on jury duty. I was hoping to be excused so I could get back to Dartmouth in time for the start of school. So we were all sitting there, bored and flipping through magazines, when we heard this loud crash. Nobody could tell where it came from because the windows in the room faced away from the Twin Towers. Nobody told us anything. We couldn't leave. We couldn't use our cell phones. We all just sat there. Then came this sound, boom-boom, and this sort of wave of high-pitched screams from the streets outside. So we knew something had happened. A court officer came in and said we were all released, and we'd get credit for that day's service, and we should leave the building as quickly as we could. When I got downstairs on the street, I saw smoke coming from behind some buildings, so I started walking that way." He swallowed hard. "Then I saw the towers were on fire."

He turned to me. His eyes filled with a kind of agonized need, reddened and filled with tears. He didn't want to tell the story, but he couldn't stop himself.

"I tried to call Kathy, my girlfriend. She worked for an insurance company in the North Tower." His eyes jerked away from mine and lifted towards the ceiling. "But all the cell phone circuits were jammed. I ran over to West Broadway and I stood there watching the buildings burn." He shook his head. "People around me were backed against the walls praying and cursing." His lips curled back. "What do you think your movie will do for them?"

"I... I don't know."

His voice became a ragged shudder, his eyes shining.

"I watched people jumping and dying. Praying she wasn't one of them. I don't think she was. But I was too far away to tell. Then the first building started coming down, and everybody turned and started running." His head fell back on the pillow, and he began to weep. He moaned, "I turned and ran!"

"Of course. What else could you do?"

"Nothing. But that doesn't matter. I still felt like the biggest coward in the world!"

His body shuddered as he wept. I pressed my warmth against him for support, my cheek on his shoulder. I wondered if I should let go of his cock, but in fact, the more he wept the more rigid his erection became. I thought that must have something to do with the release of some suppressed authentic feeling, mainly grief. With my other hand I gently brushed his hair back and placed my palm on his forehead.

"A.J., I'm sorry I said it looked like a disaster shot from a movie. Of course, I didn't know –"

He touched his fingers to my lips and shook his head. He took a deep breath, then spoke in bursts of sobbing, staring at the ceiling.

"I ran up West Broadway until I was away from the dust cloud... Then her building came down... I walked home, like, in a trance, all the way up to my mother's... All day, I tried to call Kathy, but I kept getting a busy signal... Her office was on a floor above the first plane impact... We found out later all the staircases were destroyed... None of those people had a chance."

"A.J., I'm so sorry that happened to you. So, so sorry."

We lay together quietly. He was no longer crying. He dried his eyes on the sheet, sniffling, and hugged me again. I kissed him, deep and wet and lingering, and started a line of kisses down his neck, licking around his nipples, and pressing my lips on his tight abs. His cock throbbed in my hand as my lips inched closer to it.

"That night I went downtown again," he was saying. I stopped kissing at the rim of his reddish pubic hair. "I sat on the front steps of her building until dawn the next day, hoping by some miracle she'd come walking home. Limping home. Crawling home. Delivered in an ambulance. I didn't care, I just wanted her back. I called the hospitals. I called her parents. I never heard from her again. No trace of her was ever found. We were together the night before, making plans for her to visit me up at school. The next day, she was gone. And she still is." His voice tightened. "When I think of what her last moments must have been like —"

"I'm so sorry, A.J. I didn't know you suffered such a terrible loss."

"Yeah, well, now you know." He shook his head. "I'm sorry to unload all this on you, but your movie brought it all up again."

"If you'd rather just cuddle for a while that's okay with me. Or if you just want to lie here and talk. Or if you want me to leave..."

"No," he said, pulling me up to him. "I'm okay now."

We made love, but it wasn't the ecstatic debauching of an uptight and unsophisticated man that I'd hoped to lay on him. I went to bed with him hoping to have fun, but what I got was a flood of repressed grief triggered by my movie. I don't mean the sex wasn't good, just strange. He'd shared the worst trauma in his life with me then he used sex with me to drug the hurt. And I was fully engaged, not a detached observer the way I had been in bed with his father. He was eager, he fucked me for a long time, and even though I didn't come, I can't say I was disappointed.

Afterwards, we laid back catching our breath.

"That was" – he searched for a word, and I hoped to hear something rich and vulgar – "unprecedented."

Huh? "Translation, please."

A bashful laugh. "I don't usually last that long." He was proud of himself. How cute.

 "Why tonight?"

"You made me feel like a super stud. I didn't want it to end."

"That's the way it is when you eat the forbidden fruit."

"Oh c'mon, Adrienne. When God punished Adam and Eve, I doubt they enjoyed it, sexually or otherwise."

"No, but they enjoyed eating the apple."

"They broke the rules, and they paid the price."

"Right, and you can be sure they ran behind the nearest bush and got busy."

"Well, if they did, it was Eve's idea."

"Isn't that always the way? The woman is always the spark, isn't she? The instigator. Making trouble, making love. Leading righteous men astray, helping them to find their power to fuck all night. Tonight was kind of Biblical, if you think about it."

"If you've actually read the Bible... oh, never mind."

"Don't you see that telling me that story made you free to feel more? Cleaned out a lot of stuff you've been keeping down. You see? I can bring out the best in you."

So, I thought, where's my reward? He fucked me, but how much had he been with me?

He said, "Was it good for you?"

"Wonderful." Hopefully, better next time. I reached down and pulled the sheet and blankets up over us and lay back. "In fact, I think I'll sleep here tonight."

"If you even try to leave, I'll burn your clothes. What time do you need to get up?"

"Whenever you do." I laid my head on his shoulder. After a while, thinking he was asleep, I fitted myself into a warmer place beside him.

I was just drifting off when his voice came out of the dark.

"Hey, what about my book? Did you read it yet?"

"Of course. Very inspiring. A very different Uptown. I'll tell you more tomorrow."

"Those things I said about your movie..." He started to apologize.

"It's okay. I understand."

"Yeah," he murmured. "That's what scares me about you." We laughed together, each for our own reasons, and cuddled closer.

The next thing I knew, I opened my eyes, and it was morning. A.J. was standing by the window, naked, squinting in the brilliant sunlight reflected off his backyard garden blanketed in freshly-fallen snow. He saw I was awake, and grinned.

"Good morning, Adrienne Monet."

In spite of everything that happened later, horrors that are burned into my soul forever, that's how I will always remember him, the morning light on his golden body, the smile he turned to me, and the delight in his voice, softly saying my name.

"Any more run-ins with my nasty little spawn?" Jonathan said, as he smeared cream cheese on a toasted cinnamon-raisin bagel, the smell of which was turning my stomach. We were eating Sunday brunch at Starbucks on Eighth Avenue in my neighborhood. Outside the window, people shuffled past on the slushy sidewalk, heads down as the wind coated them with wet snowflakes.

I'd canceled on him the day before to see A.J. off from JFK for a book tour, so I felt obligated to see him today. But after spending the night drinking tequila and dancing with Barky at a girl's bar downtown until dawn, I'd had about two hours sleep. All the nutrition my queasy stomach could handle was three aspirin washed down with a café au lait and soda water chaser, and until the pills began working, my brain throbbed with every beat of my heart.

Inside the café it was warm and dry, and Diana Krall was making beautiful music on the sound system.

"No run-ins," I said. Then, the test: "But after the Crockett thing, I was curious, so I had dinner with him to see what he's like."

Jonathan's knife froze with a fat glob of cream cheese on the end.

"You asked him to dinner?"

"No, he called me. He wanted to do a rematch on some right-wing talk show. Of course, I said no."

"I'm sure he loved that."

"Why'd you go to his book signing and act so silly, Jonathan?"

"I know, I know," he said, munching. "But I couldn't resist." He chuckled, savoring the memory.

"After the Crockett show the backlash against A.J. was just crazy. People loved hearing him get humiliated. He's really hated, isn't he?"

"Yes, and like all the rest of MAGA, he thinks he's the victim. He's misguided, haughty, and has no conscience. He's proud of his reputation as a right-wing bomb thrower."

"I think he's confused fame with notoriety. Although these days, it's hard to tell the difference."

"A friend once said to me if A.J. ever fathered a baby it'd be born with horns and a tail. I couldn't disagree."

I couldn't tell if he was joking or if he really saw his son as a satanic terrorist. But one thing was depressingly clear. I'd better forget about letting father or son know about my affair with the other. I'd told A.J. that I'd had a one-night hookup with his father, and after his initial disappointment, he'd let it go. The real danger was Jonathan, sitting across from me muttering bitterly. He was so consumed by hurt and anger toward A.J. that if he ever found out I was involved with his son his reaction would be unpredictable, but certainly bad.

"...such a supercilious little shithead," Jonathan sputtered. "Over the years I've forced myself to ignore all the nasty things he's said about me. It's like an evil spell he can't escape."

That was also true of him, but I was too hung over to say so.

"Cream cheese," I said, handing him a napkin. "Corner of your mouth."

"So you had dinner," he said, wiping. "What did you think of him?"

"It's a sad story."

"I should have handled it better. I felt so guilty about abandoning him that after a while I just avoided the whole thing. So it didn't take much for Rosa Lee to poison him against me."

"Keep avoiding him, Jonathan," I said gently. "It's not just that he hates you. You symbolize something he hates. I think that's how he sees a lot of people."

"For what they stand for?"

"For what he thinks they stand for. You're better off having nothing to do with him."

"And I don't." He stood and zipped up his full length down coat, from his ankles up to his neck. "I've tried my whole life to heal the mess I made of our relationship, but it's hopeless. Why reach out to him, just so he can bite my hand?"

He held up my leather jacket and I slipped into it. He wound my red wool scarf around my neck, then gave me a quick kiss on the lips.

"Some things can't be fixed," I said. "You just have to let them go."

Out on 8th Avenue in the swirling snow we took shelter beneath the marquee of the Joyce Theater.

"Don't you live around here?" Jonathan said.

"Around the corner."

"I'm free the rest of the afternoon," he said, in a certain way.

"I wish I was, but I'm not. I'm editing."

"On Sunday?"

"'Fraid so."

"Speaking of which, when do I see a cut?"

"I'm screening the rough cut for Joel Garner tomorrow at two thirty."

"You're showing him the rough? Is that wise?"

"Probably not. The cut'll be awful, it always is, but he's been bugging me for a look, so what the hell? It's not about seeing a cut. I think he just wants to be included. Why don't you come?"

"Sure. Any chance I can to see you—"

I didn't take the cue. My ears and fingers and feet were getting cold, I still had a headache, and I didn't want to talk about our relationship. In a half hour, just enough time for the aspirin to start working, I was supposed to meet Barky up at MOMA to see a Louise Bourgeois exhibit due to close soon. I had to catch an E train soon at 23rd and 8th, Sunday subway service was slow, and whenever I was late Barky got pissy and sulked. Now I had Jonathan acting that way, too.

"You know, I daydream sometimes," he said, "about our future. Working and living together? Maybe even getting married?"

"Jonathan..." I closed my eyes and saw stars. "What do you expect me to say to that?"

"We work together so well."

"Excellent work."

"And we make great love."

"Yes, we do."

"Wait until people see Josephine and David onscreen."

"It did work out well, didn't it?"

"Adrienne, you know I love you."

I sighed, buying time. Do I lie and encourage him, or risk being honest?

"Jonathan, working with you, that was some of the best work I've ever done. I'd work with you again, any time. But right now, I'm giving you all I can give. Try and understand."

At the subway stairs at 8th and 23rd, I embraced him warmly and gave his cheek a friendly kiss.

"I've got to go to work," I said. "C'mon, take the train uptown with me."

"No," he said. "I'll walk. I need to sort some things out."

"Okay."

"Like you and me."

"This snow is supposed to get worse –"

"C'mon, Adrienne. We're both artists. You're one of the best directors I ever worked with. Think of the partnership we could have." He bit his lip, and then seemed to decide. "C'mon, marry me. We could be happy together."

I sidestepped as well as I could.

"That would make me the supercilious little shithead's stepmother, wouldn't it?"

"We'll just ignore him. He won't have any place in our life."

I wished I could tell him he had no future with me. Trapped, resenting it, I got upset with him. Maybe it was the headache, but I couldn't help it.

"You pop the question while we're standing in a blizzard, and you want an answer right away?"

He looked crestfallen. "Well, okay. Take whatever time you need."

"C'mon, cheer up." I gave him a farewell hug. "And in the meantime, please stop setting yourself up for heartache over me, will you? It hurts me too." His lips twisted, he sighed and turned away. "Jonathan, wait." He walked off, shaking his head, leaving me worried again about how far I could trust him.

He showed up at the Cinema Arts Building on Monday afternoon to see the rough cut I was screening for Joel Garner. Jonathan sat closest to Garner, he and the playwright were friends. For the entire 128 minutes Garner sat upright in his seat, watching intensely, turning to look at me a couple times.

When the lights came up, he didn't stand up with us. He sat for a moment in sullen silence, a graying middle-aged disgruntled grump. Finally, he got up, turned away from us, and stalked out shaking his head.

Out in the lobby he turned on me.

"They threw my script away for *that*?"

Calmly, I said, "They being the producers and the director? Yes."

"Well, I get it. You wanted a dumbed-down version the yahoos would understand."

No, I almost said, that was Egon's version, which Garner had obviously never seen. I mean, who was he to criticize my work? He couldn't write a camera-ready film script from his own play, but he was attacking me. Rough cut screenings are always disappointing, but this unprofessional personal abuse was rude and inexcusable, and Jonathan was standing there like a dummy, watching. Instead of notes from the playwright, I got a reminder that the biggest egos often belong to the biggest mediocrities.

I shrugged and smiled, indicating I was invulnerable to his insults, on the outside, anyway.

"You know what else I see in your film?" he said. "I see a lot of pandering to this shit that's going on lately."

"What shit is that, Joel?"

I wrote the script last summer, before Weinstein, before #MeToo broke, so to accuse me of pandering was absurd. But demands for dignity and justice and respect had gotten louder lately. Women were in no mood to take anything from men anymore. Men, and Joel had all the symptoms, were feeling the change in the weather.

He didn't have the guts to look me in the eye. He just shook his head and stared at the floor.

"The way you pumped up the female roles. The way you gave Ruthie all of Abel's lines and made their story all about her."

Yes, because in his play Abel was an unappealing paranoid bully, driving his loving and bewildered wife crazy. But I was getting nothing useful from this conversation, so it wasn't worth prolonging.

"I was compensating for Lee's limited abilities."

"Putting Sawyer's wife onscreen —"

Jonathan put his hand gently on Garner's shoulder.

"We decided that worked better than having me talk to a character nobody sees, Joel."

Garner sneered, "What, you think the audience can't use its imagination? Less is always more. I also don't like the way you played her, Adrienne. Too late to do anything about it now, I guess."

"Well Joel, thank you for your feedback."

I would've bested him in the pointless fight he was asking for. But I chose silence and waited for him to go away.

At the elevator Garner got on, shrugged, and threw up his hands.

"I guess this is the best I can expect from a woman who thinks men are dogs."

The doors slid closed. Good riddance. Bottom floor, Purgatory. Please step off, sir. We've been expecting you.

"He just doesn't get it, does he?" I said. We were alone in the up elevator. "It's a miracle the film even got made."

Jonathan gave me a one-armed hug around the shoulders. "He brought an attitude in with him. That's all he saw. He's in that mindset a lot of men are in now. He didn't actually see the movie."

"He didn't see me, either. To him, I'm the 'Men R Dawgs' woman."

I shouldn't have let Garner disturb me. Worse, he didn't say anything about the film worth remembering. Add the usual rough-cut blues and the two hours I wasted, and I felt the day slipping through my fingers.

I needed to be alone. But Jonathan tagged along to the Alpha Bitch offices and I was reluctant to ask him to leave. I sat behind my computer and tried to look busy. He stared out the window, looking over Times Square as dry snowflakes blew on the wind. I so wanted to be free of him and to get back to work.

"So? The cut?" I said, just to break the silence.

"Rough cuts are a drag, everybody knows that. Listen, I have a script. A gem, I assure you. It's a post-middle-aged romantic drama, set in present-day Paris. Let's spend Christmas in Paris. We could easily write off a two week visit as a location scout."

"That's three days from now," I groaned. "I already have plans." Specifically, five days and nights in a hotel in Miami Beach with Barky, just the two of us in our own world.

"What could be lovelier than Christmas in Paris? Plus, if I can get Delphine Tessier to commit, European money is all but guaranteed."

"Well then, it's better if I'm not in the way, isn't it? Besides, I promised to spend time with some friends that I don't get to see very often."

"You made plans for Christmas and didn't talk to me?"

"You didn't talk to me either, until now."

"My script takes place during the holidays," he said.

"I'm tempted, but it's too short notice. I'm sorry."

"Yeah, but after the holidays I've got looping with you for a couple days, and I go back onstage with the play. This is the only time I can fit in a trip." He spread his hands, offering. "C'mon. I know how much you love Paris. It's Christmas! Music! Art! Fine dining! I lived there for almost twenty years. I know my way around. There'll be lots of people for you to meet. Please come. We'll have fun."

"You're torturing me. Why did you wait until now to ask?"

"Have you thought about my proposal?"

"It's not a decision I can rush into. You shouldn't either. Go to Paris. Have a great time." The look on his face said I'd just made that impossible. "Come back with lots of stories."

Or, even better, don't come back at all.

FOUR *The night of January 9, 2018*

Officers Harris and Nunez sit me in a chair at Jonathan's dining room table with my hands cuffed behind me. My wrists are sore. I'm sweating and I feel dirty. My nose is running, and I can't wipe it, and the ends of my hair are stuck on my snotty upper lip. The left side of my face is numb where Jonathan slapped me.

I hear police talking in the next room and bursts of staticky walkie talkie voices. The crime scene investigators and medical examiner's people are collecting evidence in the living room and working on the bodies of A.J. and Jonathan. I try hard to hear what they're saying.

"Well, hello again, Miss Monet."

Detective Ferino and his partner Detective Peavey stand in the doorway. So Jonathan wasn't just drunk, and he wasn't just talking. He did call the police. He would've told them I killed Egon. He really did want to destroy me. Realizing this, whatever burden of guilt I feel just got lighter.

"Hello Buddy."

"It's Detective Ferino, remember?" He pulls out a chair and sits across from me, his hands laced together. "Are you all right?" he says with a look of concern, so sincere, and so fake.

"My hands hurt."

"Detective Peavey, remove the handcuffs, please."

My hands free, I massage my sore wrists.

Peavey says, "How's that?"

"Good, thank you."

Ferino hands me a napkin from a place setting on the table and I blow my nose, then get up and stretch my legs.

"Are you all right?"

"No." I brush my hair back. "I still can't believe what happened —"

"Stop." Ferino raises a hand to silence me.

That surprises me. I was about to ask when he wants to hear what happened. But if I'm too eager to talk the police might think I'm eager to lie, so I sit with my hands in my lap and say nothing.

"In a few minutes we're going to the precinct. We'll talk about it then. First, I'm going to read you your rights. Please sit down."

I sat at the head of the table.

"My rights? Am I under arrest?"

"We're taking you into custody to talk about what happened here."

"What does that mean?"

"It means you're coming with us," Peavey says.

"Why can't we talk here?"

"You have no say in that," Ferino said. "You have the right to remain silent..." He reads the card. "Do you understand these rights as I've explained them to you?"

"I do." Of course I do. Now anything that comes out of my mouth besides a sneeze can be used against me in court.

"Sign here." He gives me his pen.

I heave a deep sigh. "Okay." I sign the Miranda card. "I didn't do anything wrong, Buddy."

"You understand the rules now? Anything you say —"

"You still think I killed Egon, don't you?" He glances at Peavey and doesn't answer me. "I'm going to call my lawyer."

"Tell him to meet us at the precinct."

"This is so unnecessary. I didn't do anything wrong."

"Nobody said you did." He stands up before I can say anything else. "You'll get a chance to talk about all of this. Oh, and uh, nice tan. Where'd you go for Christmas, someplace warm?"

Jonathan flew unhappily alone to Paris for Christmas, hoping to persuade Delphine Tessier to star with him in his movie. It was risky, letting him get too far out of reach, but being rid of him for a while felt like an early Christmas gift. I kissed him goodbye at JFK and wished him good luck. Riding in the town car back to the city, I thought of how great it could be if he and Delphine fell in love again. He'd move to France, he'd forget about me, and my problem would be solved. Which was sheer nonsense, of course. It was a burden living day by day knowing that if the mood happened to strike him, Jonathan Lehane could wreck my life with one phone call telling the New York city police where to find his gun and what I used it for. But at least for the next couple of weeks he'd be far, far away.

Then Barky called to tell me Garth wanted to take her to Minnesota for the holidays to meet his family, and she'd decided she had to go.

"I hope you don't hate me, Adrienne. I really can't say 'no' to him."

It hurt more than it should, knowing she still saw her future as Garth's wife. I managed to be nonchalant.

"Of course not," I said. "Have a great time."

Crushed, I canceled our car and hotel reservations in Miami Beach. I was wondering how I'd spend a blue and lonely Christmas in New York until A.J. called and invited me to Palm Beach for the holidays. It was, no joke, an invitation from Heaven. To stroll on sunny beaches with my handsome lover in his tropical pastel Republican moneybags paradise, beside a turquoise sea with the palms swaying in the breeze, was just what I needed to restore my soul.

Except I couldn't. If I was out in public with A.J. Upton, inevitably somebody would recognize us, and remember that I was the woman who deballed him on the radio. One Tweet of a cellphone video and the news would reach Jonathan in a flash. He was already sulking because I dodged his marriage proposal. If he found out I'd hooked up with the son who's been publicly ridiculing him for years, he might react in ways I didn't even want to think about.

I didn't see how I could go to Palm Beach with A.J., until I hit on the most obvious solution. I called him, told him I was coming, and he was happy. Then I made some hurried preparations, simple but expensive, and *voila!*

Our holiday began after work on Thursday with dinner in a small café on Lexington Avenue in his neighborhood. I hoped he would be excited by the change in my appearance, but he just looked puzzled.

"When did you become a blonde?"

"Like it?"

"Those dorky glasses, too. And you're in a pantsuit. What happened to my punky girlfriend in leather and jeans? When you walked in, I thought you were somebody's secretary."

"If you didn't recognize me, then I think this'll work."

"What will work?"

"I'll meet your friends in Palm Beach, right?"

"So?"

"The Crockett thing."

"Oh that." He shrugged. "That was a month ago. Nobody cares now."

"The tabloids will. If you hook up with anybody, it's news. Unless it's me, the madwoman creator of '*Men R Dawgs*' who beat you up on the radio. Then it's big news."

He shrugged. "Who really cares?"

"I care. I don't seek publicity the way you do. We've already been news once and I hated it. I don't want us to become public property. Looking like this, I can be with you, meet your friends, and it'll be cool. It'll be fun to play somebody else."

"Suit yourself." From A.J., a guilty pleasure grin. "It'll be like cheating on Adrienne with a hot blonde."

"Yes! We'll leave Adrienne in New York and I'll be your new girlfriend. I'll invent a whole persona."

As we walked to his house, we talked about the woman I could play.

"Nothing too radical," A.J. said.

I pitched my voice deeper.

"I was thinking transgender."

"Not funny, whatever your name is."

"My name is Bob, but you can call me Roberta."

"The important thing is, people would expect a girlfriend of mine to basically agree with my views."

I affected a Southern drawl. "That'll be easy. I'll buy a MAGA hat and a pair of Trump sunglasses when we get to Palm Beach. Hell, buddy, I can play a ditzy blonde right winger, no problem."

"I wouldn't be with anyone the slightest bit 'ditzy,' Adrienne."

"How about a girl without a political thought in her head? Or a high end, very expensive hooker?"

"Oh man."

"I'm an actor, you know. I could play a hooker. How about, 'Hooker to The MAGA Elite'? I get passed around at the highest levels. I can tell you who's packin', and who's lackin', and who can ball all night."

"I think we're headed for trouble here. Look, you can't take this too far. People will figure out something's up and they'll wonder what kind of weirdo I'm turning into, running around with–"

"No worries. I get it. A smart, elegant, low key fascist bitch."

"Yeah. Underline 'low key.'" He dug out his keys and unlocked the front door. "You know, this is going to be good. A nice vacation from New York and your liberal feminist crap."

"Only in public, my love."

In his living room, a beautifully trimmed Christmas tree glistened, decorated by his domestic staff, topped by a kitschy porcelain angel with a nauseating beatific smile whose halo grazed the ceiling. Under the tree were two gifts for me, a cashmere cardigan from Bergdorf Goodman so ultra-black it glowed in its white wrapping tissue, and a small blue Tiffany box from which I lifted a thin platinum chain necklace with a small round pendant ringed with tiny diamonds.

Putting on a show, I stripped to the waist. I took the sweater from the box and made sure to coo as I rubbed the cashmere under my chin and over my bare breasts. I slipped it on, leaving the top three buttons open so the diamonds glittered against my chest once he'd fastened the clasp.

"It's all so beautiful." I kissed him. "Thank you so much." He didn't know me well enough yet to give me anything personal, so he fell back on his money and gave me gifts any rich man might buy his woman. Still... Bergdorf's, Tiffany, diamonds... I was touched.

I gave him the complete set of Monty Python DVDs and a Hohner Marine Band harmonica with a gift certificate for lessons.

"I love the Pythons!" he said.

"I thought you could use a laugh. And with your exceptional oral talents, a harmonica seemed perfect."

We sat on stools at his kitchen island looking out over his garden covered in snow and he poured us glasses of Burgundy, 1981 Petrus, dense, rich and delicious. I complimented him on his taste.

"It's been my favorite wine ever since Rush sent me half a case for my 35th birthday."

I drank half my wine, set my glass down, then slid off my seat and intruded myself between his knees.

"Okay," I said. "My new persona has some new rules."

"Uh oh. Here we go." He circled me with his arms and pulled me close. "What rules?"

"You have to ask for my consent for whatever you want to do. Or what you want me to do. You have to say what you want. And maybe I'll consent, and maybe I won't."

"Oh sure. I bare my soul and you jerk me around. Isn't that called cock-teasing?"

"It's not teasing. Just say what you want."

"No way. It'll feel too much like begging."

That made me laugh. "How would you know? You've never begged for anything in your life."

Still, he resisted. "Why do you want me to do this?"

"Sex talk from a Jesus freak. Could be a real turn on."

He looked at me like I was hopelessly damned.

"Nothing is sacred to you, is it?"

"Whatever it takes to drag you out of your comfort zone."

"What for?" he laughed, uncomfortably. "Why?"

"Because I can. And because you need it. So, are we playing or not?"

He leaned in to kiss me, but I put my hand on his chest. "Something you want?"

"Okay. I'll play. Can I have a kiss?"

"Yes. But not here." I took his hand and led him upstairs. In his bedroom, I set down my glass. "Okay." I was feeling the wine. "Come and get it, Uptown." The kiss was warm and earnest. The strength in his arms circling me was thrilling and a little frightening. "You don't mind if I call you Uptown, do you?"

"I kind of like it. It works with my image."

"What image is that?"

"Oh, Conservative Intellectual. American Tory, maybe."

"How about Fascist Rabble Rouser?"

He rolled his eyes. "You fucking liberals. You're so sensitive about everybody else's dignity, but when it comes to conservatives, there's no limit to the ad hominem invective."

"Isn't that your specialty?"

"You liberals—"

"There are no liberals here, A.J. Just me. But if fantasizing that I'm the enemy makes it fun to fuck me, I'll play." His hands idly stroked my back. "Sex outside of wedlock, wow, and with a liberal. Everybody knows you Bible-smackers are hopelessly drawn to the pleasures of the flesh that you call sin."

"Don't insult my religion, all right? How would you feel if I called you a stuck-up little feminist bitch?"

"Ooo, now that'll get things going. So here's your reward." Another lingering kiss, unasked for. We were making progress, even though he had to get pissed off to play. I hoped he'd remember this was a game. In his ear I whispered: "So, tell me what you want."

A menacing growl. "I can't wait to fuck you again –"

"Good A.J., good, but don't jump to 'fuck' right away. We'll get there. Take your time." I unbuttoned his shirt. "Small, delicious steps." I raked my fingernails through his chest hair. "Do you like this?"

"Oh yeah," he breathed, flinching as I pinched his nipples. His hands gripped my rear end and pulled me tight against him.

"Hey, fella. Are those your hands on my ass?"

"Mm hm."

"You didn't say 'May I?'"

"May I please have permission to grab your butt, Blondie? It's sort of hard to resist."

"Sure, since you said 'please'. With a quid pro quo, of course."

"Name it."

"Take off your shirt and pants. The sight of you naked does indescribable things to me."

He chuckled. "I readily consent."

He stripped off his shirt and pushed down his trousers, which he kicked aside. His underwear surprised me. The first time we made love he wore boring plain cotton boxer shorts, but tonight he was stuffed into a thong with barely enough cloth to package the expanding contents.

"I love the way you're covered in hair. Like a beast."

He took me by the shoulders and walked me backward a step. "Stand over here and strip."

"I didn't hear you say please."

"Please. And don't you dare say no."

He sat down on an ottoman where he'd have a front row seat. I removed the platinum necklace and peeled off my sweater and placed them on the bureau.

"Okay so far?"

"Keep goin'. Please."

I peeled down my dress slacks and stepped out of them. Then, my panties.

"Wow," he said. "You went totally blonde."

"God is in the details."

Naked, I sidled over to the ottoman and stood in front of him. I slid my bare foot under his bulging briefs and tickled his balls gently with my toe. His eyes closed, and he sighed.

"Now," I said. "What do I have to do to bring out the animal in you?"

"Tell me you support abortion, gun control and open borders."

Bent over laughing, I stepped over our clothes on the carpet and fell onto the bed. I pulled down the linens and lay back. He tossed his underwear, turned the lights down to a glow, and got in beside me.

Before I could speak his lips were on mine. "I love tasting the wine on your breath." I lay back, held in his powerful embrace, his kisses hard and intense, his hand spreading my thighs and playing with me until his fingers were slippery.

I pushed him onto his back and straddled him, lifting his hands to hold my breasts. His touch was soft and tentative compared to how his father, on our very first kiss, seized my breasts as if he owned them. I kissed him again, then slid down and gently kissed and stroked the generous inheritance from his father that A.J. should have been more grateful for. He closed his eyes. He was too self-conscious to gasp too loud. Just as I was wondering how to get him fully engaged, he surprised me. He got up on his knees and leaned back on the headboard, pulled me over, and held his cock to my lips.

"Suck it." I didn't need to be told, but it was thrilling to hear him say it.

"I didn't hear you say please."

"Suck it now!"

I assumed the position of a supplicant, down on all fours. I could see he got off on that. I started soft and intense, disappointed he didn't moan, because cock sucking is more satisfying when you can hear the pleasure you're giving, but at least he spoke. Suck it, he kept saying. Powerful words from a shy boy. When he held my head and began to push in and out of my mouth, I knew I had him.

I got him quivering with excitement, then I backed up and pulled him down on the bed with his face between my legs.

"My turn."

I first experienced this cunnilingus variation with the Rutgers professor of French named 'Adrienne' who rented me a room in her apartment when I got out of the hospital after giving birth. She was my first serious female lover, and I adopted her name as my own. Barky had become adept at the practice once I showed her how, and I wanted to see if A.J. could learn a new skill.

"Put your middle finger into me," I said, "and curl it up so you're touching me with your fingertip, very lightly. Use your index and ring fingers to spread my lips." I felt his warm breath on me. "Now, with just the tip of your tongue, lick me, right up here."

He got the idea. At one point he stopped and looked up, concerned. "Are you okay?"

He must've thought I was writhing and gasping in pain. "I'm trying to be respectful," I said, "and not scream 'Oh my God Oh my God.'"

"Oh, go ahead," he chuckled, "it's not real blasphemy," and went back to licking me.

"Oh yes. Right, right, right. Oh God!"

Waves of pleasure rippled through me, my body was warm and moving against the strokes of his tongue. He was grinning, excited and emboldened by his power to make me feel so good.

But good lovemaking means never doing any one thing for too long.

"Okay, Uptown. On your back."

"I didn't hear a request."

"That's an order. Now."

I threw a leg over and straddled him, then carefully, a little at a time, enveloped him, taking him in, lifting myself up and sliding him back out, up and down, until I just barely got his cock inside me. I began rolling my hips. Beneath me, he began to thrust upwards, seizing my ass, holding me in place. That sent me over the edge, and my insides became one deep sweet shudder. Seeing this excited A.J. to emphatic thrusting, biting his lower lip, a weird, distressed look on his face that meant he thought he'd burn in Hell for this, but it would be worth it.

I lay down on him chest to chest, rubbing my naked body on his hairy pecs and belly, and rolled him over on top of me.

"Come on, Uptown." I crossed my ankles over the small of his back. "Don't you want to see God?"

He kept thrusting into me, harder and deeper. My insides melted and heat and sweat broke out all over me and I came for the first time with A.J. with blinding intensity, crying out loud enough to be heard in the heavens. When he gasped that he was about to come, I parted from him and slid down his body. Looking him in the eyes, I stroked his cock and massaged his balls. His body went rigid from head to foot and with an anguished look on his face he groaned, and he came.

We laid together under the linens in the heat and smell of our bodies, quiet, utterly at peace, and finally, asleep.

The next morning we steamed in his home spa and showered together, got dressed in jeans and sweaters, and ate breakfast. His appetite was appalling. He gobbled a bowl of oatmeal drenched in maple syrup, topped with two fried eggs, sunny side up and runny, and a bagel smeared with peanut butter and jelly. I ate a few chunks of melon, a slice of whole wheat toast, and coffee, and he still finished breakfast before me. He called for an Uber black car to pick us up at noon and take us to JFK airport for a two o'clock flight to Palm Beach.

"Where's Billy?'

"I gave Billy the holidays off. I only need security in New York. Palm Beach is friendlier territory."

Wearing red MAGA baseball caps and sunglasses, we settled into first class seats behind copies of *The National Review* and *Vanity Fair.* Our fellow passengers, high on holiday excitement, paid us no attention, and passed the flight playing with their laptop computers and tablets or wrangling their kids.

A.J. yawned. "I don't know what's happening on the social scene." We banked toward Palm Beach International and began our descent. "This is kind of short notice, but I'll make a few calls."

"If it's just me and you in the sunshine, that's fine with me."

"I do have to visit Roy. This is the only time I get to see him."

"Doesn't he ever come to New York?"

He shook his head. "Too many undesirables."

When we reached North Ocean Boulevard, he directed the Uber driver to take us past Roy Upton's mansion. We stopped for a moment outside a tall iron gate in a wall of dense green privet. Beyond it, I got a glimpse of a large French Regency chateau, gleaming white in the sun.

A.J.'s house was one block from the ocean, a two-story tan stucco Mediterranean with a red-tile roof and an iron balcony around the second floor. Parked under the porte cochere was a black two-door Bentley with a tan convertible top. The swimming pool in the back garden was secluded behind tall foliage and the patio was shaded by tall Royal Palms.

"I have a fantastic Cuban guy who takes care of all this," he said, waving his hand at the meticulous landscaping. "He's a real artist. I bought this place so I could get away from Washington and New York."

"Good idea. Get out of the political media theater racket for a while."

He gave me a WTF look, lifted his suitcase and led me toward the house.

"Why did you say it like that?"

"Like what?"

His upper lip curled. "'Political media theater racket.'"

"What about it?"

"That subtle mockery in the way you said that."

"Oh, I'm sorry. I didn't mean to be subtle."

"It's an honest way to make a living, Adrienne."

"Have you often had doubts about that?"

"I – no, what do you mean, have I had doubts?"

"Well, I made a simple comment, and you got all defensive."

"What have I got to be defensive about? My book is on the *New York Times* bestseller list. My blog traffic is a quarter million views a week. Every time I appear on *Fox* or *CNN* or *MSNBC* their numbers spike."

"So do your 'Pants On Fire' numbers on the Politifact Truth O'Meter." That was true, I checked.

He unlocked and pushed the back door open.

"The audience I've cultivated supports my values –"

"A.J., it has nothing to do with values. It's not political, it's emotional. They love the outrageous things you say about people they'd like to insult. Or worse."

"Outrageous, but true."

"Like I said, that's debatable."

He stared at me for a moment, then laughed.

"Well, Miss Monet," he said, spreading his arms, "make yourself right at home."

He took me to a lunchtime Christmas party on Saturday at the home of his friend Butterworth Newby, the youngest son of the Houston Newbys, and publisher of the conservative magazine *Druthers, a Journal of Ideas.*

"In the 1800s his family got rich from cattle ranching," A.J. said, "and then got even richer off oil and natural gas. We roomed together at college."

As we pulled up in the Bentley our host waved to us from the sunny lawn of a sprawling pink mansion, the largest in a row of houses facing the ocean. It was hard to believe the men were the same age. A.J.'s college buddy looked in his 50s and worn-out, his salt and pepper hair thinning and his upper body sinking into the broad waistline of his tennis shorts.

"Hoss!" He threw an arm around A.J.'s shoulder. "'Nuther one'a my Dartmouth boys!"

"Those were great times, Butter, up there at Dartmouth."

"Once upon a time, a hotbed of seditious conservatism." Butter smiled. "These days, I don't know." He turned his grin on me. "And who's this lovely lady?"

Quickly, a lilt in my voice and stressing every syllable, I said, "Very perceptive friend you have here, A.J."

Butterworth Newby laughed. He seemed ready to laugh at anything.

"My name is Emma Van der Berg. And you? You're called?"

"Just call me Butter."

"Butter! Just to say it, it feels fattening."

"Feels fattening!" He laughed. "What is this lovely accent you have?"

"I'm Dutch."

"Well, welcome to my humble home. What do you do, Miss Van der Berg?"

"My work is uh, analyst you could say, for the Forum for Democracy in my homeland. You are familiar with the FvD? Thierry Baudet?"

"Fascinating guy," Butter said. "Looks like he's givin' ol' Geert Wilders a run for his money."

I turned with a frown to A.J. "A run?"

"Competition. He's up and coming on the Dutch right, and Wilders is fading."

"Oh yes, very much so," I said, turning back to Butter. "Baudet is the future of Holland if Holland is to remain Holland."

Chatting on their way into the house, A.J. and Butter put their arms around each other's shoulders and fell into guy talk. Despite his warm welcome, I caught Butter giving me long glances as we mingled with the other guests. I wondered if he recognized me or was jealous because I was with his buddy. I imagined them in college, A.J. laying the prettiest girls and Butter settling for the homely best friend.

A.J. took me around and introduced me. Butter's cousin Jeff, an orange-haired, freckled and skinny guy in madras Bermuda shorts and a pink polo shirt, needled A.J.

"So, when's the rematch with that babe from the Crockett show? What was her name?"

"Adrienne Monet," A.J. said. He made it sound like a bad tasting fruit.

"Right, right," Jeff laughed. "Man, she really cleaned your clock."

"Oh, I wouldn't say that."

"What do you say, Miss?"

"Oh, I don't know." I acted bewildered. "I'm just here for the holiday from Holland. Sounds like an interesting story, A.J., you must tell me later."

Jeff said helpfully, "You can hear the whole thing on You Tube."

"Adrienne Monet and I will cross swords again," A.J. said. "Stay tuned."

My masquerade was working. I recognized a few New York media personalities mingled among the older Palm Beach guests, *Druthers* staffers that Butter flew down for the holidays. They didn't seem to know or care about The Netherlands or me. That made it easier to keep up the chatter in my faux Dutch accent. On the rear terrace the editor-in-chief and his wife lay baking in the sun and ignoring Butter's invitations to join the party. One or two junior editors hung out at the pool with their wives, trading wisecracks, dangling their feet in the water and splashing each other. I recognized a couple of the magazine's brand-name writers from talk show appearances. They were already drunk, doing a kick line and singing a parody of the Village People's "Macho Man," a song Trump sometimes played at his rallies.

Colored, colored man,
I wanna be, a colored man!

A.J. didn't dare join the singalong, but he stood by laughing and shaking his head. The Black waitresses and waiters moved smoothly and silently in and out of the party.

I poured myself a glass of fruit-bomb California cabernet from a row of bottles on a buffet loaded with platters of cold lobster and crab, big glass bowls of salad and fruit and bread, cheese boards, and steel trays of meat, then took a spin around the room.

I side-stepped A.J.'s friends when they tried to engage Emma politically.

"I think politics in my country is much more decentralized and complex. And not quite so angry as my friend here."

"Emma calls what I do 'media theater,'" A.J. said.

"Media theater!" A tall blonde, obviously a Palm Beacher, introduced herself as Rachel. She turned her glow towards me. "You are so right about that!" Golden-haired, blue-eyed and slim, she had a dazzling smile and confident poise that told you she knew she was the most attractive woman at the party. A martini glass of some red booze dangled from her fingertips.

Emma found it easy to be warm and friendly to Rachel. Adrienne saw through her from the minute she sauntered into the room, dressed very Ralph Lauren in faded blue jeans and a white peasant blouse and a belt with silver and turquoise conchos, and reeking of privilege: the spoiled daughter of a rich family, great looks and great body, and an utterly conventional mind shaped at the finest schools where she no doubt dated the most desirable men, and now a career in marketing or some shit, handed to her on a silver platter to keep her busy between graduation and marriage, working for a rich friend of the family who hoped she'd become the trophy wife of his nitwit son. Every word she spoke sounded shiny and fake, like play money. She and Emma were the only blondes at the party amongst the frumpy brunette wives, a pair of short-haired techies who might've secretly been a couple, an Asian woman whose laughter was contagious, and a shy Latina who clutched the arm of a man, I guess her husband, who hardly acknowledged her presence.

The men openly looked Rachel up and down, and I couldn't help fantasizing about getting her alone and making my own pass, just to see her stammer and blush:

Really? You've never been to bed with a woman, Rachel?

Have I? Uh, no. No...I uh...Heh heh

Oh, I'm so sorry. Now I have embarrassed you.

Well, it's just... I've never had this kind of conversation –

Maybe we Europeans are a little more open-minded about such matters, unlike our American friends.

I'll say. Woo! I've never been that open-minded.

But maybe you might feel like you want to try something different sometime? You're a beautiful girl, you could have any lover you wanted, and you might like it...

A threesome with Rachel and A.J. Probably a good way to get arrested in this tightass town. Or maybe not. When you mix wealth, religious piety, and sexual repression you often get the wildest of perversions.

I grinned at Rachel and shrugged.

"A.J., he takes my opinions so seriously, even when I tease him." I took his arm but didn't try to walk him away from the conversation. If he resisted, it would be mortifying. "I should be flattered, I think."

"Hmm," Rachel said, "what woman wouldn't be? So how have you been, A.J.?"

"Oh, working hard, you know." Out the side of his mouth he said, "Takes a lot of work to keep a media theater career going."

"I know how hard you work," she said. "It's good to see you taking time off for yourself. Was that your idea, Miss –?"

"Emma Van der Berg."

"From New York?"

"No, Amsterdam. I'm in America to study populist movements, perhaps for ideas for our movement in the Netherlands."

"Well, politics is totally beyond me, I have to admit. But you'll certainly get an interesting perspective hanging out with A.J.," Rachel said. "You make a very attractive couple."

I just grinned. Don't push me, bitch.

"I'm going to steal A.J. for a moment, I hope you don't mind." He looked at me and shrugged. I just smiled and shrugged back at him as Rachel linked arms and he let her lead him away.

She monopolized A.J. for the rest of the party. I pretended not to notice. She was confronting him, sulking and whimpering, obviously about some unfinished business. A.J.'s discomfort was amusing to watch. He looked sheepish, as if he'd been caught doing something, he defended himself, but mostly he went hurt and silent. He was no match for her anger. I decided not to rescue him from whatever mess he'd made for himself.

Instead, I circulated amongst Butter and his guests. Ultimately, I found the whole gang kind of silly. They were so languid, so truculent, sulking about one grievance or another. The only interesting talk was the difference of opinion about Trump, who was in Palm Beach for the holiday and just down the road at his mansion. The New Yorkers who knew him the longest and the best were still astonished that he'd become president. The Palm Beachers would chuckle and hint that Trump was an unwelcome and vulgar intrusion into their society, but half-jokingly, in case the wrong people were listening. None of them seemed to care about his impact on the rest of America. Some of their rancor was unintentionally funny, and so was the hopeful speculation that Ann or Rush might drop by and liven up the party. I soon got bored listening to these rich or wannabe rich people with their mystic nationalism and self-pity, ranting and griping about matters they felt impinged on their plush, pastel bubble of a world. Politics and their perceived victimization obsessed these people the way people got addicted to computer games – the real world hardly intruded.

When it was time to go, I said goodbye to everyone, certain they'd forget all about Emma Van der Berg as soon as I was gone. I walked away reluctantly. I liked, no, I loved, no, I was becoming covetous of A.J.'s life-style – not the ugly parts, the racism and class snobbery and the politics of resentment and contempt, but the material parts, the Upper East Side townhouse, first class travel to the getaway house in Palm Beach, the beautiful clothes, the Bentley, the peace of mind from financial security. I was being given a look inside a new world. Of course, A.J. would never let himself be separated from the friends in his class. But I wondered if I could create a life with him that kept them on the margins. The real problem would be Jonathan. I couldn't stay hidden, or blonde, forever.

"Well," A.J. said, walking to the Bentley after Butter said goodbye. "Looks like you were a hit with my friends."

"Do you think so?"

"I could tell."

"Nobody guessed who I really am."

"Nope. You played it just right," he said, mocking my accent, "Miss Van der Berg."

Once we were riding in the car I asked, "So where's Mrs. Newby?"

"There have been four Mrs. Newbys, but no-one at the moment. Butter pays more in alimony than I earn in a year. There are some kids here and there."

"He seems sort of lonely."

"Yeah, well, he's got the magazine. That's something, I guess."

"And who's Rachel? No, let me guess: your former fiancé."

"Only in her mind."

"Ah. Differences in interpretation. Always keeps life interesting."

"Until it gets tiresome. Not with you, though. Life with you is like living with my finger in a light socket."

"I like that image."

"I thought you would."

"How long did you have your finger in Rachel's light socket?"

"A gentleman never tells."

"Uh huh. So what happened there, Uptown?"

" 'Way too much money."

No problem with that over here.

The day before Christmas was warm, with a dry breeze under a brilliant blue sky, and too beautiful to waste hanging around the house. We drove down below Miami to Coral Gables and he took me strolling through the Fairchild Tropical Botanical Gardens. In earthly splendor, we wandered all afternoon, stopping once at an outdoor café to drink coffee. The rich foliage, and loamy air full of bird songs, the sunshine and warm breezes in the gardens, were soothing and healing. A.J. became impatient with my frequent stops to inhale the bouquet of a flower or take photographs of birds or sculpture. So when we were deep in the silence of the bamboo grove of the Coconut Palm Collection, I stood him up against the railing of a rustic wooden bridge, pulled down his khakis, and surprised him with a slow, teasing blowjob while he kept a worried eye out for any nature lovers. After I'd sucked him off, he was a gasping, weak-kneed wreck.

At a more relaxed pace, we resumed our walk through the gardens. He kept casting sidelong glances at me with a loony grin. I'd blown his mind, too.

"You're a real adventuress, aren't you?" he said. "Did you swallow all that?"

"My first Holy Communion in a long time."

"My God!" he laughed. "You are so evil! What have I done?"

On Christmas Day we returned from church services and A.J. didn't want to do anything but eat and drink, make love, and relax in the sun beside the pool. I was restless all day, so after dinner I searched the Internet and found what I was looking for. Tuesday was a perfect beach day, with clear skies and hot sun and a dry offshore breeze. We drove down I-95 through Sunny Isles to the beach at Haulover State Park. We parked in the north end lot, walked under the highway through a dim, piss-smelly tunnel and came up on a road bordered by mangrove. A few wooden steps through it led to the beach.

I took A.J.'s arm and we walked out onto the sand, crowded with sunbathers.

"Over there looks good." I led him to a patch of empty sand. I tried not to laugh at the look on his face as he realized most of the sunbathers were nude.

"Where are we?"

"At the beach, silly."

"And what do you propose we do here?"

I unfolded a fresh bed sheet for our beach blanket, kicked off my sandals and pulled off my pink polo shirt.

"I thought you wanted to get some sun."

"No," he said. "You're not really –"

"Yes, I am." Off came my lace bra, my linen shorts, and lace panties. I folded my clothes into my backpack as A.J. watched me, aghast.

"Are you crazy?" he said.

"I thought you'd already decided that."

I stepped up and hugged him. His hands fluttered in midair, apparently forbidden by some higher authority to touch my bare flesh in public.

"C'mon, Uptown. Off with those clothes. You'll see. It feels so-o-o good!"

"Put your clothes back on, or I'm leaving."

"Go ahead." I sat down cross-legged on the sheet and dug in my backpack for the sunblock. "If you leave me here, I'll catch an Uber to the airport."

"Yeah? Don't forget to get dressed first."

"You can ship my luggage home."

He looked around, uncertain. "This can't be legal."

"This beach is clothing optional. It's a state park."

"They spend taxpayers' money so people can do *this*?" Astonished, he gazed up and down the beach crowded with naked hedonists, sunbathers, people playing volleyball, swimming, strolling, and harmlessly frolicking, including a tall skinny man wearing nothing but a red Santa hat, a fake white beard, and a chrome cock ring.

"Are you gonna strip or not?"

"Uh uh. No way. Not me." He disrobed down to the Speedos he wore under his madras shorts. "That's as far as I go."

"What are you afraid of?" I stretched out at his feet, enjoying his discomfort. "If you get aroused, just lie on your stomach."

"That's not it," he said, squatting next to me and peering around. "Suppose somebody recognizes us?"

"Nobody knows us here."

"Yeah well, you're in disguise. I'm not. They'll take a cell phone video, upload it to the Internet, and five minutes later, there's A.J. Upton, lying on the beach beside a naked blonde in all her bare-ass glory."

"Yeah, that'll be terrible for your image."

"Even worse if somebody I.D.'s you too."

"We look great naked together. That's more than I can say for most of the people here."

"Which means we'll attract the most attention."

The closest sunbathers were a short distance away, a couple in low slung chairs and straw hats. They were old and fat, bright red, and arguing in guttural German.

"Seriously Adrienne," he said. "'*Nearer My God To Thee*' has just begun to sell. A picture of me lying around nude with you would —"

"Sell more books."

"— destroy my moral credibility."

"Didn't Adam and Eve come into the world without clothes?"

"Adrienne, lay off the Bible, okay?"

"Do you think the Garden of Eden was the first nudist colony? 'They were naked, and they were not ashamed.' It's the one line from the Bible I can quote."

"The Garden of Eden was not a nude beach in Florida."

"Oh, don't be such a prude." I handed him a tube of sun block. "Remember, we blondes sunburn easily, so don't leave any part of me uncovered." He didn't, and when he was finished, he had to lie on his stomach.

I opened the music library on my phone to Ella Fitzgerald singing the Cole Porter songbook, laid back, and zoned out. After a while I turned over on my stomach. A.J. lay on his side reading *The National Review*. I faced him with a rolled towel under my cheek. The hot sun baked the tension out of my body, and I fell asleep.

When I woke up, I gazed around, remembered we were on the beach north of Miami, and glanced at A.J. He'd removed his Speedos and lay on his stomach, wearing sunglasses and a Yankees cap, propped up on his elbows, nervously scanning our surroundings.

I sat up cross-legged. "How long was I out?"

"Quite a while."

"What a cute butt you have," I said. "I hope you put a lot of sun block on those buns. They're white as a pair of eggs."

"I did," he said, looking worried. "Probably time to put on more, though." I grabbed the sunblock before he could, squirted some on my palms, straddled his thighs, and kneaded his glutes.

"How's that feel?"

"Very nice."

"What about your cock and balls?"

"Yes, my, uh, private parts are covered, thank you."

"Time to do it again. Turn over."

"Here?"

"Roll on your side facing me. Nobody'll see us."

He looked nervously around, then rolled on his side and draped a towel over his waist.

"Whoa. I'm gonna need more goop." Which I applied with smooth, even strokes.

He took a deep breath and shuddered. "I can't believe we're doing this in public."

"Nobody can see. How's that feel?"

"Like I'm dangling over the fires of Hell."

"You're not exactly dangling."

We stretched out under the sun again, and soon he was snoring beside me. I picked up his copy of *The National Review* and leafed through it. There were articles about Scott Pruitt, about the proliferation of unconventional names for children that were confusing conservatives, a look back at the film "Bonnie and Clyde" fifty years later that declared they were the original amoral anti-heroes, and a review of the latest Star Wars film, *"The Last Jedi,"* which the critic called "infuriating garbage." I rolled up the magazine and smacked A.J. on the butt. He woke with a start.

"The sun's getting hot. Let's go for a swim."

"I'm up for that." He reached for his bathing suit, but I snatched it away and dragged him to his feet.

"Okay," he said. "Hand it over."

"Come get it."

He lunged for me, but I dodged around him. He chased me down to the water and dove in after me. He pushed my head underwater and grabbed for his bathing suit, but I held it out of reach.

"Come on, sea nymph," he said. "Hand it over."

"Make me feel good, and I'll consider it."

Out past the surf line, up to our necks in the cool water, no-one could see us jerking each other off.

"Isn't this the most incredible feeling?"

"I can't believe we're doing this. Oh my God!"

In the afterglow, dripping with cool sea water, we strolled back to our blanket, attracting the attention of two guys, mahogany-brown body builders lounging under an umbrella, who stared as we passed by.

"Oh God," he said. "They recognized me."

"No they didn't." I dropped my towel. "They're checking you out, Queer Bait. In case you haven't noticed, most of the guys on this beach are probably gay."

"How can you tell? By the way they're dressed?"

We spent the day like that, needling each other between naps. Later, as we were putting on our clothes, his cell phone rang. He frowned at the screen, hesitated, and answered.

"Hello? Father, hello, yes, Merry Christmas. I am, yes. Uh, over the weekend. Well, I planned to call you, but I wanted to relax for a couple days. Yes, with a friend. A new friend. Yes, Father, female. Today we're in Miami. No, we're at the beach. Well, we won't be back up to Palm in time for dinner, how about lunch tomorrow? She might like that, yes. Twelve noon? Okay." He listened and said, "Hello?" He shrugged and hung up. "Same old Roy. Never says goodbye."

"He and your mother don't live together?"

"He and Mummy don't get along," he said as he buttoned his shirt. "The marriage sort of cooled when he went to prison. But he's Catholic, so, no divorce."

"Prison? What was that about again?"

"Something to do with stock manipulation." He kicked his feet into his Cole Haan slip-ons. "It's complicated."

"Oh. Too complicated for my female brain to process?"

"I didn't mean that."

We gathered up our stuff and headed for the path to the parking lot.

"He pulled a few slick deals and got caught. But the prosecution was definitely political. Elliot Spitzer was on a witch-hunt against Wall Street and Roy got burned at the stake. Part of his sentence is that he can never work in finance again. Just like Elliot Spitzer had better not get caught with another whore."

"Roy doesn't seem to be hurting, judging by that house."

"No. He's loaded. And he loves going rogue. He considers his stretch in the slammer a badge of honor. In The Movement he's admired because he was persecuted by Spitzer and did his prison time like a man. He didn't complain, he didn't rat out anyone else, and he's still filthy rich. So now he concentrates on his main project, establishing Christian America. He spends a lot of time raising money for conservative causes."

"So you're seeing him tomorrow?"

"Tomorrow for lunch. You're invited."

"That's nice of him."

"Not really. He wants to check you out. See if you're a worthy companion for me."

"And who am I supposed to be, Adrienne, Emma, or somebody new?"

"Just be yourself." I got the message; he didn't dare deceive his stepfather.

Was it risky, to meet Roy Upton as Adrienne Monet? Only, I thought, if he starts talking to Rosa Lee again, which seemed unlikely, or even more unlikely, got in touch with Jonathan.

"You think he'll like me?"

"Hard to say."

"Think I'll like him?"

He chuckled. "I'd be surprised."

"It's another perfect day in South Florida!" chirped the gal on the radio. A.J. touched an icon on his phone screen and the tall iron gates swung inward and admitted us into Roy Upton's world, where I was willing to bet the sun was required to shine every day. A.J. drove across a gravel plaza and parked beside two exquisite cars which he informed me, with a smug grin, were a yellow Rolls Royce convertible and a black Maybach sedan.

"I'll bet I can guess which one your father drives."

"Oh, Father doesn't drive," he said. "Those are for guests."

Just then, a white Rolls Royce with smoked windows turned into the plaza and rolled to a stop. A.J. glanced at the Bentley's dashboard clock. "Stroke of noon," he said, grinning. "He's a maniac for punctuality."

A uniformed Black chauffeur stepped from the car waving and said gaily, "Hey Mister A.J.! Merry Christmas!"

"Hiya, Charles. Merry Christmas."

The chauffeur opened the rear door, Roy Upton swung out, and I found myself looking into the merriest, friendliest face I'd ever seen. He had a large head on a trim body, his thinning white hair was plastered across his sunburned skull, and two wildly overgrown eyebrows hovered over his brilliant blue eyes like clouds. His nose, short and twisted, had been broken at one point, and deep creases ran to the corners of his mouth. Roy Upton smiled devilishly, showing dazzling teeth, but I suspected his sunny expression could quickly sour into merciless disapproval. He wore a white polo shirt and trousers and deck shoes, and as his chauffeur unloaded his golf clubs from the trunk of the car, Roy puffed on a large cigar that even my untrained nose could tell was of the finest quality.

"Well well," he growled as he stared at us from under those eyebrows.

"Hello Mister Upton." I held out my hand. "I'm Adrienne Monet." He looked at me for a couple seconds, and I almost thought I'd committed some social faux paux, then he seized my hand in a bone crushing grip. "Thank you for the invitation to lunch."

"Call me Roy," he said. He turned to A.J. and gave a bow. "My good man! Swell to see you again!"

"And you too, sir."

They shook hands formally, meaning it and at the same time mocking the gesture, then broke into laughter and hugged, slapping each other on the back.

Roy's lips were close to A.J.'s ear.

"Good to see you, son. You're looking fit."

"You too, old man." He smacked his father's hard, flat belly. "Seem to have this under control, eh?"

"A man who can't control his appetites can never be a real man. Wouldn't you agree, Miss Monet?"

"Call me Adrienne."

"Wouldn't you agree?"

"I wouldn't trust a man like that. You never know whether you're dealing with him or his appetite."

"And wouldn't you agree that'd carry certain risks for a woman?" he said.

"For anyone, Roy."

He nearly spoke, then shook his head.

"C'mon, you kids," he said. "I just played 18 holes at West Palm with the president. I'm hungry."

We ate lunch on a back yard terrace at a large table, sitting in a cool breeze under a wide awning. A lush lawn shaded by tall palm trees stretched away to a high white wall. A maid in uniform served the first course, a small cup of a deliciously rich soup of tiny French lentils and spinach. Roy called for Emilio, his personal chef. A husky, cheerful man who said he came from Nice and wrote music in his spare time, Emilio served the wine, an insufficiently aired Bordeaux to my taste, and chatted with us a while before returning to the kitchen.

"How's the book selling, son?" Roy said.

"A little slower than I'd hoped."

"Do more press," Roy grumbled.

"That's how we met," I said. "On Gunner Crockett's radio show."

"Yeah-up," Roy said. "I heard all about that." He turned and said to A.J., "Are the conservative book clubs buying?"

"Not all of them."

"I'll make a few calls," he said, disturbed that a book by his son was not the Number One bestseller it deserved to be.

"Thank you, Father, I'm sure that'll help."

"My whole life I've been accumulating and spending capital. Financial, and human. I'll never live long enough to call in those favors for myself. Why not for my boy?" He grabbed A.J.'s shoulder and shook it. "How're the reviews?"

"Mixed. They love me in the Red states and in the heartland. I'm doing a big tour there in February. Until then, New York, L.A., DC. Big media markets, but not much of a market for God in those places."

"Yeah-up. Right where they need it the most. Some people will always be determined to defy the Divine Plan."

"The only review I really care about is my royalty statement. But I'm keeping score of those who write negative stuff so —"

I said, "Forget about that, A.J."

The men stopped and looked at me as if they'd forgotten I was there.

"When you get a bad review, shrug it off. Never let them know they got to you. Trust me, it's less wasteful than getting into public feuds."

"Good advice, son," Roy said.

A.J. seemed taken aback for a moment. "'Public feuds' is what I do."

Roy laughed. "Miss Monet, I understand you make movies."

"I've just finished shooting my latest."

"Is that the one about 9/11?"

"Yes. The way it was experienced by everyday people."

"Oh, one of those," he said, his voice trailing off. "Someday somebody'll make a film that tells the truth about what really happened that day."

That sounded like an invitation to hear a conspiracy theory. No thanks, not with lunch.

"I didn't know we would meet," I said, "but I have the latest edit on a DVD with me. While I'm in town I'd love to screen it for you and hear your reaction."

A quick glance passed between father and son. "I don't think I'll have time to see it now," Roy said smoothly. "I'll see it when it comes out in the theaters and maybe I'll give you a call."

"When we hold a screening for special guests, I'll invite you."

He grinned, deflecting me, eyes twinkling.

The rest of the lunch was just as tense and disappointing. The meal was grilled beef, which I ate to be polite, with peas, French fries, sorbet and coffee. I shrugged off the insulting freeze-out from Roy, but the way A.J. shrank from a brash character into a meek, obedient stepson was contemptible. The old man was a congenial host, but I wasn't invited into the conversation with his stepson. When I did try to speak Roy looked right through me. He'd checked me out, obviously thought I wasn't good enough for A.J. and worse, he didn't respect me enough to tell me to my face. Two weeks later, when A.J. and Jonathan were dead, I'd realize the events that led to their doom began that day at lunch with a God-fearing, cigar-smoking billionaire in his white palace in the sun.

Next to A.J.'s swimming pool we rolled two chaises out of the hot sun and into the cool shadow cast by the house. We laid back on the warm cushions in a post-lunch languor. Soothed by the dry rustling of the palm fronds overhead, I drifted into a dreamless sleep.

A splash woke me up. A.J. had tossed his clothes on his chaise, and he was paddling naked in his pool with a grin on his face. Naked in the pool, like father, like son. How I'd love to needle him with that! He pulled himself up on the pool edge. I grabbed my iPhone and shot a ten second clip as he leaned back and shook the water out of his hair.

"You know, you're right," he sighed, with his eyes closed and face to the sun. "This is habit forming."

I rolled to my feet and grabbed his hand, pulled him up, and dragged him indoors and upstairs to his bedroom.

"Hey, I'm dripping all over everything."

I threw him a towel. While he dried off, grinning as I stripped off my clothes, I wound my tee shirt into a whip, and snapped his bare rear end.

"Ow! Hey!"

"*Touché!*"

"What was that for?" He wrapped the towel around his waist.

"Sometimes I like playing rough. You gonna do something about it?" I hooked my fingers into the towel around his waist and pulled him to me and kissed him. But I ended it, "Agh!", with a sharp bite to his lips. He angrily pushed me away.

"Hey!" he said, anger flashing. "Don't do that, damn it, I have to go on television."

"Well, do something about it."

"Man, you're acting weird," he said, removing his towel, touching it to his lips and seeing there was no blood, then folding it neatly.

"Where are your balls, man?" He looked stunned. I shoved him backwards. His arms flailed as he fell back on the bed. He threw the towel at me but missed.

"Hey, did we come up here to make love, or what?" he said, trying to sit up.

"What is it you think we're doing, Mynheer?" I put my foot in his chest and pushed him back down.

"C'mon, Adrienne –"

"I am Emma to you, Mynheer Upton, and I find your behavior much too timid. You're so polite! I almost bite your lips off, and what do you say? 'Oh, please don't bite me again, my love.'"

"I didn't say 'please.'"

"Ooo! He fights back."

He rolled his eyes. "Oh, come on –"

"Oh come on," I mocked him, drawing it out into a whine.

He stared at me, hurt that I was treating him this way. I jumped on the bed and straddled him.

"Pain, that is your thing, right? You like inflicting it, don't you?" I hit his face with three light slaps meant to sting and insult. "You Americans. Like little boys. Where are your balls, little boy?"

I saw the fury coming in his eyes. He swept me face down on the bed, pinned me with his shin across my back, and stung my buttocks with a hard spanking.

"Is this what you want? Huh? Huh?" Each smack on my ass sent an exciting shock from my toes to my hair roots.

I reached up and grabbed a handful of his hair. I pulled him down beside me.

"Ow!"

"Mynheer!" I whispered. "Is that the best you can do?"

I woke up lying on my belly, hot and throbbing, my legs tangled in the linens, my breasts and rear end tender and my body aching here, there and everywhere. A.J. lay half on top of me, both of us in oblivion following a mind-blowing orgasm. He was snoring softly on my shoulder, his warm fuzzy thigh heavy on mine. The sunlight had moved since I last noticed, the room was shadowy and cool. I had no idea of how long I'd been out. I had to squirm and struggle to pull myself out from under his weight. I rolled over on my back, kicked my legs free of the sheets, and as the ceiling fan turned lazily, I savored the cool breeze on my naked body. I reached out and ran my hand up and down his back.

Slowly, he woke up. He gave me an astounded look.

"Oh my God," he laughed, embarrassed at what we'd done and not quite sure it was okay. We dragged ourselves out of bed, showered together, picked up our clothes and silently pulled them back on. We left the house by the backdoor and walked up the street to the beach holding hands. Not a word was spoken.

The afternoon had turned gusty and chilly under thick gray clouds. The turquoise sea was rolling with whitecaps. We strolled along the beach and I pulled my sweater up to my neck and the cuffs down over my hands.

"So. Big Daddy Upton's a real piece of work."

"What do you mean?"

"An authentic, filthy rich, Wall Street wheeler-dealer right wing plutocrat."

"You make that sound so negative."

He was sincere, but I laughed anyway. "Do you think he liked me?"

"I don't know," he said. "He wasn't just checking you out for my sake. He's always been afraid I'll make a mistake that'll embarrass the family."

"Is that why he asked if your friend was female?"

Ignoring that, A.J. said, "Roy thinks family reputation is like a stock price. He's always on guard against any devaluation."

"He's determined to make your book a bestseller."

"He'll do it, too. Whatever strings he has to pull. Between Roy, and the life I might've had with Lehane, I'll take Roy any day. And by the way, any ideas I may have learned from him, I've thoroughly questioned. I know you don't believe it, but I do think for myself."

I decided not to challenge that.

"It feels like your mind is somewhere else," he said. "Are you okay?"

"I feel like I've just been conquered." I stared out over the ocean, the surf rising and curling over down along the shoreline. So," I bumped him with my shoulder, "you liked what we did in bed just now, didn't you?"

His face fell. "Hey, wait a minute," he said. "All of that was your idea, not mine."

"But you liked doing it."

"Well yeah, even though now I feel totally corrupt."

So this was what victory felt like, a rush of pleasure that I kept to myself.

"Well, putting the Bible aside a moment, it felt good, didn't it?"

"No. Well... okay, yeah, I mean, it did when we were doing it. Now I'm not so sure. I thought I was hurting you."

"Sometimes there's pleasure in pain."

"I was just giving you what you asked for."

"Then don't ruin it by apologizing."

"You said you were into it."

"You got into it, too. I'm sore as hell."

"Pleasure from pain." He shook his head, like, WTF?

"Oh, totally. But remember. It's a game. It has rules. The only time you're allowed to spank me or call me a bitch or a cunt or anything like that, is in bed. Understood?"

"Aw, that's no fun —"

I grabbed a fistful of his shirtfront and pulled his face close to mine.

"I mean it. Just try it, and you'll see how much I mean it."

"Okay, okay." He held up his hands until I let go of him. "Man! What are you always so angry about?"

In my lifetime I've tried many times to answer that question, only to be frustrated by the inherent deafness of the lower primates.

"If you have to ask," I said, "you'll never understand."

He was quiet until we left the beach and stood waiting to cross the street.

"That first time we had dinner, when you invited me to have sex with you, what'd you mean by 'half-queer bohemian filmmaker'? Or were you just trying to shock me?"

"I like to sleep with women too," I said.

"You're serious?"

"I'm serious."

"Oh." He thought about it, then said, "Of course, I like sleeping with women. So I guess I understand."

"No, you don't." I laughed, then I gave him a playful shove into the trunk of a towering palm. "But it's sweet of you to try."

On our flight back to New York, I curled up sideways in my seat pretending to read *"Bad Behavior"* by Mary Gaitskill and gazing at A.J. as he dozed with a peaceful, contented smile. Of course I knew that my attraction to this rich brat and the friction between us I enjoyed with such erotic pleasure wasn't entirely healthy. But here we were, flying home, and I was daydreaming about a marriage of his world and mine. I imagined our wedding portrait, happy and smiling in the "Vows" section of the Sunday *Times,* over a story about the improbable marriage between the *"Men R Dawgs"* creator and the right-wing attack dog. Our everyday life would be a passionate psychological, social, emotional, and yes, political tug of war on an opulent battlefield. He was a prude in certain ways, but once he was fully broken in, I knew I'd be able to tempt him over to the wild side. I've never needed a man to complete my life, not even during my brief marriage. But I wanted this one and the life that came with him. Soaring high above the clouds, I was determined to get everything I wanted: my career reborn, my sexy arrogant maddening husband, and my brilliant angry beautiful Barky too, even if she chose a life married to Garth, pushing their kid along the Hoboken waterfront in a fancy baby buggy.

Babies... Ever since I nearly died having a child at seventeen, I believed the doctor when he told me I probably couldn't have another. Maybe he was really being honest with me. Maybe he was trying to suppress the white trash birth rate, I don't know. The guilt and remorse of giving up my baby girl for adoption was enough to stop me from ever thinking about having another child. But now I hoped the doctor had been wrong. My period still arrived more or less on schedule every month. As our plane began its wobbly descent through dense gray clouds over Long Island, I decided that if I could, I wanted to have a baby with A.J. I'd never told him about my abandoned child, by now a young woman somewhere in the world, hopefully living a better life than I could have given her. A child with A.J. would make us a complete family, might even make him a better man, and make me a better woman. Our child would be more beautiful than either of us, have the best care and love and attention, get a first-class education, and have all the things in life that I never had. It could all work out perfectly, if I could just find a way to solve the Jonathan problem.

Hello, cold gray New York winter. Goodbye Palm Beach, sunshine, and blue skies. Goodbye to my blonde Dutch girl masquerade, and bonjour Adrienne Monet, film director, my hair restored to its natural dark luster. I packed up my Emma Van der Berg costumes and dropped off the clothes at the Salvation Army used clothing store on 8th Avenue on my way uptown to Alpha Bitch Pictures.

On the day after New Year's, in a looping studio on West 22nd Street, Jonathan and I stood side by side at microphones in a soundproof booth, looping a scene that happens early in the story of David Sawyer's romance with the ghost of Josephine. In close-up on a screen, they lie in bed, speaking softly to each other.

                    SAWYER

I think I loved you before we ever met. I had an idea
of the woman I wanted to spend my life with. Smart,
accomplished, down to earth, beautiful, warm and
humorous, someone who'd know what to take seriously and
what to laugh off. And one day, there you were.

                    JOSEPHINE

I wasn't looking for a man, much less a husband. And
then when I least expected it — (A warm laugh).

                    SAWYER

I wish we had met when we were younger. We would've had
more time together, kids, the whole thing.

                    JOSEPHINE

What we had were the best years of my life.

                    SAWYER

No, no, what we have, what we still have...

We tried several readings and shadings. Finally satisfied, I took off my headphones and ran my fingers through my hair and tried to massage the tension out of my scalp.

"Happy?" Jonathan said.

"Yeah. We got it. Okay. Next."

"We have more to do?" he said, looking at his watch.

"There's something I want to try. It's that shot we did downtown on Day 16, Sawyer and the ghost of Josephine walk and talk up Rector Street on the sidewalk alongside Trinity Church."

"I remember that day."

"I want to improv new dialogue."

"What's the idea?"

"A bigger turning point than what I've written."

"How long is the take?"

I pushed my monitor button. "Hey Mikie?" I said to the ADR director. "The walk and talk. Can I see it once? Without the audio?"

It's a simple wide shot. An office building is on the left side of the street, Trinity Church is on the right side, and an iron spiked fence runs along the churchyard. Up the sidewalk comes Sawyer, walking with the ghost of Josephine toward the camera, talking, getting larger in the frame, but too far away to read their lips. At the end of the playback, Jonathan shrugged. "Sure, fine."

"Take One," I told Mikie in the booth. I turned to Jonathan. "I'll start it. Ready?"

He took a sip of water. "Yes."

"Action," I said.

The scene began on the screen in front of us.

                              JOSEPHINE

This is going to be a difficult conversation.

                              SAWYER

Difficult? Why?

                         JOSEPHINE

I don't know how you'll take this.

                         SAWYER

Take what?

                         JOSEPHINE

I want you to let me go.

                         SAWYER

Let you go where?

                         JOSEPHINE

No, no. I mean, I want you to let go of me.

                         SAWYER

What are you talking about? Wait a minute —

                         JOSEPHINE

What I mean is, this thing you've created between us?
It has to end. For your sake.

         SAWYER (a long silence, then...)

Where is this coming from?

                         JOSEPHINE

Accept it, my darling. The life we shared is gone. In
its place, you're clinging to something that's not
real.

                    SAWYER (shaken)

It feels real to me.

                    JOSEPHINE

I know. Please, David.

                       SAWYER

So, I'm a little needy. I've got an overactive
imagination. Besides, don't you think I can tell what's
best for me?

                      JOSEPHINE

Better for you to accept reality. I'm gone. You can't
have me anymore. You'll never see me again. I know
that'll hurt, because our time together was so good,
and I'm so sorry. But for your sake, this has to end,
so... goodbye.

Sawyer and Josephine walk silently to the corner of
Rector Street and Broadway. They turn to each other. In
the finished edit Sawyer will be stunned to see
Josephine's ghost fade away before his eyes.

    "Good for you?" I asked Jonathan.
    "Fine," he said, his voice shaking. In the booth Michael and his assistant
busied themselves at their console. He cleared his throat. "Yeah, I'm okay, I'm
fine. Again?"
    "I don't think I need it. Do you?"
    "No," he said. "Where are you going to use this?"
    "I'm not sure yet." I took my headphones off and hung them up. "But it's
a turning point that has to happen." I left the booth before he could reply.
    We got ourselves buttoned-down, zipped-up, and scarf-wrapped to face
the cold afternoon. We left the ADR studio at dusk and hustled under dry

snow flurries toward Sixth Avenue, moving through the sidewalk crowd of people heading home from work.

"How was Paris?"

"Lonely. And Paris is the worst place in the world to be lonely."

That was aimed at me, but I didn't respond. Now that we were alone, I expected him to say something about the meaning of the scene we'd just improvised.

But instead, he said lightly, "So, how was your holiday?"

"Dull. I hung around the city. Tried to ease off work. But I couldn't. Sorry I missed your calls."

"How'd you get so tan?"

"My Christmas present to myself. Two sessions on the tanning bed. It's chic to have a tan in January, don't you think?"

"Not much sun in Paris. But I'm excited, because I did some business on the project I told you about."

"The love story."

"'*Autumn Reprise*'. Two movie stars who once were young lovers in Paris, an American man and a French woman, reunite late in life, look back at what they had, heal old wounds, and give each other the courage to face aging and mortality."

"And Delphine Tessier to play The Woman? Wow."

"It's sort of our story. She and I."

"And she likes it?"

"She's committed."

"Congratulations."

"She'll help raise the money if I need her to."

"In Europe, I assume. Hollywood would never finance a movie like that."

"And I can't think of a better director for this picture than you, Adrienne. You and Delphine working together, that's got exciting possibilities."

That took me by surprise.

"Well, okay, let me read it."

Just what I didn't need, another 'Yes or No' question from Jonathan. He wanted more than just to spirit me away for a romantic adventure in Paris. I would be his director, which was safer than hiring a French director who might seduce Delphine artistically or in other ways and brush him aside. As the writer-producer and star and the director's lover, he could make sure the movie would be shaped around his performance.

"I've been working on it for years, writing and waiting for the right moment," he said, pulling a thick manila envelope from his backpack. "We can platform off '*Lonely Sky*' and start putting the money together for it."

"Okay." I tucked the script under my arm. "I'll read it. Thanks."

When I got to my office, I read the first scene, then I told Megan to hold my calls. I read the script to the end, then went back and read certain scenes again, with a sinking feeling. "*Autumn Reprise*" was one of the worst screenplays I'd ever read, a glib chatty two-person slice-of-life that was a mere 90 pages. The use of Paris as a setting was without imagination, nothing but a place for them to walk, talk, dine, ruminate, reminisce; they could've been in Hoboken. There was no plot development beyond the initial setup: Jonathan's character leaves behind his stalled acting career and goes to Paris to push back against aging and mortality by trying to revive his romantic and creative relationship with Delphine's character, a superstar of French cinema, herself in the autumn of her life and illustrious career and in a spiritual crisis like him, questioning whether the life she's led has been worth anything. We know all this by page 30, and everything after that is reiteration, sixty pages of ways to say the same things.

There was no excuse for that screenplay to be so weak. There could have been depth and richness in those characters, they were movie stars and citizens of the world, yet they certainly had the same doubts, fears, and insecurities as everyone else. But Jonathan's writing didn't reveal those riches. It was a love story, so each scene had to turn to some degree on whether they'd reunite or part forever. But Jonathan had written too much reminiscence, and squabbling over old hurts, instead of the characters giving each other the courage to face the dilemmas of old age and the dread of approaching death. In the end, they part company in the Gare de Lyon, knowing they may never meet again. (Cringe.) I suspected Delphine Tessier told Jonathan, "Of course, *cheri*," out of kindness, or maybe she wanted to work with him again, but not because she liked the script. Unlike Jonathan, she was an icon, with dozens of films to her credit, so maybe she felt a ho-hum film wouldn't matter.

It wasn't hard to understand why Jonathan was so passionate about "*Autumn Reprise*". He could work out unresolved issues with the great lost love of his life, on a film set where they'd have wide creative freedom. No doubt working on this script, writing conversations he wished he could have had with Delphine, had been his medicine, exploring unfinished business, and keeping him going as he approached the winter of his life. But just because writing a script feels like a therapeutic catharsis doesn't mean it's well written or will make a good movie. *"Autumn Reprise"* needed a total rewrite. And then there was the fact that to commit to directing it would mean further involvement with Jonathan for at least two more years of my life, maybe longer.

I lay on the sofa in my office, watching lights flash on the ceiling from the giant screens over Times Square. I wondered if involving myself with *"Autumn Reprise"* could be a way to contain Jonathan. He must have sensed that I was tired of him and his solution was to throw his third-rate script at me like a net, assuming, given what we were hiding, that I wouldn't dare decline. And he was right. Over my desk at home was a stack of unproduced scripts, any one of which I'd direct tomorrow. Yet I couldn't risk turning down his awful script. It was so obvious this Paris project was a way he could cling to me, but if I allowed it, the trade-off was that he'd never betray me, at least while we were shooting together. I decided that for now it was safer to keep him close until I figured out how to persuade him to accept me and A.J. without payback of the worst kind. The only way I could see was to commit to *"Autumn Reprise"* and to stall.

"I love their situation," I told him in the ADR studio on Wednesday as we got ready for looping. "They're fascinating, sympathetic characters. They got into my dreams last night. But I was dreaming about their potential, not anything you wrote. It's a very mediocre screenplay, Jonathan. It's not ready to shoot at all."

He frowned. "Read it again."

"I don't need to. You tell us too much about them too early and leave nothing for the gradual revelation of deeper character. The rest of the script has a randomness that quickly goes flat. They walk, they talk, but they never throw each other any challenges. There's not enough at stake. The story could show that aging is scary and difficult and has to be faced with courage and dignity. It could say it's a hard choice. Rage against the dying of the light? Or gracefully accept your fate? To explore those ideas, the script needs events and conflicts and less talk about their past. In every scene the suspense has to be whether the reunion has a chance to succeed, and they'll face mortality together, or they'll fail. The script doesn't have those tensions yet, and it doesn't have a climax with any real impact either."

He stood there, disturbed, his eyebrows saying So now what?

"It's a great idea. I want to direct it. I really do."

His face lit up in a wide smile.

"But only if I'm free to rewrite the whole thing."

"Well, all right," he said, deflated. "How much time do you think you'll need?"

One Sunday morning as I woke up in Barky's cluttered, chilly apartment, I was aware of a gentle hand brushing my hair off my cheek. I opened my eyes and there was my pale goddess, her red hair flaming on the pillow, grinning at me with bright, hungry eyes. As the heat came on and the radiators clanked and sputtered, we made slow, half asleep, stinky, dragon-breathed morning love.

We squeezed together into the shower stall in the kitchen, turned the hot water 'way up, soaped and sponged and shampooed each other, toweled off, and dressed. As I was checking my messages, Barky came up behind me, her auburn mane combed back in a wet pompadour and kissed the back of my neck.

"I just texted Garth. I told him I've got a cold, so I'm staying in the city today."

"Doesn't he want to come in and be with you?"

"Uh, no. He's very germaphobic. It's okay. He'll go watch the Giants game at the sports bar with his buddies."

"Why not just tell him you're spending the day with a friend?"

She gave me a look, then shrugged.

"It's complicated."

"Okay."

I'd sensed that something unpleasant happened with Garth's family in Minnesota over Christmas, so I didn't ask for more. We had a precious Sunday to spend together and I didn't want to spoil the mood. A.J. was visiting his mother, Garth had been put off, and I'd ignored two messages from Jonathan.

Outside the window beside the kitchen table was a blustery January day. Bright sunlight flickered through gray and blue clouds streaming across the narrow sliver of sky between the neighboring rooftops. Barky went down to the bodega on the corner and brought back the Sunday *Times* and a cold wave of ozone as she pulled off her down jacket. She dropped the advertising circulars, news sections, sports, and business pages onto the recycling pile, put the rest on the kitchen table, then draped herself across a chair. I read the Sunday Review, Arts & Leisure, Style, Real Estate and Metropolitan sections eating whole grain toast with coffee, and Barky had oatmeal and a protein shake while she pored over the Book Review from cover to cover, including the ads.

"What do you want to do today?"

"I don't know." Barky tossed the Book Review aside. "Do you have any ideas?"

"Let's walk the Park from top to bottom. We could use the exercise."

"Perfect! I love the Park on windy days like this when the light keeps changing. And we'll find some place to have lunch."

"And tonight I need to see at least one movie before the weekend's over. I still haven't seen 'Phantom Thread' and it might be Daniel Day-Lewis's last movie."

After breakfast I took an Uber downtown to my apartment and changed into warmer clothes and walking shoes. Touching up in the bathroom mirror, I congratulated myself on finally achieving something: a happy life, with a rich and original film in post-production, ongoing negotiations with the Lily Channel to produce and direct Season 2 of "Men R Dawgs", love with a beautiful girl, enmeshed in irresistible erotic friction with a wealthy gorgeous man, and with an offer to make a film in Paris. Could life get any better?

I was on my way out the door when A.J. called. Since we'd come home from Palm Beach, we couldn't get enough of each other. We fought over things like politics, the culture wars, and everything else under the sun, by phone and text and email, then let the hostilities climax in hot sex after hours.

"Adrienne?" A.J. said. "I'm at brunch with Mummy. I've been telling her all about you, and I thought it would be nice for the two of you to meet, so say hello."

Before I could say anything, the phone was passed and a woman's voice, rather loudly, said, "Hel-lo?"

"Hello. I'm Adrienne."

"Adrienne what, my dear?"

"Adrienne Monet."

"Monet. How lovely. Like the painter?"

"He was my father's great great grandfather."

"I have one of his paintings in my living room."

"Now that's exciting."

"The way A.J. speaks of you I can tell he's quite taken with you, my dear. So, since you two are an item, I'd love to meet you. Do you think we can do it soon?"

"I'm kind of busy, but, sure. I'd love to."

"Why not tea tomorrow? Say around three o'clock? If you're not too busy?"

"It's a date."

The Upton family apartment was on the eighth floor of a classic turn-of-the-century building on Park Avenue in the East 70s. A.J. had told me there were twelve rooms, and when the maid let me in on Monday afternoon, I could believe it. From the reception hall I could see into the spacious living room. Golden afternoon sunlight streamed through the sheer curtains onto a thick Persian rug. The Neo-Colonial furnishings and decor were in the Republican Power Elite Chintz style, and over the fireplace hung what certainly looked like a Claude Monet painting of a river in spring. So this was where A.J. grew up...

"I'm so glad you could come!"

My first sight of Rosa Lee Upton was a shock. She was shrunken and wrinkled and looked older than her early sixties and she rubbed her hands together continually, as if they were cold. Her hair was a smooth blonde helmet, and her thin body in a platinum sheath was as unremarkable as her face. But she radiated a sunny energy, and she had the same bright blue eyes she'd given her son. What a plain-looking girl she must have been beside the charismatic Jonathan Lehane, swept up and unable to believe her luck, then shattered when he abandoned her and their son for a more intriguing and worldly woman.

"I'm Rosa Lee!" She gripped my hand in both of hers, which were dry and bony.

"I'm so pleased to meet you, Mrs. Upton."

"Oh, call me Rosa Lee. Goodness, what a beautiful outfit. *Tres chic!*"

I'd primped for the occasion, and wore a white blouse with tiny blue dots, a navy-blue wool midi-skirt skirt, black pumps, a black overcoat, and a black beret pushed back holding my hair off my face.

"I like that style, the hem on the calf," Rosa Lee said.

"Sort of the brainy girl's idea of how to look sexy."

That made A.J.'s mother laugh. "Not too much leg, huh?" Which made me laugh. "Were you the brainy girl in school? I know I wasn't."

"I made the grade. But I knew very early what my career was going to be."

"A.J. said you make movies," Rosa Lee said. "You're directing his father, I believe."

"We're all finished now."

"Was he any good?"

"He was. I'm hoping the film —"

"Lucky you," she said abruptly, taking my arm and guiding me into her world. Okay, so she didn't want to hear about my movie; after all, her hated ex-husband was the star.

In a book-lined alcove off the living room, we sat on sofas across a wide coffee table. A portly red-cheeked maid served tea from a silver service. Rosa Lee told me she'd listened to my confrontation of A.J. on the Crockett Show and she'd laughed at how cleverly I'd analyzed him and deflated his smug opinions.

"I was probably too tough on him," I said, "but I had to defend my work."

"Oh, he's a big boy. He can take it. If anything, he needs to hear more of that. He certainly dishes it out to people."

"Yes, he does. But when he starts in with his political stuff, I just give it right back to him. Or I pretend to yawn. Drives him crazy."

She laughed. "I'm sure it does! My son doesn't understand the difference between an interest in politics, which can make for acceptable cocktail chatter if nothing else, and clinging to ideology, which turns people into insufferable bores."

"Well it's never boring with us. We both seem to enjoy the friction."

"So that's how you get along so well?"

"Mostly." I just grinned and, leaving out the gleeful insults and rough sex, I said, "And despite all that, we also make each other laugh a lot."

"Well!" Rosa Lee said, chuckling. "That's the secret, isn't it?"

Rosa Lee seemed to enjoy my company. She gave me such a glow inside, put me so at ease, that I told her more of my fictional biography than I usually shared, embroidering it with stories, some of them true, some improvised on the spot.

After tea, we bundled up in our overcoats and took a walk in Central Park so Rosa Lee could smoke a Pall Mall. She offered me one and I smoked it to keep her company.

"A.J.'s stepfather has been an unfortunate influence on him," Rosa Lee sighed as we strolled. "I don't share Roy's political leanings, and I dislike how they've affected our son. It just didn't seem normal for a young boy to be idolizing an old fool like Ronald Reagan and reading those ridiculous novels by Ayn Rand." She pronounced it Ann.

"Maybe someday he'll outgrow all that."

"There is something else I think you should know about, just between us." I nodded, leaning closer to her, honored she would confide in me. "For years now, A.J. has been telling a story about losing his girlfriend in the World Trade Center attack. And I've warned him that sooner or later someone is going to prove that story isn't true, and he's going to be very embarrassed."

I said casually, "I hadn't heard that story," hoping my surprise and confusion didn't show. "But thank you for sharing that. Just between us, of course."

By the time we got back to Fifth Avenue at dusk we were arm in arm and she was telling me how glad she was that we met. While her doorman hailed a taxi, Rosa Lee stood chatting with me outside her building. We air-kissed and promised to get together again soon. In the taxi, I turned to get one last look at this strange woman, but she was already walking inside.

Rosa Lee had such poise and was so well-spoken, she inhabited her elegant home so naturally and she seemed so assured in her opinions and inquisitive in her questions that I really wanted her to like me. I wanted to pull out my phone, call A.J., and tell him all about my visit with his mother, but I didn't. I was trying to understand what kind of mother tells her son's girlfriend that her son is a liar. Was she trying to discourage me because she felt, like Roy, that I was unworthy of their son? Or was she disdainful toward his need to feel like a victim? Ironically, even if his 9/11 story wasn't true, she had made me realize A.J. and I weren't that different. We both appreciated the power of a story, true or false.

The next day after an afternoon staff meeting, I spent some time in my office looking over the page proofs of the *"Lonely Sky"* book that Barky had sent over. I read my essay introducing the book and decided my account of the tragic loss of Egon Swift was perfect. I had debated whether to be magnanimous and polish Egon's legacy. But too many copies of his awful script were in too many hands, and if I gave in to the impulse to praise him, and a copy got posted online or written about, I'd look ridiculous. So I limited myself to describing how Egon's killing was such a shock to the crew, and so painful for his family, friends and fans. Before I went back to editing, I couldn't help but linger over pictures of me working with the cast and crew. They reawakened my pride in our movie and made me miss our hard work and camaraderie. The pictures of Jonathan and me as Sawyer and his ghost wife made me miss those days when we worked together so well, and to wish he wasn't so needy and frustrated with me now.

My iPhone rang. The screen read A.J. UPTON.

"Hey. Man of my dreams. What's up?"

His voice was tense in a way I'd never heard before.

"I need you to get over here."

"Uh, okay. Why?"

"Please, Adrienne. Just get over here."

"You sound upset. What's wrong?" But he'd hung up.

The midtown streets were gridlocked in traffic, so a taxi or Uber would take forever. I trotted across Broadway to the subway, took the R train up to 59th Street and Lexington Avenue, hustled through a maze of passages and stairways, then transferred to a No. 6 to the Upper East Side. I kept taking deep breaths and tightening and relaxing my whole body, telling myself not to worry until there was a reason. But there was a reason; I'd heard it in his voice.

He'd left his front door ajar for me. I heard A.J.'s voice, loud and indignant, through the open door to his office off the entry foyer.

"This interference in my personal affairs is inexcusable!"

"Oh sweetheart," Rosa Lee Upton's voice cajoled from a speakerphone. "I'm only looking out for your welfare. Is this how you thank me?"

I stepped into his office as he obviously intended. He threw me a serious glance.

"I'm a grown man, mother. I can take care of my love life without any help from you."

"You've always dated respectable young women from decent families."

"Yes, and they bored me to death."

His mother, so full of tart observation and humor with me the day before, now was seductive, and tender.

"Something's changed about you, my dear, and I don't like it at all. After everything I've told you about her, you still don't see this Adrienne Monet for what she is."

"Oh really? And what's that?"

"A low-class gold digger and a smooth, confident liar." What? But only yesterday we... I leaned against the door jamb, staggered. "In Roy's opinion you deserve better, and for once I agree with him."

A.J. replied in a strange, almost childish whine, pointing to me as if his mother could see.

"I don't care that she gave up her baby. I don't care that she changed her name. And if you plan to say anything else, I don't want to hear it."

"She didn't know I'd had her investigated before she came to tea," Rosa Lee said. "And she sat with me and told me one lie after another about herself. Only troubled women with a lot to hide are such brazen liars, A.J."

My hope to become Rosa Lee's favored daughter-in-law turned to a chip of ice in my heart. What a fool I'd been, so eager to impress her that I completely missed how dangerous she might be.

"You said you wanted to meet her," he said. "I never thought you'd do something like this."

"Sweetheart, she's not right for you. You're headed for disaster if you keep up this foolishness."

"And you just had to involve that son of a bitch, didn't you?"

"According to my investigator and the police reports he got for me, she and Lehane are having an affair. I simply asked him to tell her to leave you alone."

Panic set my mind on fire.

"Yeah, well, he came here this morning and I threw him out," he said. "He's lucky that's all I did. He was stinking drunk."

"Well," Rosa Lee said, "by the way he reacted, I'd say his feelings for this Adrienne Monet, or whatever her name is, are out of control."

I was paralyzed by indecision. I had to get to Jonathan before he did something vengeful that couldn't be undone. But I also had to know if the future with A.J. could be saved.

"I know all about him and Adrienne, and I don't care."

"You don't care?"

"No! And you can't tell me what to do! I have my own money now!"

"There's more you don't know. She and Lehane —"

"Goodbye mother!" He hung up.

I was no match for her. Rosa Lee, so warm and girly and friendly yesterday, had practically called me a snake curling up where it was warm. And the old bitch called me low-class. That hurt the most.

A.J. came to me, shaking his head.

"I'm sorry. But I thought you should hear it for yourself."

I nodded. "Why did she get Lehane involved? What else did she tell him?"

"Whatever would make him squirm, I'm sure. For thirty years she's hated him so much she'd kill him if she could get away with it."

"It's all true, you know. The baby, changing my name, re-inventing myself. But there's nothing invented about my feelings for you. I wouldn't do that to you."

"Listen, you need to hear something." He punched a button on the answering machine on his desk. "How's this for insane?"

Lehane's voice, hoarse and hesitant, croaked out of the speaker.

"A.J. (Sigh) It's your father. I need to have a conversation with you. Immediately. Your mother tells me you're very involved with Adrienne Monet, and we're worried that you don't know what you've gotten into. I know Adrienne Monet, much better than you could ever hope to. (Pause) She's a beautiful woman, she's a talented artist, she's great company, she's an original spirit. (Sigh) But she's also a very dangerous person. (Pause) You have no idea how dangerous. I hope you'll let me save you from making a tragic mistake."

I shook my head. "He's angry. He's confused..."

A.J. snorted. "Also very drunk."

"Well, I was honest with you, wasn't I? About me and him?"

"According to him, you're having an affair."

"That's not true. I told you what happened."

"First, he said he's in love with you, then he warned me not to fall in love with you. Well, it's too late for that."

In the typical Hollywood rom com, next would be my close-up, and I'd bite my lip and try in vain not to cry.

"Did he really ask you to marry him?" he said.

"Yes. Of course I said no."

"You heard what he said on the voicemail. He called you a dangerous person."

"I can't imagine why. Is that the worst thing he said?"

"He accused me of hooking up with you just to humiliate him!"

"Of course. To Jonathan, everything is about him. What else did he say?"

"It wasn't a very long conversation."

"Try to remember. I need to know everything."

"Why?"

"I'm going to see him."

"You're going to see him?"

"There's nothing between me and him. He needs to be told that again."

"All right. I'll come with you."

"No. I have to go alone."

"He's drunk. You don't know how he'll react."

"Yes I do."

"You might be in danger."

"If I bring you, I will be."

He looked unsure.

"I'm going to bring him back to reality. I'm going to talk to him as his director and as his colleague, not as his lover, or anybody who ever wanted to be. But you can't be there. The war between you will get only in the way."

I had to go find Lehane, but I let him hold me tight for a few seconds at the door.

"Your mother is the one who worries me," I said, "hiring detectives and meddling in our relationship."

"I love her to death, but Mummy can be a terrible old snob. Just ignore all that stuff you heard. It doesn't matter."

"In the long run, she might be the bigger problem. Please don't let her ruin a beautiful future for us."

"That future's already here." He kissed me, deep and lingering, as much a statement as a kiss. "Be careful."

"I'll call you later."

I ran down the sidewalk to Lexington Avenue, hoping to catch a cab across the park to the West Side instead of waiting for an Uber. After what I'd just heard, it worried me that Jonathan hadn't called or texted me. Lehane, Lehane, where the hell are you? He was out in the city, somewhere, angry, drunk, and unpredictable.

The bar on Columbus Avenue where he sometimes hung out was packed and noisy as I squeezed my way through the after-work crowd. He was sitting alone at a table in the back, swirling a glass of whiskey. He saw me coming, kicked out a chair for me, and sat back, glowering.

I sat down and held out my hands, which he ignored.

"I came here for you."

"Oh really?" A brief sneer. "For me?"

"Is that so hard to believe?"

He slurred, "It sho' is, Baby Jean... I mean, Bobbie Jean," he corrected himself, scoffing drunkenly at his mistake. It wasn't the name that offended me. It was that mocking drawl, suggesting I was some kind of hick.

"A.J. played me the message you left for him," I said. "He let me listen to his mother talk about me on speakerphone. I'll bet she told you the same things."

"You mean about your illegitimate daughter," he said with a mean glint in his eyes, "and how you got rid of her?" He wanted to hurt me and must've thought that would wound me the most. "You never told me that part of the story."

"How can a child be illegitimate?" I needed to recover peace, trust, and understanding between us, but a part of me, less hopeful and perhaps more genuine, refused to take any shit. "And you know all about getting rid of children, don't you?"

"How dare you —"

"We all put things behind us, Jonathan. Things nobody has any right to judge. I gave my baby a better chance than she would've had with me." A waitress approached with an inquiring look, but I waved her away. "I came to New York. I changed my name. So what?"

"This isn't about Bobbie Jean Blivka, or Adrienne Monet, or whatever your name is. It's about a much bigger lie."

"What lie?"

"You told me you didn't even like him. But according to my rancid, treacherous ex-wife, you're in love with him."

"I wanted to tell you about me and A.J., I just didn't know how. You hate each other so much. And don't we have enough to deal with already?"

He looked blankly at me for a moment.

"What do you mean, we?"

That was chilling.

"Don't you know by now how much I respect you, as an artist and as a man? How could you think I'd let A.J. use me to humiliate you?"

"So now that he knows about us, how does he feel about you?"

"His feelings haven't changed."

"They will when he thinks about it," Jonathan said. "He's going to hate you for fucking his contemptible father."

"He doesn't care about that. It's no big deal."

"No big deal?" Disbelief, tinged with sadness. "That's all I am to you?"

"It's no big deal to him. Certainly not the big deal you're making out of it."

"It is a big deal to me. You're a big deal to me."

"I never encouraged you to think we could be –"

"Yeah? Why? Why didn't you want more with me? What's wrong with me?"

"Nothing's wrong with you." He was slipping into self-pity and I couldn't stop him. "Do you really need me to tell you that?"

"Well then, what happened?"

This was getting embarrassing. Debasing himself like this could be dangerous for both of us if he got out of control.

"I met someone else. Hasn't that ever happened to you?"

"You never loved me the way that I loved you."

"You needed more than I could give."

"You played a cruel game with my heart."

"You gave it to me to play with."

"No, playing Josephine was your idea."

"You wallowed in unhappiness over me, then used it on camera. Brilliantly."

"And this is the thanks I get," he muttered, his jaw clenched. "Just watch, this story'll be all over Page Six. Me, cuckolded by my own son, who ridicules me every chance he gets."

"Don't you think you're overreacting?"

He shook his head. "Women. You claim you want men who are in touch with their feelings. Then when you get one, you despise him for being sensitive, like it's a weakness."

"I don't know what women you're talking about. That's not me." He'd pushed me too far. "Nobody else knows about me and you, so stop worrying about Page Six. Why can't you just be a man and accept the situation?" He reacted like he'd been slapped. "I'm sorry you found out the way you did, but you weren't listening to me." The words flew out of my mouth before I could stop them: "You even proposed marriage, for God's sake."

He gave me a look that could kill.

"Oh, sorry 'bout that." He got awkwardly to his feet, threw money on the table, grabbed his backpack, and walked out. Well, I hadn't planned it that way, but now Jonathan had his answer.

I trotted outside, where the gloomy afternoon had turned to black Manhattan evening. Cold wind pierced my clothing. I tucked my hair into my jacket collar and pulled it up around my neck and stuffed my hands in my pockets. I stayed a few steps behind Jonathan up the sidewalk toward Central Park West. Despite his drunkenness, Jonathan was upright, steady on his feet, moving with his jaunty, sexy walk.

In the lobby of his building he didn't acknowledge me as I waited beside him for the elevator. We rode up to his penthouse in silence.

He offered to hang my jacket in the hall closet.

"No thanks. I don't know how long I'll stay."

He sighed and shook his head. He opened a closet and hung his backpack on a hook. He stood frozen, peering silently at the hanging clothes. Then, in a sudden frenzy, he tore off his overcoat, crushed it into a ball.

"God damn you!"

He hurled it with both hands into the closet. He seized the door and, swinging with his whole body, slammed it shut with a crash as loud as a gunshot that made me flinch. The jamb shattered, molding fell to the carpet, and the door swung outward, quivering on its hinges.

He glared at me, spat "How's that?!" then headed for the living room, snarling over his shoulder, "Manly enough for you?"

Ordinarily that would have been enough to make me turn and run. But I couldn't. I had to steer us to a safer place.

The lamps filled the living room with a rich, golden glow. Out the glass doors to the terrace, Central Park was a dark forest dotted with blue lights, and from the buildings on Fifth Avenue lights gleamed like campfires on a distant cliff. Jonathan poured himself a whiskey with a shaky hand, spilling some on the bar, the bottle clinking on the rim of the glass.

"Will you please stop drinking?"

He looked at me, swallowed the drink, and put the glass down.

"I was so glad when you became director." He shook his head, steadying himself with one hand on the bar. "And for the longest time," his voice caught, "I tried to believe you didn't shoot Egon to take his job. I really did. That was before I saw your true nature."

"I went to Egon to try to save the show and almost got raped for my trouble."

He lit a cigarette and took a deep drag and brushed that aside.

"Bullshit. I think what really happened was, you wanted the job, so you stole my gun and you killed him. You didn't even tell me so I could protect myself. I had to catch you at it." He shook his head, then exhaled with a sigh. "And now you and my son are out to make me a public joke. And the worst part of it? I've lost you, and I'm losing A.J. again. And believe it or not, I care about that. Losing you both. That's hard." He gasped a short, high-pitched sob. "It's hard to feel you've got nobody."

"You're not losing me." I had to calm him down. "If we just give this a little time —"

"Oh, fuck that!" Jonathan cried, slashing the air with the cigarette. "Fuck give it time! Time for what? Time for you to figure out your next move? Don't even bother. You have no moves left. You just don't know it yet."

"What do you mean?" Silence. "Jonathan? What don't I know?"

"You don't deserve my loyalty anymore."

"That's not fair. I gave you everything I had. Ask anybody we worked with."

"Yeah, you're very popular, aren't you?" He sneered. "A friend to one and all. You've got the whole world fooled. But not me, not anymore."

"How many times do I have to tell you it was self-defense?"

"Stop insulting my intelligence! I know why you shot Egon. For all I know you were fucking him, too."

That did it.

"Oh, sure. I lured him into my web, fucked him, killed him, drank his blood, and then I stole his job!"

That shut him up for a second. He just stared.

"I don't have to fuck or kill anybody to get a job!"

"Well," he said, pleased that he'd got me so upset. "You won't be able to fuck or kill your way out of the trouble you're in now."

I was afraid to ask.

"I called those detectives. They're on the way, so you may as well wait here. Because it's over, Adrienne. I'm giving them the gun. I'm going to tell them you admitted you shot Egon. I want to clear my conscience and get closure for Egon's family, which is something I care about even if you don't. I'm wiping the Adrienne Monet mess off my shoes and moving on."

How I wish I could've smiled, shrugged, come back with something witty, even elegant, the way the hero always does when facing certain doom. But in reality, I was losing my grip on myself. I must have looked stunned, because he grinned. I dropped into an armchair, with my head in my hands. So it was over. And why? Because he couldn't handle unrequited love? Because he felt betrayed and rejected? Boo fucking hoo! Meet the real Jonathan Lehane, the lover scorned. Not so pretty now, is he?

"If you do that," I said evenly, "I'll have to tell them you put me up to killing Egon and taking his job so you could get back in the movie. And how you gave me the gun to do it."

"If I turn you in for murder, I can make a deal for a lighter sentence. I'm getting myself out of the trouble you put me in."

"By forcing us to lie and accuse each other? Great plan, Jonathan. Weren't you saying just the other day how much you love me?"

"That was then." He glanced at his wristwatch. "They'll be here any minute."

My impulse was to run and buy myself time to think about what to do. But leaving him here alone to talk to the police would be suicide – mine. I was staggered by his spite and hatefulness and I was on the brink of tears.

"After everything, our work together on the film, our affair, I can't believe you're doing this to me."

"Believe it."

"What about Paris?"

"Oh, right. Paris." His eyes narrowed to mean slits. "You're fired."

"Jonathan, what you and I had together, the journey to make our film, I wouldn't have missed that for anything. We've done great work. You could win an Oscar. And I really do want to make your Paris film. But I've been telling you every way I know how that there's no future for you and me as lovers. So why sic the police on me now? Have you thought about what having me arrested will do to me? To our film? Can't we drop all this and just be friends?"

He refused to look at me.

"I'm going to marry A.J., if he'll have me. Come to our wedding and dance with the bride. Be an adult and give us your blessing." I reached for him. "Life's too short –"

He lunged at me and slapped my face. It knocked me backward, I stumbled and fell down and my glasses went flying. My head spun, shocked and stinging. He stood over me, livid, furious, his fist cocked to hit me again.

"Be an adult? Is that what you said to me, you bitch?"

I grabbed my glasses off the carpet and scrambled back out of reach.

"Get away from me!" I was so shocked I could barely speak. "Just get away!"

I fled to the bedroom and locked myself in. In the bathroom I sank to my knees on the tiles, lifted the toilet seat, and threw up my lunch. I rinsed my mouth and drank some tap water and immediately threw that up too, leaving my empty stomach painfully cramped. I splashed cold water on my face, toweled off, and put my glasses back on. They fit okay, but that slap in the face could've broken them and put my eye out. The red mark across my cheek was livid and my body was trembling. I rinsed my mouth and blew my nose – no blood, at least – and dried myself off. I went through the bedroom and stood at the door wondering what to do.

The doorbell rang and my heart leapt. The police! You took too long, Adrienne. After a moment, male voices came through the wall, low and menacing, rising in volume and intensity. Then there was scuffling in the hall, the sounds of two men pushing each other around and cursing.

"Adrienne!" A.J. called out. "Adrienne!"

No! I was so upset that he was here I couldn't stand still. I flung myself around the room in frustration, waving my fists and cursing under my breath.

"Adrienne! Where are you?"

"Try the bedroom," I heard Jonathan say, suggestively.

"Adrienne? Let me in!"

I unlocked the door, and he burst in and closed it behind him.

"What happened?" he said. He put his arms around me and held me. His cheek was cold from the streets. I lost myself and started sobbing. He leaned back and peered at my face. "He hit you! I'll kill that son of a bitch! C'mon, I'm getting you out of here. I should've never let you come here alone."

"It was nothing, I'm okay. We're working it out. I'm all right. Go home. Please. Let me handle this."

"I'm not leaving you here alone with him."

"I'll be fine, A.J. Please, just go home and wait for me."

"I'll settle this."

"No, wait –"

He pulled away from me and left the room. I didn't want to be rescued, I just wanted him to leave and let me handle it. I expected to hear cursing and punches being thrown but there was only silence.

I found A.J. in the living room. Jonathan was outside on the terrace, leaning on the parapet, his anguished face lifted towards the starless sky.

"Stand by for a Shakespeare soliloquy," A.J. mocked. "Oh, the pain of it all!"

"Please leave. Having you here is making things worse."

"Come with me."

"I can't. I have to finish this."

Jonathan came back inside. He closed the sliding glass door. His eyes, glaring around, stopped on A.J. across the room. Then he looked at me.

"Will you please let this go?" I said to Jonathan. "If we can't get along, we should all just get out of each other's lives."

"You'd like that, wouldn't you?" Jonathan said, his voice flat and loud. "Walk away from all the shit you've caused. Well, not this time."

He reached under his sweater and pulled the gun from his waistband. Suddenly I was standing in the worst place in the world: between two angry men, father and son.

"Dear God," A.J. gasped.

"You said you'd get rid of that thing," I said, scared and not thinking.

"No, I didn't. I said I wouldn't destroy evidence."

"What?" A.J. said, incredulous.

"I took it out last night to kill myself. But why should I? Over you? You're the cause of all this. And you're the one who should pay." Jonathan raised the gun and pointed it at me.

"Jonathan, please..." I was in a nightmare, desperate to run, feet stuck to the ground.

"Come to your senses, man!" A.J. said. His voice shook. "Put the gun down!"

"Jonathan. Be reasonable, please."

"Reasonable? Listen to her. Be reasonable! What do you know about her, anyway?"

"I know I love her."

"Really?"

"So you're wasting your time with these theatrics."

I knew what was coming. "Jonathan, please don't –"

He spoke to A.J. but he was looking at me.

"Do you know she murdered the director of our film and took his job? Stole this gun, shot him, then she put the gun back and said nothing to me until I forced the truth out of her. I still might be arrested for murder."

"Don't believe him, A.J."

"She told me herself she shot Egon Swift," Jonathan said.

"A.J., he knows it was self-defense."

"Wait a minute." The worst silence I had ever felt in my life. "You actually killed someone?"

"Not the way he's saying."

"There, you see?" Jonathan said. "Adrienne always has her version of everything, and she's never to blame. Well," he said, gloating, "you can tell it to the police when they get here."

I turned to A.J. but he backed away, looked aghast at me, then at his father. To try to tell him the truth – the threat from Aldo and why I borrowed the gun, how my sympathetic appeal to a meth-crazed Egon backfired, the assault that forced me to shoot him – would be too complicated, especially with a gun in my face.

"A.J.," I said, "Egon tried to rape me. Jonathan knows it was self-defense but he kept quiet so we could make a movie. This whole time, he's been holding what he knows over my head." A.J. looked bewildered. "And now because he can't have me, he's going to lie and tell the police I'm a murderer."

With more time I might've made him understand. But I had to get the gun out of my face. I tried to look Jonathan in the eye, but his gaze was unfocused. Only the dead black eye of the gun was steady.

"Haven't I given you the best I have?" I said, trying anything to get through to him. "And now look at you. Full of self-pity, and all because you refused to hear what I've been telling you."

"You're always so fucking honest, aren't you?"

"Because you need it!" I said, overcome with anger and contempt. "Forget this fantasy that anybody cares about this! Nobody cares! Quit blaming your son because he's angry with you! You know you deserve it! And quit pointing that gun at me! If you're going to shoot anybody, shoot yourself! You think anyone will care? They won't!"

Then I caught myself, and when I spoke again, it was as soft and sincere as I could make it, tears and all.

"But I'll care. I've seen the best of you, Jonathan. The real you. And this isn't you. This is not you."

I didn't know if that worked or if he just got tired and he weakened. But he lowered the gun.

"You know what? You're right." He slumped, and his head hung low. "I can't do this anymore," he croaked. "I'm sick of the whole thing." He raised his head and stuck the gun under his chin.

I stepped back... and waited.

A.J. cried, "Come on, man, put the gun down! We can work this out! This isn't that bad!"

Jonathan said, "This is what you two want, isn't it?"

"Listen to me," A.J. said. "I'm sorry it's come to this. I'm sorry for everything I said about you. It was childish to let my hurt and my anger run away with me. I realize now when I was trying to hurt you, I was also hurting myself. Please... Dad..."

Jonathan stared at us, speechless, his eyes shining.

"Jonathan," I said. "Give me the gun, please."

"Adrienne!" A.J. said. "Stay away from him!"

"It's all right. Jonathan knows it's all right. We could never do each other any harm."

I came closer, speaking softly to him, his head tilted back by the gun muzzle jammed under his chin.

"When 'Lonely Sky' opens, the world will finally see what a fine actor you are. Your career will be reborn," I said. "Don't you want to make 'Autumn Reprise'? Work with Delphine again? Work with me again? I know I've hurt you, but give me a chance to make it up to you. You've been such a brave artist these past few months. Life is always messy when you live from the heart. Be brave now, and don't do this to yourself. Give me the gun, please? You've been drinking, you haven't slept, you're not thinking clearly. Give me the gun before someone gets hurt."

Jonathan began sobbing, his face clenched in pain. The gun muzzle remained jammed under his chin.

"I'm still here for you. You slapped me in the face, but I'm still here, aren't I?" He stared at me silently. "Let me have the gun. We'll all go to dinner and talk this out."

In tears, Jonathan shook, breaking down. The words caught in his throat.

"If only..."

"It's going to be fine. A.J. said he's sorry. Now maybe there's even hope for you and him. You've got your son back! Everything's going to be all right."

Staring at his son across the living room, Jonathan lowered the gun until it hung in his hand by his side.

Behind me, a loud sigh of relief came from A.J.

"Oh, thank God!"

"A.J.?" I said, "I think everything's going to be all right."

I stepped over and gently took ahold of Jonathan's shoulders.

"It's not true that you have nobody."

I hugged him. His whole body was trembling. I kissed him on the cheek. He never looked more handsome, more beautiful, than at that moment. His eyes gazed into mine, huge with sadness and a fragile, hopeful trust. I felt so sorry for him. But the police were on the way, and Jonathan would not be strong enough to keep our secret any longer. In my mind, a chorus of voices rose to a painful volume, telling me my time was up, prison would be a living death, and "Lonely Sky" would be the last movie I ever made.

He let me take the gun from his hand. I'd forgotten that it was so heavy.

"Look at you," I tsked. "You left a bruise on your neck. Let me see."

He lifted his head back. I gripped Jonathan's shoulder tighter, jammed the gun under his chin, and pulled the trigger. The blast filled the room and slammed my ears. His body twisted out of my grip, and he collapsed to the floor. I took a step back.

"Oh my God..." A.J. was gasping behind me. "Oh my God!"

My ears were ringing. A.J.'s voice seemed to be coming through the wall of the next room. I lowered the gun and rubbed my aching wrist.

"I had to do it."

He was frozen, not even breathing. He stared at Jonathan's body.

"But... he gave you the gun."

"He would have told the police any lie he could. He would have tried to destroy us."

"But..." A.J.'s mouth moved but no sound came out. Calmly, I tried to lead him toward our future.

"We'll tell the police he killed himself because he found out about me and you. Okay?"

A.J. stared at me, at his father's body, then back to me in disbelief.

"You've been calling him a narcissist and worse for years. Our story fits right into that."

"Adrienne," he begged. "How can you be so calm?"

"Okay, A.J.? Tell me you can do this. Our future depends on it."

"Yes, yes..."

"You know how much I love you."

"Yes. And I love you too. Don't worry. Don't worry about anything."

My heart lifted, it soared. It was A.J. and me, the two of us, against the world.

He said, "Money is no object. I know the best defense attorneys in America. The kind that won't stop fighting to get you off. Or at least, they'll keep you from going to prison for very long. And I'll wait for you. I swear I will."

My heart broke, and the pieces fell into some unknowable place inside.

"I'm so sorry, A.J."

"I said don't worry. It's going to be all right."

"No," I said. "No, it's not."

I pointed the gun, shaking in my hands, at his face, that beautiful face. He couldn't believe what I was doing. I couldn't believe it either, but I knew I had to do it. He shook his head, puzzled.

"Adrienne?" He reached for me.

The gun fired again with an ugly bang and the bullet hit him with a wet smack in the forehead. Time froze. To my director's eye, it was a perfect MEDIUM SHOT from the shooter's point of view: A.J. rocked back on his heels, his arms flung out and his mouth wide open in a silent scream, and fell below the frame line, exposing a broken, blood-spattered mirror on the wall, and a woman lowering a gun, staring at her reflection in horror.

FIVE *The night of January 9, 2018*

The detectives leave me alone in Lehane's dining room and I call Bruce Berger. I dial him on FaceTime because I want him to see how I look. His phone rings and rings. Where is he? Doesn't he see my name on caller ID? Is it that he doesn't want to get drawn back in? Has he dropped me as a client? Suddenly Bruce's face is on my screen. Behind him a TV announcer talks excitedly over a noisy crowd. He's in a sports bar, I can almost smell the aftershave and the beer, yelling over the noise to someone, laughing.

"Hey, I'll take that action! The game's not over yet!"

Then he looks at me, scowling.

"Yeah! Hello?"

"Bruce, it's Adrienne."

He peers at me. "Miss Monroe — I mean, Monet."

"I'm in trouble."

"So call your lawyer."

"That's what I'm doing."

"You don't have anyone else?"

"I don't want anyone else."

"So what's the trouble?" he says, his eyes on the basketball game on the TV screen.

"Jonathan Lehane and his son are dead."

That gets his attention. I go to the doorway to the living room, turn my phone camera around, and show him the bodies and the police and EMTs.

"I saw them die. The police are taking me in —"

The crowd in the bar behind Bruce erupts, whooping and whistling and hollering. His face gets big in my screen and he shouts over the noise.

"Are you under arrest?"

"I don't think so. I don't really know, I'm scared, I'm confused —"

"Did they read you your rights?"

"Yes."

"That same two detectives?"

"Yes. They're taking me in for questioning."

"Don't say anything to them! Not one word! Understand?"

"Yes, Bruce. I know."

"I'm on my way."

Finally, something goes right. Okay, Bruce is a condescending sexist, he hates it when I follow my instincts instead of his advice, he tried to dump me as a client, and he's been drinking. But tonight he's the best friend I've got.

Ferino and Peavey come back and now they're all business.

"Put away the phone Miss Monet," Ferino says. Peavey cuffs my hands behind me.

"Do I really have to wear these?"

"Our discretion, Miss Monet," he says. I get it, he wants to make a state-ment. He's going to parade me in handcuffs in front of the media hoping that will erase the memory of the ad in the *Times* criticizing his investigation and the embarrassing article in the *Voice*.

Peavey grips my arm and walks me through the living room past the med-ical techs and crime scene investigators. They're too busy to even glance at us. Going down in the elevator between the detectives, I mentally rehearse how I'll present myself when the doors open.

Ferino brings me slowly through the lobby so the press can see us coming and get the best angles. It takes all my self-control to look calm and untrou-bled as we walk into the storm of shouting voices. On the sidewalk we're as-saulted by a blinding explosion of camera flashes from the photographers. We're mobbed by reporters, photographers, and video cameramen, jostling and spilling into the street, trying to get an angle on the *"Men R Dawgs"* woman. The detectives push them aside and walk me to their car. Beside the detective car Billy, A.J.'s driver and bodyguard, is red-faced and shouting at the two uniformed cops, Harris and Nunez, probably because they won't let him go up to the penthouse. He turns and sees me between Ferino and Pea-vey. Billy's sunglasses hang under his chin and for the first time I see his eyes. Pure rage.

Peavey puts her hand on top of my head, so I don't bump it on the door frame. I squat down and drop onto the back seat and discover there's no way to sit in handcuffs without crushing my hands behind me. Yelling faces, blinding lights, and camera lenses crowd the windows. Peavey gets in beside me and shuts the door. She buckles my seat belt over me.

"Let's go."

In front of the precinct, Ferino pulls into a parking space that's been dug out of the snow. Peavey goes around and opens the door and grips my elbow, so I don't slip and fall on the icy street with my hands cuffed behind me. Ferino swaggers into the building, ignoring Bruce Berger, who's pacing the sidewalk talking on his phone. Berger and I lock eyes, and he nods.

Inside, Peavey takes us to a small conference room and removes my handcuffs. Berger starts texting. I sink onto a chair and rest my head on my arms on the table but I'm too agitated to relax. As Peavey leaves, she offers me a cup of coffee, which I gratefully accept. A uniformed officer comes back with it in a china cup and sets it in front of me, then leaves. The coffee is black and smells freshly made, and the aroma is comforting, but Berger raises a warning hand.

"Don't touch that cup unless you want to give them your fingerprints."

"I don't care. I need something." But I realize I'm being uncooperative again. "How's this?" I pull my shirt cuff down over my fingers and pick up the cup. It immediately slips from my grip, clunk, and spills a steaming black pool of coffee across the table.

"Not so good," he says.

"Shit." This feels like a bad omen.

The spilled coffee stinks up the room. I don't need the caffeine anyway. My mind is already so on overdrive that it's a struggle to stay focused. My body feels disgusting, overheated and sweaty under my clothes. Berger pulls a chair close and sits beside me. I can smell alcohol on his breath.

"Okay. So they read you your rights?"

"Yes."

"Did you make any statements to the police?"

"No. Nothing."

"Were you the only witness?"

"It happened right in front of me, Bruce."

"What happened?"

"Lehane shot his son. Then himself."

"Why? What happened?"

"They were fighting over me. I was involved with both of them."

"So how are you now? Right now?"

"I don't know. I'm scared."

"Okay. Now listen. When they want you to tell them what happened —"

"Yeah, I want to –"

"No Miss Monet." Berger leans in, getting eye to eye with me. "Listen to me. We know they want to arrest you for Swift, but they don't have enough evidence. So they're frustrated. That means they're out to get you, you understand? In a minute we're going to sit down with them. They're gonna act like you're a witness. Don't believe it. You are a suspect in the killing of two men."

He sits back for a moment and watches me, waiting for that to sink in. Then he leans toward me.

"You're the only person who knows how they died. Do you know what that means?"

"I know what it means."

"What does it mean?"

"It means I control the narrative."

"No, Miss Monet," he says with utter disdain. "It means the only person who can convict you, *is* you." He sits back and watches to see if I heard that, then rubs his face, brushes his moustache, and sighs. "All right. When we go in there, don't say one word unless I tell you to. Understood?"

"Okay."

"You have to mean it this time."

"I do, I promise."

"I can't let you go in there if you're just gonna start blurting things out."

My heart is pounding. I'm so adrenalized I feel like I'm coming unglued in every direction, and he has no confidence in me.

"I'm losing it, Bruce. I don't know if I can do this."

"Get yourself together. 'Cause otherwise, I'm not gonna let you say anything. And that'll lead to more problems, because they can keep you here. You wanna spend the night with them hammering away at you?"

"I just want to get this over with."

"Then snap out of it. Take a minute. Close your eyes. Breathe. Get yourself under control."

He sits back and crosses his arms, waiting for me to collect myself. I tell myself one more time how I will describe the way Jonathan and A.J. died. I don't like to lie, but sometimes life forces you to. I'll tell as much of the truth as I can afford and only replace a few facts with new facts that work better for me. Ever since Egon got shot, I've wished I could tell somebody what happened and hear them say it wasn't my fault. But I know that's impossibly naïve. Tonight was chaos, and now I'm eager to tell them what happened and hopefully impose order on this chaos. Which means Berger is right. I'd better stay quiet, because if I start talking, I might never stop.

In the interrogation room, Berger and I take seats at a Formica table across from Detective Peavey. She flips through scribbled pages in a notebook. Ferino, who leans on his elbows at the head of the table, won't take his eyes off me. We are joined by a grouchy-looking, bottle-blond Latina almost bursting out of her gray suit. I figure she must be some kind of prosecutor.

I try to do a slow deep breathing exercise, but it doesn't really calm me down. Only an hour ago I decided not to kill myself because I thought I could handle the police. Now I'm not so sure I can even handle myself.

"January 9, 2018, the time is 7:32 p.m.," Ferino drones for the video. "Interrogation of Adrienne Monet. Present are Detectives Artemis Peavey and Buddy Ferino, Assistant District Attorney Jenny Garcia, and Miss Monet's attorney Bruce Berger."

Ferino reads my Miranda rights again.

"Do you understand these rights as I've explained them to you, Miss Monet?"

My reply is high-pitched, agitated.

"I do."

"With these rights in mind as I have explained them to you, are you willing to speak to us at this time?"

"No." I turn to Berger and he shakes his head. "My lawyer says no."

Garcia looks at Berger irritably. Detective Peavey sits back, shaking her head.

"That could make this a very long night, Miss Monet."

"Hey Bobbie Jean," Ferino says. "Two men died tonight. Violently. You say you were the only witness. So tell us what happened."

"Detective Ferino," Berger begins, "stop pretending my client is here as a witness. You've played that game long enough. The last time you questioned her you accused her of killing Egon Swift. Is that investigation still open?"

Garcia gives Ferino a warning glance. He says, "It's still open."

"And she's still a suspect?"

"That's right."

"You led her to believe she was a witness in that case, too. And Miss Monet cooperated without an attorney present or being informed of her rights."

"If she's innocent," Peavey says, "she doesn't need those protections."

"No? After you got her help, you searched her apartment, put her through a line-up, and accused her of murder, all without a shred of evidence. So Miss Monet will not say anything about Egon Swift or answer any questions about him. Understood, Miss Monet?"

"Yes."

"You only answer questions about what happened today."

"Okay."

"And keep your answers brief."

"I will."

Ferino has his fingers laced on the table before him. He nods to Peavey.

"Okay," she says. "Tell us what happened."

"They were arguing."

"What about?"

"Me."

"What about you?"

"Since last fall I'd been trying to get Jonathan to accept that our affair was over. But he wouldn't let go. In the meantime, I'd met his son and we started dating. We were planning to get married."

Peavey says, "Please tell us about those relationships in detail."

"Don't answer that," Berger says. "Just describe what happened today."

"Mister Berger," Garcia says irritably, "you're not running this interview."

"You want to waste time asking questions we won't answer? Go right ahead. You're lucky she's even talking to you. You can blame your cops for that."

"How can we understand what she tells us about today," Garcia says, "if we don't understand those relationships?"

I looked at Berger and he paused, then relented.

"Keep it brief."

Peavey says, "You told us in a prior interview you and Lehane had a personal and professional relationship."

"Yes."

"It started last summer when you were making a film together."

"Yes."

"And when did you meet Mister Upton?"

"Around Thanksgiving. A.J. went on TV and mocked his father and the movie we were making. I called in to a radio interview he was doing, and we traded insults for a few minutes. The next day he called me asked me out to dinner."

Garcia says, "Seems counterintuitive."

I shrug. "Men."

Ferino says, "Did he know you'd been involved with his father?"

"I told A.J. the truth about Jonathan. And I told him it was over. I was working with Jonathan to finish the film, but that was all. I kept the relationships separate because A.J. hated his father ever since he abandoned him as a child."

Peavey says, "And when did Mister Lehane find out about you and his son?"

"Last night. Yesterday, A.J.'s mother invited me to tea. I thought we got along great. But A.J. told me his mother called Jonathan last night. For the first time in, like, twenty years. She told Jonathan about A.J. and me. She demanded that he break us up."

"Why'd she do that?" Peavey says.

Berger says, "You'll have to ask the mother about that."

"Oh don't worry," Ferino says, grinning at me. "We will."

Peavey says, "So Lehane found out only last night about you and his son." "Yes."

Ferino said, "From his ex-wife."

"Yes."

"Ouch."

I turned to Berger. "And she found out about Jonathan and me from some police reports that she just happened to have." He nodded but directed my attention back to Ferino.

"You said you and Upton were engaged. When did that happen?"

"New Year's Eve."

Peavey says, "Did Mister Lehane know you were engaged to his son?"

"I told him today. It made him angry. He still had feelings for me. He felt betrayed."

"Betrayed by you?"

"Yes. He and A.J. already hated each other."

"Things were bad between the father and son?"

"Very bad. Like I said, Jonathan abandoned his wife and son when A.J. was a young boy. A.J.'s hated Jonathan ever since. Very publicly."

Peavey nods, listening intently. Ferino looks like he doesn't believe a word I've said.

"A.J. said Jonathan came to his house today. Drunk. He tried to break us up, but A.J. threw him out. Jonathan accused him of stealing me away. A.J. said his mother also called him and said a lot of derogatory things about me."

"Like what?" Ferino says.

"He wouldn't say. He didn't want to hurt my feelings. It didn't matter to him, anyway. He told her to mind her own business."

"So, then what?" Peavey says.

"I went to see Jonathan to try to calm things down."

"And when you found him, how was he?"

"I found him in a bar. He was drunk."

"Did you have anything to drink?"

"No. We talked a little bit. Then we went to his apartment."

"You've been there before?"

"Yes."

"So, you're familiar with Mister Lehane's apartment?"

"I've been there before."

"Then what happened?"

"He kept drinking. He wouldn't let go of the idea that we could be a couple. He was angry. He was sad. He was spiteful. One minute he said he hated me for taking up with A.J. The next minute he said he loved me. I tried to –"

Berger said softly, "Slow down Adrienne. Take your time."

I took a deep breath, wishing I had a cigarette, and continued.

"I tried to get him to quit hanging on. I tried to get him to accept that A.J. and I were going to be married. That's when he slapped my face."

"He assaulted you," Peavey says.

"Yes."

Ferino says, "Then what?"

"I locked myself in the bedroom. I was so upset I threw up. While I was in there, I heard yelling. It was Jonathan arguing with A.J. He came to help me, even though I asked him not to."

Remembering A.J.'s gallant protectiveness, I hug myself, and I begin to cry. I'm embarrassed to have my feelings so exposed, but I'm also thrilled because the feelings are real and so far, I've been telling the truth, mostly. Berger reaches over and grips my forearm.

"Take your time, Miss Monet."

"I could see nothing was going to get settled. The two of them fighting was only making things worse. I tried to get Jonathan to let it all go and move on. But he looked at me with such hatred. And then he pulled out a gun."

Ferino says, "You knew he owned a gun, right?"

"No."

"Where'd the gun come from?"

"He had it in his belt, under his sweater. He said he took it out last night because he was going to kill himself after the phone call from A.J.'s mother. But he said since I was the cause of all the trouble, he wanted to kill me instead."

My mind is clear, but my weeping gets worse.

"I tried to calm Jonathan down. But then A.J. lost his temper. He called Jonathan a coward for threatening me."

"With the gun in your face?" Peavey said.

"I begged him to shut up. He was just making Jonathan angrier. He told Jonathan to get on with his life, and to accept that I didn't want him anymore. He told him to quit feeling sorry for himself."

"Then what?"

"A.J. called him a weakling for refusing to accept the situation. They were yelling back and forth. Jonathan was waving the gun at A.J. and right in the middle of all that yelling the gun went off and A.J. got shot." I turned to Garcia. "He said he didn't mean to do it. He said, 'I just wanted him to shut up!' He said he didn't mean to shoot. It was an accident."

Across the table, Peavey and Ferino lean in toward me. Garcia wears her distress on her brow.

"So then what?"

"I couldn't move... I thought I was next... Then he said, 'I can't do this anymore...' He put the gun under his chin."

"'I can't do this anymore'?" Peavey says.

I nod. "He was crying. He was shaking. He said he'd lost A.J. years ago. He'd tried his whole life to patch things up and now he'd killed his son. His life would never be the same again."

"Then what?"

"He said, 'I love you. I will always love you.' Then he pulled the trigger."

"Shot himself?"

"Yes."

Ferino says, "How did Lehane fall to the floor?"

I take a moment to breathe, relieved that part is over. "He sort of collapsed, and fell on his back."

"Did he drop the gun?"

"I don't know."

"Did you touch the gun?" Ferino says.

"No."

Berger pats my forearm. "That's enough, Miss Monet."

"Lehane told us he didn't own a gun," Ferino says. "Why did he lie?"

"Don't answer that," Berger says.

"Why did he lie, Bobbie Jean?"

"She said she didn't know he owned a gun."

"She knew him well. Maybe she knows why he lied."

"How do you know he lied?" Berger said. "Lehane's interrogation was months ago and that was about Swift. How do you know he even had a gun then? He could have bought it at any time in the past few months. He could've bought it this morning."

Peavey nods, conceding the point, which irritates Ferino.

"Okay, Miss Monet," he says. "You've been helpful. We appreciate it. What we need now are your fingerprints and your jacket, and we're going to take you downstairs for a gunshot residue test –"

"Forget that," Berger says loudly, irritated. "Miss Monet, don't say one more word."

"She says she didn't do anything wrong," Ferino says. "If she's got nothing to hide, why not cooperate?"

"No," Berger says. "Even if you find DNA or GSR that only means she was close to Lehane when he fired the gun. It doesn't prove she fired it. And revolvers give off more GSR than an automatic."

Garcia says, "The law allows us to tell the jury her refusal to consent is evidence of guilt."

"Or, it's evidence she doesn't trust the police, with plenty of reasons not to."

Ferino says, "Look, if it all tests out negative, no prints on the gun, no DNA on her jacket, no positive on the residue test, okay, I'll buy her story." He looks from my lawyer to me. "I'll believe she didn't commit double murder."

"My fiancé?" I say, before I can stop myself. "You think I killed my fiancé?"

"That's enough, Miss Monet," Berger says.

Ferino gives me a stone-cold look. "I think you're capable of anything."

"Fuck you."

"That's enough," Garcia says loudly.

I shout back at her.

"How would you like to be accused of killing the man you love? The man you're gonna marry? How would you like it?"

"Detective Ferino," Berger puts his hand on my forearm. "You're taking it to the edge again."

Ferino just grins and shrugs.

"Bobbie Jean?" he says, smooth and low, like he never heard my lawyer. "Did Lehane tell you he called us today?"

I stare at him, giving him nothing that could be an answer.

"Did he tell you we were coming to see him?"

I don't answer. I very loudly don't answer.

"He gave us new information about the Swift killing."

"That's it," Berger says. "Charge her with a crime, or let her go."

"You know what Lehane told me? He told me you shot Swift. Which is what Swift told us before he died."

"Not one word, Miss Monet."

Ferino shakes his head, smirks, stands up and straightens his jacket.

"The clock's running, Bobbie Jean, so you better start telling the truth. We won't always be this nice."

He turns to Garcia, who gets up and motions to Detective Peavey. As they all head for the door, I ask my lawyer, "Can I leave?"

"No." Ferino turns and looks at me. "We're gonna talk about how long we need to keep you here tonight."

"Take your time, Buddy."

I sit there for the next half hour worrying about what will happen. Berger watches the basketball game on his phone. Suppose they keep me here indefinitely? The past hours have taken everything out of me. By the time Ferino comes back, I've got nothing left but anger to keep me going.

He looks like a man who has just lost an argument with two women.

"Miss Monet," he says curtly. "Thank you for your cooperation. You're free to go."

I get quickly to my feet, avoiding eye contact with him.

"We will talk to you again."

"Through my office, please," Berger says.

Ferino scoffs. "Oh, of course."

We leave the precinct out the main door and find ourselves mobbed by a crowd of reporters and photographers rising up from the sidewalk, trapping me and Berger with our backs against the door.

Microphones are thrust in our faces. Shouted questions roar at me from all sides.

"*What happened?*"

"*Were you a witness?*"

"*Why did they let you go?*"

Berger takes my arm and tries to clear a path. Nobody moves an inch. The only way I'll get out of here is to make a statement. It's the last thing I want to do, but at least I can be first to frame the deaths of A.J. Upton and Jonathan Lehane for the public record.

"If I don't say something," I yell in Berger's ear, "they'll follow me home and camp on my doorstep!"

"They'll do that anyway!"

"*What happened?*"

"*Who shot who?*"

"*Why did they let you go?*"

I shout at the crowd over the noise they're making.

"The police will have to tell you what happened!" I say, cringing at how shrill I sound. "That information should come from them! But I just want to say this!" The mob quiets.

"Jonathan Lehane had just given the greatest performance of his career," I say, with tears in my eyes. "A.J. Upton had just undergone a spiritual trans- formation and published a brilliant book about it. Then tonight a terrible thing happened between a father and son who'd had a complicated and vio- lent history. They died just as their lives and their careers were getting better. And that's a tragedy."

The questioning erupts again. Above it, Berger shouts, "That's all, that's all!" He pushes into the crowd and I walk behind him, head down, micro- phones inches from my face. We make our way slowly until we break free from the hollering throng. He hustles me down the street to the avenue, stalked by trotting video crews and photographers.

"The car's over here."

He leads me to a sleek Mercedes sedan idling at the corner with his driver at the wheel. The driver clicks the door locks down, and we fasten seat belts. Camera lenses and faces fill the windows. Berger nods to his driver, and the car surges ahead, leaving the noise behind.

My cell phone rings. It's Barky on FaceTime. She's sitting at her kitchen table, looking incredulous.

"Adrienne, what the fuck?" she says. "I just saw you on New York 1. You looked terrible. What's going on?"

"A nightmare."

"Is it true? Jonathan is dead?"

"So is A.J. Upton. I was there. I saw the whole thing. And I was questioned by the police. They think I did it."

"Are they insane?!"

"No." I glanced at Berger, who was watching me closely. "They're just police."

Barky shakes her head.

"Look, I know I'm not very warm and cuddly –"

"Oh, you always undersell yourself."

Beside me, Berger chuckles.

"I mean it, Adrienne," she says. "Seeing you on TV just now made me realize how much you mean to me. If you're in trouble, we'll deal with it together. You shouldn't be alone tonight. You want me to come over? You want to come over here?"

That brings up the tears again. I want to lunge through the phone and hug her.

"I'll be there as soon as I can."

Berger sits back and seems to relax. "Will you be all right?"

"Yeah... No... I don't know."

The adrenaline from the police interrogation has drained away and I'm losing the energy to speak, or even to think.

"Your friend's right," Berger says. "You shouldn't be alone tonight."

Barky's apartment is a railroad flat over a Chinese restaurant in an old tenement building on Second Avenue in the East 60s. She buzzes me in, and as I climb the three flights, to my surprise I feel comforted by things that used to annoy me, like the garlic and ginger aroma in the stairwell, the tin-clad stairs that rattle underfoot, the dirty walls gone for years without paint, the bicycles and shopping carts chained to the banisters, the fluorescent fixture over Barky's landing that flickers fast enough to cause a seizure.

Barky is waiting, leaning on the door jamb, barefoot in jeans and a flannel shirt, her hair a coppery tangle. I fall gratefully into her arms.

"You'll feel better after we take a hot shower," she says.

Out of the shower, both of us in sweat clothes and robes, she pours me a glass of red wine.

"So," she says gently, "do you want to talk about it?"

I'm well aware Barky's not just lending me a kind ear. She wants to know if she's fallen in love with a crazy person. To tell her I was forced to kill three men to defend my dignity and freedom, to horrify and maybe lose her, would be more than I can take right now.

"I was at Lehane's. He wrote a screenplay. He asked me to direct it and we were talking about it. Then A.J. showed up, and they had a terrible fight. Jonathan shot A.J. Then he shot himself."

"Oh my God." Her face flushed, and tears came to her eyes. "In front of you? You could've been killed."

"There's more to the story. Just give me time. Right now, I just want to forget tonight ever happened."

"I don't care about the details," she says. "I care about you." Which makes me feel like a real shit for lying to her, but I know in time I'll get over it.

A.J. falls away from me, blood spouting from the wound in his forehead, his face fading into darkness. My hands reach for him but grasp only emptiness...

I jerk awake beside Barky, gasping and sweating under the blankets, my heart hammering against my ribs. Outside a car swooshes down Second Avenue, a siren echoes in the distance. The heat in the building is turned down and the cold air chills my face and pinches the tip of my nose. I raise my head and look around.

Something's gone wrong in my brain. I'm horribly dizzy. Up on the ceiling and across the walls stripes of dark and light through the venetian blinds seem to vibrate, and the walls and ceiling keep moving. I'm lying motionless, but my body feels like it's spinning in space. I'm going to throw up, and my bladder is painfully full. I have to get to the toilet at the far end of the apartment or stay here and soil Barky's bed.

I force myself to sit up, then stand. I hold on to the window frame beside the bed for support, shivering in my sweaty bedclothes. The floor feels like it's moving, and I rock and sway, like I'm falling to one side, then the other. My stomach is trying to make a fist. I stagger to the back of the apartment, holding on to furniture and door jambs and trying not to knock over the books piled everywhere, the piles of magazines and manuscripts overflowing off her cluttered desk.

The toilet is in a corner of the kitchen, in a closet so small that when I sit on the icy seat I can reach out and touch the walls to keep my balance. I pee long enough to make the rivers rise, and the relief is excruciating. Then I turn and kneel at the toilet and start throwing up. When my stomach settles down to dry heaves, I wipe my sweaty face with a handful of toilet tissue, blow out acidic snot that burns the inside of my nose, and flush it all away.

I crawl on all fours out of the closet and across the ice-cold tiled floor of the kitchen, retching on my empty stomach, my hair stuck to my sweaty face. I brace my hands and knees wide, but the kitchen floor keeps trying to pull out from under me and dump me on my side. I feel like my body is under attack from my brain. Suppose this never ends? A dust ball on the floor in the moonlight through a dirty window, the decades of dirt ingrained in the tile floor, are proof the world is doomed.

I crawl to the kitchen sink, grab the edge, and pull myself to my feet. Swaying side to side in the mirror, I force myself to smile. My smile is even on both sides of my face, there's no weakness in my limbs, and my head doesn't hurt. So, this isn't a stroke, it's just intense vertigo.

I brace myself with one hand and with the other I splash icy water on my face, brush my teeth, and rinse my mouth. I wobble back to the bedroom without falling and lay back down on the futon. The sheet on my side is ice cold, and as I shiver in my sweaty bedclothes, the room seems to shake all around me.

Barky wakes up and reaches for me.

"Are you all right?" she says, brushing my bangs off my forehead. "Oh wow, you're soaking wet."

"I had a dream. I was reliving the killing. I'm dizzy and I'm so cold."

"Ssshh. Be still." Barky gets out of bed and brings back a clean bath towel. With her help, I strip, and she rubs me dry. She helps me pull on socks, a pair of sweatpants and a hoodie. Back under the blankets, she wraps her warm body around me.

"Lie still, get warm," she says. "Everything's gonna be all right."

Do I really not have to be so tough any longer? I cling to her and cry for a long time. Before long, my weeping heats us up and an unexpected peace and comfort come over me.

"What Lehane did, right in front of you, was terrible," Barky whispers. "To destroy two lives like that, a person would have to be insane. Or evil."

I sleep for a while, then I wake up and need to pee again. I feel so heavy I can hardly push myself up into a seated position. Crying has relaxed some of the pressure in my head and I'm no longer dizzy, just very spaced-out. I get out of bed and wrap Barky's flannel robe around myself and shuffle unsteadily to the kitchen, my feet protected from the cold floor by thick crew socks. I use the toilet, then light the stove under the tea kettle.

I sit at the kitchen table, huddled in her robe. The mug of chamomile tea steams in the cold air and warms my insides. All I want is to pass this night in peace and quiet until daybreak. But my lover's remarks won't leave me alone. Her soft voice whispering *Insane? Or evil?* echoes in the emptiness of my soul, the soul I'm afraid I lost tonight. If Barky ever learns the truth of what I've done, I'm afraid I will lose her too.

One more time I assure myself that justice is on my side. It was Aldo's fault that I'd even had the gun the morning Egon got shot. Egon would have degraded me, in God knows how many ways, if I hadn't stopped him. Was there any doubt that I had to do it? Afterward, I didn't trust the police, an instinct that turned out to be absolutely correct. I've tried to trust people my whole life and they always let me down. I trusted Jonathan with my secret, and we were okay for a while, but when he couldn't own me, he became spiteful and weak and he tried to take away my freedom. He would have distorted my story of self-defense, twisted it completely against me, and gotten me charged with murder.

And A.J. Oh, A.J. All of it was gone, our passionate arguments, my delight in our beauty as a couple, my Christmas masquerade among his friends in Palm Beach, his foolish laugh, his awakening sensuality rising to meet mine in bed, my fantasy of marriage and a child and entrée into his upper-class society of comfort and privilege; all of it was gone, destroyed by the cruelty and snobbery of Rosa Lee and Roy Upton and by Jonathan's weakness and injured vanity. They all made A.J.'s death inevitable by forcing me to choose between killing the one man I'd ever really loved or going to prison. Then again, I have to admit A.J. hadn't been on my side one hundred percent, not the way I needed him to be.

I slip back into bed and lay there until I accept that I'm not going to fall asleep again. I quietly get up and dress, then sit for a moment at the kitchen table and write a note for Barky on her shopping list pad.

It's four in the morning. I can't sleep so I'm going to the office. But what I really want to do is just curl up next to you for the rest of my life. Thank you so much for getting me through last night. I couldn't have made it without your love. I'll bring mine back to you as soon as I can. All of it... A.

Down on the sidewalk the air is ice-cold. In the gray hours before dawn, sparse traffic is rolling down Second Avenue. A person in a puffer coat and hoodie sprints out of the path of a downtown bus, two men wheel cartons on hand trucks into the deli on the corner. I have the urge to go down to Chelsea, but I know if I go home, even to shower and change clothes, I'll lock myself in my apartment, turn off the phone, crawl into bed, and never go out again.

At the deli I buy an apple and a poppy bagel with lox and cream cheese and copies of the *New York Times* and the *Daily News*. The counterman keeps looking at me strangely. Did I say something wrong? I flag down a taxi and flip through the newspapers as we cross midtown through the empty streets of the office canyons of Manhattan to Broadway and 49th Street.

There is nothing on page one of the *Times*, but the *Daily News* has made last night's horror a Page One story. "TWO DEAD IN CPW PENT-HOUSE/'Men R Dawgs' Director Questioned in Murder-Suicide." The story says the police confirmed I was the only witness to the "carnage" of the night before, but they've released no details. In one photo EMS workers are rolling the bodies on gurneys to the morgue wagon. In another I'm being put into the police car in handcuffs. People will get the wrong idea about me from that picture, but there's nothing I can do about it.

As I walk through the dark Alpha Bitch offices flipping on lights, I startle Jenny McPeek. An insomniac and obsessive worker, she's already in the editor's chair.

"Oh my God," she says. "I didn't expect to see you today. Did you get my texts? No? Oh, come here, come here."

She gives me a hug, and a sympathetic sigh.

"Thanks. I needed that."

"Do you still want to do the screening at ten o'clock?"

"Absolutely."

"We'll be ready."

I go to my office, hang up my scarf and jacket and hat, and close the door. I feel so safe and warm here it makes me sleepy. I kick off my boots and curl up on the sofa in the warmth and the darkness, bolstered with pillows, and lay under a heavy fleece blanket pulled up to my chin. From the editing room down the hall I hear voices from the movie. I take a deep breath and sigh. It always felt so good, waking up with A.J.'s arms around me, his warm fuzzy chest pressed against my back. This morning I miss him so much that I can't hold it in any longer, and I start crying. The weeping washes me out until I fall asleep, drained.

When I wake up, gray daylight is glowing through the venetian blinds and the traffic down on Times Square is at full honk and roar. I quickly become fully awake, buzzing with anxiety. Darkness turned into day while I slept, and I feel like I've somehow been caught off guard and unprepared. I roll off the sofa and go out to the kitchen and make a large cup of coffee and take it back to my office. While I eat my apple and bagel, I check my messages. Marshall, Lenny, Juno and Whit Allwether have all left voicemails on my phone, all of them concerned for me. I make a note to schedule calls to them later. I dwell for a long time on a text from Nikki Xiu sent last night, offering to postpone our dinner meeting tonight. A second text from her, after midnight, simply says, "Call me if you need anything."

I boot up my computer, Google search "Adrienne Monet," and find out the story of the last 12 hours of my life has gone global. Reports about the actor Jonathan Lehane committing suicide after murdering his estranged son are all over the news websites and morning TV news shows. They all focus on the notorious creator of "*Men R Dawgs*" who witnessed the bloodshed. A YouTube video of my brief eulogy on the steps of the precinct has gotten over 100,000 views. On top of the local news, there are stories with my picture on the websites of the *Times* and *The Washington Post, the Drudge Report, Salon, The Huffington Post, New York Magazine, The Guardian of London and Le Monde of Paris, The Hollywood Reporter* and *Deadline Hollywood*. A clip of me in handcuffs being perp-walked out of Lehane's building is all over the Web and TV.

The *New York Post* story says that Rosa Lee Upton, mother of the "slain conservative firebrand," is mourning in seclusion and awaiting the arrival of A.J.'s stepfather Roy Upton from Palm Beach. The sympathetic portrait of those two as suffering parents drives me into a rage that, in my weariness, I turn against myself. It was so stupid of me to be impressed with his mother. How could I have been so naïve as to think I would be accepted by A.J.'s class of people? Why didn't I see that our jovial tea two days ago had been a cruel trap? Am I still the hick from the sticks I thought I'd left behind in New Jersey? Rosa Lee and her bankster husband looked down their noses at me, interfered in my relationship with A.J., and started the series of events that got their son killed. They should suffer.

My office kids start trooping in at eight o'clock and are surprised to find me at work. There are hugs all around, and they're ready to do whatever I need.

Marshall calls around nine o'clock.

"Yo, checkin' on my girl, whatup?" I tell him I'm okay. I deflect his eagerness to hear the gory details, denying him the juiciest gossip to dish at lunch with his fellow sharks, who'd then spend the afternoon letting everybody know they have the inside skinny on the hottest story of the day. "Yeah, I had lunch with her agent, and he told me she said..."

At the front desk the phones ring more than usual. I tell my girls to say I'm not in the building. All morning they redirect media calls and requests for interviews to Marshall to deal with. Hugging is rampant at Alpha Bitch this morning, but we all stay focused on the work.

During a break in the editing, I go to my office and click back on the Web. The right-wing media is gushing with extravagant eulogies, angry accolades, and righteous outrage over the tragic death of A.J. Upton. The drumbeat at *Fox News* is the loudest: A.J.'s courageous, patriotic voice was tragically silenced by an act of madness, murdered by the decadent, hedonistic, Hollywood limousine liberal father who abandoned him as a boy, killed him in the prime of his manhood, then took the coward's way out and committed suicide. For the first time in my life I can appreciate *Fox News*. They're selling my version of last night's tragedy for me, and with feeling.

"Lenny Victor on line 1," Megan announces over the intercom. "Again." I avoided his earlier calls. But if I don't pick up, he'll just keep calling, or worse, come here to the office.

"Oh, hi Lenny," I say, giving him a sad, forlorn singsong. "How are you?"

"Never mind me," he says, "how are you? You didn't return my calls. We're worried about you."

"Oh, well, I'm okay, I guess. I guess I'm okay, I don't know. I'm here. I'm working."

"Should you be working?"

"What else can I do?"

"I couldn't believe what I read this morning. You saw the whole thing?"

"I did."

"What the hell happened?"

"The police and my lawyer told me I can't talk about it."

Politely refusing Lenny was a pleasure, because he feels entitled to know everything. He grunts.

"Murder – suicide? Jonathan must've gone insane. And when we heard you were a witness, we both went 'Oh my God, poor Adrienne.'"

"Yeah, well... I just have to keep going. One day at a time, y'know?"

"Look, I'm sure this is rough now, but you'll be all right. You were tough enough to take over this movie and get it made. And me and Juno, you know we're here for you."

"Well, thank you Lenny. I never doubted I could count on you." *Not...*

"Listen, about today. Juno and I were thinking" – uh oh – "and maybe this would be better for you too, considering what you've been through. I'm gonna cancel the screening this morning."

I cut him off. "No, you're not. It has to be today."

"Adrienne, I'm told your building security already threw one photographer out because he tried to bribe his way up to your office floor. That's how crazy it's gotten. You should watch out for camera drones at your window."

"Stop! Lenny, you're making me paranoid." The understatement of the day.

"But it's just that Jonathan'll be up there on the screen, the man we worked with all those weeks, and, you know —"

"You think it'll be easy for me?"

"Why put us through that?"

"I need feedback. I need to keep going. We're a team. Y'know?"

"A couple days, that's all. What's a couple days?"

"Lenny, I was there last night. The whole thing happened in front of me. Then I was questioned by the police. That was horrible in a whole other way." If I give him details, he'll blab it to anyone he wants to impress with his insider's knowledge. "I'm still shaky. I've hardly slept in over twenty-four hours. If anybody needs a day off, it's me. But I'm here, and I'm working. I'm screening the film at the scheduled time, and if people don't show up, I'll be unhappy. Pass the word."

But the screening is a waste of time. Judging from the hugs and kisses I get before the lights go down, my crew members came to offer me emotional support, not evaluate my work in progress. There isn't a real creative meeting afterward, just a group chat and a slow stroll to the elevators. They try to be helpful, Lenny and Juno, McPeek and the assistant editors, Terri my sound designer and Gabriella my amazing director of photography, and I'm grateful, but they don't tell me anything I haven't already thought of, and I've just made everybody feel worse about Jonathan's death. I almost say I'm sorry that I insisted they come to work, but after they leave, I'm glad I didn't. I try to run a happy company, but sometimes I need to be tough.

I lay down again on my couch, tired and disappointed. I should've spared myself too. As soon as I saw myself playing those intensely romantic scenes with Jonathan, I began to feel sorry for myself, resenting him for forcing me to make some terrible choices last night, and feeling what it all cost me. When the film was over, I hadn't really watched it either.

I realized that from now on I have to carefully control how I think about A.J. and Jonathan. No remembering the good times, no musing about the lives they might have had, no moaning about the emptiness I feel or suffering what I've lost, and no sadness for their friends and loved ones. That kind of thinking will only undermine my chances of surviving all this. I can't afford to let go and relax. As I lay there staring at my office ceiling, I start getting nauseous, so I get back on my feet. My posture feels somehow tentative, like I could collapse at any moment, and I begin to fear a return of the vertigo from the night before.

So I pull on my jacket. Once I'm moving around, I feel more grounded. I need to get out of the building and take a walk and get stabilized. I need a brisk hike through cold, crowded Times Square, to become part of the rush and crush of humanity, to shake up my senses and lift me out of this desolation. I decide to walk over to Rockefeller Center, eat lunch and drink coffee and watch the ice skaters for a while, then return to work with a clear head and stronger nerves.

I step off the elevator into the lobby and find my producers talking in hushed voices with those detectives, Ferino and Peavey. I can't believe they all just happened to bump into each other. Lenny and Juno shoot me guilty looks, which tells me a meeting with the detectives had been scheduled.

"Detective Peavey, Detective Ferino," I say. "It's been so long."

That gets me a silent stare from Ferino.

"If you'd've come a couple hours ago, I could've showed you the film. We just had a screening."

"We're not here to watch movies," Ferino says. "Let's go folks." They all move toward the front door.

"Hey Lenny? Juno?" The Victors turn to me. "Be sure to tell the truth."

Ferino whirls around and lunges at me.

"Hey Bobbie Jean!" he says, loud and hoarse. He turns every head in the lobby. He gets so up in my face I can smell the coffee on his breath through the cloud of his peppery cologne. "Don't ever do that again!"

His anger almost forces me back a step. "Do what?"

"Coach a witness! That's tampering! That's a crime! Understand?"

"I told them to tell the truth." I shake my head at his outburst. "Doesn't that help you?"

"I don't need your help!" Behind him Detective Peavey takes a step, almost speaks, then hushes up. Lenny and Juno look stunned. "Just keep your fucking mouth shut when I'm trying to do my job!"

"Looks like the job's doing you, Buddy."

"*Detective Ferino.*"

I smile, knowing he'll hate that. He turns around and pushes Lenny and Juno out the front doors on Broadway. They disappear into the crowd streaming down the sidewalk. People in the lobby are staring at me, so I just grin and shrug.

Lunch beside the Rockefeller Center skating rink is the restorative I need. But after a while I see heads turning in my direction and a lot of people holding up their smart phones taking my picture, so I leave sooner than I want to. When I get back to the office someone shows me a cell phone video on Twitter of Ferino's attack on me, and the office is ringing with media calls again. I look surprisingly photogenic in the video, and I never lose my cool while Ferino sputters and snarls.

That evening I keep a dinner meeting with Nikki Xiu. She had offered to postpone the dinner if I needed to, but she is not someone I would ever keep waiting. We meet at a small, elegant restaurant on the ground floor of a new office building in Chinatown. She's dressed in a bespoke black jacket, and slacks. I'm wearing my favorite black evening sheath and a string of pearls. I compliment her choice of café, which is empty except for us. She says her family owns the place, in fact, owns the whole building.

She agrees to end my collateralization of *"Lonely Sky"* since I finished shooting under budget, and we shake hands. The dinner is business for us, but she treats me with tact and delicacy. After all, it's been only 24 hours since two men died in my presence.

I tell her the same story of murder and suicide I gave the police and shed a few genuine tears.

"I can see you're still in shock," she says. "And your recovery will take time. But I predict this experience will enrich you as an artist. Despite everything, you had the intense passion and focus to last through the making of your film." She sips her Da Hong Pao tea. "At our fund we finance a select number of film productions in Asia, Europe, and the U.S. And I must tell you, the people we choose to work with all have the same intensity and determination as you. You'll meet them, and you'll see you belong with us."

"A film director is all I've ever wanted to be. It's not just a career. It's who I am."

"I know."

She smiles and grips my hand. Oddly, I don't mind her touching me. In her voice is genuine concern.

"The day we met, when I spoke Chinese with Whit Allwether, weren't you curious about what we said?"

"No, not really." Does she think I was offended? "I got the outcome I wanted."

"I told him I was certain that you shot Egon Swift so you could take his job. I told him if you were willing to kill for the job, you should have it."

This was an invitation to tell her, the boss, everything, and I admit I felt a powerful impulse to finally tell all to someone. But I swore to myself I would never give anyone that kind of power over me again.

"Nikki...Uhhh," I laugh nervously. "That's a misunderstanding."

"No. I don't think so." She lets go and pats my hand, and takes a sip of tea, watching me over the rim of the cup. I'm afraid I've insulted her by telling her she's wrong, but she grins as if to reassure me.

This is too much to take in all at once.

"What'd Whit say?"

"Well..." She shrugs and laughs quietly. "What could he say?"

On the sidewalk we air kiss and say good night. I need fresh air, so I walk up to Dominique Ansel's bakery on Spring Street, hoping to buy a couple DKA for breakfast. But it's too late and the place is closed, so I head over to Hudson Street and hop in a taxi heading uptown.

I think my meeting with Nikki Xiu went well for us both. She said the latest cut of *"Lonely Sky"* had her intrigued. I'm relieved that my revenue from *"Men R Dawgs"* will no longer be in jeopardy, and I haven't had to pay a single dollar for an overage. Most important, my relationship with Nikki has reached a new level of candor and honesty.

As we walked out of the restaurant, I tried once more to deny that I'm a murderer, for the record, just to see if this was Nikki's idea of a put-on.

"Nikki, I'm afraid you're giving me more credit for ruthlessness than I deserve."

"No," she said, "I don't think so." Her driver held the Escalade's door open. "But don't worry. You're going to make it big, Adrienne. And nobody who makes it really big is pure."

I walked away feeling both strong and vulnerable, the way you feel when you have an ally with awesome power you hope will never turn against you. She seemed to respect me, not despite but because I killed Egon, and without saying so, Jonathan and A.J. too. She'd just offered me membership in a club I was surprised to learn I was qualified to join, as if I'd just passed an initiation, and had been handed my ticket for a seat on the luxury jet, the one in which people like Nikki fly above the rules.

So, the start of a beautiful friendship. She'll finance my movies, and as long as they make money, we'll be in business. Apart from that, her idea of me is mine to worry about. Knowing that somebody thinks I'm a killer is no longer so hard to live with, and clearly has its advantages. Still, I'm not sure I heard what she was telling me. That she admires my ambition, my courage? Or that she's in control and has the power to blackmail me if she ever needs to? I don't think it's cynical to imagine that in her world, far above the reach of the police and the laws, wealth and power are the only values, moral judgments are inconvenient, and all that matters is getting what you want by any means necessary.

The back seat of the taxi is warm and stuffy, and the fruity stench of the dashboard air freshener irritates my sinuses. I crack open the window and the air is cold but at least it doesn't smell like fake cherries. I open my overcoat and scarf and sit back, enjoying the breeze on my face and neck as we head uptown. I'm just beginning to come down from the past 24 hours, and the wine I drank at dinner is helping. I'm ready for a hot bath and a long winter night's sleep.

At 14th Street my driver begins growling in a guttural language, turns, and gestures angrily out the rear windshield at the driver in the car behind us who keeps flashing his bright lights and blowing his horn. I roll up the window to cut out the noise. We continue forward, safely and within the speed limit, as the obnoxious driver behind us, probably some New Jersey person fresh out of the Holland Tunnel, keeps making a fuss.

At the next red light the car whips around and stops beside us. The driver's door flies open. Aldo jumps from behind the steering wheel and dives at me, wild-eyed, pleading. He crashes against the window and I jump halfway across the back seat.

"Adrienne! I found you! I gotta talk to you! Please!" He grabs the handle of my door, but it's locked. "Pull over!" He pounds on the window. "Pull over!"

I lean forward and yell through the partition to the driver.

"Get me out of here, please!"

The lights up 8th Avenue turn green. My cab takes off a couple lengths ahead of Aldo, who jumps back in his car and chases us.

"Stop here!" The cab swerves to the left at Eighth Avenue and 20th Street. I throw money at the driver, bolt from the cab, and run west down the eastbound street. Aldo screeches to a stop on the avenue, jumps out of his car leaving the door hanging open, and begins running after me.

"Adrienne! Stop! Stop and listen to me!"

He races after me, his open overcoat billowing around him like the wings of some crazy beast. Annie Levy's office fucked up! They were supposed to let me know if he got out of jail! I run madly, frantically, for the safety of my apartment a cross-town block away.

A loud pop echoes off the brownstones. I look over my shoulder. There's another pop and a flash from a pistol in Aldo's hand. The bullet rips the air an inch from my ear and shatters the light on the front stoop newel post of a building. I duck and cower behind the stoop.

Behind me an engine roars and tires squeal. In a blur, a car streaks past me and bumps up on the sidewalk, blocking Aldo. Detective Ferino jumps from the driver's seat with his gun and badge drawn.

"Police! Stop right there! Show me your hands!"

Aldo skids to a stop, his hands in the air. In one hand he holds a small black gun. He gives Ferino an insolent cock of the chin.

"Who the fuck are you?"

"NYPD! Put the gun down!"

I peer over the stoop banister.

"Adrienne!" Aldo's wail echoes down the block. "Why are you doing this to us? Why can't we be like we were?"

"Put the gun down now!" Ferino roars. "Drop the gun and get down on the ground!"

Aldo looks anguished, trapped.

"You made me do this Adrienne! You made me do it!"

He turns and darts between two parked cars and into the path of a speeding van. The tires scream, and the loud crash as the van strikes him makes me flinch. Aldo is hurled into the air off the front of the van. As his body crash lands on a line of CitiBikes, the gun in his hand fires a shot that pops a tire on a parked Range Rover.

Ferino holsters his gun and hustles into the street. The van driver, a bearded young guy, marches back and forth in the middle of the street with his head in his hands. I creep out from hiding, and I run for home, as the drivers stuck behind the van begin blowing their horns.

I sit dazed and breathless in my kitchen. Aldo had been dangerous and unstable, but for a while he also had been a sexy, exciting man in my life. Why did he have to go crazy over me, and bring this down on himself?

The doorbell rings. I know it's Ferino and I don't want to answer but I really have to. I have to keep control of the situation. The doorbell rings again. Time to get this over with. I'm as ready as I'll ever be for whatever might happen.

I press the intercom button. "Hello?"

"Detective Ferino, NYPD," he mutters, his voice echoing in the vestibule. "Let me in, Miss Monet."

"Go away."

"No. Not 'til I take your statement." He keeps ringing the doorbell.

Before I make him even more angry, I press the door release button. I leave the door ajar and go back to the kitchen. When I ran, I tore the seam of my favorite evening dress nearly up to the hip. I finger the tear wondering if the dress, which has great sentimental value, can be repaired. I mean, if this dress could talk...

I pull a chair out from the table and sit down, hands folded, my torn dress hiked up as high as I dare. When Ferino walks in, the first thing his eyes go to is a lot of leg. The first thing I notice is that Detective Peavey isn't with him.

He glances into the living room and the bedroom. He comes into the kitchen with his hands in his coat pockets.

"You look very nice, Bobbie Jean."

"Don't call me that, or you'll have to leave."

"You didn't have to get all dressed up for me."

That's not even worth a comeback. He sits in an empty chair at the kitchen table.

"So, is he dead?"

He nods. "Yeah."

"What'd you tell the cops?"

"Disturbed individual fired shots at a woman I had under surveillance. Suspect ignored my order to drop his weapon. Tried to evade arrest, stepped into the path of a speeding vehicle."

"What about the woman?"

"Fled the scene. I gave them your name and address."

"They'll find me in his records anyway."

"I'll let them handle the rest. I wanted to get up here. Are you okay?" Like, he cares.

"No. Look at my poor dress."

I extend my leg and his eyes linger for a moment.

"It could have been worse," he says. "We searched his rental car. We found plastic sheeting, a roll of duct tape, and a shovel."

"My God."

"And he had a gun. So, who the hell was he?"

"His real name's —"

"I saw his I.D. I mean, who was he to you?"

"A guy who's been stalking me for, like, a year."

"Old boyfriend?"

"No. Much less."

"From what he said on the street it sounds like you were his one and only."

"He was a very fucked up kid."

"You had him in tears."

"He came from a rich family. He never had to grow up."

"Well, he won't be stalking you anymore."

"About a year ago he attacked me with a knife. I had to get an order of protection."

"Those things never protect anybody."

"No shit."

"First Lehane, then Lehane's kid, now this guy. Men who get hung up on you, they don't do too well, do they?"

"That's not my fault."

"Maybe it's your sunny personality. Or maybe you're a porn star in the sack." I can't believe what I'm hearing. "Let's face it, you're no super model, and you're not the cuddly type either."

"Well, neither are you, Detective Ferino. God, I'm still shaking. I need a drink. You?"

"Why not?"

I place two glasses and a bottle of Barolo on the table.

"Aren't you on duty?"

He shrugs. I pour him a glass of wine.

"Is this okay? A cop paying a social visit to a murder suspect?"

"This isn't a social visit. You were almost a murder victim."

"For the second night in a row."

He ignores that. He sips the wine. He makes an appreciative face, because it's a very good Barolo. "Okay, let's hear it."

I keep it simple: Aldo followed my taxi up from Soho, then chased me on foot.

"If you hadn't stopped him" – I shudder – "I might be dead. Tonight was the third time he's tried to kill me. I guess I should thank you."

"I'm glad I stopped him. If some lunatic kills you, I won't have the pleasure of sending you to prison."

"Oh. Is that why you're here?"

"Yeah, why else?"

"So you had me under surveillance?"

"Not exactly. I was nasty to you today in front of your producers. I thought I'd apologize." I'm sure this is bullshit, but I play along.

"Yeah, okay. Apology accepted. Now maybe you should leave."

"Tell me something." He swirled his wine, apparently in no hurry. "Do your girlfriends also have a hard time letting you go?"

"That's none of your business."

So he knows I go to bed with men and women. I can see how that excites him. His curiosity feels dangerous, and it's not the kind of danger that turns me on.

The wine is beginning to affect me.

"Y'know what I want to know?" I say. "Would you have shot him? To protect me?"

"I'm just glad it wasn't necessary."

"You investigate people killing each other all the time. How can you stand it?"

He shrugs. "It's what I'm trained to do. It's like any job. Parts of it are okay. The rest you do because it's the job."

"Do you ever think about the kid you killed?"

He clears his throat. "All the time. And his buddy, who I crippled. But those kids shot first, at me and my partner. I had no choice."

"Maybe you didn't mean to kill him. That's just how it turned out. Who could blame you for defending yourself? Everybody's got a right to that."

He stares into his wineglass a moment, then sighs.

"Some people think I'm a racist, trigger-happy cop. But I'm not. IAD took 'way too long to clear me, but I knew they would. I feel bad that the kid's families were hurt too. They're suing me, and that'll drag it out longer, but it'll be dismissed."

"You think so?"

"Clear cut case of self-defense. But I still hurt a lot of people. And I left one dead and one in a wheelchair. I have to live with that."

"It doesn't matter that they were drug dealers and they had guns?"

"Not to me. There's only one thing I want now. I want my reputation back. I'm a good cop. I've got the commendations to prove it."

"Want me to write you a reference?"

He doesn't like that. He gives me a hard stare and the edge in his voice sharpens.

"Y'know, not every killer feels guilty. Some people are pretty cold about it."

I just shrug and swirl my wine. "I wouldn't know." I toss that off a little too nonchalantly, and I can see it gets under his skin.

"Murder is the worst thing a person can do," he says. "A society that doesn't punish murder is no place to live."

I nod, seriously.

"After I killed that kid, my standing in life changed. With my fellow officers. With my family and friends, they looked at me different. With myself. Even with God – I do believe in God, now and then." He hesitates, maybe that was too candid. "I was taught by the priests only God has the power to give and take life. But now I'm somebody who took a life." I tilt the bottle and refill his glass. "Where that leaves me, I don't know."

"Well, sometimes people do bad things for a higher purpose. That doesn't make them bad people."

He says coldly, "Is that how you excuse what you did?"

"What did I do?"

"Cut the shit, Bobbie Jean."

"I don't know what you're talking about."

"Yes, you do. You think my killing a dope dealer and you murdering three innocent men is the same thing?"

"I never murdered anyone."

"Sure you did. And what was the higher purpose?"

"This is just your mania again."

"Mania for what?"

"Putting me in jail." I glance at my wristwatch, spread my arms and yawn. "But not tonight, unless you're going to arrest me. It's time I went to bed."

"Yeah." He drains his second drink. "I think I'd better go. Thanks for your hospitality."

I lead him down the hall to the entrance. I turn and grin expectantly. I know why he's really here, and I know what he really wants. And he knows that I know. But he doesn't know what I want, and I think I'm about to get it.

"Well? Detective Ferino?"

Men are so predictable. He pushes me back against the door, reaches one hand behind my neck and takes a handful of my ass with the other and kisses me, hard and urgently. His mouth tastes like wine and is rimmed with coarse whiskers. His body feels solid and trim through his clothes.

"What are you doing?" I gasp, pushing against his chest, but not enough to repel him. The first stirrings of fear begin to excite me.

"Don't ask stupid questions."

Once I feel his hands greedily roaming my body, once my arm is wound around his neck and my tongue is in his mouth and our chests are pressed together, I know he won't be able to stop himself. I'm in his arms, in his smell, in his breath. Between wet ravenous kisses I keep whispering that he should leave, while I stroke his hard cock through his trousers.

I let him drag me into the dark bedroom. I swipe at the switch and the lights go on. I grab the remote control off the bed and set it aside. He pushes me down on the bed. He yanks my dress up to my waist, tearing the seam even further, and rips away my panties.

"Buddy, what are you doing?"

I'm shocked that he can see my exposed crotch, but before I can cover myself, he reaches down and grabs me between my legs and squeezes until it hurts. I grab his hand, but I'm too weak to pull it away.

"Ow, what are you doing?" It comes out loud, with a gasp.

He lets go, sniffs his hand, and grins. "Nice." I try to get up and he keeps pushing me down as he kicks off his shoes and pulls down his trousers and briefs.

"That wine went shtraight to my head." My voice is slurring. "I only had one glash, didn't I?"

"I don't remember."

"That's because you drank more than me," I say, adding a dopey chuckle.

He kicks his pants away and rips off his jacket, his cock poking out through his shirttails.

"Okay Buddy... This has gone too far!"

"The name," he snarls, "is Detective Ferino."

He pulls a condom from his shirt pocket and rolls it on with a couple quick strokes.

"Uh uh! You're not sticking that thing in me, Buddy. You need to go. Now!"

He's so excited he's panting. He climbs on the bed, looming over me, holding me down and forcing my legs apart. He rips my dress and bra down off my shoulders. My breasts pop out and he slobbers kisses all over them. His cheeks are like sandpaper. He grabs my face.

"I'm gonna teach you a lesson," he says, his eyes an inch from mine. "You think you've got everything under control, the way you look down your nose at me, and I'm just another guy you can jerk around. Well, now you're gonna find out who the fuck you're dealing with."

I reach down between us and stroke his cock and tickle his balls with my fingernails. At the same time, I keep pleading.

"Don't do it, man, please don't..."

He sets his knees, braces himself on his elbows over me. Then, before he can even get inside me, his body convulses, and he groans. In my hand, the condom on his cock gets warm and slippery.

For a moment neither of us says anything. Then I pull back my hand and say, "Uh oh!" Frantically, he takes ahold of himself and roughly forces a little of his cock into me and it hurts, but he is already going soft. He slides back out without me even pushing. He gets up on his knees. His cock hangs, limp and spent in its gooey latex bag, like a defeated man hanging his head in shame.

"Fuck!" he yells.

"Nope!" I laugh. "I don't think so!"

"You laughin' at me?" He swoops down and slaps my face. It stings and brings tears to my eyes. "Come on, suck me. Get me hard again."

"No way!" I squirm back, kicking away from him. "Leave me alone!"

The look on his face is mortified, defeated, powerless, all at the same time. He wants to say something, but all he can do is mutter.

"What the hell am I doin'?"

"See?" I say. "You're doing what you wanted all along! Investigating me! Interrogating me! I told you all you wanted was to fuck me! I'm an innocent person and —"

"Shut up!" He lunges and smacks me again, but my guard is up and the blow glances off my arms. He stumbles back off the bed. "I gotta go."

"You better be careful. You're 'way too drunk to drive."

"I need the bathroom."

He grabs his clothes off the floor and goes in. Through the open door, I hear the rustle of clothing, his belt buckle jingle, the toilet flush.

He stands in the bathroom doorway and looks at me, curled up in bed, rubbing my sore face and whimpering. He looks like he wants to speak but can't get it out. When he leaves, he closes the door, quietly.

O n a frigid sunny afternoon I catch a taxi up to the Upper East Side for Lehane's funeral. From the back seat of the cab I pick up a discarded *New York Post* and start to casually browse. On Page 5, I find myself looking at a quarter-page photo of myself.

I'm on the street, dressed in a black knitted cap with my hair flowing down over my shoulders, a striped tee shirt, my leather jacket, and my headphones slung around my neck. In the picture I'm scowling, probably wondering who the hell let this the photographer on my set.

The incredulous headline says IS SHE TO DIE FOR? How many readers must be looking at my picture and thinking Who? This scrawny little thing? The more I read, the more I realize with a sick feeling that what little anonymity I may have had is over.

"'*Men R Dawgs*' creator Adrienne Monet was the reason the long-standing feud between actor Jonathan Lehane and his son, conservative writer A.J. Upton, exploded into fatal violence on Tuesday evening, according to an NYPD report obtained by the *Post*.

"The report, its authenticity confirmed by a source close to the investigation, says Monet told investigators she was carrying on simultaneous love affairs with both father and son. She told police the two men quarreled over her, the actor shot his son, then killed himself in remorse."

I am about to redirect the driver to Barky's building when I realize she's probably already heard about or read the story. I pull out my phone, call, get no answer, and leave a voicemail.

"Call me. I really need to see you today. We have things to talk about."

Things? Like me falling in love with A.J.? Dreaming about marrying and having a child with him? Things like lying to her about how A.J. and his father got killed? Things like that?

"In an early December TV appearance," the *Post* says, "Upton ridiculed Lehane's radical-left politics and his role in a film directed by Monet. She responded by calling into his guest appearance on Gunner Crockett's radio show. They traded insults, and afterward they began an affair, according to what Monet told the police.

"The police report says Monet was the only witness to what police have not yet officially concluded was a murder-suicide. Monet has not been charged with a crime, but police say the investigation is continuing.

"Monet could not be reached for comment."

No doubt Buddy Ferino is behind this. He can't arrest me, so he gave the *Post* the police report so the public will see me as a slut if I ever accuse him of misconduct after his clumsy, out-of-control performance in my bed, not that I would ever want that gross episode to become public. For a moment I have second thoughts about going to Lehane's service, but as my taxi pulls up to the funeral chapel, I decide the eulogy I have asked to deliver is the best way to answer the story.

Outside the funeral chapel, Lehane is getting more attention dead than he ever got alive. Police sawhorses hold back a deep crowd of onlookers and the media, a thicket of microphones on booms, outstretched arms holding recorders, camera strobes flashing, and questions yelled as mourners arrive. I put on my sunglasses and I step from the car into a barrage of brilliant lights so intense I'm almost blinded.

"Okay! It's her! It's her!" The women reporters caw like excited crows. "Adrienne! Hey Adrienne! Can we have a minute?" I keep walking and rough voices bark, "Did you fuck 'em both?! Over here! Did you do 'em one at a time or together?"

Composed and unsmiling, I stroll down the gauntlet of ugly snarling faces. Inside the main room is full of mourners. There is a pew with an empty seat on the aisle. I don't know the people I sit beside but I can feel their sidelong glances.

When it's my turn to speak the room falls quiet. I can hear my footsteps as I walk to the podium and stand over Lehane's closed coffin on a bier surrounded by white flowers. Many of these people must have seen the *Post* story, and they hush to listen to the woman who reportedly caused two lovesick men to quarrel over her, ending in a fatal confrontation. Who knows what kind of seductress they expect, but I've dressed plainly in a black shift, black pumps, and no jewelry, just an ebony barrette holding my hair back.

"For an actor's career," I say, my hands clasped in front of me, "it usually helps to be more than attractive. But God help you if your beautiful face is all people want, leaving your struggling creative soul yearning for the chance to show what you have inside, to show how much truth you're able to bring out in your work." I gaze down on the coffin bearing the remains of the man I killed, remembering for a moment the affection I'd had for him before it turned to fear, then scorn. "I only knew him for a few months, but that describes the Jonathan Lehane that I worked with. It was the main issue in the art he lived to create. Could the world see past his beauty and into his passionate soul and original mind? I assure you, he achieved that and much more in the final role he played, onstage and on film. Now his life has come to a tragic and premature end. But while we mourn his death, we can take some solace by remembering that when he was among us, Jonathan lived life to the fullest, was good to his friends and committed to his art, and he was on the humane side of many issues. The way he approached his work and the way he lived his life are his legacy and can serve as an inspiration to us all."

I step down from the podium as a low murmur of conversation rises. I go straight out into the lobby, dialing for an Uber. Good eulogy, I decide, for a man I ultimately detested. On any occasion except a funeral that speech might have gotten a round of applause.

I walk calmly to the car through the howling mob of press out on the sidewalk. On the ride downtown I hear a ping! and find a text from Barky.

"Things to talk about? Yeah, I guess we do."

Barky opens the door for me and lowers her eyes and turns away before I can hug her. She takes her seat at the kitchen table and I sit across from her. She looks so lovely, in a thick black turtleneck and Lulu Lemon yoga pants. Her eyes are red and swollen from crying, and she looks so hurt that I ache for her.

"I've been unbelievably stupid," Barky mutters.

"First of all, the media have it all wrong." I want to explain myself, so she doesn't have to ask a lot of humiliating questions. "The affair with Lehane was over last fall before I even met you. But when I backed off, he wouldn't let go. And about A.J., yeah, we were a lot more involved than I told you. He actually asked me to marry him and I said yes. I'm so sorry I didn't tell you everything."

I'm ready for her to say she feels betrayed and to tell me it's over. But she reaches out and takes my hand in both of hers.

"You were going to marry him? And you saw him get killed? No wonder you were out of your mind that night."

Her kindness, her concern for me, are more than I deserve. The tears are hard to hold back, but my story stays the same.

"Lehane found out about me and A.J., and he just lost it. He was drunk. He almost shot me, but I guess he hated A.J. even more. And after he killed A.J. he just gave up."

She stares at me, slowly shaking her head.

"I failed you Barky. You deserve better. I didn't tell you about me and A.J. because I wanted you so much, and I was afraid you'd be hurt, and I'd lose you. And besides, you had Garth, you were going to get married —"

She raises a hand to stop me. "Adrienne —"

"— but I still should have told you. You and I were getting into each other. And this thing was happening with A.J. and I was already hiding it from Lehane, and it was just easier to hide it from everybody when it got serious. I wanted to tell you, I just didn't know the right way or the right time. I'm so sorry. Can you ever forgive me?"

"There is no Garth," she says wearily.

"What?"

"Not anymore."

"Why? What happened?"

Barky stares out the window beside the table.

"He found out I cheated on him."

"He found out about us?"

Barky shakes her head. "About a week ago I hooked up with an ex-boyfriend, a guy I lived with for a while when I first came to New York. He lives in Texas now, but he was in town on business and staying at a hotel. It wasn't any big thing. I didn't even spend the night with him, I came home. It was harmless, a little adventure, that's all." She grinned crookedly. "Before I met you, I probably wouldn't have had the nerve."

When she saw I was amused, not angry, she shrugged helplessly.

"Last night Garth and I were having dinner in the Village and my ex sent me a text. I was in the lady's room and my phone was on the table. Garth recognized the name and he read the text. All this stuff about how I've gotten so erotic and comfortable with my body, and hey, how about a replay next time he's in town, that kind of shit. When I got back to the table Garth handed the phone to me, grabbed his coat, and walked out. I ran after him and he broke up with me right there at the Christopher Street PATH station. He was so hurt. He never wants to see me again. I call, I text, but I'm sure he's just deleting the messages. And now I'm wondering if I blew a good thing, or if I'm lucky it's over because he's so fucking young and tender. Y'know, at Christmas his parents treated me like I was robbing them of their son. They were really cold." She runs her fingers through her hair and tosses it back. "I'm so sorry, Adrienne. You probably feel like I cheated on you, too."

For a moment, we stare into each other's eyes.

Then I shrug and say, "We are both so *bad!*"

Barky bursts out laughing, which makes me laugh, and soon the two of us are laughing through our tears.

"We never made any promises to each other." I grip her hands. "You have nothing to apologize for."

"What a mess!" Barky says. "You're not mad?"

"No. I'm the one who's been stupid."

"You don't hate me?"

"I love you."

"Oh, Adrienne. I love you too. Really, I do."

I stand up and pull Barky to her feet.

"We need to talk about a few things."

"Yeah," she says. "Like, of all the men in New York, how the fuck could you fall in love with A.J. Upton?"

"It's a long story."

Barky steps into my arms. "Later."

She moves into my apartment, and for the next few days we're never apart except for work. Then MetroTerraNova sends her to London on business and our love has to subsist on texts and emails and a daily FaceTime call. I try to lose myself in work but even finishing my movie feels like drudgery. I'm also feeling sorry for myself because I was warned by Roy's security guards to stay away from A.J.'s funeral. I'm tired of reporters harassing me for comment about the deaths of Lehane and his son. Every night I go to bed hoping to sleep, but I lay awake, afraid that if I relax and let down into my unconscious, I'll be captured by the ugly things that lurk there.

So this night, worn out after a long workday, I trudge home stepping carefully over the rutted, frozen slush on West 20th Street, trying not to slip and fall. I'm facing another night alone. But the temporary cure for my blues is only a half block away: reheated Coq au Vin over brown rice, a glass of Zinfandel, a soak in a hot bath, then early to bed in the warmth and quiet of my apartment, texting love notes for Barky to read when she wakes up in London. Then, if I'm lucky, a long night's sleep.

I've heard nothing from Ferino since the night he made a fool of himself in my bed. So when I reach the vestibule of my building, I'm shocked to find him waiting there with Detective Peavey. They've caught me off guard, and quickly my fatigue turns to anger. Maybe I'll ask him in front of his partner how it feels to return to the scene of his recent humiliation.

"Let's go Miss Monet," Ferino says. "We have new evidence we need to talk to you about."

"I'm not talking to you."

"We're going to the precinct, then you can talk or not talk. It's up to you."

My keys are in my hand and he's blocking the door.

"I've had a long day. Get out of my way, please."

"Let's go," Ferino says. "You can call your lawyer on the way."

"I'm not going anywhere."

He gets in my face, loud. "We're not asking! Let's go!"

"Fuck you!"

I push against him and reach again for the door. Peavey grabs my arms from behind and I drop my keys into a mess of dirty slush at my feet. The vestibule spins around me, and my face is pushed against the cold tiles of the wall and they cuff my hands behind my back. Ferino scoops up my keys and stuffs them, dripping slush and dirt, into my jacket pocket, then wipes his hand on a handkerchief that smells like his cologne.

Berger appears outside the holding cell in the precinct where they've seated me. He stares wearily, shaking his head.

"You look terrible. Are you okay?"

"No. I'm sick of this whole thing. They brought me here in handcuffs like a fucking criminal. I'm tired, I'm hungry, I'm cold, and I'm mad."

"Why'd they bring you in?"

"They say there's new evidence."

"Which case?"

"I don't even know."

"Okay. You know how this goes. You take your cues from me. Right?"

"Right."

Ferino leans against the interrogation room wall, typing on his phone and chuckling. Berger and I take seats at the table. Ferino comes over and sits directly across from me so we're face to face. By now my loathing of him is hard to contain. I'm totally capable of saying or doing the wrong thing, so I get up and move to the other side of my lawyer.

Ferino watches with a self-satisfied chuckle.

"What're we playing here, musical chairs?" He's relaxed and confident and he has the energetic advantage over me, God damn him.

I hear Peavey and Garcia talking out in the hall. They come into the room and sit beside Ferino at the table. The last time they brought me here Peavey was professional and reasonable. Now there's an evasive look in her eyes that worries me. She was too rough when she handcuffed me. What changed?

Ferino raises a large manila envelope, shakes it over the table, and out with a clatter falls Jonathan's journal, or what's left of it, a spiral binding with a front and back cover, and no pages. That's because I tore them out, ripped them up, and flushed them down the toilet knowing the police were on their way. I couldn't figure out how to get rid of the stiff covers and wire binding, so I just wiped it off and stuffed the notebook back where he'd kept it. That was a mistake, but with two men dead on the living room rug I was in a hurry.

"Know anything about this?" he says.

"No."

"We found it in Lehane's backpack. Why would a man carry around a notebook with all the pages torn out?"

"I'm as baffled as you are."

"What was on those pages you had to get rid of?"

"I've never seen that before."

"There's no fingerprints on this at all," he says. "And it smells like window cleaner. Don't you think that's unusual?"

"You tell me. You're the cop."

He tries to stare me down, and fails, and I feel a little better. Finally, he slides the notebook back in the envelope and sets it aside.

Peavey looks up from her notes.

"Miss Monet, we have some follow up questions about your previous statement. When Mister Upton got shot, how close was he to Mister Lehane?"

I glance at Berger. He nods.

"You mean, like, how many feet apart?"

"I mean where was each man in the room?"

"Jonathan was near the bar. A.J. was near the couch at the other end of the room."

"So what, a few steps apart?"

"A few. It's not a very big room."

"Facing each other?"

"Yelling at each other."

"Standing basically in the same places their bodies fell?"

"Basically, yes."

"And where were you?"

"Between them, but off to the side, near the fireplace."

"And you were facing which way?"

"I was trying to talk to Jonathan."

"And you said at that point Lehane was pointing the gun at you, is that correct?"

"Yes. That's why I was talking to him."

Ferino says, "So tell us again how Mister Upton got shot."

"A.J. called Jonathan a coward. He said he was a weakling who wouldn't let go of me. He called him a loser. And Jonathan was yelling at him to get out."

"He was still pointing the gun at you?"

"Yes. And the two of them were just getting louder and angrier. There was all this built-up rage. I'm sure you know A.J. ridiculed Jonathan publicly for years and Jonathan hated it. But he was also heartbroken because A.J. refused to try and repair their relationship. A.J. told Jonathan 'Give me the gun!' and that's when Jonathan turned the gun toward A.J."

Peavey says, "Mister Upton was where in the room at that point?"

I see where they're going with this. A.J.'s blood splattered the mirror on the wall and all over the couch.

"I wasn't looking at him. I was talking to Jonathan and trying to calm him down."

"Would you say Mr. Upton was more in the middle of the room at that point?"

"When Jonathan pointed the gun at him, he must've stepped back. They were so angry, yelling at each other. Things were crazy. A.J. said to Jonathan, 'Give me that gun or I'll take it from you.' And then the gun went off."

Ferino says, "What'd you do?"

"I ducked. I turned away. When I looked up, A.J. was shot in the head and he was rolling off the couch onto the floor. Jonathan was just standing there with this blank look on his face, like, in shock. He said he didn't mean to do it."

"Okay. And how close were you to Mister Lehane when he shot himself?"

"Close."

"How close?"

"I had my hand on his shoulder. Trying to get him to give me the gun."

"And what did he say at that point?"

"He said, 'I can't do this anymore.' He said, 'I don't deserve to live.'"

"Which I'm sure you agreed with," Ferino smirked, "since he just shot your rich boyfriend."

"Fiancé."

"Yeah, yeah, whatever."

He's irritating me, but it's okay, it's energizing.

"And I didn't agree with him. Jonathan wasn't my lover anymore. But he was my friend. He was the star of my movie. We had plans to make another film together. His work was getting better all the time. When we finished filming, he just got a little intense and needy, that's all. I thought after he spent Christmas in Paris, we could settle things peacefully between us and between him and A.J. But he wouldn't listen. I didn't know what to do. I just tried to be my best self and hope I could talk sense into him. I begged him to give me the gun."

"Did you touch the gun?" Ferino says.

"No. I already told you that."

A couple silent seconds go by.

"Are you sure about that?"

"Yes."

"You didn't touch the gun, at any point?"

"No. Like I said."

"Then why did you wipe the gun with toilet paper and put it back in Lehane's hand?"

"I don't know what you're talking about."

"Oh yes you do."

He's right. I know exactly what he's talking about. I was in a frenzy that night, with two dead men at my feet, blood all over the room, and a warm gun in my hand. I wiped the gun carefully, but I didn't have the time or presence of mind to arrange the *mis-en-scene* perfectly.

I turn to my lawyer. He keeps his game face on, but I know he fears I'll crash unexpectedly.

"It's a simple question, Bobbie Jean," Ferino says. "Why did you wipe the gun with toilet paper and put it in Lehane's hand?"

"I didn't wipe the gun."

"Yes, you did. Your fingerprints were on the gun, weren't they Bobbie Jean? Because you shot Jonathan Lehane. Maybe Upton, too."

"I didn't shoot anybody."

"Well, somebody shot them. The only person who could've done it is you."

"I told you how it happened —"

Berger cuts me off. "Are Miss Monet's fingerprints on the weapon, detective?"

"No. Nobody's are. Not even Lehane's, even though the gun was in his hand."

Berger looks incredulous.

"You're telling me," he says, "this is about an *absence* of fingerprints?"

"We found fibers on the gun matching the toilet paper from the bathroom. There wasn't a single useable print on the weapon. There was nobody else at the scene. Obviously, she wiped the gun. The question is, why?"

"I..." Reflexively, I start to answer. But I have no answer. I glance at Garcia, and she's staring hard at me.

"Miss Monet," Peavey says, "physical evidence doesn't lie."

"What evidence?" Berger scoffed. "You can't prove she wiped the gun."

"Lehane fell to the floor from a standing position," Ferino says. "The way the gun was in his hand? Laying on his open palm? That was all wrong for somebody who fell that way. But not if she wiped the gun and put it in his hand. So quit wasting everybody's time Bobbie Jean! Why'd you wipe the gun and put it in the man's hand?"

They all stare silently at me, even my lawyer. A desperate but plausible explanation occurs to me. I have no idea if they'll believe it. But they know I'm lying about not wiping the gun and if I keep lying it will make things worse.

"All right." I squirm and sigh. "I touched the gun."

"Stop," Berger says.

"But it's not what you think."

"That's all, Adrienne."

"So you admit you shot him," Ferino says.

"No. No."

"I need a moment with my client," Berger says, standing up and practically dragging me out of my chair. "Come with me."

Out in the corridor, what I'm planning to say comes out in barely a whisper, and after listening, Berger rolls his eyes and says it'll be better if I say nothing. But now that I've admitted I touched the gun I'm in real trouble. My explanation is reasonable, actually sort of pathetic, and he still wants me to keep quiet. He's pissed off that I'm not listening to him again, and when we go back, I'm afraid his commitment to my defense will waver.

"Okay?" Ferino says when we sit back down. "You shot Lehane."

"No." Calmly, patiently, I explain. "After Jonathan shot himself, he fell down. The gun fell out of his hand, and I picked it up."

Not the answer he's expecting. "Why'd you do that?"

"Adrienne," Berger says. "I advise you to stop talking."

"Bruce, there's an explanation for this. It's sad, it's humiliating, but it's the truth."

Garcia says, "Miss Monet?"

"A.J. was dead. And now Jonathan was dead. And it was all because of me. I felt so guilty, so horrible to have caused all this. I felt like I had nothing left to live for." I stare at them across the table. In the mirror behind them I looked wide-eyed and scared. "I picked up the gun. I was going to shoot myself and be done with it."

Ferino just about gagged on this.

"Come on! You expect us to believe that?"

"But I couldn't do it. And then I realized I'd left my fingerprints on the gun and that would be taken the wrong way. Especially since you cops have been playing me from the start. So, yeah, I wiped off the gun and put it back in Jonathan's hand."

Ferino looks down the table to see if Peavey and Garcia are buying this.

"C'mon Bobbie Jean," he says. "Your lover was dead. Your rich boyfriend was dead. Oh, sorry. Your fiancé. You had the gun in your hand. Why didn't you just shoot yourself?"

"I couldn't. I even went out on the terrace. I stood up on the parapet. I was going to jump."

"Hey, why not?" he says. "You said you had nothing left to live for, right?"

"I realized I did have something to live for. The only thing I've ever lived for. My work."

"Your work. You mean your movie."

In the silence my eyes well up with tears and they run down my cheeks. "Yes," I whisper. "My movie. My work." I sit back wiping the tears away. "Why is that so hard to understand? It means everything to me." I sob silently, rocking slightly in my chair. "I'm sorry, but I've lost two people who both loved me. I saw them destroy each other right in front of me. I'm a long way from over it and you're making me relive it all over again."

"Let's get this over with, please," Berger says. He puts a reassuring hand on my shoulder.

Ferino gives Peavey the nod to continue. Peavey just stares at me. All Garcia's face betrays is her effort to show no feeling. Ferino looks disgusted with them both.

So he says, "Lehane found out about you and his son and it broke his heart, right?"

"I don't know what it did to his heart."

"He called me. Did he tell you that?"

"I answered that the last time I was here."

"That's when he told me you killed Egon Swift."

"If he did, he was lying." Although, remembering how Jonathan had felt so angry and betrayed, I'm sure he would have told them anything to hurt me.

"I told you detective," Berger says. "Nothing about Swift."

"We were on our way to Lehane's apartment to talk to him. But before we could, you shot him. Why'd you do that? Because he killed your fiancé? Or did you kill him so he couldn't tell us you killed Swift?"

Finally, I turn to my lawyer. "Do I have to listen to this?"

"Stay calm," Berger says. "Say nothing."

"Miss Monet," Peavey says. "Our Ballistics people matched the bullet that killed Swift to Lehane's gun."

Ferino says, "Just like you knew it would."

Berger takes my arm. I don't know whether to feel reassured or restrained.

"That's okay," Ferino says. "Stay calm. Say nothing. Just keep listening to me with that tragic look on your face. Lehane knew all along that you shot Swift, didn't he? And he kept quiet about it. He loved you, you had a movie to make, whatever the reason. Then he found out you were screwing his son and making a fool out of him and he decided he wasn't gonna be your alibi any longer. I don't believe he killed his son. I don't believe he killed himself. You knew where the gun was. You'd already used it to shoot Swift. Lehane was going to pay you back big time for screwing his son and humiliating him and you had to silence him before we got to him. Unfortunately, poor Mister Upton was a witness. One minute he's your fiance, the next collateral damage. Lucky for you their famous father and son feud seems to support your bullshit murder-suicide story. Do I have that about right?"

My lawyer says, "Silence, Miss Monet."

But Ferino has it completely right. It's been my mistake to let my contempt cause me to underestimate him.

"How'd you sweet-talk your way in close enough to blow Lehane's brains out? That must've been some trick. Come on, Bobbie Jean, tell us how you did it."

He thinks he's got me going now, and he presses harder. "And poor Mister Upton. How did it feel, to shoot your future in the head? Tough choice to make, wasn't it? Just to keep your ass out of prison, you killed your chance to marry into the elite. Too bad about all that stuff you're never gonna have, the fancy homes, the name, all that money. Felt pretty bad to kill all that, didn't it, Bobbie Jean? But not as bad as life would be in prison, right? They don't let you make *movies* in prison."

By now I've steeled myself to where nothing going on inside me shows.

"And of course," he says, "when Swift came out of his coma, and before he died, he told us you shot him."

"Bullshit," I say calmly.

"It's true. Right Detective Peavey?"

"That is right, Detective Ferino."

"Now it's my turn to say bullshit," Berger says caustically. "He I.D.'d her? And for three months you never mentioned it? Not once?"

"We had our reasons."

"Poor Buddy." The slow, sad way I shake my head, pitying him, will piss him off. "You still don't get it, do you?"

"Miss Monet..." Berger says.

"Jonathan wasn't my alibi. I was his."

That stops Ferino cold. Garcia sits upright. Peavey looks surprised. Berger doesn't seem to know what to say, but I bet he wishes I'd told him this in private. But it's too late for that. The interrogation is going against me and I have to turn it around.

"Miss Monet," Berger says, "I'm warning you –"

"I'm sorry, Bruce, but we have to get this over with. We shouldn't even be here."

Somehow, I manage to remain calm, wide-eyed and innocent.

"Jonathan told me he shot Egon. He said it was self-defense."

"When did he tell you this?" Peavey says.

"Around the end of October. The night before we wrapped shooting. He couldn't hold it in any longer. He said the day after he was fired, he went to see Egon. He tried to get his role in the film back, but Egon refused. He said Egon got nasty, and y'know, we did find out later he had meth in his bloodstream. Jonathan said he offered to buy Egon out to save the film from being ruined by an inferior director. That caused a violent argument. Jonathan said Egon attacked him and he shot him in self-defense."

Garcia says, "He told you this at the end of October. Three months ago."

"Yes."

"And he asked you to lie for him?"

"No." I feel bad enough accusing Lehane of my crime. I can't dump any more dirt on his memory.

"He asked you to keep quiet?"

"No. He said he planned to turn himself in. So I decided not to get in his way. He didn't ask me to lie or keep quiet."

Ferino says, "That's impossible to believe."

"Maybe because you don't want to," Berger says. "But it doesn't change the facts."

"Jonathan loved me. I felt protective towards him. If you'd seen the humiliation Egon put him through on the set in front of everybody –"

"She's lying," Ferino says to Peavey and Garcia. "But do you see what she's doin'? She's so craven she's blaming a man she killed for another murder she committed."

Nobody comes to my defense. Not even my lawyer.

"Besides," he says. "A man goes to beg for his job back and he takes a gun with him? Are you kidding?"

"He said he took it because he was afraid of Egon's temper. And it looks like he was right."

Garcia says, "Did you know Mr. Lehane was going to try to get his role in the movie back?"

"No. In fact, I didn't know Jonathan went to see Egon until the October night when he told me what happened. I asked him, 'Why are you telling me this now?' He said he'd decided to wait until the filming finished and then turn himself in. He thought if he came clean and explained that it was self-defense the law might go easy on him. He said he wanted our future to be clear. He thought we still had a future as a couple. I don't think he was being very realistic."

Ferino says, "And this was before or after you met Mr. Upton?"

"At least a month before."

"So Lehane told you he shot Swift. Do you know if he told anybody else?"

"I don't know."

"Miss Monet," Garcia said irritably, "you knew last fall how Swift got killed and you kept quiet this whole time? Why didn't you say anything until now?"

"Jonathan said he was going to turn himself in. I didn't think it was my place to say anything. And I cared about him. I felt protective —"

"Oh yeah? Toward him, or your movie?" Ferino sneers, shaking his head. "Bobbie Jean, are you really gonna blame a murder you committed on another man you killed? Are you really that big a moral zero?"

I don't need Berger to tell me to keep my mouth shut.

"Either you took the gun, or Lehane gave it to you. Maybe he wanted you to kill Swift. You both had something to gain. But he didn't shoot Swift. We have security camera video that show the front door of that building for the whole time when Swift had to have been shot. And Lehane wasn't there, not ever. But they do show someone who could have been you."

"Or anyone else," Berger intones wearily. "And cameras do malfunction."

I murmur, "Jonathan told me he shot Egon."

"Well, Egon told us you did it."

"Yeah," Berger scoffs, "when he was delirious and dying."

"Lehane also told me you did it."

"When he was angry, and he wanted to hurt me. And you were so out to get me that you believed him. Not very smart, Buddy, letting yourself get played like that."

Ferino jerks to his feet so abruptly his chair crashes to the floor and everyone at the table flinches. He swivels away from the table, but the room isn't large enough for him to pace off his fury. Peavey seems uneasy with him pacing behind her.

Garcia leans forward on her elbows.

"If you knew Lehane committed that murder, Miss Monet, you should have gone to the police three months ago."

"She had no legal obligation to do that," says Berger, "and you know it."

"Not in New York state, but she's admitted she's violated Federal law against misprision of felony. She could be looking at a fine and three years in jail."

"Not on the mere failure to report. Most courts require active concealment and there's none in her case."

"It also comes close to obstructing justice. It might even make her an accessory after the fact."

"It's not obstruction. She decided on her own not to report a crime. She didn't conspire to be silent or hide the facts. And she's not an accessory. She had no prior knowledge, she never assisted, she never acted to cover up, and she never lied. She says she and Lehane never spoke about hiding the crime. From what I've been told, the detectives never asked her about Lehane's movements that morning."

"That's right." I turned to Peavey. "You asked what we did once I went back to his apartment."

Garcia says, "My every instinct tells me you conspired with Lehane to keep quiet about this."

"God help us if instincts ever become evidence," Berger says.

"If I had my way," Ferino says with his back turned to us, staring at his own angry face in the mirror, "I'd arrest you right now for obstruction of justice."

"And I'd get it dismissed before it even came to trial," Berger shoots back.

"All we know about any of this," Ferino says, "is what she tells us."

"Or doesn't tell us," Peavey says.

"You didn't ask the questions," Berger says, seeming to enjoy their frustration, "so she didn't tell you what she knew. Maybe that's not good citizenship, but it's not a crime."

"Right," Ferino says, sneering. "And then there's the all-important reason she and Lehane kept quiet. For the movie they were making."

"Well, we all love movies, don't we?"

He turns, steaming, and stalks out the door.

Garcia leans back, staring at me and shaking her head. She taps Peavey on the arm, and they get up and leave, whispering hurriedly.

We sit there for almost an hour. I turn off my phone and stuff it in my jacket pocket, so I'll quit looking at the time. Berger is up and pacing, ignoring me, texting on his phone. I huddle in my jacket in the chilly room. I've got a hunger headache. I'm exhausted, sweaty, and ripe under my clothes. God, please get me out of here, so I can get some food, get cleaned up, and finally get a peaceful night's sleep.

The door opens. I don't like the grin on Ferino's face. Behind him Garcia and Peavey enter, looking like they're delivering bad news.

"Adrienne Monet," Ferino says, hustling around the table and standing over me, "you're under arrest for the murders of Jonathan Lehane and A.J. Upton. Stand up, please."

I can't believe this is happening. I look to Berger and he sighs and shakes his head. At me? At the situation he couldn't save me from? I get up and look Ferino in the eye.

"Are you kidding me?"

"You see anybody laughing?" He grips my arm to turn me around, but I jerk my arm away and step back from him. "Don't do that, Bobbie Jean. We can add resisting arrest, too."

I turn around and he pulls my wrists together and cuffs them.

"You're arresting an innocent person, Buddy. Isn't your personnel record bad enough?"

"Let's go," Ferino says, taking me by the arm.

"Don't say anything else, Miss Monet," Berger says. He turns and says to Garcia, "You don't have this, Jenny, and you know it. Not even close."

"We'll see what the grand jury says."

"Oh sure. Put her through the meat grinder. In the end she walks away, free but financially ruined. You people —"

"Let's go," Ferino says, pushing me toward the door. Peavey and Garcia stand beside the door, avoiding my eye as he leads me past.

Ferino walks me through the detective squad room to the surprised and approving nods of his colleagues at their desks.

"Prison's not so bad," he says loudly, playing to his fellow cops. "You'll have the rest of your life to write a screenplay about the whole thing. And think of all the interesting characters you'll meet."

He pushes me through the door to the precinct holding cell as the squad room behind us echoes with men's laughter.

The courtroom for my bail hearing is a zoo. I'm the exotic creature on display, but the really dangerous animals are in the gallery. The front rows are packed with reporters and photographers, shoulder-to-shoulder, scandal-sniffing dogs seduced by the scent of celebrity, sex and death. A Limousine Liberal Movie Star! His Conservative Attack Dog Son!

Murder! The notorious creator of "*Men R Dawgs*" in handcuffs! Did she really have sex with both father and son, then kill them both, like a female mantis who eats her mates after copulating?

I stand beside my lawyer at the defense table, sleepless and spaced out. All I need to do is hold my tongue and hang on to my sanity and trust Berger to get me out of this nightmare. I say a silent prayer asking God to please make this just a formality so I can go home, and not just an intermission before I'm locked in another squalid prison cell.

Last night they moved me from the precinct to a group holding cell downtown, where I was almost driven out of my mind by a chubby Latina prostitute pacing around ranting and raving about police brutality, a moaning Black mother with a split lip whose children had been taken from her, and a White woman in a soiled wrinkled business suit slouched and jittery and babbling incoherently, the perfect picture of a coked-up mess. Sitting there feeling bad for my sisters in misfortune, it reminded me how easy it is for a person to get lost. Take a wrong turn, make a wrong choice, agree to a bad deal, and your life can detour into any one of a million dead ends, in a cold indifferent world where you're alone, running on your wits and ambition.

The detectives are watching from the back wall by the courtroom entrance. Peavey's arms are folded and she's wearing a blank stare, but Ferino is grinning at me. I'm sure he hopes all this press coverage will erase the doubts about his investigation. I wish at that moment I had his balls in my hand again. I'd squeeze them until he begs me to stop.

Then I'd say, "Nope."

Berger enters not guilty pleas to two counts of first-degree murder of witnesses to a prior crime. The courtroom rumbles with talk, gaveled down by the judge, an elderly woman with large glasses that make her eyes look large and startled.

"Bail, Ms. Garcia?"

"The People request remand, Your Honor," Garcia says. "The defendant is a celebrity with access to resources that make her a distinct flight risk."

"Mister Berger?"

"Your Honor," Berger says, "as to the first count, the murder of Mister Lehane as a witness to a prior crime —"

The judge snaps back, "The subject is bail, counselor."

"— no connection between Mister Lehane and any prior crime has been established. The first count is absurd, and therefore so is the second. I ask the court for an immediate dismissal."

Garcia strikes back. "We will present evidence to the grand jury asking for indictments on these two counts of first-degree murder, and possibly a third murder charge."

"Possibly a third charge? Possibly? Why don't you establish that an actual crime happened before you charge my client with killing a witness to it?"

"The Medical Examiner ruled Swift's death a homicide," Garcia fires back. "We believe remand is appropriate, Your Honor."

"Your Honor," Berger says, "no bail at all is excessively harsh."

"This defendant is a distinct flight risk, Your Honor," Garcia says. "She has a passport, access to funds, she's unmarried, without children, and with no ties to the community —"

I turn and cut her off, loud and emphatic.

"My ties to this community are just as strong as yours! I have a movie about New York to stay here and finish! It's a tribute to the spirit of the people of New York after 9/11, starring the man that you're falsely accusing me of killing!"

The judge bashes the gavel.

"Bail set at one million dollars! Surrender your passport! Next!"

I call the Alpha Bitch office and tell my assistant Megan where to find my passport in my apartment and to bring it to my lawyer. Berger reaches out to Nikki Xiu through her New York office. I found out later she had Whit Allwether send a $100,000 certified Emerge International check for the deposit on my bail to a bondsman before lunch time.

But I still have to wait, exhausted and anxious, all day in another cell while my bail is processed. Evening comes down, and I begin to fear I'll spend another night behind bars. I finally get to go home late that night. Barky sets out Chinese takeout and wine on the kitchen table. I've eaten almost nothing for the past 24 hours, but all I can do is pick at the food. I really need to calm down and rest. Finally, Barky drags me to bed. She falls right asleep, but I can't. When I'm in bed at night and the world is quiet, that's when I'm most likely to drown in my own dark depths.

So I get up, slip quietly into the living room, and curl up in the Eames chair, reading text messages of support from my office kids. I also discover on the *Hollywood Reporter* website the reason why Lenny and Juno weren't in the courtroom this morning to support me.

The headline above a picture of an unshaven, grinning Lenny Victor reads, "Two actresses accuse film producer of sexual misconduct." Two young women are suing Lenny and Victor Productions for $100 million, saying that five years ago, when they were teenagers, they were invited to read for a Victor production at Lenny's house in Los Angeles. The audition turned out to be a pool party for three during which Lenny took cocaine and offered them the drug, disrobed and exposed himself, groped them, tried to pressure them into getting high and swimming nude, and to engage in three-way sex. They refused and fled from the house. After that, they say he spread defamatory lies about them in the industry and hurt their acting careers.

Nothing in the young women's complaint surprises me. I'm sure it's all true. The story disgusts me and I can't escape the memories it arouses, even though the wee hours of a troubled night are the worst time to relive my history with Lenny Victor.

But some memories are so overpowering they can't stay suppressed. Neither can my guilt for not speaking out or fighting back. I was a freelance production assistant when Lenny came on to me. I wanted to work in film and Lenny Victor Productions was a successful and growing company. The occasional shame I felt at my behavior was not as strong as my pride in being a tough little slut, telling myself after all the sex I'd had in and out of high school, fucking Lenny was no big deal. I never told anyone, either, and I've had moments when I felt ashamed and complicit in the abuse others who came after me surely must have suffered.

Whatever these two young women are doing now, I'm sure it isn't what they came to Hollywood to do. If I had stood up to Lenny would life have turned out any better for them? It's tempting to think so, but probably not. The reality is, the most common currencies in the world are power and sex, and those who profit and those who pay has never changed.

When I was nineteen, I didn't think about the damage that having sex with Lenny was doing to my soul – that came later. I thought that by enduring, and sometimes even enjoying his misconduct, it proved I had the guts to do what was necessary to get ahead. But I was also afraid he would kill my career if I resisted him or went public. I was just beginning the life in New York I left home for, and I was working my way up from the bottom of the film production world. Lenny gave me work and introduced me to people I needed to know, some of whom eventually invested in my first movie. I avoided him as much as I could, but that wasn't always possible. My mother used to have a cheerfully cynical saying: "Sometimes you just gotta tootle the flute and swallow the music."

I recited that pearl of wisdom more than once during those early days while I was on my knees or while Lenny heaved and groaned on top of me whispering obscenities in my ear. I shut down my feelings and did it and hoped I was paying the dues that would push my career forward, although I admit I had mixed feelings about working with Juno while fooling around behind her back with her arrested adolescent of a husband. I tried to chalk it all up to experience, even to a writer's research, but that wasn't a final answer. I don't know if I'll ever have one.

I feel a sudden urge to get raging drunk and smash everything in sight. Instead, I get dressed, slip into my shoes and winter coat, and leave a note on the kitchen table in case Barky wakes up. I go downstairs and tramp the cold streets, down through the West Village and Tribeca and back up to Chelsea, until I am tired enough to crawl back into bed and fall asleep just before daylight.

When I reach the office, I receive a text from Juno. "Call when yr in. Need to talk." Well, well. I think I hear the terse voice of a woman who can no longer hide from the truth about her husband.

"Honey, I need your help," she says, without a greeting. "Have you seen this fucking story in *The Hollywood Reporter*?"

I have loathed Juno for so long that feeling sisterly sympathy for her takes effort. Still, I try.

"Yeah. I'm sorry you're going through this."

"I'm sending you a statement for you to sign." It sounds more like an order than a request. "I need as many people as I can get to sign on and rally 'round Lenny, so we can stop what these so-called actresses are trying to do."

For a moment, I am in disbelief. Then, reality catches up. Of course – this is Juno.

"What are they trying to do?"

"How can you ask that?"

"It's just a lawsuit," I say. "If you stay silent and don't prolong it, the media attention will die down. It'll get resolved in court, and —"

"Adrienne," she says, now angry with me too. "What is wrong with you?"

Through the looking glass we go. What's wrong with me?

"What do you mean?"

"These two tramps came trotting over to our house wiggling their tiny heinies and parading themselves in front of my husband. I mean, what did they think was going to happen?"

"They say they were there to audition."

"Oh, bullshit. You know what happened. They threw themselves at Lenny, and when they didn't get the roles they wanted, they decided to get even."

"Five years later? Do you hear yourself, Juno?"

She shuts up for a moment, and her tone toward me hardens. "You sound like you believe them."

"What I believe isn't important. Forget about this statement, it'll only encourage the media to dig up more dirt on Lenny. Let it die. Settle it out of court."

"You believe them, don't you? Admit it."

"Juno, I get it, you're standing by your husband —"

There are tears in her voice.

"You're God damn right I'm standing by him. This lawsuit could destroy our lives, along with our company and everything we've worked for. If it wasn't for Lenny, I'd still be carrying a clipboard and wearing a stopwatch around my neck."

"If it wasn't for Lenny you wouldn't be so angry and afraid right now," I say. "C'mon Juno. You've known about Lenny for years."

"What I know is that Lenny has a problem with drugs. It's the drugs that caused his behavior."

"Are you serious?"

"And I'll tell you what else I know. If it wasn't for Lenny, you'd have no career at all, and you know it. Without us, you'd be nothing."

I can't let her get away with that.

"You're absolutely right," I say, calmly. "And I paid a price for the help you gave me. Lenny made sure of that."

"Oh, now you too?"

"Ask Lenny. Ask him about the fun times he had with me on that velvet couch in your old apartment."

Her turn to be silent.

"Maybe I do owe him my career. Every time I sucked him off, he babbled about how he cared about me, and would help me become a success in the business –"

"You're a liar!"

"— and lately I've been trying to remember, was I so naïve that I believed him, or was I just making a deal with the devil to get ahead?"

"You little —"

"But my deal was nothing, compared to the deal you made to close your eyes. Now it's time to open your eyes, Juno. It's time to get real."

I can't take any satisfaction from this reckoning with the Victors, thirty years in coming. It actually feels sad. Juno chose to be blind to her husband's abusive and criminal behavior toward women, and for her silence she got a successful career and rich life uncomplicated by the truth because she ghosted anyone who refused to enable her blindness. Now I feel no triumph, I just feel sad to be hurting another woman, even one I dislike.

Finally, she finds her voice.

"You ungrateful little cunt."

"You should thank me for telling you the truth..."

I'm talking to a dead connection.

"...when nobody else will."

So much for Juno. She's trippin' if she thinks anyone will 'rally round' Lenny. If anything, the lawsuit will bring out of the shadows even more women that Lenny abused. All day his defiant, clueless response to the lawsuit is widely quoted.

"According to the Bible and the Boy Scout handbook, I've committed sexual misconduct thousands of times since puberty – with myself, ha ha ha."

A jerkoff to the end.

The day the grand jury decision is due on the murder charges against me, I wake up feeling weak, wishing I could just stay in bed. But I force myself downstairs and into a cab to the gym and get pumped with a weight-lifting circuit on the machines, then a three-mile run on the treadmill. When I get home, feeling ready to do battle with whatever comes, Barky is up and we have breakfast. She chuckles at how I'm dressed, in work boots and jeans, a tee shirt, hoodie, and a leather jacket.

"All you're missing is a hardhat and a jackhammer."

"Thanks to my night in jail, I know how to dress, if that's where I'm going today."

When I come up from the C train the cold wind at my back pushes me along West 49th Street to the Cinema Arts Building on Broadway. The paparazzi and camera crews crowding the sidewalk surge up to me, yelling shit. I feel like a gazelle in a YouTube video surrounded by a pack of snapping snarling wild dogs. I march into the side entrance through a chaos of flashing strobes and the building security guys push the photographers back outside the door.

The mood in the Alpha Bitch offices is tense and subdued, but I bear down on the work with McPeek in the editing cave and push any worries about today aside for a while. In the back of my mind, it's like I'm waiting for a biopsy report, or like the sleepless two weeks you once had to wait in the old days to get HIV test results from Bellevue after you'd been careless. All-wether calls to tell me that Nikki Xiu has directed him to arrange a buyout to take *"Lonely Sky"* away from Victor Productions before Lenny and Juno's sexual misconduct scandal harms the picture. Rather than realize this is a lucky break, I'm sure Juno will feel even more victimized, although of course they'll take the money. Good or bad, lawyers are expensive.

At lunch, nobody on my staff talks about my court case. There's nothing to say until the grand jury verdict is announced. All afternoon I shuttle between my office and McPeek's editing cave, where sound effects selected from a vast digital library are being mixed into the soundtrack. Today she's working on the torture sequence from "I'm A Stranger Here" and experimenting with different screams, which can be heard throughout our offices. We're a long way from a final cut, but as McPeek finishes a sequence she sends me a link and I watch it on the server, grateful for the distraction.

My wristwatch alarm goes off at four o'clock and fear grabs me by the throat. I decide to take a walk. I need to be alone. I get downstairs, and then I change my mind and head back up to my office, lay back on the couch and practice emotional detachment while I wait to hear my fate. It doesn't take long.

My cell phone rings. BRUCE BERGER.

I sit up on the couch. My voice is a weak whisper.

"Hello?"

"Miss Monet?"

"Bruce. Did you —"

"The grand jury no-billed you."

"Oh God." Crushing fear nearly forces the breath from my lungs. "That sounds so bad."

"No, no, it's good news."

"How is that good?"

"It means no bill of indictment."

"Okay, so what do I have to do?"

"Nothing. The DA's office had a press conference scheduled but they just canceled it."

It's benign…your blood test is negative.

"So that's it?"

"You're in the clear on Lehane and Upton."

I don't believe it. There must be a catch.

"Can they still arrest me later?"

"Not unless important new evidence shows up."

"What'd Ferino tell the jury?"

"Defense lawyers aren't allowed in the grand jury room. But whatever case Ferino and Garcia presented, the grand jury didn't buy it."

"Wait. What about Egon?"

"I don't think they have a case. What's it been, almost five months? Homicides are usually solved in the first 48 hours, or not at all."

"My God. I'm like, shocked. I've been so afraid for so long." I pause to get a grip on myself. "That cop, Ferino, he's really out to get me. I expected a different outcome."

"Juries can be unpredictable. Let's just be thankful for the one we got."

"Thankful? I'm thankful I have you as my lawyer, Bruce! Thank you so much for everything!"

"You're welcome. Have a good life, Adrienne."

"If I don't, you'll be the first to know." He hangs up, laughing.

I sit there, too stunned to move. Every day, to stay in the moment and focus on the grind of making a movie, I've had to put my fear of arrest out of my mind. To sleep at night, I've tried not to imagine how I might be punished for the things I've done. Now that's all gone. I am out of danger. I am free to pursue any future I want for myself. A mood of anger, of defiance, rises in me, strength mixed with fresh hope. My film, finished, will be successful. My life and career will rise again. Life will again be charged with possibility, maybe even for happiness.

I leave a voicemail for Barky.

"It's me. I'm out of trouble. The grand jury decided not to charge me with anything. Call me, I want to hear your profane, beautiful voice." She calls back, excited, and we talk about how soon we can get out of town and take our first trip together.

When I open my door to the Alpha Bitch offices my staff stands up and they cheer. Champagne corks pop and come bouncing out of the kitchen, and everyone crowds around me, telling me how happy they are for me. Megan hugs me and says tearfully, "It was so cruel, what they did to you, after all you've been through." Enid the receptionist, basketball-tall and lanky and droll, says, "So cool you escaped the bloody jaws of fate, Boss." She lives with her parents out in Rutherford and writes horror novels at night. Roger, our production assistant and runner, hugs me and says, "What a relief, huh?"

Lana stands on the toes of her Converse sneakers and hugs me. "I think there's a movie in all this, don't you? If you need somebody to write it with you, here I am." Hustling, always hustling, these NYU film school graduates. We all drink a lot of champagne this afternoon, but the work stays on schedule. I care so much about these people, yet as I accept their congratulations, I wonder how they'd feel about me if they knew the truth.

The offices are dark and silent. Nothing moves except the screen savers on the computers. My employees have all gone home, and I'm alone, strolling around swigging from the last bottle of champagne. It's warm and flat, and I don't care. Alpha Bitch Productions is my world, and I don't want to leave. I read again the text that came earlier from Nicky Xiu: "Purity is the refuge of second-rate minds." I keep telling myself that after all these months of tension and fear, I'm not in jeopardy anymore. I should be relieved, but I'm not. I've gotten so used to living with dread that letting down my guard feels dangerous.

My conscience is supposed to torture me. That's the price that I'm supposed to pay, right? But what good will that do? Suppose I suffer guilt and sorrow for the rest of my life, my anguished conscience churning inside me like a sickness, day and night? Will that bring the three men I killed back from the dead, or ease the grief of their loved ones? Guilt and sorrow and regret are the price I'm supposed to pay. But the truth is, I don't feel any of that, and it isn't just the wine. It's because the truth is perfectly clear to me, and anyone who values their dignity and freedom would understand. I was constantly forced to choose: let Egon degrade me and lose my dignity, or defend myself; let Jonathan betray me and cost me my freedom, or silence him; allow A.J.'s well-meaning and law-abiding witness testimony to land me in jail, or sacrifice his life and our future to stay out of prison. I was forced to do some bad things, but all for good reasons. That doesn't make me a bad person, does it? I mean, are we only the shitty things we do, or are we more than that? With no one else to ask, I'm the only one who can answer that question, and only one answer is possible if I don't want to lose my mind.

I look over the empty desks and chairs, raise my bottle in a silent toast, and finish the champagne. God bless my staff, these kids who work so hard and look up to me, especially my girls, starting their careers in a brutal business. I'm so glad we're not going to be pulled apart. In my whole life I've never felt like I had a real family or a real home, and yet, here it is, all around me.

A few days later I wake up and discover I've slept through the alarm. WNYC-FM says the weather is cold and windy with snow on the way. I usually start the day feeling sluggish and irritable, but today there's no time to go to the gym and burn off my morning fog. My stomach isn't open for business yet, so I postpone breakfast until I get to the office. Instead of my usual butch outfit, I slip into a clingy cherry-red wool-cashmere dress. I pull on my work boots and wrap myself in my three-quarter length down parka and leopard print Pashmina scarf.

I kiss Barky goodbye and clomp out of my building and down the front steps. I toss a bag of trash in the can next to the stoop and turn toward 8th Avenue, deciding to take a brisk walk, up 8th Avenue until my head clears, then catch a C or E train the rest of the way to Times Square.

But sitting at the wheel of his car a few parking spaces up the street is Detective Buddy Ferino.

I can just imagine his disappointment after he failed to get me indicted. His grand jury testimony must have been the equivalent of his clumsy performance in my bed.

He leans out the window, grinning.

"Bobbie Jean! I've got something you need to hear!"

"I've got something you need to hear," I say. "Fuck off."

I keep walking.

"I can prove you killed Egon Swift."

I stop walking. I'm queasy, I'm pressed for time, and now this?

"What are you talking about?"

He motions to the passenger seat. "Get in."

"Not a chance."

"Okay, just stay there and listen. After the grand jury blew it, I went back over all the evidence. Here's what I found."

He turns on the dashboard CD player. I hear my voice coming out of the car stereo speakers. *Hi, Egon, it's Adrienne.* It's the voicemail I left on Egon's cell phone after I shot him.

Ferino sits there grinning as it plays, his fingers tapping on the wheel, pleased with himself. Does he really think this innocuous message is significant? I begin to wonder if he became unhinged after losing with the grand jury.

"Yeah?" I say. "So?"

"Just before the end. Hear the little chime? Hear those doors opening?"

He raises the volume very high. I hear the chime and the doors opening in the background but they're easy to miss because my voice is so much louder.

"Okay, so?"

"I must've heard those sounds a dozen times at the scene that day. The sounds the elevator makes when it gets to Swift's office."

That hits me like a punch in the stomach. I shrug and try to act unconcerned.

"Yeah, and about a million other elevators in New York, including the one in my building, which is where I was when I called him. You cops! Why can't you ever admit you're wrong?"

I back off and turn toward 8th Avenue. He gets out of the car and trots around in front of me.

"I'm not wrong. I was just in your lobby." He nods toward my building. "Your elevator doesn't have a chime."

"Well, it did last summer when I left that message." So lame, Adrienne, and so easily disproven. "I guess it's out of order." Oh my God, what's happening? "What're you saying?" But of course, I know.

"You were there. You shot Swift. Then you called his cell phone and recorded that message to cover your ass —"

"You're fantasizing again."

"— but the elevator got there before you were done. We've got forensic experts who can match the sounds on the recording with the elevator at the crime scene. And if they can't, the FBI lab at Quantico ought to be able to nail it down, especially with three murder cases riding on it. This is routine stuff for them. I'm gonna use your own voicemail to prove you were at Swift's that morning. Add to that, Swift's deathbed I.D. of you, plus your access to Lehane's gun, and all that you gained by killing Swift. That ought to be enough for an indictment."

"Experts," I scoff, to hide my growing terror.

He's right. As careful as I tried to be after I shot Egon, I obviously wasn't careful enough. My throat closes and my voice is so tense I can hardly talk.

"They can really do that?"

"Yeah. They really can."

"Well, all the experts in the world can't change the truth, and I've got the truth on my side."

"No you don't, and you and I both know it. You're a killer, Bobbie Jean."

"Okay, so what am I? Under arrest? *Again?*"

"No," he says. "I'm gonna let you sweat while I put together an airtight case."

"Aren't you afraid I'll get on a plane?"

"And what? Run away from your movie?"

"So when are you planning to arrest me? I'll put it on my calendar."

"First I'm gonna get that forensic report. Then I'm gonna take the Swift case to a grand jury and get an indictment." He jams his hands in his overcoat pocket and grins. "Then I'm comin' for you, bitch."

"Bring it on, Buddy." But my voice trembles so badly I'm not convincing, even to myself. I try to get away from him, but he sidesteps and blocks my path.

"With the forensic report on the voicemail, plus Lehane's gun and you taking Swift's job, I can get a grand jury to indict you for killing him. And I think there's a good chance you'll be convicted. Then I'll find a way to refile charges that you murdered two other men to cover up the first murder. And this time, I'll get an indictment. You killed Lehane so he couldn't I.D. you for killing Egon Swift. And Upton saw you kill his father, so you had to kill him too. That's life without parole, times two."

He sidled up close, eye to eye.

"Better hurry up and finish your movie."

It's too early in the morning for this. Dear God, if I never get anything more in this life, can you please make this go away?

"Aren't you afraid I'll tell the NYPD about that night at my place?"

"Your word against mine?" He laughs. "Who do you think they're gonna believe? A decorated cop? Or a murder suspect?"

A quick thought occurs, of myself on the witness stand, trying to explain to a jury how I got the gun and why I shot Egon. All I see are frowns, and disbelief in their eyes. I take a moment to get ready for what I now have to do.

"Well, what do you expect me to do now?" I sneer. "Confess?"

That takes him by surprise, and he responds exactly as I hoped.

"Are you saying you did it?"

"I'm saying I want this over."

"If you confess, you'll get a lighter sentence."

"Wow, what a bargain. A lighter sentence for a crime I didn't commit."

"Maybe what you did to Swift wasn't a clear-cut case of murder."

"I didn't do anything to him! But the fucking stress is killing me! I'm going broke paying my lawyer! Okay? So you win! Is that what you wanna hear?"

The wind stiffens and the first flakes of a major snowstorm swirl around us. The fresh, raw morning cold makes me shiver, and for a moment I feel just as distressed as I sound. I pull my coat tighter around myself.

"I'm just saying I want this over and I might be willing to make a deal." I whine, I can't help it. "I'm fuckin' sick of this."

"Let's go talk to Garcia. We'll do it right now."

"I have to talk to my lawyer first."

"Okay. Have him bring you in."

"I guess that's the only way to end this." I shrug, hoping he believes I'm as resigned as I'm acting.

"You may as well end it now. Because I'm gonna get you, sooner or later."

"I'll talk to Bruce."

"Yeah. Do the right thing," he says. "Finally."

He nods, pleased with himself, gets in his car and drives away.

The moron. He should've gotten his evidence, then arrested me. But he needed to get in my face and prove something, and now he's given me all the time I need. I ride back up to my apartment on the elevator with no chime, and I call Megan at the office and tell her I won't be there until later.

But before I get down to work, I check the date, January 30, 2018, on the menstrual tracker app on my phone. My period is two weeks late. In the bathroom, I take down the pregnancy test kit from the medicine cabinet and cross my fingers.

SIX *One day in September 2022*

Paris, on a beautiful late summer morning. In the kitchen of a spacious apartment on the Rue Ernest le Fevre, golden sunlight shines on a large wooden table where two people are seated at breakfast. A very pregnant redheaded woman nibbles a piece of toasted baguette and sips a cup of lukewarm green tea, the only food her delicate stomach will accept first thing in the morning. A four-year-old boy of exceptional beauty dressed in jeans and a red sweatshirt, Rory Upton Monet, is deeply absorbed in drawing on a tablet. I've finished my early morning writing in my studio down the hall, meditated and said my prayers and daily affirmations, and I join them, my family, for breakfast.

The red-haired beauty, my wife Evangeline Barksdale, is due to give birth next month.

"*Bonjour, my darling.*" From Barky, a big smile as she raises her lips for my kiss. She's had to be very tough through a difficult pregnancy, and as the day of delivery nears, she's holding herself together and hoping it'll soon be over.

She shifts uncomfortably in her seat and brushes back her thick auburn hair. She'd planned to cut it all off when the doctor confirmed she was pregnant, but I begged her to keep it. I've always felt that women who cut their hair short once they marry or become pregnant seem to be doing a kind of penance and giving up on their sexiness.

"*Bonjour, Rory, mon amour.*"

"*Bonjour Mama,*" my little boy sings.

"How is our big boy this morning?"

"*Je suis un garçon très heureux, maman,*" he says, engrossed in drawing.

"This morning you'll go with Mama Barky so she can see the doctor about your baby sister."

The stylus freezes in his hand.

"She's almost here."

His stare makes the silence heavier, then he shrugs.

"Wow. I can hardly wait."

"When she's born, you'll feel different."

"She just better not touch any of my stuff."

Barky and I laugh at that, and he looks up at us and grins. He loves when we find him entertaining.

Barky says, "Better get ready, we're leaving for the doctor's soon."

Rory lays down the tablet, slides off his chair, plants a sudden kiss on Barky's cheek, then heads for his room.

"He asked me the Papa question again this morning," Barky says.

"I still don't know what we should tell him."

"We'll have to deal with it sooner or later. I can feel it coming. I had coffee yesterday with Genevieve and Helene and I asked them what they told Caroline. I think she was just about four, too."

"Did they say her Daddy came from a sperm bank and they don't even know his name?"

"No, but they were caught unprepared. They ad-libbed something about her father living in another country because of his job or something. But that just opened up more questions. Caroline's having a real hard time because her girlfriends have fathers in their lives, and she doesn't."

"So what did you tell Rory?"

Barky pushed herself to her feet.

"I told him to talk to you."

"A.J.'s death was so public," I said. "We better settle this soon. He's got a browser on his tablet. He may already know all about it. What worries me is, he's still too young to know how A.J. died. Killed by his father? What would that mean to a kid?"

"A lot of confusion. He already thinks his new sister is from the same father."

"He's such a happy kid. I'd hate to cast any dark clouds."

I watch them prepare to leave, framed in the vestibule door, pulling on jackets, slinging on bags. Rory hops into the kitchen and kisses me goodbye, on the lips as usual, then races out the door. I stare at the space where he stood, already missing him. Our life in Paris is so different from what our life would have been like if A.J. was alive. We'd be much wealthier, of course, and we'd still be in New York, but I wouldn't be able to marry Barky. For Rory, it would mean visiting me on movie sets with his tutor, Upper East Side pre-K, summers at Rosa Lee's house in Bridgehampton, winter visits to Palm Beach and Roy Upton's mansion, a life like his father's, with wealth putting everything desirable within reach, and insulating him from anything bad. Sounds pretty good, on paper. For me, life in New York would be living in a town full of ghosts, with the real risk of getting arrested again. The life the three of us have made in Paris is richer and healthier than any life a kid could have in the ongoing nightmare that is America.

I stand in front of the mirror for my daily moment of truth. I look like I got dressed with my eyes closed in faded jeans, a white tee, and my black acrylic sweater that I bought at Reminiscence on McDougal Street with my first paycheck in New York. I've worn a big hole in the right elbow from resting it on my desk as I write. This afternoon I'm doing a photo shoot on the Right Bank for an important magazine profile of my life at 52 years old. I don't want to overdo it, but I can't show up looking this scruffy.

So I lay out my clothes on our bed, then slip into a charcoal wool-crepe St. Laurent maxi dress with five gold buttons up the torso, echoed by a stack of gold wrist bangles. I pull on and lace up my gold Converse sneakers. I'll let the photographer's stylists do what they want with my hair. My face looks 10 years younger than my age, and my body is harder than ever to keep in good shape, but my hair, black with silver highlights, is still one of my good features. It's grown back in full since last winter, when I took a supporting role in a dark fantasy *"Game of Thrones"* clone mini-series for German TV, playing the leader of a platoon of female warriors. The part paid well, the script was tolerable, and the work was fun, but they chopped my hair military short and it's only now back to its normal length. I brush it and hold it back with my extra-large sunglasses perched on top. I take a closer look in the mirror at the chic Parisian woman I've made of myself. In my face, most of all in the eyes, I search for a glimmer of optimism but find only the weary, searching look of a troubled soul, ready to step out into the world hoping she can be her best self, or at least successfully fake it for another day.

I need to go down to my European manager and publicist Jean-Pierre's office near the Place Contrescarpe for a situation report on the day's business. Riding down from Menilmontant in the back seat of a Mercedes with an Uber driver, I sit back and try to cheer myself up by remembering the reception *"Autumn Reprise"* received at Cannes in May. Nikki Xiu brought me and our film to the festival and took me to all the important parties, where the press fluttered around us and not a word about my nasty reputation was whispered. After the screening, I took a bow to a standing ovation from an international audience, which was a huge moment for me. I was treated like an artist and no longer like a true crime freak from the tabloids. The affirmation I got from that moment in Cannes has energized and driven me ever since.

Up until then, I hadn't gotten much respect. *"Lonely Sky"* got good reviews, did better than expected box office for an art film, and got three Oscar nominations – Best Adapted Screenplay, Best Director, and Best Actor for Jonathan Lehane – but no wins. Despite the nominations, despite having an acclaimed film in the theaters, people in the media still treated me like a suspected murderer who has eluded law enforcement, or as the angry feminist bomb thrower who created *"Men R Dawgs"*, my reality TV trash triumph, now in its fourth season. The only upside to *"Dawgs"* was money. I sold the series to the Lily Channel and got rich, then richer still when they created versions in the UK, Spain, Germany and Japan.

I hoped moving to Paris and shooting *"Autumn Reprise"* would be a welcome escape from New York, but it turned out to be very nerve-wracking and physically challenging. COVID was raging and French filming was shut down by the government from March to May 2020, right in the middle of pre-production. When we regrouped and began filming, it seemed like a virus of aloofness and short tempers had spread. Each day working with Delphine was a war of creative interpretations and listening to her male co-star complain about her. The tight-fisted investors fought me over every Euro. The two-month shutdown pushed our schedule into the summer and the devastating heat of Paris in August. It was like working in purgatory. Then I got knocked flat by the virus myself for two weeks, and I came back to directing utterly exhausted, but I got the job done.

Since Cannes I've done no press. But starting with a magazine piece timed to drop when *"Autumn Reprise"* opens in December, Adrienne Monet will be back in the news. I've got a chance with this new movie to remove the stigma from my name, and I'll do whatever it takes to no longer be synonymous with crime and scandal. For example, just now my driver keeps glancing at me in the rearview mirror and I can tell he recognizes me.

My phone buzzes in my purse.

"Bonjour, mec."

"Adrienne! There are paparazzi in the street in front of my building! I went out for cigarettes and they were all over me when I came back!"

I naturally assume this has something to do with Jean-Pierre's very public love life or with his former fame as a star football player. He was a French sports hero, his prowess on the field broadcast around the world, his handsome face on magazine covers, in TV interviews, and on the Internet, but in 2018 he ruined his knee in the World Cup semifinals. Now he's turned his celebrity into a business, working from his home, handling public relations and other matters for a select clientele in cinema, sports, and the arts. He's handsome and open-hearted, devoted to my career, and, I may as well tell you, other key aspects of my well-being.

"Did you talk to them? Did they say what they want?"

"They want you!"

We're just circling the Place Contrescarpe. A half block down the narrow Rue Mouffetard is a crowd with cameras and microphones on booms at the entrance to Jean-Pierre's building. I ask the driver to pull over for a moment and, looking fascinated, he does.

I say, "How do you know they want me?"

"They all know I manage you and they want to know where you are."

The media pack forces walkers off the sidewalk into traffic and they have to squeeze past, looking highly indignant.

"Something is happening," I say. "Something is happening in my life, and I don't know what it is."

"I've heard nothing."

"All right. I'm almost there. We'll figure it out."

I ask the driver, cursing under his breath and blasting the horn as we inch through the crowd of journalists, to stop right outside the entry. I put on my face mask and pull down my sunglasses.

I step out of the car and into a riot of yelling voices. Flashes of silver light engulf me. I squeeze through the crowd, pushing aside cameras and those microphones with fuzzy wind guards. At the door I turn, take off my mask and push up my dark glasses and give them a wave, a dazzling smile, and a kiss, then vanish inside the vestibule.

Upstairs, Jean-Pierre opens the door. He reaches out and takes me in his arms. With his lean muscular body against mine, his hand on my cheek, the greeting and kiss that goes on for a long time, I've just entered a safe space. I should explain that once Barky told me the anxiety, depression and loss of libido that came with her pregnancy made love making undesirable, I began hooking up with Jean-Pierre once in a while. He had always been seductive and flirty toward me, and one day I simply turned around and gave him what we both wanted. He knows we can never do more than play, and he accepts that. His large, airy bedroom at the back of the apartment has been my refuge all summer.

"Did you find out anything yet?" I say.

"Not yet, not yet."

His office is next to the living room. At the front of the room is an armchair beside doors open to a Juliet balcony over the street. The first place I go is to the espresso machine alcove for a double. On an empty stomach a little caffeine goes a long way. At the back of the room, Jean-Pierre sits at his desk in front of a large computer screen, searching. I sip a little coffee, then take a chair beside him.

"Okay, okay," he says. "This must be it."

"Let me see."

With a troubled look at me, Jean-Pierre pushes back in his chair. I roll in closer and peer at the screen. It's the *New York Post* website.

The story is about Buddy Ferino. And me. And it's bad, it's got pictures of Egon and Jonathan and A.J. and me, and the whole ugly history of the making of *"Lonely Sky"* four years ago. It's even got a picture of Barky and me together.

"And the day was going so well."

I feel Jean-Pierre's arm go around my shoulders.

"I need to talk to Rhonda, like, now."

"Adrienne, in New York it's, like, four o'clock in the morning."

"I don't care. She's my publicist. She should have called me. Please just keep calling 'til she answers."

I take myself to the armchair near the open doors, sip some coffee and light a Gitane, and open the browser on my phone to the *New York Daily News*. They also have the story on their home page. I picture the bundles of tabloids being dropped by the thousands all over New York city in the pre-dawn dark.

Over at his desk Jean-Pierre is purring to Rhonda, my publicist in New York.

"Yes yes, I know the time, I'm sorry, but for Adrienne this is urgent—"

I say, "Tell her to Face Time me. Now."

A minute later Rhonda appears on my phone, her hands rubbing her face and pushing her thick bangs out of her sleepy eyes.

"The street downstairs is full of paparazzi."

She speaks, a deep sleep croak. "The story broke really late last night."

"So why didn't you call me?"

She raises a hand, yawns, shakes her head, and rubs her face awake.

"The time difference, Adrienne. I didn't think I should call you at four o'clock in the morning."

"Okay, so, a text? An email? Something? I'm totally unprepared for this. I got to the office and found myself surrounded. I just now saw the stories. Where did they find him?"

"In his car. At a rest stop on the LIE."

"What's the NYPD saying?"

"Nothing official, not yet. My brother-in-law Marty's a detective so I called him to see what I could find out. He said they found an empty whiskey bottle, a gun, and a note. They're not saying what's in the note, but Marty called you 'the bitch who killed him.' So be prepared. The NYPD's already focused on you."

"Focused on me? And not three murders? Still unsolved? Four years later?"

"Apparently Ferino had a detective agency on Long Island that wasn't doing well. He was under investigation by the Nassau County DA. He was being sued by a client —"

"Well, okay! So he could've shot himself for a lot of reasons! Right?"

"Yeah, but the police must've told the press there's something about you in the note."

"Why do you think that?"

"Because every story mentions the sex tape."

"Oh shit. What do they say?"

"The usual. He was investigating you for murder, you set him up, and destroyed his career."

"They've been saying that for four years."

"Well, now for the part that really sucks. The sex tape's a hot item on the Internet again." I wish I wasn't on Face Time because I grimace, and it shows. "I Googled it. 'Adrienne Monet sex tape.' There's a whole page of links."

"Okay, okay."

Now even more people will see the video I secretly shot the night Ferino tried to fuck me in my own bed. When it leaked, I stopped eating in restaurants because men at nearby tables would watch the video on their phones and wave them to taunt me. After someone in the NYPD leaked the tape, I knew it would have eternal life on the Web, but it's reappearing now at the absolute worst moment.

"There's nothing I can do about this?"

"Just don't feed it," Rhonda says. "Right now in paparazzi dollars, a picture of you is worth big bucks—"

"Then I just made some photographers a lot of money. You know, until today I was living a quiet, peaceful life with my wife and son. Barky's just about to give birth. This stress is the worst thing that could happen now. This isn't fair. I don't belong in this story."

"Oh, come on, girlfriend. I'm on your side, you know that, but get real. To the NYPD you're still a suspect in three murders. You got the cop who was investigating you in a compromising position that cost him his job. His life fell apart and now he's killed himself and left a note. It's a good bet he blames you for something. How could you not get dragged into it? I'll tell you what I tell all my clients. A scandal never dies, so be sure it's one you can live with."

The media will be camped on our doorstep. I need to call Barky and warn her.

"I gotta go. I gotta figure out what to do today. I'm doing a photo shoot for a magazine piece this afternoon."

"What magazine piece? I didn't set that up."

"I've known the writer for five years. She's written about me before and the stories have always been okay. She asked for access, so I said okay."

"Do I know her?"

"Cassandra St. George? She's American—"

"And she lives in London."

"You know her?"

"Oh yeah. She used to cover crime for one of the New York tabloids before she switched to entertainment writing. I have a client, the star of a new series on Hulu? And we gave her access for a profile. Afterwards the kid came to me, like, literally shaking. She got him to spill secrets, things he'd never told anyone. And of course everything he shouldn't have said ended up in the story. Now he won't even look at another reporter."

"Sounds like he said too much. But that's not her fault."

"I'm just saying be careful."

"In May she spent a week with us in Cannes. This summer she came to Paris a couple times and we got along great. We're going to talk one more time at the photo shoot. If it even happens, now. The setups are all outdoor scenes around Paris."

"You're not serious. I hope you're gonna cancel."

"I can't. There are deadlines. I can't delay the story. It's timed to drop when 'Autumn Reprise' opens."

"Oh God," she said with a weary sigh. "So tell me, are people still wearing masks over there?"

We agree to talk later. I phone Barky but she doesn't answer so I leave a voicemail. "Call me as soon as you can. It's important. Be careful around the apartment, the press is after me."

I put down the phone, curl up deep in the armchair, and close my eyes, wishing I could just... something, I don't know what.

Jean-Pierre pushes his chair back from the computer, leaving Buddy Ferino's picture on the home page of the *New York Post* staring at me from the screen. He comes over and slouches on the sofa.

"I never knew this story! Fantastique! You're really something!"

"'Something'? Like what?"

He looks amazed and amused.

"*La bad girl americaine.*"

"So are you sorry you got involved with me?"

"Not for one minute. I'm here for you. You know that. One hundred percent. I'm sure I can turn this to sympathy for you with the European press."

"It feels good to hear you say that."

"It's so unfair. I mean, a cop shoots himself, but you're to blame?"

"He had issues. Is that my fault?"

"But still, they blame you. Did you put the gun in his hand? No."

I wish it was that simple. I know I'll appreciate whatever he and Rhonda will spin for the press. But let's be real. I'm going to be blamed for something. I gave the police the sex tape, derailed his investigation for a while, and watched from a distance as Ferino's career fell apart and he left the NYPD. I felt vindicated after the way he treated me, but I was also relieved, because he'd gotten too close to the truth.

"So, do we have any actual business to take care of?"

"A little." He hands me song demos on a thumb drive from Carlotta Novi, the Italian pop diva I've been writing songs with. "I'll listen and I'll call her." Did I still want to meet for drinks with a publisher interested in my autobiography? "Reschedule that for me, will you? If I call him, he'll keep me on the phone for half an hour. If he's seen the news, he'll understand."

I find Bruce Berger's phone number in my Contacts and text him to call me as soon as he can.

I roll out of the chair and slink over to Jean-Pierre on the sofa. He starts to get up, but I push him back down, hike my dress up to my waist, straddle him, and give him a hard urgent kiss.

"I need you now," I say, and he grins.

We pull each other to our feet, and we kiss again, longer and warmer than our kiss at the entrance. Jean-Pierre is a lovely, sensitive man but he's also a cheerfully opportunistic stud.

"Make me forget about all this for a while."

"Oh?" He cocks a hip, rebelliously. "You think you can order me around?" He mimes picking up a phone. "Hello hello, deliver me a fuck, please! Not too young, not too old! Medium rare!" He laughs and pushes me into the bedroom.

The sex is as hot and exciting as I could hope for, stripping off each other's clothes, crashing onto the bed, a ravenous sixty-nine, then he fucks me in one position, I fuck him in another, on and on. Pinned beneath him as he rides me, my legs wrapped around him, I close my eyes and begin to fall away from everything worldly and melt into pure sensation, pure pleasure. I'm at the edge of total, throbbing oblivion, when my mind intrudes. I worry about the stories in the New York newspapers. I get anxious about whether I'll be on schedule for the rest of the day. A stubborn knot of tension grows inside me that I strain to expel. I wrap my arms and legs tighter around him and I try and try, and try even harder, but I can't let go. Even when he lifts me off the bed as he finishes, there is no orgasm for unlucky Adrienne this time.

We sprawl and catch our breath, spread out on the sweaty sheets. I stare at the shade bumping on the windowsill, swayed by the breeze. The cool September air raises goose bumps on my bare flesh. I try not to berate myself because I can't relax and let go. I'm so frustrated I'm ready to cry or smash something if that'll make what's jammed up inside let go.

"No good?" he says.

"*C'est magnifique.*"

"Liar."

He rolls towards me and pulls me against him. He raises himself on an elbow, and I feel the excitement from his hand between my legs from head to toe.

"Okay?"

"Oh yes..." I groan.

"Not too Trumpy?"

I don't how a French boy comes up with this stuff. All I can do is laugh and that helps me relax.

"Breathe, Adrienne. Let go."

His fingertips stroke me, lightly and slowly, then hard and urgent. The sweetness rushes through me with an upsurge of sensation so complete, and I bury my face in the hair of his chest and sob from deep inside in relief. After a while I crawl off him, spent, feeling so open and vulnerable that it scares me.

"Don't ask me to speak," I say. "I can't even think."

He laughs, a bass rumble from deep in his chest.

"You know," he says, "I can't figure you out."

"Don't try." He hovers over me and I pull him down and kiss him, long and deep. "Figuring me out is the last thing you want."

"Perhaps because you have too many dirty little secrets." Clearly, this excites him about me.

"Who doesn't have secrets?"

"I learned more about you from reading the news this morning than from a year of working for you. You have a rich, as you'd say, back story. But like I always wonder about everyone, what is being hidden? What is withheld? What is she not letting me see?"

He's more like me than I realize. He knows seeing only what someone allows you to see isn't seeing them at all. The real person is always under the mask.

"Seriously, Jean-Pierre. You'll never figure me out. Please don't even try."

"But studying you is fun. It's a pleasure."

"Oh? More than the other pleasures we share?"

"No. Don't be silly."

"Well, what else about me is there to find out?"

"When I find out, I'll let you know."

He kisses the tip of my nose, sits up and swings his legs off the bed, lights one of my cigarettes, and pulls on his jeans.

I don't have time to bathe, nor do I want to. I want to go through the rest of this day smelling his body on mine, exuding the lingering aroma of lust, my body sticky with sweat. I hope the smell of pheromone off me excites people so much it makes them dizzy.

I get dressed and refresh my makeup. I'm running late now but I'm reluctant to leave. It saddens me to think I will probably lose Jean-Pierre someday. When that day comes, I promise myself that after a fine lunch with plenty of wine and hashish we'll make love all afternoon, then part with tears and regrets.

He orders me an Uber, and when the driver texts that he's downstairs, we hold each other for a moment. He kisses me and whispers *"Bon courage"* in my ear, and we separate, feeling like two halves of something being pulled apart. Head up, I stroll smiling through the throng of shoving shouting paparazzi to the safety of the car.

P aparazzi riding scooters behind and alongside the car yell and point cameras at me through the windows, and there's a Fiat tailgating us with a cameraman popping out of the roof shooting video. My Uber driver, Middle Eastern and steaming and cursing under his breath, speeds up the Rue Cardinal Lemoine toward the river, heading for the photo studio of Herve Dumas in the Rue Marbeuf on the Right Bank.

I phone Barky, but again she doesn't answer. Her appointment with Dr. Gerard should be over by now and she's probably home working in her studio, so maybe she's in a Zoom meeting with a client. Thanks to the public's true crime fascination with the unsolved murders in the shooting of the film, her *Making of 'Lonely Sky'* book was a bestseller and got a lot of media attention. That led to a steady stream of freelance editing and design offers. She worked hard every day, still gave me complete love and support all through my pregnancy, and after Rory's birth she took over his primary care while I shot two more seasons of *"Men R Dawgs"*, one in New York and one in Los Angeles, and she organized our life so I could film *"Autumn Reprise"* here in Paris.

Marshall got her a big-bucks book deal for *Making of 'Autumn Reprise'* that made it possible for us to pick up our happy life and transplant it here in Paris.

The life we left in New York had been a nightmare that put both of us under an unfriendly media magnifying glass. When *"Lonely Sky"* opened, the NYPD still hadn't solved the murders of Egon Swift and A.J. Upton, or explained Jonathan Lehane's suicide. So the good reviews and box office for my first film in ten years were ignored. Instead the press wrote about the unsolved crimes, and more about me as a suspect than a film director, even though the charges were dropped after the grand jury didn't indict me. Then somebody in the NYPD leaked the sex tape, and when that story broke, the scandal became the bigger story. It also boosted ticket sales, and so with the box office rising each week nationwide, Nikki Xiu shrugged off any moral taint the scandal may have left on our film, even though some nasty reporters added "amateur porn actress" to my description. When Ferino was fired, I was reviled as the destroyer of a decorated cop's career, but I think his behavior on the sex tape made the more lasting impression.

This new press attention will surely drive Barky into a rage when she should be peacefully preparing for childbirth. Ferino's suicide will bring back every headache from the *"Lonely Sky"* period of our life. When we first got together Barky was shocked by the press. She's since learned from bitter experience, but the unfairness of it is still harder on her than on me. Our life went through a few nerve-wracking months after Roy and Rosa Lee filed a lawsuit for custody of Rory. The lawsuit was Barky's unwilling and unwanted public outing. The Uptons claimed that because A.J. never married me, and because of my "immoral" relationship with Barky, I could not be trusted to be a responsible mother. That brought a Twitter storm down on us, and that's when photographers started ambushing us in public. Photos of us started appearing here and there, orchestrated I'm sure by Roy's people. We were trolled as greedy lesbians trying to seize A.J.'s estate by controlling his heir. Roy and Rosa Lee lost their custody battle, but they immediately filed another suit to block my legal right to supervise Rory's inheritance of his father's $50 million estate until he's 21 years old. I told the court I don't want or need the money, but I am his mother, and legally that should be all that matters. We still don't know yet what the court will decide.

In the midst of all that legal and publicity shit, Season 2 of *"Men R Dawgs"* dropped. Critics called the show more caustic and sexist and scornful of men than the first season, and we went through a new period of vicious social media trolling and death threats. To be the target of hostility was nothing new to me, but Barky hated the attention. For a time she wouldn't leave the apartment. In New York, where people are generally tolerant and mind their own business, she was accosted by strangers on the street, again probably orchestrated by Roy Upton, harassing her and taking pictures. Her parents came in from Connecticut to try to talk sense into her. They told her I was trouble. She told them: "Yes she is, but we're in love."

I know two things about our marriage. I owe Barky everything. And I don't deserve her trust. The night I lied to her and said Jonathan killed A.J. and himself, she said in all innocence *To destroy two lives like that, someone would have to be insane, or evil.* I still don't know if I'm one or the other, but I live in fear she might somehow learn the truth. At the same time, on some level, I must wish I could come clean with her. One night on our honeymoon on Ibiza, I woke up from a nightmare trembling and sick with fear. I had dreamed I was an old, weak woman, dying in a hospital bed. Barky was my aged loving wife, sitting a vigil by my side. Suddenly the urge to cleanse my soul before it was too late was overwhelming. In my dream, I took her hand and looked into her eyes, begging her to understand, and croaked, "Egon, Jonathan, A.J. – I killed them all. I had to. I had to, because..." Her eyes lowered in shame, hurt at my betrayal of her trust, and she backed away from me, fading further into darkness. I laid there gasping and heartbroken, as if Barky had really left me.

Suddenly in a narrow block of the Rue Monge a van backs out in front of us then jerks to a stop. We swerve and miss it by inches. The scooter riders weave around the van and keep photographing but the Fiat hits it with a loud crash and the video cameraman catapults with his camera out of the Fiat and crashes into the van. My driver pays no attention to the shouts and screams and car horns echoing in our wake.

I've kept the photographer Herve Dumas and his staff waiting, so I'm not surprised to get a call from Clarice, his assistant at his studio.

"You're on your way, I hope?"

"We're crossing Pont Alexander now."

"Oh, but that is not so close. Tell your driver not the Champs de Elysees, we hear it's very jammed." I lean over and tell him that as we come off the bridge.

"*La circulation sur Les Champs Elysees est tres dense!*"

He barks loudly "*Je sais! Je sais!*" and immediately swings a violent left westward onto Cours-la-Reine.

"Okay. He knows."

"Yes, I can hear," she says with a laugh. "He's not happy."

"We're being chased by paparazzi on scooters. A car with a video crew crashed into a van. Please tell Herve I'm afraid I've ruined the chance to shoot outside today."

"Oh, but we cannot change the schedule now. Permissions have been obtained, fees paid, locations arranged, I don't see how—"

I'm not going to debate this with an assistant.

"When I get there, I'll talk to Herve."

We jolt to a stop in front of the studio on the Rue Marbeuf, a fashionable street of expensive boutiques and chic cafes. The photographers scramble to the sidewalk, begging me to stop and pose. I dash from the car and shimmy through a line of motorcycles parked at the curb. The security guard opens the entrance for me then pulls the heavy wooden doors shut.

In the lobby Clarice tells me Herve is waiting in my dressing room and she escorts me there. Inside, there is the usual fruit bowl, bottles of water, basket of croissants, coffee, bottles of wine, fresh flowers, and one skinny, lank-haired photographer dressed in black, including his face mask. I'm sure Herve is feeling pressured by my lateness, but he's calm, leaning against the wall with his arms crossed.

"Ah! Finally you're here," he says.

"I'm so sorry I'm running late. The New York media are being vicious to me again. I've been talking with my publicists about how to deal with it."

He takes a deep breath and nods solemnly.

"Yes, we know. We've seen the stories. That kind of publicity, it must be terrible for you."

"Paparazzi chased me all the way here."

"They've done worse to others, as we know."

"I can handle it. I'm more concerned for my wife. She's about to give birth."

"It's ironic, isn't it? The media. We despise them, yet here we are, at the glamorous end of the same shitty business."

We both laugh, sort of. "So," he says, "we'll stay in the studio today."

"Oh? Clarice said plans have been made that can't be changed."

"She did?" Have I just gotten Clarice in trouble? "No. We have no choice. Paparazzi will follow us everywhere. Their pictures will be in the media and on the Internet before the magazine comes out. None of my images will be fresh."

"Herve, I'm sorry. This was so unexpected."

"This problem is not of your making. We'll deal with it. The costumes will still be as we planned. Maybe we'll find a way to do outdoor shots in iconic places we can control. Or Photoshop you in."

"Please, let's do that. Paris is my home now. I want people to know that."

For some reason it feels pretentious to have said that, but there is no time to worry about it.

"I'm sure this will all calm down in a few days."

"I'll keep my schedule flexible. I'm in Paris for the foreseeable future."

"'The foreseeable future.' A questionable concept these days, isn't it? If the future is anything like the present, I don't want to foresee it, do you?"

"Let's just hope we all have one."

He ponders that. "Who knows? Okay. Wardrobe and hair and makeup are down the hall and the studio's upstairs. Clarice will walk you through."

"Thank you. You're being so gracious."

"Let's have a great afternoon." He stops at the door. "Oh. You have a friend waiting."

"That must be the writer. If you see her, would you ask her to come in?"

Cassandra is already dressed for her flight to London tonight in sweatpants and hoodie and running shoes and a flowered face mask. Even so dressed down she's an impeccably groomed brunette beauty, with a vitality that makes rolling a suitcase and slinging a backpack over her shoulder look sexy.

"Hey."

"Hey. Would it be okay if I kept my bags in here?" she says.

"Anywhere you like."

She rolls the suitcase into a corner and balances her backpack on top. She turns and looks me over and nods. Seeing I'm unmasked she says, "Can I take this thing off?"

"Sure."

She removes her mask, then steps up and hugs me and kisses both cheeks.

"It's great to see you again!"

Affection? Or the kiss of death? After what Rhonda told me I don't know whether to be open with her or be on my guard. Do I look like I need a hug? Is this misdirection, is she about to crucify me with her story? We've gotten along well, but lovey-dovey stuff from any reporter makes me suspicious.

Five years ago when "*Men R Dawgs*" dropped, and I was news again after ten years of obscurity, Cassandra and I sat talking for hours on a park bench in Chelsea sipping iced cappuccinos from the Empire Diner. She wrote a story in *New York Magazine* that acknowledged frankly that the show was crap, but vulgar enough to be a hit, and her profile of me did me no lasting harm. We had a very strong rapport. She wrote an insightful story on the opening of *"Lonely Sky"* focused on my career journey and the film and not on the true crime drama that came to be known as "The *Lonely Sky* Murders." Now she's writing a new profile, timed to drop when *"Autumn Reprise"* is released, that should reintroduce Adrienne Monet to the world as a filmmaker whose life and career matter.

"So," she says. "How are you holding up?"

"As well as I can, considering everything's fucked."

"Yes." A theatrical sigh. "Sometimes the past just won't stay where it belongs."

"So Herve rescheduled. We're shooting in the studio."

"Smart move. Outdoors would have been a real circus."

"Yeah. A fucking Circus of The Damned. I've already been chased all over Paris by those vultures." Hey, calm down, I tell myself, and remember you're speaking about the media to the media.

"It would've made a crazy scene in your story, though. While they were chasing me, one of them even had a car crash. It was pure slapstick."

"Oh dear," she says, hesitantly. "So you haven't heard."

"Heard what?"

"The cameraman."

"The one in the Fiat?"

"Yes. He was killed."

"Oh no." I feel sick. Nothing slapstick about that, Adrienne. And now I'm an even bigger, uglier story. "Of course I didn't know."

"It just made the news. And of course all the stories say he was chasing you."

"A picture of me is not worth someone getting killed over." Now I just want to push everything away. "Listen, we have to finish the interviewing today, okay?"

"We will, I promise. We should have time after Herve's done. I saved the best for last. I just have a couple things to ask about. A few general questions and a little more about 'Lonely Sky' and that's all."

"Great," I say. "Am I going to need an air sick bag?"

Prepping my hair and makeup and getting into wardrobe takes over an hour. The girls wash, dry, spray and stiffen and blow out my hair into a wild mane. The foundation makeup turns my face into a blank mask, my eyebrows are darkened and sharpened to points, and kohl-blackened lids make my eyes look deeper and more confrontational. In the mirror I look like a plastic mannequin based on Adrienne Monet. Two Wardrobe assistants dress me in a pinstriped gray double-breasted suit jacket over a frilly white blouse, a black bandana pushing my hair up in a wild tousle, and baggy trousers with wide cuffs rolled up over black patent leather work boots. I personally call the look The Gray Flannel Banshee. I step on to the set, a sky-blue cyclorama, and a heavy silver man's wristwatch is latched on my wrist. They put a huge fuming cigar with an inch of ash in my hand for me to fool around with.

In any photo session I always try to give the camera more than just my face. Herve stalks back and forth shooting and peering down into the screen on his camera. I mug for him, pose with the cigar and blow a perfect smoke ring.

"Beautiful!" Herve says. "Very careful! Don't knock off the ash!"

I lose myself posing, and in the dance I'm doing with Herve, until he finally stands up straight, nods, and says *Fantastique!* He ducks into the computer tent to look at the pictures next to a portly, bearded young man who had been introduced to me as Neil Lampry, the New York stylist the magazine hired to produce this shoot. The pictures scrolling on the iMac screen reflect on Herve's glasses so I can't read his expression, but Neil keeps tugging and flipping back the cashmere gray scarf draped around his neck, murmuring to Herve and nodding his head. He catches me staring at him and gives me a tight grin and thumbs up.

Clarice allows me a few minutes before prep for the next setup, and I spend it in my dressing room, washing the cigar taste out of my mouth with a few sips of wine and continuing Cassandra's interview.

"When I heard Detective Ferino killed himself I was devastated," I answer to her most obvious question. "I literally asked God, 'How many people does this movie have to kill?' No matter what the police say about me, I cared deeply for all three men connected with my film who died. That whole time period was terrible for me and now the media are trying to make me relive it all over again. That's hard enough, but when they suggest I'm a murderer and they don't know what they're talking about, I wonder, where has basic decency gone?"

I steer the conversation to my life at present, my happy marriage to Barky, our beautiful son and the expected birth of our daughter. I talk about how amused I am that her book about *"Lonely Sky"* became such a bestseller that a low budget American director is begging to option it and, absurdly, wants to make a film about the making of the film, sort the behind-the-scenes genre meets True Crime. He says he wants to be guided by the still photographs and my introduction, but Barky's afraid he'll just sensationalize the unsolved murders of three dead men. He's been trying to get an interview with me, as if I would ever –

Just then Barky returns my call and Cassandra goes back to the set.

"So, do you know what's happening?" I ask.

In a brisk voice with street noise in the background she says, "Uh, yes, unfortunately."

"Where are you?"

"We're just getting home."

"Everything okay?"

"Yes. Doctor Gerard says I might even deliver early."

"Okay. We'll be ready. Just don't let this new craziness bother you."

"I'm trying Adrienne, but it's not easy."

"How is Rory?"

"He's fine."

"I'm sure they'd love to get pictures of him. So be careful if you go out. The media blowing up this story is so frustrating."

"How are you going to handle it? The PR, I mean."

"Jean-Pierre and Rhonda are working on it. Otherwise I'm just ducking the media for now. We'll figure it out."

"How's the shoot going?"

"Good. Cassandra is here and we'll finish the interview today."

"Say hello for me, will you? And call me later?"

"I will. Call me if there are any problems with the press."

"See you later. Love you."

"Love you too."

I promise to call her when I'm finished, and we'll sit down for a family dinner she plans to cook.

Herve's staff is quick and efficient. My hair is washed and dried smooth, so it flows over my shoulders. Over the next several hours we shoot three costumes: a street look of tight black midriff blouse, white bolero hat, and puffy white cargo pants; a near-nude, dressed in a black lace teddy and black patent leather platforms, and an evening gown of black silk with puffed shoulders and white darts at the hips. I text Marshall to tell the magazine editors they cannot use the teddy shot on the cover, then send him another text, canceling the first.

During the dinner break, Cassandra wants my take on how life has treated Lenny and Juno Victor. I pour two glasses of wine and answer with a magnanimity made easier by not having thought about them for a long time. The Victors, even Lenny's violation of me in my youth, are part of a past I think I've integrated successfully and can live with.

"I feel sorry for Juno, with so many women accusing Lenny of assault. But at the very first trial the judge decided Juno knew Lenny was a sexual predator and just looked the other way. I hear they're in danger of going broke, but Juno refuses to divorce him, even to protect her own wealth from the judgments against Lenny and their company. The sad thing is, they've made some good movies, and the success of 'Lonely Sky' might've helped if the studio hadn't been forced to buy them out. But at their age, and with Lenny possibly going to prison, it's hard to imagine how they'll survive."

My phone vibrates. The screen reads BRUCE BERGER.

"It's my lawyer in New York," I tell Cassandra. "I need a couple minutes." She leaves.

"Hello Bruce."

"I've already heard from the Manhattan DA. They want you to come in for further questioning."

"Is this a joke?"

"No joke."

"I have nothing to say about Buddy Ferino killing himself. I've had no contact with him in over four years. There's nothing else to tell them."

"There's something about you in Ferino's note. I don't know what it is yet."

"I was interrogated a half dozen times by two sets of detectives. They searched my apartment. They tried to indict me for killing Jonathan and A.J. and they failed. What else do they want from me? And now that sex tape they leaked is all over the internet again. Make sure you tell the DA they owe me an apology."

"We knew it might get leaked when we gave it to them."

"My publicist spoke to a detective who called me the 'bitch who killed him,' quote unquote."

"It will get worse. The NYPD is absolutely out to get you. But you're not in any immediate danger as long as you stay in France."

"What if the DA tries to force me to come back?"

"Without an indictment, I doubt the French would extradite you."

"What if the Feds charge me under their law for failing to tell them Lehane shot Egon?"

"A., they won't, even with the publicity value they've got better things to do, and B. it's a low-grade misdemeanor, a fine and for a first offender probably probation for 1-3 years."

"You don't think they'll pursue it?"

"It's not worth their time, but if the Feds try anything, you're still safer there."

"This couldn't be about The Voice Mail, could it?"

That's what we call the message I left on Egon's cell phone after he got shot, the recording Ferino hoped was proof I was in Egon's office that morning. The police forensics lab confirmed with near 100 percent certainty that the background sounds on the recording were made by the elevator in Egon's building. For a time it looked bad for me, but I'd thought my story through and gave them a plausible explanation. I admitted to the detectives who took over from Ferino and Peavey that I had remembered wrong when I said I'd called Egon from home. Actually, that morning I got as far as the lobby of his building and pushed the elevator button, then I decided not to go up to his office. I was pissed off because being called to work threw my whole holiday weekend off. So I called him, and when he didn't answer, I left him the voicemail. While I was recording the message the elevator arrived in the lobby, empty, and went back up, empty. After I left the voicemail, I went home. They didn't believe me, and they insisted the person in black on the gallery security video, who doesn't exit the building for 11 minutes, was me. But the judge ruled that out because the video quality was too poor for a positive identification.

"The Voice Mail is a dead issue," Berger says. "You gave a perfectly reasonable explanation. The first story, okay, you were mistaken, but you admitted it."

There's a knock on my dressing room door. "Adrienne, we're ready for you."

"I have to go."

"Since you routinely ignore my advice, let me end this by repeating myself," he says. "Stay in Paris."

"No problem there. And you know you're welcome to visit any time."

When I see the last costume and set up, all I can do is laugh. Fully outfitted, I'm wearing a sheer black lace top over a black pushup bra, skin-tight black leather slacks, six-inch platform clogs, a diamond buckle on a black leather belt hanging loose on my slim hips. My hair is brushed out loose and flowing, and my bright red lipstick matches my tiny leather shoulder bag.

On set, Herve poses me against a white cyclorama seated on a huge chrome Harley Davidson motorcycle. When he directs me to, I grab the handlebars and try to look like I'm roaring off against a sunset cyclorama, as a wind machine blows my hair back. The last shot of the session is me posing on the bike as a fog machine sends brilliantly lit white vapors swirling around me.

By the time Herve is satisfied and we wrap, it's late evening. I need to get home and Cassandra needs to catch her flight to London. I've already missed dinner and Barky and Rory will be missing me. Cassandra comes in just as my iPhone vibrates. The screen has Chinese symbols.

This is awkward. I don't want to tell Cassandra to turn around and go back outside, but to ask Nikki Xiu to wait is unthinkable.

"Hello Nikki."

"You need to say something," she says.

"What do you mean?

"A statement. About that dead cop. Your silence is being filled with a lot of negativity. I thought you'd know how to handle this. I want this mess long forgotten before '*Autumn Reprise*' opens. This must not distract from our film. We don't need another '*Lonely Sky*' situation."

"I won't allow that to happen. I'll do it tonight."

"It's what's best, Adrienne. For everyone concerned." She hangs up.

"Sorry," I tell Cassandra. "I just need a minute to write a press statement." For a moment I wonder what I can possibly say that won't make things worse. Finally I type out a first draft of something quickly on my phone, then I call Rhonda. It's 4 p.m. in New York, early enough to make the evening news cycle.

"I have a statement I want to make. I'm ready to Tweet it."

"Read it to me."

"Here it is. 'Despite having been stalked and assaulted by him, I feel sadness and regret over the death of Detective Ferino. New York City has lost a brave and courageous protector.' How's that?"

"No, lose the first part."

"I was stalked! I was assaulted!"

"You really want to say that about a man who committed suicide?"

"It's the fucking truth! Too bad if that's inconvenient!"

"If there's anyone on the NYPD who doesn't hate you, this'll fix that. Besides, it'll remind people about the sex tape."

She's got a point. At the vanity table Cassandra sits looking at her phone and pretending she's not recording this. I can imagine this scene ending up in her story.

"Well, so how about this? 'That poor man. I kept telling him I was innocent, but he wouldn't believe me. He obviously had issues he couldn't resolve.'"

"That's almost as bad."

"But why?"

"It's condescending."

"All right. I'll just say the 'brave and courageous' part."

"Okay. And keep the part about sadness and regret."

"I'll keep it. Nobody'll believe it. In fact, I don't mean one word of it. But I'll say it."

My thumbs fly over the letters. I read it to make sure there are no mistakes or typos then I send it to her before I change my mind.

"There. It's done. Let me know how it plays."

Cassandra pours us both more wine and checks the time on her phone. "There's one last thing we need to talk about," she says, clearing her throat. "I waited for this until you were done shooting because I didn't want to distract you."

"Is it good news?" I look and feel very tired in the mirror as I remove my makeup. "Right now, I could use some."

"Well, I hope you think it's good..." She sighs, her voice wavers uncertainly. "So, a source at the NYPD leaked me a transcript of one of your interrogations. The one where Ferino confronted you with your real name and background? And how you gave up your baby for adoption?"

For a moment I think I'm going to be sick. This is the very last thing I want a reporter to know about me. Cassandra! What a turnaround.

"Is this what you call saving the best for last? And now what? You're writing some kind of exposé?"

"No, but I'm not writing a typical clichéd celebrity profile either. When I followed the leads in the transcript, I found the story of Bobbie Jean Blivka really emotionally powerful. I think our readers will too, when they know the whole story. It's a deep human-interest story with a very 'up' ending, your life today."

Well, Rhonda warned me, and I've been too trusting, once again.

"So you are planning to write about this."

"If I could ask first, what happened to the father?" She was being maddeningly polite.

"The father. You mean the rapist."

"Why was he never prosecuted?"

"He was a drug addict and a lowlife. He died of an overdose before the baby was born."

"He died." She stares at me a moment then snaps out of it. "So you never got justice."

"No."

"Did you consider having an abortion?"

"Of course. My mother wanted me to. And that would've been the easy way out. But spiritually, I was afraid to do it. I didn't want it on my conscience."

"It must've been very hard to give birth to a baby girl and give her up for adoption."

"I'd rather you didn't write about this."

When she didn't respond I tried another approach.

"I felt like I had no choice. I was eighteen, I was homeless, and I was broke. My baby deserved a better life than I could give her."

"A better life, yeah, of course," she nodded, seeming to be deep in thought. I got the feeling Cassandra was hearing a different story than the one I was telling.

"I mean a normal life. That was much more important to me than her being a child of rape."

I'm talking too much, and now she's getting emotional, too. Cassandra is staring at me, her face reddening and tears coming to her eyes. Empathy? Or method acting? Before I can understand this odd reaction from a reporter, her phone signals an incoming text, and she glances at it and groans in frustration.

"My car is waiting. I've got a plane to catch. Damn it!"

She rummages in her backpack, pulls out a manila envelope.

"Okay. I had hoped we could sit and do this properly, but today ran so late, and now I have to go. But while I go back to London and write, I want you to have this paperwork." She hands the envelope to me. "I did a deeper dive into the adoption story."

"I thought we were friends, Cassandra." A futile thing to say to a reporter.

"Adrienne, what I'm trying to tell you is, I've found your daughter."

Bad enough poor Bobbie Jean Blivka will be reborn, but now the child she gave up for adoption will even amplify the story, the one I never wanted told.

"I didn't ask you to do that."

"Don't you want to know?"

"It's just that I haven't thought about her. It's too painful. And anyway – how do you know she, this person, is really mine? You have proof?"

I open the envelope. There are documents inside. "What's this?"

"This is why I had to come back to see you in person. In there is your daughter's birth record. She was born at Middlesex General Hospital in New Brunswick, New Jersey. And so was I. On the same year, the same day, at the same time." She took a deep breath and said, "When I saw that, I almost passed out."

It took me a moment to understand what she was saying.

"Last spring, when I flew over to see you at Cannes? One of those nights we were talking, you tossed an empty nicotine vape in the trash. I got it, and I had our DNA compared." At my reaction, she insisted, "I couldn't not do it, Adrienne. After I saw the birth record, I had to know. The DNA report's in the envelope, too. You can see for yourself what it says."

"What does it say?"

"It says I'm your daughter," she stammered, breathlessly. "I mean, take a good look at us."

We turn and see ourselves side by side in the dressing room mirror, but I'm too stunned to see whatever she wants me to see. Her phone chimes again, incoming text.

"Look at the documents, please? Then call me? I'll come back to Paris or you'll come to London, but we'll do this the right way. Okay?"

It's too much, too much, 'way too much. I lean on the vanity table to support myself.

"And this is what you're going to write about?"

"Yes, of course. I mean, what a story! You know the typical celebrity profile. The kind of stuff they're always about." She rolls her eyes and speaks rapidly, sneering. "Drug abuse, mental health, dysfunctional family, gender dysphoria, crooked management, career ups, career downs, child rearing, divorce, money problems, body image anxiety, bulimia, anorexia. Feuds! Do you have any idea how fucking sick I am of writing that shit? But here, on a normal reporting assignment, I've discovered my birth mother is the talented, notorious, fascinating film director Adrienne Monet! Is there a better story here than that?"

"Are you sure you even want to be associated with me?"

"Absolutely!"

She hugs me, fiercely, and I put my arms around her. She pulls out her iPhone and takes a picture of us, then I do too. When she steps away, we're both too incredulous for tears.

"I'm sorry, I've got to go. I've got a husband and daughter waiting in London. I'll come back. I promise."

"You mean I have a granddaughter?"

"Yes! Ride to the airport with me. I'll show you videos on my phone."

"I can't. Barky needs me now. I should have been home hours ago. Take a later flight. Or even better, come home with me. Stay over."

"I can't. Tomorrow's my daughter's birthday. I'll email you pictures from the party. And let's get back together soon!"

"But I want you to meet my wife. And your half-brother."

"I will! I promise! Soon!"

I watch her, so chic and so beautiful, rolling her suitcase to the door. She turns and waves. What'd she say? Sometimes the past just won't stay where it belongs?

Then I'm alone, just me and the paperwork, and an empty wine bottle.

It's after 10 p.m. when I finally leave Herve's studio. No-one is left, just me and the security guard. He lets me out onto the street where an Uber is idling. There are no paparazzi in sight. As we glide through Paris back towards Menilmontant, I'm sad and pissed off that I was robbed of what should have been a perfectly lovely day. I woke up this morning excited about the weeks ahead, with *"Autumn Reprise"* about to open on a wave of film festival acclaim, my New York years behind me, my personal life happier than ever with a beautiful son to raise and my wife about to give birth to a baby girl, and life in Paris, the city of my dreams, as perfect as I can make it. I was finally on the verge of a future in which I'd be respected for my artistry and not gossiped about for the scandals I thought I'd put behind me.

And now all that is gone. I'm an object of sick curiosity again for all the pathetic people still fascinated with what reporters keep calling "The *Lonely*

Sky Murders." And soon Cassandra's article will dredge up an older secret, the sad story of Bobby Jean Blivka from South Brunswick New Jersey, a ghost from a painful past that even the sudden appearance of my long-lost little girl can't banish. I had no illusions about the slant of Cassandra's story. Sure, my current happiness will be touched on, but the story will be all about a journalist rediscovering her long-lost mother.

I decide to get out of the car on the Avenue Gambetta, a few blocks from our apartment, to walk and clear my head before I get home. It's a cool night, and the daytime odors of perfume, roasted coffee and cigarette smoke, diesel exhaust, street drains, and the aromatic smells from cafes have been replaced by a sweet fresh night breeze. I stop at the corner of the Rue Ernest Le Fevre, and quickly step back from an alarming spectacle. Down the block in front of my apartment building the entrance is lit by bright lights. A TV satellite truck is parked along the curb, reporters and photographers block the street and angry motorists are leaning on their horns. My neighbors will hate me for this. After a whole day of being chased, I want to tear into the paparazzi and fight my way into my home. But with one of them killed chasing me this afternoon, they'll be out for my blood. So I walk calmly across the street and around a couple of blocks and through the garden yard behind our building to the parking garage door and use my pass card to enter. The garage is cold and silent, spooky with shadows the weak fluorescent light makes deeper. I ride the elevator to our floor, luckily encountering none of my neighbors, and let myself into our apartment.

I slip off my Cons in the foyer. The parquet floor is delightfully cool under my bare feet. The kitchen is warm and dark, the only light comes from over the stove. The memory of the dinner I missed, roast lamb with garlic and Middle Eastern spices, lingers in the air.

I sit down at the table to read a sweet note from Barky telling me my dinner is in the oven. I run my fingers over the table, the beautiful wooden antique farmhouse table that was our first purchase when we moved to Paris, the setting for so many dinner parties, serious late-night conversations, sunny breakfasts, birthday celebrations, anniversaries, reunions. It's too late to eat, so I wrap my dinner and put it in the refrigerator until lunch tomorrow. All I want is a glass of Burgundy from the bottle that's always on the table next to the salt and pepper shakers and sugar bowl.

The parlor is dark, but the curtains are pulled back and the windows are open to the night air. I sit back on the window seat and put my feet up. To be in my quiet home with the dark wrapped around me is exactly what I need right now. Across the street the wind moves the shadows of the trees that the streetlamps cast against the wall of the building. In its lighted windows a woman in a blue gown brushes her hair, two young boys wrestle in a parlor, a Black man sits at a desk in front of a computer without moving, an old man plays a harmonica, a woman in a red overcoat and hat stares expectantly down at the sidewalk. Thump thump thump, loud hip hop on a car radio, moves slowly down the street.

I assume my wife and my son have gone to bed. But as I walk toward the next room, I smell the shampoo that always lingers after Rory's bath. In the living room under two large prints of Andy Warhol's "Flowers," Barky lies back on the sofa with her head on a pillow and Rory nestles under her arm wearing his cape and mask, his head resting on her belly, both of them deep asleep. The wide screen TV is still on. They've been watching *Les Chroniques de Zorro*, Rory's current passion. Onscreen is the smiling face of the young hero who fights injustice. Curled up half in Barky's lap, Rory's breathing seems to be in sync with hers. I turn off the TV and DVD player, and he stirs.

"Mama?" He holds out his arms and I lift him off Barky, who wakes up and yawns. I carry Rory to his bedroom, take off his mask and cape, and lay him on his bed, where he curls up and falls asleep again.

In the hall Barky is up, stretching, and we embrace.

"Thank God this day is over," she says.

"That's exactly what I'm going to do. Give thanks."

"Coming to bed?"

"Soon."

She kisses me and pads sleepily away.

I drop my shoulder bag next to the desk in my studio and ease back into the Eames chair beside it. It's a weird thing to say, but if I was forced to, I could live in this one room for the rest of my life. Everything I need to keep working is here. This summer I'm writing a screenplay of psychological, cosmic horror, so on the table next to me is a stack of reading to maintain the mood: a book with Thomas Ligotti's *"Songs of a Dead Dreamer"* and *"Grimescribe"*; two novels of cosmic horror by William Sloane, and *"The Complete Fiction of H.P. Lovecraft."* Tonight it's too late to continue reading where I left off. In this room where I am always working, always driving to achieve something, it sometimes feels good to sit back and do nothing.

A lot of my life and work is on these walls. Over my desk is a blowup of the crew picture taken on the day *"Coma"* wrapped. All I have to do is look at that picture to fall in love with film making all over again. A huge close-up of a waif-like Willi Adams stares out from the poster for *"Girl in the City"*, one of two movies she made before she withdrew, disgusted with fame, and managed to disappear, even in this age when anybody can be found. The poster for *"Bust"* is all I have left of my ex-husband since the lawsuit was settled, and I prefer it that way. *"Gimme Some Sperm"* is maddeningly easy to find online and so are the nasty reviews. No need to even search for the Victors, they'll be gossip bait forever. I hung the *"Men R Dawgs"* poster, the one I love with the chubby hubby on a leash, on the end wall over the filing cabinets. The poster from *"Lonely Sky"* is Jonathan's haunted profile, with the Muslim family in an upper corner and the East Village hipsters at the bottom, all of it set against a large ghostly image of my face, my eyes just beneath the title.

I sip my wine and drift back to the memory of this morning's romp with Jean-Pierre. Once Barky gives birth I will have a choice to make. The thought of telling Jean-Pierre I'm unavailable makes me sad, like I've already lost him. But does it have to be that way? Can't I be a perfectly good wife to Barky and a good mother to our children 24/7 and still indulge myself for an hour of fun now and then? It's not like we're in love, or that he's a threat to my marriage.

I open my phone to the selfie I took with Cassandra and upload it to my iMac so I can see it on the large screen. She looks so avid, so excited, and beside her I look, frankly, old and bewildered. Cassandra's article won't surprise Barky. I told her about Bobbie Jean Blivka long ago, including my pregnancy and the adoption. But I wonder how she'll react when I show her the photo and re-introduce Cassandra as my long-lost daughter. One thing I love about Barky is that she's unpredictable. When we first met, I was pretty sure my advances would be rejected, and they were, until one night when Barky came over, having changed her mind. And look at us now.

My phone chimes, it's an incoming text from Rhonda. It's 6 p.m. in New York.

"Prepare yourself for the worst."

I click on the link to the *New York Post*. The headline screams, 'A KILLER WALKS AMONG YOU,' over that picture of me on the set they ran the day of Jonathan's funeral.

The article says Ferino's suicide note has been leaked to the press. I could have predicted the things he says in the note.

"There is no doubt Adrienne Monet murdered Egon Swift, Jonathan Lehane, and A.J. Upton. I tried very hard to make the case against her, but I couldn't, and that's the biggest regret of my career. Not that it matters now.

Hopefully a brother or sister officer will take up the case where I left off and get justice. Until then, just be aware that a killer walks among you."

The condolences for Ferino that I texted to Rhonda are several paragraphs down in the story, placed in such a way as to make my response almost insignificant.

Ferino, who was so intent on recovering his own good reputation, has made sure my future will be a horror show. Between Rhonda and Jean-Pierre they'll spin this as the delusion of a man just prior to shooting himself, but the media attention will be suffocating anyway. Once more I will have to refuse to be dragged back in time. I will have to refuse to be captured or defined by my past. All I can do is stay present, live forward and trust in God to bring me through this moment, especially in those hours in the dead of night that are the worst.

I plug my phone in to charge, then try to wipe away all thoughts of the past or the future. I set my bracelets aside and sit on the meditation stool at the end of the room and finish this day as I do every day since moving to Paris. I clasp my hands together and bow my head.

"Hello God. It's Adrienne again. I know this relationship is still new for us both, but please, hear my prayer. Thank you for this gift of another day of life, and for helping me to try to be my best self today. Thank you for my beautiful, beautiful wife, for all the love and the happiness we've shared, and that I hope we'll share for many years to come. Thank you for Barky's healthy pregnancy, please bless her and keep her safe as she gives birth to our baby girl. Thank you for our beautiful little boy, the light of our lives, the greatest miracle that's ever happened to me. Thank you for enabling Cassandra to find her true mother, and for reuniting me with the little girl I lost. Thank you for our beautiful home, where we've been so happy for so many years, and for the chance to live in this city of eternal delight and beauty. Thank you for the blessings of good friends, and respected colleagues. May they all be safe and healthy and at peace. Please watch over the souls of my late departed loved ones, Jonathan and A.J., and let them rest in peace. And Lord... there is so much fear and anger, hatred and contempt, disrespect and inhumanity in this world today. Please let a spirit of love and forgiveness flood the hearts of all people. Enable us to be more compassionate and more empathetic. Let us each find in our hearts the peace, love, and understanding that may yet save this cruel and troubled world.

"Amen."